THE CATCH

EASTERN SHORE SWINGERS
BOOK 2

PHOEBE ALEXANDER

Mountains Wanted Publishing

PO Box 50

Harrison, DE 19951

www.mountainswanted.com

Cover design by Teresa Conner of Wolfsparrow Publishing

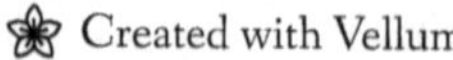 Created with Vellum

As we prepare to celebrate making it through our first year together as husband and wife, I just want you to know that I'll never forget you were the one who gave me new literary mountains to climb.

And thanks to you, I continue to soar to new heights.

I love you.

ONE

"So, what's it like working at a swing club?" the man asked as he bent to sign his membership forms. His wife teetered on stilettos next to him looking nervous.

"It's pretty cool so far," Paisley laughed, "but I'm still pretty new at it." She smiled at him reassuringly as his wife hesitated over the documents spread out on the table.

"I feel like I'm signing my life away." She frowned, looking up, first to her husband and then to Paisley. "Are you sure this is private? We're not going to show up on some list or something?" Her eyes were wide with worry.

"Member privacy and confidentiality are very important to us," Leah, Paisley's boss, said from the other side of the room. She walked over to the couple and introduced herself, shaking their hands warmly. "We do everything in our power to make our members feel safe and secure."

"Okay," the woman answered, watching her husband's face spread with a relieved grin. "If you're sure, honey...."

"You only live once!" the man bellowed happily, wrapping his arm around his wife and squeezing her to his body.

"That's exactly right!" Paisley nodded in agreement. "You only live once!"

❦ ❦ ❦

*I*t's *not the* actual *weekend that's such a thrill. It's the* promise *the weekend holds that's so exciting.*

As the clock struck five that Friday afternoon, a glorious sixty-plus hours of opportunity stretched like an endless ribbon of highway just begging to be explored. Paisley tossed a red chiffon dress onto the growing heap of rejected clothing and wrangled her plump body into yet another option. She admired how the shiny black fabric hugged her ample curves.

This is the one. Definitely. It gives me nice cleavage too!

How many times had she hung on the promise of a weekend? At thirty-six, she was technically past her prime for weekend shenanigans, yet the weekend was *sort of her thing.* In her line of work, opportunity hung in the air like a heady perfume every Friday night. Anything could happen before dawn on Monday morning.

Along with promise came pressure. This was Paisley's first weekend managing the club solo since she'd first started her job nearly a month ago. She shadowed the owners, Leah and Cap Sheldon and Casey Fontaine, for the prior three weekends. There had been one-on-one meetings with Leah about protocols and procedures, and she'd led a team meeting with the bartenders, the security personnel, the DJ, and the hosts. But now she was on her own for the first time.

"So, do you have any questions?" she asked Bob and Cindy, that weekend's hosts. Hosts volunteered their services in exchange for a free annual membership.

Cindy batted her long, glittery eyelashes at Paisley. "Is it true you used to be a burlesque dancer?"

She tried to stifle a surprised laugh. "Now, who told you that?"

"Oh, it's just a rumor flying around," Cindy explained. "You know how it is." She winked. "We'd love to see you dance someday! Maybe you could give a demonstration or teach a class?"

"It's a small community," Bob added. "We like to get to know people, that's all. I know you're from New York. It's probably not like that there."

"No, it certainly is not." Paisley humored the couple with a warm smile. "But, for the record, yes, I danced for a few years to save up for college. You know how it is!" This time it was her turn to wink. "Maybe I could teach a dance class some night. That would be a lot of fun!" She would add that to her list of ideas for Leah.

"I think the Sheldons made a really smart hire," Bob observed. "You really seem to know your shit." His wife nodded her blonde head in agreement.

Paisley wondered if it was a genuine compliment, or just a bit of brown-nosing. "Well, thank you! I'm a little nervous about tonight, so thanks for that vote of confidence!"

"Relax," Cindy encouraged her. "You've got this!"

The music coming from the DJ booth was throbbing through the club like a heartbeat. Paisley had a circuit of checkpoints, a routine she learned from Leah when she shadowed her the previous weeks.

She'd start at the bar and check in with Erik the bartender; then, walking the perimeter of the dance floor, she'd give a nod to the security guards, Trent and Jason, before looking in on the lounge area. After that, she walked the hallway leading to the play rooms. Her last stop was the hot tub room at the back of the club before returning to the bar again.

By midnight that the club was a lot more crowded than it had been the previous weeks. It was Memorial Day weekend, long considered "the start of the season" in Ocean City. The hosts had registered already thirty couples with "guest memberships," which was the three-month plan out-of-towners generally purchased.

Casey will be pleased! Paisley thought, and no sooner had the words floated into her head than the woman appeared through the side door of the club.

Whoa, that's totally freaky! I seem to have conjured her up. She saw Casey, one of the club co-owners, standing there near the DJ booth, studying something on her phone. Seconds later, Cap, another owner and her boss Leah's husband, joined her.

"What are you two doing here?" Paisley gasped, her heart beating as hard as the bassline of the music pumping out of the DJ booth. She had the sinking feeling her bosses didn't trust her to run the club on her own just yet. *Or they could just be checking up on me?*

"I had to get away from the in-laws," Cap shared with a shake of his head and an eye roll. The fishing boat captain was still wearing swim trunks and a tank top, even though the night had turned chilly. Paisley could feel the nip in the air rushing in from the stage door when they entered the building.

"Aren't they asleep by now?" Casey wore a skeptical

look, glancing at the delicate gold watch around her wrist. Even this late at night, she looked exquisite with every hair in place and her makeup perfectly set. *She's still wearing nylons and high heels.* Casey was at least twenty years older than she was, and she was still dressed to the nines. Paisley had ditched her heels at 10 PM.

Cap's mouth turned up into a sheepish grin. "I just wanted to see how you were making out, Sugar," he admitted, flashing his dimples at Paisley.

"Great minds think alike!" Casey laughed. "I got in from my conference earlier than I thought, so I thought I'd look in and see how things are going."

"Things are running smoothly. Here, come take a look!" Paisley ushered them down the corridor that ran behind the bar, and they entered the club from the other side. The bartender was so busy schmoozing a couple of topless ladies that he didn't even notice the trio of managers sliding past him.

"Looks like things are in full swing!" Casey bellowed, amused at her pun. She hesitated on the other side of the bar, her attention captured by two women dancing in the cage.

Paisley's eyes zeroed in on the pair, the smaller of whom was clad solely in rhinestone-studded panties that sparkled when they caught the flashing lights.

It's like a disco ball on her coochie. Paisley was equally mesmerized.

The other woman was dark-skinned with large, natural breasts, a narrow waist and full hips that writhed in time to the beat of the music. They made a striking couple on their own, but were made even more striking by the colorful lights bouncing off the bars of the black metal cage, creating ever-changing patterns on the dance floor.

The ladies didn't escape Cap's notice either. He didn't say a word, but Paisley glanced down at his crotch and could have sworn she saw an impressive bulge growing.

Would it be wrong to fuck my boss? Maybe Leah wouldn't mind? I mean, after all, she is kinda busy growing a baby. She might be glad for the help.

Paisley imagined a man like Cap would have a voracious appetite for pussy. There was just something about him...and she was rather adept at picking up on those sorts of vibes.

"Um, still with us, Cap?" Casey playfully jabbed at his arm. It seemed to snap him back to reality. The two women laughed as he recovered from his daze, then he shrugged and wandered off toward the lounge.

At the end of their tour, Casey took Paisley's hands into both of hers and clasped them tightly while her perfectly outlined lips spread into a grin. "You're doing a fabulous job, Ms. Parker! I'm truly pleased!"

Paisley couldn't help but feel relieved. Sometimes she didn't realize how uptight she was getting until the tension was released. Casey's praise felt nearly as good as an orgasm. Paisley's shoulders felt noticeably lighter, her joints looser.

"We're going to stay and help you clean up." Cap had returned to their side and patted Paisley on the shoulder.

"Oh, you don't have to do that!" She liked the way his thick, rough hands felt against her smooth skin. *Maybe he's curious about me too?*

"Go take care of your wife, my dear," Casey directed him with a kiss on his scruffy cheek. "We've got this."

"They're all asleep anyway, and I don't have a charter till nine tomorrow. I'll stay for a bit." He winked at Paisley, who took it as an affirmative. She'd spend the last two hours the club was open letting her mind run wild with that fantasy.

The activity in the public areas tapered off after one o'clock. At a quarter till two, the rooms began to empty one by one as everyone packed up their toys and prepared for the mass exodus. The smiles on everyone's faces were beams of gratitude shining down on her.

There's something really rewarding about helping other people get laid. I get a lot of vicarious pleasure from it, but I still wish I'd found someone to take home with me...

She scanned the premises to see if any single men were lingering about, anyone she might be interested in sharing a drink with. *If not a single guy, maybe there's a couple who didn't find their unicorn tonight?*

She was kinda in the mood for curling up next to a soft, feminine body. Her tongue practically danced at the thought of lapping at a hard, wanton clit.

But, sadly, the only people still around were Casey and Cap, and the latter was just about to take his leave after being continually pestered by the former to do so. It didn't appear that any of the fantasies she'd indulged in throughout the night were poised to come true.

Paisley resigned herself to clean-up mode. She had seen a lot of things in her former life as a burlesque dancer, and she had been a guest at many lifestyle clubs up and down the east coast. Her bosses had stationed her in the office counting money and reconciling the books during her the previous weekends, so she'd never had a close-up, behind-the-scenes look at the aftermath of a swinger party until that very night. The mess was nearly enough to turn her stomach.

This is gonna require gloves.

"You good?" Cap inquired as he watched her come

around the corner with a trash bag full of god-knows-what. She was holding the bag outstretched as if it had cooties.

"Uh, as good as one can be while picking used condoms up off the floor." She smirked as she dumped the trash bag into a huge bin that had been wheeled into the hallway to assist with their clean-up efforts. "Were some of these members raised in a fucking barn or what?!"

"Yeah, sorry we spend our money on security instead of janitors," Cap laughed, though Paisley failed to find any humor in her present situation.

She slipped the ugly yellow rubber gloves off and placed her right hand emphatically on her ample hip. "I'll just have to bring in a bunch more members so we can hire a custodial staff."

"I like the way she thinks, Casey," Cap announced.

Paisley loved the way his bright blue eyes creased when he smiled. It was almost as endearing as his dimples.

"Well, I told you she was the right choice for the job," Casey agreed. "Now, go on home to the Misses. We can manage without you!" She practically shooed him out the door.

"Men!" Casey sighed, turning back to Paisley when he was at last gone. "Can't live with them; can't live without them. Can't ever get rid of them when you need to!"

Paisley laughed in agreement as she slipped the yellow gloves back on. "I hope you didn't think I was out of line when I complained about picking up the used condoms." Despite feeling good about the success of the night, she didn't want to let her guard down.

"Oh, gosh no, it is indeed a rather unpleasant task," Casey acknowledged. "So, did everything go smoothly for you tonight? Do you have any questions?"

"I think things went as well as they could."

I still can't decide if lusting after your boss when you're both swingers is a No-No. But I feel pretty certain I might have to run the risk of being wrong so I can learn the correct answer.

"So glad to hear. I believe Leah is expecting you to check in with her first thing in the morning. She's going to send her parents out on the boat with Cap's 9 AM charter so she can run into the office really quick to meet with you."

"Oh, good thinking!" Paisley laughed.

She had to admire the way her bosses' minds worked – all three of them. They seemed quite resourceful, able to find indirect solutions to issues when the direct approach wouldn't work. That was how they'd managed to open a swinger club right in the middle of such a conservative small town.

Paisley had a tendency to just plow right through obstacles. Maybe she could learn something from their more careful, diplomatic approach.

As she returned to her Mazda, now the sole car in the parking lot as it had been when she arrived, she glanced up at the night sky. She hadn't seen a sky so dark that even the tiniest stars were visible since she was a young girl. A faint band of them swirled around what might have been a constellation. For a fraction of a second, she was touched by the fleeting memory of her grandfather showing her the moon through a telescope in the cornfield behind the house where she grew up.

I guess it's just me and B.O.B. tonight, she lamented as she popped her key into the ignition. It was her nickname for her favorite vibrator, otherwise known as her *Battery Operated Boyfriend.* She couldn't believe she hadn't had sex in nearly a month.

Whoever winds up on the receiving end of all this pent-

up frustration better be a real stud, she thought with a smirk. *I'm sure going to give him a fucking epic workout!*

❀ ❀ ❀

"So how did it go last night?"

Paisley couldn't help but cast an adoring smile at the round bump protruding from her boss's stomach. It was so distracting, so wonderfully hemispherical, she nearly didn't hear the question.

Leah Sheldon made a picture-perfect pregnant woman. Paisley could scarcely imagine what her boss had looked like before the baby, her pregnant figure was so striking. *She's tall and has such long limbs, she really carries it off.*

Paisley also admired Leah's beautiful strawberry blonde hair: thick, wavy and nestled around her face like a shimmering copper halo. Just as striking was the contrast of the radiant reddish-gold with the cool, thoughtful green of her ever-observant eyes.

Paisley was still trying to unravel the mystery of her youngest boss. Despite her soft, graceful demeanor, Leah sometimes had a firm, businesslike tone that made Paisley doubt they could ever be friends.

I'm pretty sure she thinks she is too good for me. And she's probably right.

"Oh, it was great," she answered, a smile plastered on her face. "Busy, though. You can tell summer is coming soon."

"We'll do lots of temporary memberships for the summer; the three-month ones usually start selling like hotcakes Memorial Day weekend. So you'll want to make sure Casey goes over the procedure for those with you. All of the hosts should be trained in it."

"We had about thirty last night, as a matter of fact, so we got a lot of practice. But I'll make sure all the hosts are aware of the procedures."

"Oh, and there's another project I want you to get started on before it becomes a complete madhouse around here, and while I'm still available." She patted her stomach with a serene smile, as if an explanation for her impending absence was necessary.

Leah continued, "I really want the club to have a website. We have a secret Facebook group right now, but it's hard for visitors to the area to find out about us other than word of mouth. And sometimes members get the crucial information wrong, like the hours, fees, and rules. I want a website with FAQ-type stuff and photos, and also to high-light our commitment to cleanliness and security. Some-thing that looks more professional and official than the Facebook group."

"Oh that sounds fabulous!" Ideas buzzed in Paisley's head like a swarm of bees around their hive.

"But we have to be careful," Leah warned. "The commu-nity here is pretty conservative, and this is supposed to be a family-friendly resort town...though a trip down to the boardwalk on a Saturday night at the height of summer often makes me question that designation."

She simultaneously rolled her eyes and shook her head. "Nevertheless, there are several people who would like nothing better than to force us to close our doors. Anyone who handles our website must sign a non-disclosure agree-ment, and it needs to be a company we can trust to be discreet. I want the website to be classy and professional too."

"I understand," Paisley agreed. "I can put out some RFPs to local agencies, and we can go from there. And if I get the vibe they won't be down with the club, I won't even solicit a proposal. How does that sound?"

"That sounds perfect, thank you! Just use your discretion." Leah smiled so wide, her youthful green eyes showed creases at their edges. "I don't know if I've said it yet, but I'm so glad we hired you. Thank you for everything you've done so far. Cap was raving about the great job you did last night handling everything on your own."

"Of course!" Paisley beamed. "It's my pleasure."

"It really helps me to relax and enjoy my pregnancy to know we have you on board." She rested her hand on the baby bump, and her blingy wedding rings caught the light streaming in from the window in her office, sending rainbow sparkles dancing across the room.

"I'm glad to hear that, thank you." She fought to keep from blushing at the thrill of her boss's approval.

She could perform or discuss any number of sexual acts, in front of an audience even, but a sincere compliment on her knowledge and work ethic embarrassed her. *Go figure.* She wasn't used to accolades, nor dealing with such professional managers. She'd had her share of obnoxious and unfair bosses when she was in New York.

What a nice change of pace. Feeling valued and appreciated is pretty fucking awesome!

TWO

Saturday night was as successful as Friday night, just busier. Paisley reached deep inside to harness the energy and enthusiasm she had for late nights in her twenties. Back then, it wasn't truly a weekend if she wasn't out till dawn, but at thirty-six, her youthful energy was waning.

She scanned the building for any stragglers who required an escort to their cars. An hour ago, she didn't think it was ever going to be 2:00 AM. But now, the club was nearly deserted except for Casey and the hosts helping clean up. The two security guards, Jason and Trent, had each cracked open a can of beer and were sitting with their feet propped up on the bar.

"What the fuck?" Paisley muttered out loud, though she didn't mean to. She had half a mind to whip off one of her nasty yellow rubber gloves and smack them both across the face with it.

"Oh, sorry, Ms. Parker," Trent apologized with just the slightest patronizing undertone. He was the taller of the two, with long limbs, a red beard, and tattoos covering both forearms.

Paisley knew he and his business associate had some inclination toward the lifestyle, or they wouldn't have been hired, but she wasn't sure how experienced they were. The only things she knew for sure about them were that they were both military veterans and had been at The Factory since it opened.

"Get your feet off the bar, gentlemen," she answered, trying not to seethe the words. She was too tired to deal with anyone's shit after being a United Nations-caliber diplomat with club patrons all night.

Trent swung his long legs off the bar and dropped his shiny black boots to the floor with a thud.

Jason chuckled under his breath, then tried to cover up his apparent amusement with a cough. "Excuse my colleague's disrespect," he said with sincerity in his dark eyes. He was shorter and stockier, with a bald head and thick, black eyebrows. Both men were in their late twenties or early thirties, but if she had to guess, she'd say Jason was probably older.

Paisley had piled her long dark curls on top of her head so her hair wouldn't be in her way during the cleaning process. She'd kicked off her heels and stripped off the dress she'd worn all night in favor of a stretchy ribbed tank top and tiny terrycloth shorts that clung to her ample thighs. Trent was quite obviously captivated by the way her flesh jiggled as she walked away. His eyes were burning into her backside with the precision and intensity of laser beams.

"You know, if you guys are gonna stick around, you might want to consider helping out. You know, if you value your jobs and all," she called out in their general direction, whipping around on the word "jobs" to witness their reactions.

They both leapt to their feet and dove for some of the discarded beer bottles and plastic cups around the bar area, tossing them into the waste bin that stood in the hall between the bar and lounge areas.

"That's more like it!" Casey expressed her approval as she came from behind the curtains. "Paisley, darling, I'm going to head out, sweetie. I've got an open house tomorrow."

"Oh, of course, Casey. Thanks for your help. I wasn't expecting it either night. I know you have a lot going on."

Casey sidestepped the garbage bin and headed toward Paisley, who standing in the lounge cleaning the glass tables. Even though she was bent over cleaning, she could feel her mentor's critical eyes wandering over the area.

"Not sure these glass tables are the best idea," the younger woman sighed as she wiped another down with a cloth. Behind her, the forty-two-inch monitor played a scene from a porno. It looked like two bisexual men and a woman, but with the extreme close-up angle and intertwined body parts, it was hard to tell what was going on.

It looks like aliens doing it, Paisley amused herself as she glanced up at the screen.

"New tables. You can add that to your list of ideas." Casey winked, patting her mentee on the arm. "Night, sweetie."

"Night, Casey. See you Monday." She watched her boss exit, teeter to her car in her ubiquitous heels, then her headlights flashed into the club before she drove away. The whole time she was watching Casey leave, Paisley had a series of rather devilish thoughts churning in her head that involved Trent and Jason.

Is there a club policy on fucking staff? I mean, it's a swing club.

How could they possibly frown upon their staff partaking in sex when sex is what this club is for?

The pair of security guards had abandoned their brooms and were making themselves comfortable on one of the loveseats facing the screen. Their eyes were glued to the hot blonde with the fake tits sealed air-tight by her trio of male companions. And though their eyes were affixed to the screen, their hands were glued to their crotches.

"You know, that's a lot harder to accomplish than they make it look in the movies." Paisley settled herself in on the leather armchair opposite the loveseat.

Jason's dark eyes flashed from the screen to hers until they were missile-locked. "You've done that before?"

"When I was a bit younger and a little bit smaller, yes. Takes some patience on the guys' part to get the right angles and get everyone into position."

Now Trent was equally intrigued. "Damn it, that's really hot," he said, but his eyes didn't wander away from the TV. "God, I'm about to bust a seam on these pants, I'm so fucking hard."

She laughed and waved at him dismissively. "Well, don't let me stop you from doing whatever it is you need to do."

A man desperate for release was one of her biggest turn-ons... right up there with a woman desperate for release. The desperation, the longing, the sheer need was intoxicating.

The heat rose to the surface of her skin as Trent shrugged and unfastened the button on his pants with one hand. He pulled the zipper down over his noticeable bulge.

Her mouth began to water as his cock sprang forward. It was long and veiny, nearly purple with need.

This is what happens when I go too long without.

Jason's eyes widened as Paisley blazed a trail to the spot directly in front of Trent on the loveseat. It looked as though his eyeballs might pop out of his head as she dropped herself to the dark blue carpet, her thick legs pressing into the fibers. She rested her elbows on Trent's denim-clad knees and watched his long fingers moving up and down his veiny shaft.

"Need some help with that?" she uttered in a husky voice.

Back when she was dancing, admirers would often ask if she'd done porn. "I could have," she always answered. It wasn't that she didn't have offers.

"You have just the right look for BBW porn," a couple of producers told her. She'd met talent scouts through the years at her shows in New York, looking for the next plus-size It Girl. Paisley didn't regret a lot of things in her life, but sometimes she regretted not having the confidence to really go for it when she was younger.

Jason's eyes weren't the only thing growing as he trained them on Paisley's tongue, which flicked the head of Trent's cock like a snake smelling the air. He reached down and pulled out his own member, which was shorter and thicker than Trent's.

As he pulled up his shirt, Paisley was surprised to find he boasted a set of washboard abs. She wouldn't have guessed it by looking at him, but he clearly spent his leisure time in the gym. Now she had the urge to see his entire body.

Trent strained his erection toward her mouth, his eyes silently begging her to devour him whole. She wanted to make him wait, to make his cock throb with longing before satisfying his wordless request.

Meanwhile, Jason wrapped his thick fingers around his cock and began to slowly stroke up and down while he watched her tease the hell out of just the tip of Trent's manhood. Wanting to see Trent squirm some more, she angled herself toward Jason and lightly touched her lips against his swollen head. She planted a soft kiss, leaving just enough moisture for him to feel the air cool against it when she pulled away.

"You're fucking cruel; you know that?" Trent finally spoke up, the words sounding like they were caught in his throat, needing to be forced out.

She began to pull herself to her feet. "Oh, then I guess I will just go home, in that case." She flashed the pair a wicked smile.

"No!" they both shouted in unison.

Loving the feeling of being in control, she settled back down to her position on her knees. "So who wants to fuck me?"

"Really?" Trent asked, his voice still hoarse with need.

"I might like to kid around about some stuff, but I do *not* joke about sex," she assured them.

Jason didn't wait for his friend to take the offer. He leapt off the couch, cock still in hand, and dropped to his knees behind her. With his other hand, he eased the terrycloth shorts down her thighs, and she helped by kicking them off while she plunged her hot, wet mouth down on Trent's throbbing pole.

The look on his face was priceless, as he'd been watching Jason do the big reveal of her fleshy round ass cheeks and wasn't expecting her to swallow his entire length in one gulp. Paisley glanced up just in time to see his eyes roll back in his head with pleasure, and the sound that escaped his lips was one of passion so deep and primal, it sounded like it came from some dark, steamy jungle.

"Use a condom," Paisley managed to instruct without disrupting the rhythm of her long sucks of Trent's cock all the way down to the base.

Jason complied and reached into his pocket for the square-shaped package. He unrolled it onto his thick, rock-hard tool in record time. Pressing the tip against Paisley's sex, he gasped when he realized how wet and ready she was for him, even though she hadn't been touched at all.

She squealed at the intrusion when only one thrust of his hips rendered him balls-deep inside of her. Hands gripping the soft, ample flesh of her hips, he began to pound his cock into her pussy, completely breaking her concentration on her oral ministrations.

Trent interlaced his fingers through her dark curls and forced her mouth back down on his erection. Neither men were willing to let her slack off on her duties, though she didn't seem to be complaining.

Soon her moans and screams were much louder than the ones coming from the porn. She briefly wondered what would happen if Cap, Leah or Casey just happened to return to the club and walked in on the sight of her being Eiffel-Towered by the security detail.

She had a feeling Casey would laugh and Cap would be turned on, maybe even want in on the action. Leah was the only one she doubted would be amused.

She snapped back to the present when Trent suggested he and Jason trade places.

"I'm about to blow my load," Jason groaned, slowing down his thrusts. Paisley was sure she felt a drop of his sweat land on her backside.

"Trust me, you want to finish in her mouth," Trent managed. "When she's not teasing the shit out of you, she's a helluva good cocksucker."

Paisley laughed, which came out all garbled since her mouth was still full of dick.

Trent helped her off the floor, then pushed her back down on the loveseat. "Why the hell are you still wearing this shirt?" he demanded, literally ripping it from her body.

She'd read in erotic novels about clothes being ripped off heroines, but this was the first time she'd ever witnessed it happening. *Good thing I wasn't emotionally attached to that shirt*, she mused as Trent's hands began to explore her full breasts. Her nipples hardened under his touch, and when she opened her eyes, Jason was standing over her too, still slowly stroking his cock.

Trent leaned his long torso over to the basket under the glass table and grabbed a condom, which were always kept in abundant supply in every room of the club. "I'm going to fuck the hell out of you, babe. You gotta problem with that?"

A laugh caught in her throat, and she choked it down, seeing from the intensity in his blue-gray eyes that he wasn't joking. "And what are you going to do with that thing?" she asked Jason, whose fingers were still wrapped around his stiff shaft.

"He suggested I sample your oral skills," he aimed his cock toward her lips, "and I intend on doing just that."

"Well, don't just stand there, boys." She smirked at them, her eyes glassy with lust. "Get on with it!"

Trent was the perfect height to drop to his knees and align his pelvis with hers. He pulled her body to the edge of the loveseat, and, slinging her thick thighs over his shoulders, he eased his cock into her dripping pussy to make good on his promise. Jason straddled Paisley's face and guided his manhood into her waiting mouth, shoving it deep down her throat.

Pinned underneath both men, Paisley could barely move or breathe, but the action of the two bodies moving inside her, taking pleasure from her, started to build a wall of pleasure in her core that teetered on the verge of collapse. All that stood between her and a universe of ecstasy was a few more strokes.

With Jason's balls slapping against her chin, and Trent's cock slamming into her like a piston, her body exploded with pleasure. The waves rocked through her so violently that both of the men absorbed the shocks into their own bodies.

Feeling her quake beneath him sent a searing streak of pleasure radiating through Jason's balls and surging out the tip of his cock. His climax impending, he pulled out of Paisley's mouth and spewed thick white streams of semen all over her chin, neck and breasts. His knees shaking in recovery, his entire body spasmed while the last drops of his seed oozed out.

When he was finally able to move out of the way, Trent saw the mess he'd made, a thick white puddle glistening under the light cast from the giant chandelier suspended from the ceiling. He locked his blue-gray eyes onto Paisley's bright blue ones and delivered an assault to her pussy the likes of which she had not experienced in months.

Trent's body transformed itself into a jackhammer, pulverizing Paisley's womanhood like a machine. Her swollen lips were growing raw from the intensity, and she was nearly at the point where she couldn't take it anymore when finally, finally, the sweat dripping from his brow, he pulled his cock from her, ripped off the condom and thoroughly drenched her fleshy curves with spurt after spurt of cum.

Afterward, the trio found themselves suspended in time, their bodies struggling to return to homeostasis after being pumped up on lust and adrenaline, nature's most perfect drugs. No one said a word while their breathing stabilized and their hearts established their pre-romp tempos.

"Can you grab me a towel from one of the rooms?" Paisley broke the silence. She remained outstretched on the loveseat, arms spread wide, the semen on her chin starting to drip down her body like a melting icicle in the sun.

Without answering, Jason disappeared and returned moments later with a stack of towels from the laundry room behind the bar and stage area. Paisley gratefully took one and began to wipe up the evidence of their passion.

"I'm gonna jump in the shower before I drive home," she announced.

Trent had just, at that moment, recovered enough breath to speak. His body had been silently heaving with exertion for five minutes straight. "I - that was—" he stammered.

Paisley's lips spread into a smile. "Don't ruin it with a lot of words. Just go on home, okay? I'll lock up."

"That was the hottest night of my entire life," Jason said, his eyes wide and trance-like.

"Just keep it on the DL, okay?" Paisley asked. "It's best for all of us if we keep that in The Vault."

"As long as I get to visit The Vault again someday," he answered wistfully.

When Paisley came back from the shower, both men were gone.

THREE

The packed boxes in Paisley's apartment were mocking her.

The next morning when she woke, she experienced several sensations: a burning in her groin from having her thighs spread so wide, a stiffness in her joints from being stuffed into the loveseat with two men on top of her, and a striking condescension from the multiple cubes of cardboard that held all her worldly possessions.

For the former, there was ibuprofen, and for the latter... there was continued procrastination.

She glared at the boxes. "I know, I know, you're all talking behind my back about what a horrible slob I am, but fuck all of you!"

When her phone chimed with a text, she nearly jumped across the room—at first she thought the boxes were responding to her taunt. But it was only one of her New York friends texting to inquire how her transition to life in Maryland was going.

Allison was one of Paisley's coworkers from the event management company she worked at on Long Island. She was one of the few non-lifestyle folks who knew all the sordid details of Paisley's life, but she also had a wild streak a mile wide. Paisley believed her friend was just in denial about her lifestyle tendencies.

> Paisley: Well, I finally got laid last night, so that's a start.

> Allison: You've been there a month, and you just now had sex? I thought you work at a sex club. What gives, P?!

> Paisley: *laughing emoji*

> Allison: Can you get me a job down there? It's so boring here. And expensive.

Paisley considered for a moment what that might be like. So far she'd been in Ocean City for a month and had yet to make any friends. She had hoped her bosses would introduce her to a few people, or that she would hit it off with more members of The Factory, but she was afraid the former saw her only as an employee and the latter saw her only as management.

How do you make new friends when you're thirty-six?

Allison could be a lot of fun, but she could also be whiny, dramatic and draining. Not to mention the fact that men gravitated to her like magnets to metal.

For once, Paisley wanted to be the center of attention. She fantasized about what it would be like to make friends with a meek little lifestyle newbie, then bring her up in the ways of the force, the force being secret magic swinger mojo, of course.

Allison refused to surrender to the dark side. She wanted to go out to clubs, get drunk, bump and grind on the dance floor, then take an unsuspecting cute guy home to fuck, only to have him magically transform the next morning into a parent-friendly knight in shining armor who wanted a serious relationship. And she failed to see anything improbable or illogical about that scenario.

> Paisley: Oh! That would be fun. I will keep my ears open.

She rifled through a box of clothes until she located her black and white paisley tankini with the ruffled skirt and halter top. She pulled it on, gave herself a quick once-over in the mirror, and headed down to the beach, where she plopped herself onto the warm sand.

She adjusted her sunglasses, drenched her fair skin in sunblock and settled herself in for a morning of sunbathing. While she was remembering the prior evening with a certain fondness, she spotted a pod of dolphins playing in the waves about thirty yards offshore.

Things may not be ideal just yet, but they will be. I can feel it.

Paisley scanned the row of glass doors, the kind with the dark reflective film that prevents anyone from seeing in, much like the doors of The Factory. She finally spotted CM Web Development's surfboard logo, recognizing it from their website and social media platforms.

I guess it's a play on "surfing the web." And we're at the beach. How cute.

She stepped inside the sleek office with modern furniture and counters so shiny they gleamed like silver. The receptionist's chair was empty, though, and the desk bare. It appeared no one held the post.

Looking down the hallway, she counted three doors. There was no bell, so she settled on calling out in her boisterous voice, "Hello? Anyone there?"

After some rustling, a dark head poked out from one of the doors, instantly spotting her in the reception area. In two giant steps, the man's long legs propelled him to the counter. He gave her a charming, if sheepish grin.

"Hi, I'm Calvin Mitchell," he said in a voice as deep and rich as milk chocolate. "You must be Ms. Parker."

He extended his long arm with a welcoming gesture to usher her past the counter. "The second door on the left is my conference room." He wore a striped button-down shirt with the sleeves rolled to his elbows, revealing his well-defined forearms and topaz-colored skin.

Once he was settled in the gray leather executive chair at the head of the table, Paisley could study him more intently. He had closely-cropped black hair, exquisite cheekbones, full lips and light hazel eyes that glowed with intensity. She could have handled his broad shoulders or the ineffectiveness of his dress shirt at concealing his beefy chest muscles, but she was at a loss when it came to handling those eyes. They did her in.

"Ms. Parker?" came his chocolate voice again, echoing through the murky fog that had collected between her ears.

"So this is your business?" She realized as soon as the words were set adrift how patronizing she sounded.

"I'm sorry?" The corner of his mouth turned into a smirk.

Her question generated a spark of fiery indignation in his light-colored eyes, which he quickly tried to disguise with a slight cough into his shoulder and a clearing of his throat. He couldn't have been older than twenty-five, in her estimation. And he certainly didn't look like a computer geek. She was expecting lanky limbs, thick glasses, and a pocket protector, not a bronze-colored hunk with gold-flecked eyes.

"Oh my gosh, please forgive me!" Paisley giggled. Her laugh sounded like a million bubbles floating into the sky, where they hung for a moment before bursting. "You just seem really young to own a business. It's really...commendable," she plucked a word from the deep recesses of her vocabulary. "I meant it as a compliment. Sorry if it didn't come across that way."

"Yeah, well, I've been building websites since I was twelve years old." He straightened his back in the gray leather chair for a moment so she got a full sense of how broad his chest was, then he leaned forward in a smooth but swift motion, placing his elbows on the table, then resting his chin on top of interlaced hands.

His nails were impeccably groomed, but his hands still appeared strong and masculine. "Do you have a website for me to build?"

"As a matter of fact..." her voice trailed off as she found herself about to get lost in those honey-colored eyes. After a narrow escape, she reached into her pocketbook for her business card and laid it on the table in front of him.

This was the furthest she had gotten with any of the firms she had considered for the task of building The Factory's website. She knew immediately upon meeting Calvin's competition that they were too uptight and conventional to build a website for a lifestyle club. She didn't feel comfortable sharing the real business venture at the last web development office she'd visited, so she made up something about owning a handmade jewelry business. Even as innocuous as that was, she still felt like she was being judged.

Calvin picked up the card and studied it. "You don't have a website now?"

She shook her head. "Just a Facebook page, but it's woefully inadequate."

"What does 'on-premises lifestyle club' mean?" He locked his hazel eyes onto hers.

"Uh..." Her cherry-colored lips spread into a full grin, flashing her perfectly straight teeth at him. "Lifestyle, you know, like... swinging." She wasn't one to beat around the bush. Not too much, anyway.

He didn't appear the least bit flustered by her explanation, and his body didn't register even the slightest flinch of discomfort. *Impressive*, she thought, studying his eyes, the way his jaw was set, and how white his teeth were in contrast to his dark skin.

"What kind of functionality will it need? E-commerce or...?"

"It needs to have an online registration form that can accept membership dues, so yes. And other than that, just a home page, FAQ, and photos. Nothing terribly fancy. I just want it to look clean and professional."

"Well, that won't be a problem," he assured her. "I should be able to put together a mock-up by the end of the week. Can you send me the content? Hi-res photos and logos, please. Also any social media or blogs you want integrated."

"Of course," Paisley answered, finding it hard to disguise her disappointment with his business-like demeanor. She couldn't help but try to probe beneath the surface, searching for a crack in the veneer, a small clue to whether or not Calvin Mitchell had a wild side.

She found it when he walked her to the door. She was pressing the bar to push it open when he laid a warm hand on her bare shoulder. "This is going to be a badass website, Ms. Parker," he said, smooth as jazz flowing out of a saxophone. "You won't regret giving me the opportunity to build it."

Confident too, I love that... "Please, call me Paisley."

"Pretty name..." His hazel eyes were bright as gold coins as they danced over her face.

"Just let me know when you have the mock-up done." She winked, hoping to leave him wanting more. That was always her mission.

Exiting the door, she was strong as steel and didn't look back. But she could feel his eyes boring into her, more than likely affixed to her ample derriere. She thought with a sly smile: *Mission accomplished.*

FOUR

P aisley was in the midst of enjoying a delicious dark-skinned hunk with muscles galore when she was rudely awakened by the sound of her phone vibrating on the nightstand. She reluctantly traveled back to consciousness, still feeling hot and tingly between her thighs.

She'd missed a phone call from a blocked number. *Great*, she seethed, *way to ruin my dream, asshole.* She never answered blocked or unfamiliar numbers, anyway.

She also noticed she had a text: *good morning, beautiful*, from a 410 number, which she knew to be one of the two area codes for Ocean City.

Still perturbed by being kidnapped from her peaceful and erotic slumber, she answered:

> Paisley: Did you just try to call me from a blocked number?

She didn't realize the text had been sent hours before at 2 AM. The reply came back swiftly:

Unknown number: No. This is Jason, from the club.

Jason from the club. She scanned her archives for a Jason. Mental images of myriad Jasons began popping up, projected against the back of her eyelids like old-fashioned family movies. *Jason Gregory? Jason Dukes? Jason. Hmmm...*

Jason: The security guard?

Oh, that Jason. She failed to recognize him when separated from his comrade Trent, the pair who had tag-teamed her after-hours only nights before. This was Tuesday, and she felt more removed from that incident than ever. That was Weekend Paisley. She was currently operating in Weekday Paisley mode.

She put the phone back on the nightstand and ran her fingers through her tangle of matted curls. The book she'd fell asleep reading emerged from the twisted sheets, and she fondly remembered how the hero and heroine had just had a very sexy romp on the beach when she drifted off.

She stumbled into her kitchen, noting the sun was already high in the sky. *I hope no one is missing me at the office.*

While she contemplated the steps for making coffee, another text came in.

Jason: What, you don't want to talk to me?

Just that tiny annoyance started a chain reaction inside her body, resulting in a throbbing headache.

> Paisley: Is there something I can help you with?

Why do men think women being nice are leading them on, but women saying no are bitches? There's no right way to reject a man.

I shouldn't be jumping to conclusions, though. Maybe he wants something work-related. I shouldn't assume he wants some of this...

She giggled while examining the way the sunlight passing through the kitchen blinds was striping her pale breasts with dark shadowy bands.

> Jason: Will you be at the club this weekend?

> Paisley: Of course. It's my job.

> Jason: Think you'll stick around afterwards?

> Paisley: Yes. To clean up.

> Jason: Oh, so not to suck my cock again?

Dammit. Why does my intuition have to be so damn good? She exhaled every last oxygen atom from her lungs to keep from firing back a rude response.

> Paisley: That was a one-time thing.

She hoped he would take it in the spirit in which she intended, which was "I'm trying to be nice, so please don't push me."

Jason: *frown emoji* I understand. But would you go out with me sometime?

Ugh. Relentless, she sighed. *Why do men force women to go through this?*

Paisley: I don't date employees, sorry.

Finally, a glimmer of hope he'd received the message...

Jason: OK. Well, see you this weekend.

I need a few non-club members who are satisfied with being fuck buddies and nothing more.

Or maybe she could target tourists spending the weekend at the beach.

That would be perfect, right? Once I'm done with them, they'll be ready to head back home.

She'd have to figure out a strategic perch for luring in her prey.

Paisley sailed into the office nonchalantly, hoping no one would notice she was late. The only person in was Casey, meticulously garbed in a Kelly-green suit with a gauzy floral scarf artfully draped around her neck. She was on the phone and waved to Paisley as she headed into the space they'd designated as hers.

It wasn't a full-blown office with four walls and a door, but it was her own space with a beautifully stained antique mahogany desk and a comfortably padded swivel chair. She had a laptop with a docking station and internet access and a metal filing cabinet with a file for every current and past member.

Casey had given her the task of following up with members who had not renewed their annual memberships. "So, I'm just supposed to ask them why they haven't renewed?" She wrinkled her nose slightly in confusion.

"Be diplomatic," Casey advised her. "Some of them will have left the lifestyle, gotten divorced, broken up, moved away... You never know what kind of sensitive situations might be at play. Be positive and upbeat, then invite them back. Offer them a discount if they renew. Twenty percent off!"

She was planning to start working her way through the expired memberships when she saw her computer screen flash with an incoming email from Calvin Mitchell. With absolutely no effort or control on her part, a mental image of him sitting at his conference table in the gray leather executive chair flashed on like a light bulb, and a wave of electricity raced up and down her spine. She was astounded by the effect just seeing his name had on her.

She scanned the message. He wanted to meet her for a drink and go over the three designs he had created for her to choose from. *Three? I thought we agreed on a single mock-up.*

She decided to give him a call. She didn't think Leah would want to pay for extra design work.

"Hello, Calvin?" she spoke smoothly into the phone. She may or may not have done a brief stint as a phone sex operator, just another colorful entry in her vast catalog of past life experiences. "It's Paisley Parker from The Factory."

"Yes, hi, Paisley," he replied in his silky voice. "Did you get my email?"

"I did, but I wasn't expecting you to do three mock-ups. I—"

"Oh, right, well, I just enjoyed doing a fun project for once so I...I might have gone a little overboard. I hope that's not a problem. I'm really anxious to show you what I came up with."

"I'm looking forward to seeing them. I could drop by your office later if—"

"I thought maybe you'd meet me for a drink. Or dinner," he suddenly upped the ante.

She squinted as if it would help her understand what was going on. "You mean like a date?"

He chuckled, deep and rich like dark chocolate ganache oozed over a cake. "A business dinner," he clarified. "Kind of like a business lunch except later in the day. You know, since it's past lunchtime now."

"Semantics," Paisley sighed. "Where would you like to meet? I'm sure the boardwalk will be crazy busy." She was already starting to hate tourist season, and it had just gotten started. It took her twenty minutes just to get to the inlet bridge that morning.

"The club is near Berlin, right?"

"Yes," she affirmed. "Kinda in the middle of nowhere between Berlin and Assateague Island."

"Perfect. There's this crab house on the way out to the island that's pretty secluded and quiet. I can bring my laptop and show you what I've come up with. Is that convenient for you?""

She vaguely knew the place he was speaking of. She'd only been out to Assateague once and remembered passing this shack-like restaurant. She hadn't been able to discern whether or not it was actually open for business, it was so dilapidated with a faded sign and parking lot overgrown with weeds.

"Uh...I think I know where you're talking about?"

"I know it doesn't look like much, but I swear to a higher power, they have the best crabs you've ever had in your life."

She tried not to giggle at the idea of having crabs being a good thing. Sometimes she was pretty sure her sense of humor had been hijacked by the depraved soul of some fourteen-year-old boy.

"I don't know if I do crabs..." she admitted, fully realizing it was sacrilege to dislike crabs on the Eastern Shore of Maryland, sacrilege in the sense that crabs were practically a religious experience on the shore.

"Well, have you had blue crabs straight outta the bay?"

"Um..." The conversation had taken a precarious turn, one she wasn't prepared for.

"Just meet me there at six," he said.

"Six," she repeated. And then he was gone.

Casey popped her perfectly coiffed head into her space. "Did I hear you say something about crabs?"

Paisley rolled her eyes. *See, these people are completely nuts about them!*

"I'm going to look over the designs for the website with the web developer tonight," she explained. "I guess we're going out for crabs."

"Have you ever picked crabs before?" Casey asked. "It's messy. Don't wear anything you mind getting dirty."

She had to laugh. Usually when she thought about getting dirty on a date, it had nothing to do with the food they were eating. "Thanks for the tip!"

Casey smiled. Her teeth were shockingly straight and white for a woman her age. Her impeccable presentation never ceased to amaze Paisley. She glanced down at her boss's feet and saw she was wearing Kelly-green sling-backs with a kitten heel that matched her suit perfectly. *Of course.*

She always felt frumpy and disheveled next to Casey, even when she had really taken her time getting ready. Although, she had not dressed with much care that morning since she was running late. She was wearing a simple black knee-length A-line skirt with gladiator sandals and a white and black print tank top. She hadn't even bothered to put on jewelry.

She wondered if she should go home and change before meeting Calvin, but the idea of creeping slowly up Coastal Highway in the snarled tourist-clogged traffic to her apartment just to come back south again was a daunting prospect.

Black and white it is!

"Paisley?" Casey's voice knocked on the door of her overtaxed brain.

She glanced up at the older woman, her bright blue eyes sparkling with admiration. "Yes?"

"I just wanted to make sure you're doing okay," she explained, "you know, personally. Are you adjusting to life away from the big city?"

Paisley felt a little glob of emotion catch in her throat, but she swallowed it down. "Oh, yeah, of course. I love it here!"

"Are you sure?" Casey studied her expression for any signs of deceit. "You've never spoken of your family or personal life...and please forgive me if I'm prying; you can just tell me to butt out if you'd like. I just want you to know we care about our employees here. We're like a family, and we like to make sure everyone's happy, not just with their jobs, but with their work-life balance and all that."

Paisley had never had a boss ask her if everything was okay in her personal life. As a matter of fact, she'd had many bosses refuse to speak to her about personal issues that interfered with her ability to do her job.

She remembered the man who managed the club where she began her dancing career. One time he told her straight-up: "Nobody gives a fuck about your problems, little girl."

Every time she started to feel an ounce of self-pity, she would hear his gruff voice in her head. They had become a tree inside her, deeply rooted, taking its energy from her dreams and bearing the fruit of self-assurance and independence.

"I'm used to being alone," Paisley explained. "I had a roommate in New York, but he was a pain in the ass, so I'm glad to finally be able to afford my own place. I'm sure in time I'll meet some people to hang out with."

"So your family isn't in New York?"

Paisley shook her head. "No, no, haven't seen my family in a long time. Hey, I've been meaning to ask you..." She took a deep breath and considered how she wanted to phrase her question. "What's the club policy about...staff playing with members?"

She gauged Casey's reaction and decided to add, "It's just that I've been lifestyle for so long, and pretty much all the lifestyle folks around here are club members, so..."

"You know, we've never really talked about it." Casey laughed, a bit sheepish about their oversight. "I think we just expect staff to be discreet and judicious about what they do and who they hang out with. You know, just try to make good decisions."

"So that's a no?" Paisley guessed. She wasn't sure if Casey was someone she could just cut to the chase with or not. She and Leah always seemed so...proper. She might have been more comfortable having this conversation with Cap.

"I'm not saying no to it!" Casey erupted with a crystalline laugh. Paisley could see she was struggling to find the right words. "You know, a lot of lifestyle folks are mature and low-drama... and others are pretty much the opposite. As long as you've been around, I'm sure you can spot the difference."

A smile crept across Paisley's face. "Yes, I know exactly what you mean by that."

She wondered if she'd made a huge mistake when she indulged Jason and Trent in their sexy romp the other night. She wasn't sure how experienced they were in the lifestyle, though they'd been at The Factory long enough to see how it worked.

Well, if they want to keep their jobs, they'll be mature about it and take it for what it was. She refused to regret her choice to play.

The sun was starting its descent toward the horizon when she made her way to the crab house to meet Calvin. It was that time of evening when the entire earth appeared dipped in gold. Sunlight dripped from the leaves of the trees lining the road, the fields, and the little creeks and marshes that preluded the mighty Atlantic reflecting the glory of the dying sun.

Despite having lived on Long Island, the beach was a foreign concept to her, the edge of the continent slipping away under one's feet the farther one crept into the surf. And the way the waves pounded the shore, always trying to carry swimmers back onto the land made it seem like the ocean rejected human visitors.

But the attitudes toward the water down here in Maryland were different. People vacationed here. Cap made his living taking tourists out on his boat to catch striped bass and flounders. There was a sport-fishing tournament every year where they'd reel in marlins and sharks and god-knows-what other wild and dangerous creatures.

There was a reverence and awe of the ocean here that she never saw up north. And it made her curious to see what the fuss was about.

Her GPS reminded her that her destination was on the right in a quarter mile. She had lost herself for a moment in the golden promise of the sunset, but she squinted to see the narrow gravel entrance to the parking lot and whipped her Mazda into it just in time, hearing the loose gravel rumble beneath her tires.

When she parked she realized it wasn't gravel after all, but tiny pieces of broken white shells. Low clouds with golden underbellies hung over the crab shack with its weathered wood and faded sign. She only saw a few cars in the parking lot, which didn't exactly inspire a lot of confidence in the quality of the food. It was high tourist season, after all.

She didn't see Calvin and wasn't sure what type of vehicle he drove, so she ventured inside and told the hostess she needed a table for two.

"Oh, are you meeting someone?" she asked with a knowing smile. She pointed toward the large windows on the other side of the restaurant that overlooked a marshy tributary, which no doubt led to the bay.

Calvin's face was glowing from the light emitted by the laptop in front of him. She was afraid he was going to be startled by her presence as she pulled the wooden chair back from the table. But instead, his hazel eyes appeared over the screen and creased as his lips stretched into a grin.

"Well, good evening, Ms. Parker," he greeted her formally.

"Hi, Calvin," she responded, setting a more casual tone as she took her seat across from him.

The waitress came by before any other words could be spoken. Paisley stalled when deciding whether to order something alcoholic, so Calvin decided for her, ordering two cocktails from their summer drink menu.

"Hope you're hungry," he said as the waitress walked away to retrieve the drinks.

"I am, but I have to be honest, I've never picked crabs before. Casey told me it's messy!"

"It can be, but I'll show you how." He winked at her. "Before the mess, let's take a look at these mock-ups." He fiddled with the laptop for a moment, then whipped it around to face her. "This is option one."

It was simple and elegant with a charcoal gray background and the logo at the top. There were tabs for home, about, photos, FAQs, and membership. It seemed easy to navigate as Paisley clicked her way through all the tabs. "Okay, that's nice. It's clean and uncluttered; I like that."

He adjusted the laptop again and presented it to her. This option was more brightly colored, heavily drawing from the lime and fuchsia accent colors inside the club. It looked fun and flirty, and the functionality was just as good as the sleek charcoal gray site.

"It looks really trendy; I like that." She was impressed with how different the two sites felt even with the exact same content.

"Okay, here's option number three," he announced, bringing the third page into view.

She gasped when she saw it because she knew immediately. The home page looked like the inside of the club. It had the retro steampunk industrial look they'd worked so hard to achieve. Instead of tabs along the top, there were interconnected gears along the left side, each one a different area to explore. When you clicked the gear, it turned and then appeared to unlock that section of the site as if it were behind a vault. It was absolutely perfect.

"Well?" His eyes were wide as he waited for feedback.

If she'd been drinking her cocktail, she probably would have choked on it.

"Too busy? Too much?" For the first time, he had a slight crack in his confident veneer, revealing the slightest youthful insecurity as he anxiously awaited her answer.

"No, god no, you nailed it!" she gasped, the air rushing into her lungs right. "I absolutely love it! Can you send the link to me? I want to show it to the owners and get their feedback."

"Okay, we do need to talk about the domain, though. I can't get the *factory dot com*, but I can get *the factory oc dot com*. Does that work?"

"I'll need to check with them, but I don't see why not." As she gushed her approval, the waitress returned with their drinks, a glittery coral concoction garnished with a cherry and a chunk of pineapple speared by plastic swords. "Fancy!" She laughed as she popped the sword into her mouth and used her teeth to rake the fruit off.

The cocktails took the edge off, the business motivations for their meeting slowly evaporating along with inhibitions and small talk. By the time the crabs arrived at their table, they were on their second round of drinks, and she was thinking of other creative uses for the wooden mallets they'd been given. "Spider killing," she suggested. "Unruly children. Courtroom gavel?"

She eyed the pile of steaming hot crabs on the tray between them. "What's that stuff all over them? Is that sand?"

He chuckled. "No, no, that's Old Bay."

"Old Bay? You act like I should know what that is."

"Oh, it's a seasoning. People down here put it on everything, but especially on crabs."

She nodded. *More local weirdness; got it.* She grabbed the mallet and poised it over the shell of the creature, whose beady little eyes were angled right toward her. "Oh, god, I don't know if I can do this!"

"Well, it's already dead, so you might as well eat it!"

"But it's looking right at me!"

"Come on, Paisley, I didn't take you for a shy, squeamish girly-girl," he said, his words trimmed in satin.

He had this way of speaking that set him apart from anyone she'd ever known. An impossible-to-place accent, a richness to the way he enunciated every word.

"I'll show you, okay?" He ripped off the legs and claws, flipped the body over, and used a knife to pry underneath the pointy tab-like indention. Then he tore the entire thing open. "Lots of good stuff in here," he said, digging at it with the knife.

"What the hell? This is the most violent meal I've ever eaten!" Paisley laughed. "I need another drink to do this."

An hour later, they were surrounded by discarded crab parts, and the table was saturated with crab guts and butter. "So, what do you think now?" Calvin asked, grinning at her.

"Disgusting!" she answered. "And delicious!"

It was amazing the amount of ground two people could

cover in the course of picking crabs. She'd found out that Calvin originally grew up in Baltimore, but his entire family moved to the shore around the time he started college because his dad took a new job. He was the oldest of three sons, and his mother stayed at home with them all until he was in junior high, and then she went back to school to become a nurse. He'd played football in high school and was recruited by a few Division I schools to play in college, but he wanted to stay close to his family.

"Awww, that's sweet!" Paisley cooed. *Clearly the alcohol has gone to my head.*

She had meant to keep her walls a little more firmly in place, but the combination of the cocktails and those damn hazel eyes of his just made them crumble away.

"So what about your family? Are you close with them?" he asked as if it were the most natural question in the world. And it did follow logically that she would discuss her family next but...

The F word instantly sobered her. "Oh, well, I—"

She was always trying to find a new way to explain the situation that would be more comfortable for the other person. It was nothing to her, not anymore, anyway, but it really seemed to put other people on edge.

She typically tried to sugarcoat it as much as possible by saying she didn't talk to her family, or that there just wasn't anyone left but her. Unfortunately, with her only being thirty-six, it was a little hard for others to believe the latter, and it tended to spur follow-up questions, which is what she wanted to avoid.

She cleared her throat, sensing he was getting impatient for her answer, and the discomfort was already settling in. She didn't want to ruin what had been a delightful evening, so she took the path of least resistance. "Oh, they're great, but I don't see them much."

"Oh, why is that?"

Shit. He was supposed to just shrug it off and change the subject. "Oh, everyone's just so busy, that's all."

"That's too bad," he observed. She could tell he wanted to probe a little deeper, but he thought better of it, and she was grateful. "Family is a person's foundation, their roots. I don't know how anyone makes something of himself without a strong, supportive family in his corner."

Huh, she thought. *Well, I did. And I didn't have help from anyone.*

She downed the rest of her third drink and began to formulate an exit strategy. She realized what a critical error it had been to agree to dinner.

He was just so intriguing when I met him last week. And I've been so desperate to meet someone not affiliated with the club. Well, at least we got our website. That's what really matters.

After an awkward silence settled in on their table like a fog hugging the shoreline, Calvin furrowed his brows and asked her if he'd said something wrong. "I'm sorry if I pumped you too hard for information," he apologized.

"No, no, I just need to think about getting home. And I definitely cannot drink a single drop more!"

"Me either," he agreed. "I hope you don't think it was too forward for me to ask you to dinner."

"Well, I don't know if 'forward' is the word I'd use."

The sunset had left a blood-red streak sitting on the edge of the water, being pushed lower and lower by the pink and purple bands above it. Soon it would fall into the bay and sink deep to the bottom, making room for the stars to pierce the sky and admire their reflections in the watery mirror.

"So you think I'm totally crazy for wanting to date you?" he asked, that boyish vulnerability he'd shown a glimpse of earlier in the evening coming back full-force.

She had to shake her head to replay his question in her head again. *I'm pretty sure he said the word "date." What the hell?*

"Calvin, this is a business dinner...like you said, a business lunch that happens to be later in the day."

"Well, truth be told, I only said that—"

"How old are you?" She straightened up in the booth and pressed her eyes into his like she was flattening cookie dough, slowly and deliberately.

He offered up his deep chuckle like a gift, a distraction. "I don't get what that has to do with anything. Is it because of my race?"

"What?! That has absolutely *nothing* to do with it," she gasped. "You've got to be at least ten years younger than me, and in case you couldn't figure it out, I'm kind of a swinger," she hissed the last word in a whisper.

He laughed again as if this entire conversation was the after-dinner show. "I'm twenty-six," he said when he finally stopped.

"Well, I'm thirty-six, so guess what, I was right!"

The corners of his lips turned down as a seriousness gripped his features. "I like you, Paisley. The minute you walked through the door of my office I immediately felt myself drawn to you."

She wanted to pinch herself. This was not a conversation she had ever been part of. She was used to saying yes and she was used to saying no, but she didn't know what to say to a gorgeous, younger man saying he felt "drawn" to her.

What the hell does that even mean? The question hung in her mind while she tried to find another excuse besides the age and swinger thing.

"So, age is not an issue for me," he clarified. "I just want a chance to get to know you."

"Calvin," she enunciated, "I'm not really a... Uh, I'm not really the type of woman who dates men."

"What do you mean? Are you a lesbian? Do you date women?"

She didn't detect any judgment in his questions, but she still felt trepidation. Everything inside her was saying, "Shut this down," except a tiny part – probably her clit – that was thinking, *hmm, wonder if he's any good in...*

"No, I mean, I like women, but I don't date men *or* women," she finally managed.

"So, what, are you like asexual or something? I thought swingers liked sex." She was clearly a mystery that he was committed to unraveling.

She was growing frustrated by his tenacity. The very quality that had allowed him to rise to the top of his field and run his own business was annoying the ever-loving shit out of her at that very moment, and her mind was scrambling for something – anything – that would convey that this conversation was over.

She took a deep breath and blurted out, "I don't date; I don't do relationships... I just fuck. No dating, just fucking."

And that was the end of that.

FIVE

After six weeks of hard work, Paisley had been given a reprieve. Casey surprised her with a night off and gave permission for her to attend the club as a guest, not as a manager.

"That's yet another benefit of us hiring a new manager!" Casey's face wore a victorious grin. "We can rotate, and each get a night off once a month or so. Brilliant, right, Cap?"

Cap nodded. "And not to mention how deserving she is of playtime." His dimples were on full display, ocean-blue eyes sparkling like the deepest waters caressed by the sun.

Paisley didn't know what to say. She had worked weekends for years, both when she was dancing as well as when she did event management, and she never had a Friday or Saturday off, not unless she called in sick or it was Christmas. To have bosses with kindness and humanity was a brand-new experience for her.

"I don't even know what to say! I'm thrilled!"

"Think of it as a reward for getting the new website up

and running so quickly," Leah added. "It really does look amazing. It's exactly what I envisioned."

Paisley was beaming. There was something about her bosses that made her want to impress them, to surpass their expectations. Her smile faded and tone dropped down as she gave them one more opportunity to change their minds.

"I'd love to enjoy the club tonight, but only if you're absolutely sure you can do without me." Leah was planning to step in for her; she knew it might be one of her last nights to run the club for a long time as she was now in her eighth month.

Leah nodded, smiling and glowing despite her nearing due date. "Yes, I'm actually feeling pretty energetic! And besides, I want you to meet some of the ladies before the shower on Thursday. We have a really nice group of women in the club who you should get to know."

Paisley had almost forgotten about the baby shower. She knew next to nothing about babies and didn't have the slightest idea what to buy, but fortunately Casey had suggested she go in with her on a bigger gift for the new arrival. They were going to buy the baby's crib. She didn't mind forking over a couple hundred dollars. *After all, if it weren't for this baby, I wouldn't even have this job.*

She found herself facing the difficult task of staying out of work mode once she entered the club, even though she came through the front doors instead of the side one for employees. She did pause to pick up some garbage that someone had left in the lounge because she just couldn't help herself.

Okay, now I'm going to relax and have fun. She marched right up to the bar, checked in her liquor and asked the bartender, Erik, to pour her a drink.

"Sure thing, Boss!" he replied cheerfully as he sloshed vodka in a glass and topped it off with juice.

"Not 'Boss,' tonight, just Paisley." She winked at him.

"Oh, very nice. Cheers!" He grinned with his perfect, straight white teeth.

Why hadn't she ever considered what he might be hiding in those tight Wrangler jeans of his? He nailed the quintessential country boy look with a button-down shirt, metal belt buckle and cowboy boots. She could go for that look. *And he most definitely pulls it off.*

She watched him turn and reach under the bar for something. *Nice view!*

She scanned the club from her perch at the bar, across the dance floor to the far reaches of the lounge. *The world is my oyster tonight. And I'm going to make up for lost time.*

After all, she had been a perfect angel since getting down and dirty with the security guards, Trent and Jason. Couples were arriving in packs at this point, six to eight in a group. Her fun-seeking side gave each couple the once-over, looking for sparks, but her business side wished she'd brought in two sets of hosts, as Pam and Frank seemed to be having a hard time keeping up. Leah was taking up the slack, and Paisley hated seeing her pregnant body waddle repeatedly down the hallway.

Maybe putting on something more comfortable would get me in the right mood to enjoy myself. She swished the last drops of her mixed drink in her mouth before sending it down the hatch.

After leaving Erik a tip, she headed off to the women's dressing room where she'd stashed a bag with her lingerie earlier in the day. She slipped the tight black dress up over her head and pulled out a corset, tulle skirt, fishnet stockings and her high-heeled boots.

Okay, this doesn't exactly qualify as more comfortable, but it is a lot...sexier.

A size twenty-two, Paisley was blessed with a well-proportioned hourglass figure that looked amazing in a corset. The one she brought was black with red satin insets covered with black lace. It had metal clasps up the front, steel boning, and tight black laces in the back. She shimmied into it and scanned the room for someone to help her tie it.

Her eyes fell on a woman in her forties with blonde curls and heavily made-up hazel eyes. "Do you mind tightening these laces for me?" she asked as the woman finished applying her thick mascara.

Her lips curled upward as she turned to face Paisley. "You look familiar. Have you been here before?"

Paisley extended her hand to the lady. "I'm Paisley Parker, the new assistant operations manager. They gave me the night off so I could play."

"Oh, that's wonderful! You're the one they brought in to help out when Leah is out with the new baby." She pumped Paisley's arm up and down while she was talking. She quickly straightened her posture as if she was trying to make a good impression. "I'm Shannon, by the way."

"It's a pleasure to meet you, Shannon." She didn't waste any time turning to give Shannon access to the corset laces. And Shannon didn't pull any punches either, giving the laces a firm tug until Paisley's midsection was compressed to minimum size.

"Wow, okay, that's good. I can still get a little air in my lungs."

"You look fabulous!" Shannon exclaimed and headed out the door.

Paisley followed her, feeling like she needed one more

drink to really dig deep and expose her true exhibitionist side. She headed back to Erik, who was obviously rather impressed with her transformation. His eyes were immediately glued to her breasts, which all but spilled out the top of the corset.

"Good lord, Paisley!" He shook his head as he found her bottle of vodka and began pouring her another drink. "You sure know how to rock a corset."

"Why thank you, good sir." She blew him a kiss as she downed the drink in only a few swallows. Then she turned her attention to the dance floor.

A new song had just begun, and the thumping bass made her feet move involuntarily. Her body vibrated with the beat, urging her out onto the dance floor. Two other women were already grinding against each other while their dates perched on the edge of the sofa as if watching their own private performance.

As she began to approach the women, she the alcoholic buzz surged through her body. She hadn't had a drop of liquor since the night she met Calvin Mitchell for dinner, and tonight she hadn't had anything to eat, so every intoxicating molecule rushed directly to her brain. She fought off the dizzy feeling and let the music thunder through her, feeling it from the inside out instead of the other way around.

Her boots clicked against the parquet floor as she found her rhythm, and the two women opened up their tight circle to let her join in. One had wavy, layered auburn hair and deep, dark eyes to match. She was pear-shaped with narrow, white creamy shoulders and full, luscious hips. The other woman was a tall, willowy blonde who was also wearing a corset, though she wasn't nearly as well-endowed as Paisley.

Some plus-size ladies might have felt intimidated or out-of-place next to thinner or average-sized ladies, but Paisley had long ago stopped comparing herself to other women. That was one of the many lessons she learned during her time as a burlesque dancer.

Some nights she had dozens more guys slipping her bills than the fit, athletic pole dancers did. There was an audience for every look, and she had the voluptuous, pin-up brunette look down to a T.

Women of size often asked her how she managed to have so much confidence. Sometimes they seemed to be in awe, and other times the statement came with the subtext that it was wrong for her to have such a high opinion of herself. Even thinner women seemed jealous of her confidence, it seemed.

Yes, she had moments where she felt fat and unattractive just like every other woman, but the simple fact was that men loved how secure she was. They appreciated that she didn't require a constant stream of validation and affirmation. All she needed was to look into their eyes and see their desire, their attraction. That was all the positive reinforcement she needed.

And if she didn't see that in their eyes? She simply shrugged and walked away. *After all, I can't be everyone's cup of tea.*

Her goals were simply to be healthy and happy. That meant she ate dessert when she wanted, and ate a lot of healthy, whole foods too. And she tried her best to get 10,000 steps in a day. She always got a clean bill of health along with an astonished look when she had a check-up. Doctors weren't used to seeing healthy fat people in their offices, especially ones who wouldn't allow themselves to be fat-shamed. Paisley refused to see any doctor who berated her about her weight.

The woman with the red hair introduced herself as Kayla, as well as her husband, Derek, in the murky pause between one song and another. They were a younger couple, whom Paisley guessed to be in their early thirties. When Paisley was younger and enjoying her much-desired unicorn status, she always felt like everyone was so much older than she was. In some ways it was nice to be on the other side of that gap.

Derek was about her height with a beard and full head of shaggy, dark hair. He was a bit on the hipster side with thick black-framed glasses and a plaid button-down shirt topping dark-washed skinny jeans. Tattoos popped up out of his collar and extended below his shirt cuffs. His dark eyes were glued to hers as she reached down to stroke her finger down his wife's cleavage, eliciting a moan from her lips that was swallowed by the sound of the next song winding up. When she finally let her eyes meet his, she saw that look she loved: the one of anticipation, of hunger.

She led the couple down the hall, then up the twisting staircase to the second floor. Her favorite spot in the club, the jungle room, was at the end, right above the hot tub room. It was one of the bigger rooms at The Factory, its central feature a round bed with a canopy of twisted vines and mosquito netting. The aesthetic was a tent in the deep, dark South American jungle, with jungle sound effects piped in through a speaker.

In all the clubs she had ever been to, Paisley had never seen attention to detail to rival this room. It was a work of art. Calvin had even remarked on it when she sent him photos for the website.

"What happens in *that* room?" he had asked, his gold-hazel eyes wide with curiosity.

"Why don't you come down some weekend and find out

for yourself?" she had retorted, knowing full well he wouldn't.

Kayla stopped at the curved edge of the bed and stood with her hands on her hips as if awaiting instruction. This was Paisley's forte. Too often swinger newbies didn't know how to get things started, how to set the ball in motion, so to speak. Paisley stepped forward, urged on by her desire for this beautiful, naive creature standing before her.

"Have you been with a woman before?" Paisley let the words blow out of her mouth and onto Kayla's neck, then she stamped them down with her lips against the tender flesh. As the kisses soaked into her skin, Kayla's body trembled beneath her mouth.

Not waiting for an answer, Paisley tickled the ridge under Kayla's collarbone with her tongue, making the woman swoon, her knees buckling and rendering her unsteady on her pointy high heels. Paisley didn't have to look at Derek to know that a stiff bulge had already grown in his pants.

"This is only our second time to the club," he answered for his wife. "Last time we mostly observed. It's pretty new to us."

Virgins! Paisley squealed inside her head. Some seasoned lifestylers got sick of initiating newbies, of bringing them into the fold, but she reveled in it. Maybe that was why she was so well suited for her job.

She didn't answer the husband's comment directly but instead whispered to his wife, "Don't worry, I'll go easy on you...this time."

She bent down and followed up her promise with a trail of soft kisses along Kayla's décolletage. She slipped her arm around the redhead's waist to help keep her upright when her knees wanted to give way again. It was painfully obvious that Kayla had never experienced the sensual touch of a woman before, and her synapses were overloaded, firing like cannons throughout her body.

Paisley pushed her down onto the round bed, right on top of the aqua-blue satin comforter that made the bed look like an oasis of water in the deep recesses of the jungle. The soundtrack filled the room with sounds of birds, frogs, and monkeys screeching at each other, punctuated periodically by the deep, primal growl of a jaguar.

Paisley took inspiration from the symphony of wildlife, grooming her inner jungle cat for an impending pounce. She stalked her prey carefully: no sudden movements, her eyes singularly focused on the woman's outstretched limbs, ears attuned to her low moans and labored breaths. When the time was right, she'd strike.

She didn't concern herself with Derek, who watched from the corner. He had taken off his skinny jeans and now stood in his tight boxer briefs, the outline of his erection easily visible.

I'll let him join in eventually. She slowly peeled Kayla's clothes away from her writhing body with deft, nimble fingers.

Bending over in her tight corset wasn't the easiest feat, but she managed to straddle the redhead even in her fishnets and boots. She lowered herself, careful not to put any weight on her prey. Propping herself on her elbows, she lightly brushed her lips against the pair below her. It was like a key unlocking a door as Kayla's mouth opened, receptive to Paisley's tongue.

She licked the redhead's bottom lip, then nibbled at it gently before continuing her exploration down to Kayla's breasts. They were perky C cups that sat on top of her ribcage like two scoops of ice cream. Her pale flesh practically glowed under the light, highlighting the network of aqua-colored veins that crisscrossed underneath. She was breathtaking.

Paisley's eyes were like cameras, snapping dozens of freeze-frames for her memory. She'd file them away in her album of beautiful women she had bedded throughout the years.

She flicked her tongue against one ripe, strawberry-hued nipple, and Kayla nearly came unglued, her body jerking against Paisley's. Derek appeared beside the bed to get a closer look as Paisley sucked his wife's nipple into her mouth and gently suckled it before raking her teeth against it.

"Ahhhh!" Kayla gasped, half in pain, half in pleasure.

Paisley couldn't hide her devilish grin as she gauged how easy it was going to be to make Kayla come all over her face if she nearly lost it over having her nipple bitten.

She planted more kisses and nibbles on Kayla's smooth abdomen and her ample hips, pausing over each hipbone. She pressed her thumbs in and slid her fingers underneath, scooping the beauty's pelvis up to her mouth for her first taste of her pussy. She swiped her tongue directly up the tight-lipped slit and relished the moan of pleasure that escaped Kayla's mouth. Derek was now sitting on the bed stroking his cock, his boxer briefs long since discarded across the room.

Paisley delivered strategic kisses to Kayla's inner thighs and let a series of hot breaths fall against her swollen clit. She felt the bed move as Derek stood up and walked to the other side of the room. She didn't have to watch; she knew he was fumbling for a condom from the top drawer of the cabinet.

Meanwhile, his wife arched her back with excruciating

desire, nearly to the point of begging Paisley to put her out of her misery. She acquiesced by allowing a little more direct contact, the tip of her tongue painting broad strokes along her folds, letting the honeyed sweetness of her juices soak into her taste buds.

"Oh my god, you're killing me," Kayla finally murmured, her eyes shut tight and her fingers gripping the sheets.

"What do you want, babe?" Paisley looked up from her dripping wet pussy with a devious grin curling her lips.

Derek had now positioned himself behind her and was stroking his hands up and down her curves and pulling her tulle skirt down around her ankles to access her ass.

"Make me come," Kayla pleaded, her voice raw with need.

"Can I fuck you while you go down on her?" Derek asked with his condom-sheathed cock pressed against Paisley's backside. Paisley nodded as he lifted his chin toward his wife. "Is that okay, baby?"

"Yes, please...please...oh god, please," his wife repeated as Paisley's tongue went to work on her clit. "Please...please..." She said it again and again as her body began its surrender to the expertise of Paisley's mouth and fingers.

Derek wet one of his fingers and slid it between Paisley's thighs, then up into her ready cunt. "God damn," he sighed as he guided his cock into her hot, wet slit, making her moan with pleasure and sending the vibrations directly into his wife's clit.

"Do you like watching me fuck another woman?" he asked his wife as he slid balls-deep in Paisley's pussy.

She locked her eyes onto his, struggling to form words beyond primal groans. She finally managed to whimper, "Yes, yes, fuck her, baby."

Derek gripped Paisley's fleshy hips as he pounded into her, all the while watching his wife squirm beneath her talented tongue. Kayla's thighs started to quiver, her juices soaking Paisley's cheeks, her chin as she became more aggressive with her fingers sliding in and out, matching the rhythm of Derek's cock.

It wouldn't be long before an orgasm caught Kayla in a mighty whirlwind of pleasure, swirling her high above the room with its flaming tendrils of ecstasy until she was all at once doused by waves of satisfaction as every last flicker was extinguished. As her own body swelled in response to Derek's relentless thrusting, Kayla's explosion rocked through her, starting on her tongue and then radiating throughout her body until Paisley was completely drenched in her cum.

Watching his wife succumb to her climax made Derek lose control. He hammered into Paisley like a machine.

The corset restricted her breathing to the point she thought her chest might explode before her pussy did, but as fortune would have it, she and Derek reached their heights of pleasure at the exact same moment, just as Kayla had recovered enough to witness it happening: two bodies giving and receiving at the same time.

Afterward, the three lay on the big round bed, spent and grateful, with no energy for words.

SIX

Sundays were Paisley's lazy day, her only official day off work. After a glorious night at the club full of passion and fun with other people's genitalia, she was happy to wake up refreshed and satisfied in her own bed. Sleeping was tantamount to religion, and she was a devout practitioner.

Her sanctuary featured a king-size bed with the thickest, fluffiest double pillow-top mattress on the market, along with the softest, most decadent down comforter and pillows that money could buy. She loved waking up in the midst of her luxurious cloud of bedding.

That morning a momentary jolt of loneliness spiked up her spine and out toward her extremities, but it was fleeting. It had been a while since she invited someone to stay overnight. She wasn't opposed to it, though sharing her glorious kingdom of downy goodness was not something she did often. But it was nice to wake up to a strong, warm, masculine body on occasion.

She had visited Cap and Leah's house for dinner earlier in the week. It was rather generous for them to extend the invitation, especially so close to their baby's arrival.

She wasn't surprised to see that their spacious country home nestled in the pines along Ayres Creek suited them both perfectly. It was on the water, which was expected, given Cap's profession. And it looked like something out of *Better Homes and Gardens* magazine, which was also anticipated, given Leah's attention to detail. It was homey, lived in, and smelled amazing.

The baby's nursery was done in a nautical Americana theme with vintage-looking signs, stars and stripes bunting, an old-fashioned life preserver, and navy curtains with tiny white anchors on them.

"We don't know if it's a boy or a girl," Leah had explained, pointing to a few bare spots on the walls, "so we might add some baby blue or pink accents later. We'll see."

"I bet you're excited!" Paisley had gushed.

"Some days I still can't believe it's happening. I think I'm excited about all the fun parts and in total denial about all the hard work. Cap claims not to remember how to change a diaper. I told him he's going to be relearning that skill pretty fast."

"I can't even imagine myself as a mother, not for one second," Paisley admitted. "But you have motherhood written all over you. You're gonna do great!"

She looked genuinely grateful for the compliment, but then her lips curled into a frown. "Do you ever get lonely living by yourself? You've never been married, right?"

"Nah, I've had roommates off and on, and live-in boyfriends, but I'm kinda a lone wolf. I'm good with it."

"I don't know how I would have survived living alone without Glory!" She only had to speak the pup's name to send her bounding into the nursery from the living room.

She jumped up so her human could give her an affectionate scratch behind her floppy beagle ears.

"I'm not much of a dog person, but maybe I'll get a cat. Or a turtle or something," Paisley had said thoughtfully.

Now she was revisiting that idea. *There's probably an animal shelter around here somewhere. I'll google it.*

She grabbed her laptop from the chest and then hopped back into her ethereal slumber pit. She hadn't ever owned a pet on her own, although her grandparents had quite a menagerie when she was growing up. They usually referred to their zoo as a farm, since there was a goat and some chickens, along with three or four dogs at any given time and a clowder of cats.

As Paisley started her search for a feline companion, she noticed a couple of new emails in her work account. She groaned, not wanting to think about work on a Sunday, but then her responsible adult side kicked in.

The first email looked like it came from the contact form on the website Calvin had built.

In all lowercase letters with no signature, it read:

---

we know who you are, rebecca bridges. we know your secret. the factory is going down unless you meet our demands. will be in contact with further instructions.

The blood in Paisley's veins froze into tiny, crystallized atoms at the sight of her given name. No one had called her that for eighteen years.

SEVEN

Paisley dug through all of the receipts and business cards she'd dumped on her desk and had been meaning to organize. She was the poster child for organization in her office at work, but was left with little organizational energy for her small apartment. Finally, she spotted Calvin's business card with its surfboard logo and snatched it up from the pile as if she'd just discovered the holy grail.

I hope this is his personal cell number and not an office phone, she prayed as she punched the numbers in. Then she hung up abruptly before he could answer.

"Wait a minute, what the fuck am I doing?" she said aloud to the empty room.

If she called Calvin to ask if he could figure out who had sent the web form, she was opening herself up to a lot of questions. It sounded an awful lot like someone was trying to blackmail her, either that or someone was making a sick joke at her expense. If someone who knew her past really sent the form, she was quite certain Calvin was not on the list of people she wanted to explain it to.

Actually, there's not a single soul on that list.

Who knows my real name?

Her heart pounded at the possibilities. *A handful of aunts and uncles, maybe a few cousins. A few others in my hometown may remember me.*

The police? Shit.

In the fifteen or so years since she had legally changed her name – nearly half her life ago – she had thought of herself as Rebecca Bridges less and less often as time marched on. She wasn't the same person who had left her childhood world behind so many years ago.

What secret could they possibly know? Not that *secret, right?*

Is Calvin the type of person who would judge me for my past?

She weighed the pros and cons of contacting Calvin, and within minutes, she was redialing his number. This time he answered on the second ring, giving her less time to back out.

"Hi, Calvin?" she tried to sound casual and pleasant, with no traces of the panic that was strangling her.

"Yes? May I ask who is calling?"

"It's Paisley Parker. From The Factory?"

"Oh, yes. To what do I owe the pleasure?"

Damn. His smooth, sexy voice was raising the little hairs on the back of her neck. *Why, oh why doesn't he want hot, no-strings-attached sex like other twenty-six-year-olds?*

"Thank you for taking a business call on a Sunday, I appreciate it," she attempted to return the pleasant formalities.

"Is everything alright with your website?"

She paused. She wasn't sure this was something she wanted to explain over the phone, and she didn't really want to screenshot the message and have it floating around in cyberspace either. She'd feel more comfortable showing him in person and hoping to God he could figure out where it came from.

"Paisley?"

"The website is fine," she assured him. "It's just... I received a web form submission that is a little...disconcerting, and I wondered if you could take a look at it. I know it's a lot to ask on a Sunday. We can wait till tomorrow if that's better."

"I actually have a really busy week ahead," he explained firmly but with a pleasant tone.

Shit. He's still mad that I don't want to date him.

"But," he brightened, "I could meet with you later today?"

As her car crawled down the coast, she seriously considered stabbing her eyes out from the frustration of constantly hitting the gas pedal just to have to lurch to an immediate stop. Traffic was bumper-to-bumper, inching along Coastal Highway under the glaring late afternoon sun.

Once she got below 21st street, it dawned on her why the crowds were even worse than usual. The air show was in town. She remembered all the radio ads she'd heard just as jet engines thundered overhead. It sounded as though they were diving close to the beach, then zooming away from it at Mach 3.

Why are we complete idiots for wanting to meet down the beach?

A text from Calvin lit up her phone:

Calvin: Air Show. Shit. I totally forgot.

Paisley: Me too. Where are you now?

Calvin: I'm still in the parking lot at my apartment on Bayshore. There's not going to be anywhere to park over by the beach. Why don't you come here? I have a visitor tag you can use in our lot.

She couldn't prevent a rush of excitement from racing through her, even though she immediately reminded herself this was a business call.

Paisley: Address?

As soon as she received it, she turned off the congested main highway and rerouted back north. Traffic in that direction was still thick, but not nearly as nasty as heading south.

Paisley: GPS says ten minutes.

She could nearly walk there as fast. Leah and Cap had tried to warn her about Ocean City on the weekends during tourist season, but she clearly hadn't learned her lesson. She was used to New York traffic. How could this be worse than that? She should have just waited until Monday and made an appointment with him like a reasonably professional person.

Paisley knocked on Calvin's door fifteen minutes later, and when he answered it, she was shocked at how casually he was dressed. At their two earlier meetings, he'd been all buttoned up in business attire, but today, his toned, muscular limbs stretched out from olive-colored board shorts and a black screen-printed tank top.

To Paisley's surprise, he revealed two large tattoos: one on his rather well-developed deltoid and the other on the opposite biceps, which was equally impressive. His skin was such a delicious shade of bronze, and so smooth, she was having a hard time resisting the urge to trail her fingertips down his arm.

His confident grin reflected his awareness that Paisley had both noticed and appreciated his muscular physique. *Wonder what he's thinking about me?*

She wore a long, sleeveless maxi dress with a bold animal print, but her arms and shoulders were covered with a black crocheted shrug. The wild print seemed like an appropriate wardrobe choice given the time she spent in the Jungle Room the night before.

"Thank you for seeing me today," she began as he ushered her to a glass-topped table near French doors that led to a balcony overlooking the bay. She watched a heron swoop down onto the shoreline and dip its beak into the water, gently rippling its reflection. "Wow, this is a great view!"

"You should see it at sunset." He smiled at her, his perfect white teeth contrasting against his full lips.

Maybe I'll still be here at sunset?

She typically didn't censor inappropriate thoughts, otherwise she'd never be allowed any thoughts at all, but she was making a concerted effort to keep her business and personal affairs separate. After all, in the past, mixing them had always caused big problems.

She had been leery of playing at the club, but her bosses had encouraged it when they gave her a night off. *Getting involved with our webmaster who isn't in the lifestyle might be pushing it, though—even if he is hot as fuck.*

He brought over a matched pair of glass goblets filled halfway with white wine. She swirled the sweet liquid around in her mouth before swallowing. "Moscato?" she guessed, and he nodded.

"So what's up? Something about a web form submission?"

"Yes!" she exclaimed, convincing herself it was best to return to the topic prompting her visit. She pulled out her phone and dug through her work email account to retrieve the suspicious message. She held it out to show it to him.

"Uh...okay..." he said after studying it for a few seconds. "And...is this message meant for you?"

She sighed. "I'm not sure who it's for or what it means." She decided at the last second to play dumb.

"Well, we can probably get the IP address, but tracking down who it belongs to might prove more difficult. Any idea who could have sent it?"

Grateful he didn't probe any more deeply about the content of the message, she shook her head. "No, I thought the whole thing was weird."

It dawned on her that he assumed it was either a fluke or about someone else associated with the club, someone who was not her. "I don't want the owners to get upset," she explained.

"Well, someone may be trying to extort money from them, at least that's what it sounds like." He peered at the message again, his mouth slightly open while he reread it. She couldn't help but notice how full and succulent his lips looked parted like that.

Stay on target, girl, she admonished herself. "That's

what I was afraid of. I just want to nip this in the bud before it gets out of hand."

"Okay, well let me get into the database that stores the web forms. There should be a timestamp and IP address." He pulled open his laptop and typed approximately a million words per minute, his eyes racing across the screen. She wished he didn't look so damn sexy while he was concentrating.

A few minutes later he said, "Well, the ISP seems to be MediaCom, but the location isn't accessible. I'm going to have to do some more digging tomorrow when I'm at the office. Might call a buddy of mine who has more experience with this than I do."

"ISP?"

"Internet Service Provider."

"Oh, okay, well, I appreciate your help." She tried not to sound too flustered, but she was disappointed she hadn't gotten any more clues. She wasn't sure why she expected Calvin to be some sort of wizard who was able to make the disturbing message go poof into thin air, but alas... he couldn't.

And she needed more wine. She nudged her empty glass toward him with big eyes and batting lashes.

He smirked at her wordless hint and went to the kitchen for the bottle of wine he'd opened. Topping off her glass, he asked, "So, did you get into anything fun last night?"

Just like that, his business face vanished. His jaw relaxed, and his eyes narrowed a bit as he swallowed another gulp of wine. He leaned back in the chair and put his hands behind his head so she could really appreciate the definition in his arm muscles. It seemed like he was doing it on purpose, egging her on.

"Well..." she stalled while she calculated the risk versus

benefit of sharing personal information. But the wine was going to her head, so her calculations may have been a bit compromised. "As luck would have it, I didn't have to work last night."

"No? So what does the operations manager of a swinger club do when she's off work?" he boldly asked, his gold-flecked eyes gleaming with curiosity.

"*Assistant* operations manager," she corrected him. "Uh, well, I still went to the club."

She didn't mean to sound sheepish, but she knew there was an undercurrent there. She wasn't used to talking about lifestyle stuff with non-lifestyle people. *Vanilla people*, a slightly amusing label considering Calvin's dark complexion.

For the first time she wondered what his background was...*Black? Latino? White? Some combination thereof?* It was impossible to determine just by looking, and she had certainly looked long and hard.

I believe his race is "yummy."

"So you aren't going to tell me what you did at the club?" His eyes were so wide that she could see white all the way around his honey-colored irises.

"Well, I'm not sure you really want to know...as it's..." She swallowed another swig of her wine for dramatic effect. "It's...rather naughty."

"Naughty is intriguing," he insisted, a teasing smile spreading his lips. "I'm going to just keep liquoring you up till you tell me."

She giggled. "I think you're mostly there already!"

She put her wine glass down, suddenly remembering her promise to stay professional. "Look, I have no qualms about what I did. I'm not the least bit embarrassed or shy about it. However, I don't like alienating my web developer – or vanilla friends, for that matter."

He did a double-take. "Wait...vanilla friend? I don't know if that's a compliment...or not?"

"I like you, Calvin. You're a cool guy. Obviously you have some mad web skills, and we're all impressed with the site you built. But I don't want to overstep our professional boundaries. I want to stay friendly, and I don't want to leave you with a bad taste in your mouth about the club."

He sat back again in the chair, his eyes locked onto hers, carefully considering what she had just said. "So you're afraid I'll judge you?" He had a look on his face like he'd just solved a great mystery.

"Yeah, something like that." Paisley answered.

He leaned forward and covered her hand with his. She nearly jumped at the electrical current that jolted through her from the warmth of his skin. "I admit I'm curious about the club and what happens there, but let me set you straight about something, okay?"

She nodded, still soaking in the heat of his hand on hers. She couldn't believe how sober she felt, right in that moment, as if the intensity of his stare had absorbed all the alcohol in her body.

"I won't ever disclose anything you share with me in confidence to anyone else, and I won't ever judge you."

"I appreciate that." When she peered into his eyes, it felt like a deeply intimate moment, the likes of which she hadn't shared with anyone for quite some time.

It amazed her that she could fuck any number of people, but all the pleasure stayed on the surface, all bubbled up in impermeable flesh. It never trickled down into the soul. But that was the beauty of it, right? Pleasure without the risk of pain. After all, letting it seep inside was the first crucial step toward getting hurt.

She brushed off that internal monologue, blaming it on the wine. *Just come right out and say it.* "Well, I had a FFM for starters."

"FFM?" His eyes were wide again, his voice higher-pitched.

"Female—female—male," she explained without an ounce of apology. "I had a threesome with a couple to start my night. Then I think I ended up in a pile in the dungeon room. There may have been some flogging and restraints going on. A Dom was having his way with us." She couldn't help but sound excited when she recounted all of it, the memories were rushing back to her like the tide coming in to the shore.

He was surprisingly unaffected by her story. "So why swinging? Why that instead of dating?" He looked like he knew the answer already but wanted to hear the words form on her lips.

"If you've never been in the lifestyle, you wouldn't understand," she answered, not giving him the satisfaction of hearing what he hoped for. "It's liberating. It's always new. It's fun."

He nodded and took another sip from his goblet. "Is that an invitation?"

"I'm sure you'd be a big hit at the club. There'd be all sorts of ladies who'd love to get their hands on you."

He smirked. "Not you, though?"

She laughed, a twinkling arpeggio that started deep in her throat. "Well, getting my hands on you isn't the same thing as dating. You seemed opposed to the former without the latter."

He nodded. "There aren't a lot of options *here* for the latter, to be honest. Even if it is my preference."

She assumed by "here" he meant Ocean City. "No? You're not into bikini-clad coeds getting sloppy drunk and trolling for D up and down the boardwalk?"

"That's so not my style." He took a long sip of wine as if to punctuate his statement. Even in his board shorts and tank top, he projected an air of sophistication that made him seem much older than his twenty-six years.

If he led me off to his bedroom now, I wouldn't stop him. But he has to make the move. I'm not seducing the webmaster.

His expression changed as he glanced out the French doors. "Oh, look, that sunset I warned you about...it's already happening."

She'd barely noticed the gradual darkening of the room. He'd never bothered to switch on lights as the second bottle of wine seemed to render them obsolete.

The sky was glowing with the dying sun, throwing up its amber arms in defeat and stretching them across the water in one last glorious display of majesty. The echo of the orange, plum and crimson on the bay was almost too intense to process. In twenty minutes, the sun would abdicate its throne to a silver crescent moon.

Paisley stood up and walked to the glass doors. She couldn't believe so many hours had slipped by since they first looked at the disturbing message she'd received. That was a lifetime ago now, when she was sober and level-headed. Now she was drunk and suggestible, and the deepening darkness was providing a willing alibi.

He stood and opened the French doors to the setting sun, sweeping the breeze coming off the bay into his apartment. "It's better with sound effects," he explained as they stepped out onto the patio.

It was just big enough for a two-person table and a small charcoal grill but, yes, the ambiance of the swirling, dusky air and the sounds of nature did add immeasurably to the beautiful sights. She let the sounds of birds, frogs and crickets fill her ears as she scanned the bay all the way to the horizon. She didn't know it could be so peaceful this close to the cacophony of Ocean City in June.

His body heat seemed to warm the air around her, and she wondered if they could stand any closer without actually touching. It seemed like a game: how long could they hold out before their body parts brushed against each other, even by accident? She was determined to win and make him succumb first.

And finally…. his shoulder bumped against hers as he moved to stand on the other side of her. "Oh, sorry," he said, as if it were an accident, but then, his hand touched her hip as it fell to his side, and she knew it was no accident.

The final glass of wine made her skin flush, and she felt wrapped up in the weakness, the openness that accompanies a buzz. She turned to face him just as the skies softened to a peachy pink and whispered, "Thank you for sharing this with me."

He smiled. "I almost forgot why you came over in the first place, you know?"

"Oh my god, me too! It's been an enjoyable evening, despite that."

On the other side of the strip of land comprising Ocean City, the crescent moon was rising over the sea like a ballet dancer tossed into the air: slim, delicate, and seemingly on wings. Another weekend was slipping through her fingertips, and by tomorrow morning all she'd have left of it were memories.

"So...I hope that message you got was a fluke. Kinda nice that it happened, though, so I got to spend some time with you." He was so close to her that she could feel his breath falling on her. If one of them leaned in, they would be kissing.

Paisley reveled in how sincere his voice was. It was rare for her to click with a man in a way that made her want to delve deeper, to discover his story, where he came from, what made him *him.*

Maybe I can get over the not being able to fuck him thing if I get a friend out of it, she consoled herself. She tried to recall having a male friend she hadn't fucked at least once, and she honestly couldn't think of anyone. *Maybe at thirty-six I'm finally growing up?*

"Well, I should probably head back home now that traffic has cleared out," she said with a slight sniff of resignation.

"I'll let you know if I find out anything tomorrow about the IP address, and in the meantime, let me know if you get any other correspondence." He seemed a bit disappointed too; his hazel eyes had clouded over.

"Sure, of course. Hope we can hang out again sometime."

She immediately regretted saying that. It made it sound like she wanted another "date."

His hand lightly brushed against hers as she slipped by him toward the glass door. "I hope so too..."

EIGHT

By the time Thursday rolled around, Paisley was still thinking about her time at Calvin's apartment and had nearly forgotten what sent her over there in the first place. There had been no more suspicious web forms, and she hadn't heard whether or not Calvin had tracked down the location of the person who sent the first one.

She tried to brush off the entire incident as one of those crazy non-sequiturs where the dots never get connected. *I seem to have a lot of those in my history*, she thought as she headed back to work for Leah's baby shower.

The Factory was an unusual spot to host a baby shower, but Casey insisted it made the most sense. She and Paisley had decorated the lounge area with pastel decorations to try to make it look more baby shower-appropriate. At seven, female club members began showing up wearing vanilla street clothes and carrying packages and gift bags of all different shapes and sizes. It was quite the contrast from the traffic coming through the club doors on Friday and Saturday nights.

Looking at the smiling faces of the ladies spread out among the many chairs and plush loveseats, Paisley wondered if anyone who came in off the street would ever guess he or she was in a room full of swingers. She guessed not. These appeared to be ordinary women from all walks of life. From the young twenty-something school teacher to a few retired ladies well into their sixties, no one would fathom it was an affinity for sex that brought this group together.

Paisley let Casey run the show, and she was happy to do so. Casey had a gift for bringing people together and making everyone feel welcome and involved. They played the requisite cheesy shower games and started a pool to guess when the baby would come.

Leah was beginning to look swollen and tired in the summer heat but otherwise was a good sport. She had lovely things to say about each gift, holding up the tiny clothes and baby paraphernalia while expressing her gratitude to the giver.

Paisley watched the entire thing in awe. She'd never been part of a tribe of women before, a group of ladies who were close-knit and supportive of each other. The dancers at the clubs where she worked in New York were a petty, catty, fickle group. She'd learned the hard way that no one was to be trusted.

Unfortunately, in event management, things were not much different. The cattiness was perhaps more concealed, which made it more tempting to trust, but it turned out there was no such thing as loyalty.

That atmosphere had led Paisley and Allison to form a tight bond. They'd both gotten overlooked for promotions by the same two-faced, power-hungry female boss. Her name was Tonya, and she seemed to have a personal vendetta against them both. When she and Allison began to compare notes, they discovered Tonya's underhanded tactics.

They banded together to take Tonya down by going to her boss and exposing her nefarious schemes. Their victory over Tonya had solidified their friendship. Sometimes Paisley felt bad that they bonded over bringing down a fellow woman, but that was the world they knew.

Women don't like me. It was a universal truth, like the earth being round. To be brought into this club as an outsider, but vetted by prominent members, was an unexpected head start to forming friendships with other ladies in the club. They just assumed she was one of them and were at once overly familiar, which was not entirely unusual in the lifestyle anyway.

"So you're from New York," a petite brunette named Karen asked while they filled up their little plastic punch cups. "You don't seem to have much of an accent."

"Yep, from New York," Paisley answered, even though it was a half-truth and a long story all wrapped up in a convoluted tale she didn't plan on sharing.

"What did you do there?" Karen's companion Trish asked.

"I worked in event management," Paisley answered, feeling a bit like she was being interviewed all over again but knowing that these curious, well-meaning ladies were just trying to establish common ground.

"Oh, before that Paisley was a dancer!" Cindy, one of the club hosts, chimed in.

Oh, god, here we go. Paisley managed to keep her eyes from rolling.

"What kind of dancer?" Trish questioned.

"A burlesque dancer, right, Paisley?" Cindy answered for her.

She nodded and smiled, hoping that was it for the questions. Alas, it was not. Karen was suddenly animated. "Wow, that's awesome! Do you miss it? Why did you stop?"

"I think I miss the costumes the most." Paisley laughed. "They were pretty amazing!" She looked at their expectant faces and could practically see the little webs of friendship growing between them.

"Oh, I can imagine. Do you have pictures or videos?" Trish was apparently fascinated with the whole idea. She had the far-off look of someone reminiscing about their youth.

"There may be a video or two on YouTube actually." Paisley winked.

The crowd of women around her were impressed, all talking amongst themselves about how "neat" and "awesome" it was to have a semi-famous burlesque dancer in their midst.

"So, why did you stop dancing?" Karen asked again.

"I got too old for it," Paisley answered.

It wasn't the whole truth, but it was at least a fraction of it. And the limit of what she felt comfortable sharing had just been reached. She excused herself to go say goodbye to Leah. She'd had enough estrogen for one night.

"Thank you so much for helping Casey organize the shower!" Leah gushed, her tired face still managing to glow with gratitude. "And for the crib. I can't wait to get it set up in the nursery!"

"It's going to look great in there!" Paisley agreed. She gave Leah's round shape a sideways hug and headed out to her car.

The sun had slipped down onto the water like a crimson

goddess bathing in the bay, and all Paisley could think about was watching the same show just a few nights ago at Calvin's. She tried to suppress the thought of him, but the curiosity of what he was doing at that moment held her in its grasp. She imagined he was sitting on his patio staring at the sunset and remembering how he'd enjoyed it in her company a few nights before.

NINE

When she woke up, another chilling web form submission awaited discovery in her inbox. She knew as soon as she saw the bolded message that it was going to be bad, and her heart rate accelerated accordingly. This time:

Paisley Parker AKA Rebecca Bridges, we know who you are and what you did. You will pay or we go to the police and the press. How do you think the Sheldons will feel about that?

Want to avoid letting the cat out of the bag? Get together $10K. More instructions to follow.

She felt dizzy as she closed her laptop and went to the kitchen for a glass of water. The phrase "cat out of the bag" reminded her that she was about to adopt a kitten when she discovered the first message.

It freaked me out so bad that I totally forgot about wanting a cute little furry companion!

It had been almost a week since she met with Calvin about the initial incident, and she hadn't heard from him since. She had played off the email as though she didn't know who or what it was about. This time it was going to be impossible to deny that it was meant for her.

"Ten thousand dollars? Like I have that just sitting around," she said to the wall, feeling more nauseated by the minute.

Whoever it was knew her real name, which meant they most likely knew her from childhood. Whoever it was knew she had some secret to hide. And whoever it was knew that asking for an outrageous sum of money was completely beyond her reach.

Ten thousand was an amount the average person might be able to scrape together between savings and calling in favors. It wasn't so much as to be totally beyond reason. So it seemed like they really needed a specific amount of money and weren't setting the bar so high that there was no way she could meet their demands.

It could be her high school boyfriend or one of his friends, but the former had gone to jail last she heard. *I guess it's possible he's been paroled.*

The thought of him stung, making her wince. She bit her lip in frustration as she struggled to push a legion of painful memories back down to where she had successfully locked them away years ago. She had no choice but to return to Calvin for help.

She was going to be late to work, but she wouldn't lose her job over that. She would be much more likely to lose her job over this blackmail situation.

She whipped her Mazda into the parking lot of Calvin's

office in West Ocean City before heading down 611 to The Factory. She walked past the row of glass doors until she reached the one with the surfboard logo, her heart still thundering against her ribcage.

Today she found a petite redhead with an upturned nose and high cheekbones sitting at the receptionist's desk. She was dressed impeccably in a tailored navy blazer that accentuated her narrow shoulders, and she wore tortoise-shell cats-eye glasses, lending her a serious, intellectual look.

Well, well, this is a new development. Paisley eyed the younger woman up and down. *Wonder if he's fucking her?*

She tried to muster up a pleasant tone. "Is Calvin here?"

The redhead tucked a piece of her long bangs behind her ear and tilted her head. "Mr. Mitchell is on the phone at the moment. May I have your name?"

"I'm Paisley Parker." She helped herself to a seat in one of two chairs in the cramped lobby and mentally reviewed how she was going to explain the new correspondence to Calvin.

When he poked his head out into the hallway, his lips cracked into a smile upon seeing her. Wordlessly, he gestured for her to follow him. She slipped by the snooty receptionist and trailed him into the conference room, where she'd sat the first day she'd met with him.

"You look upset," was the first thing he said after he closed the door and plopped down in his gray leather chair.

"New receptionist?" She hoped to keep the focus off how she looked. She'd made every effort to pull herself together, to not appear as though she was the victim of stalking, harassment and extortion...*but makeup can only do so much...*

"Oh, did you meet Michaela? I just hired her last week."

He was back to his professional, business-like self in a pale aqua button-down shirt, gray pants and a silvery gray tie. His warm topaz skin rendered a striking contrast against the aqua and made his eyes impossibly bright.

She hadn't heard from him since she visited his apartment, and he had just hired Michaela, which made it seem all the more likely that he was fucking her.

Not that I care, of course, she convinced herself.

She pulled up the message on her phone. "I got this today." She held it out for him to read as if it were hot, and if he didn't read fast, he'd get burned.

She expected his face to register some sort of surprise, but he was expressionless. "So they *are* targeting you," he confirmed, his eyebrows raised ever so slightly.

"I'm afraid so." The panic rose up her throat from the pit of her stomach like magma tunneling its way to the top of a volcano. An eruption seemed imminent. "I don't know what to do..." She looked into his eyes for some indication that he was empathetic.

"Can you tell me what they're talking about?"

She sighed and shook her head. "Is it important? I just want to find out who it is so I can talk some sense into them. That's why I wanted to trace the IP address."

"I didn't get very far in my investigation. Looks like it came from a proxy server, and I'm sort of out of my league. I don't think my buddy has had a chance to look at it." He folded one hand on top of the other and leaned in toward her, his elbows resting on the table. "Have you considered going to the police?"

That word immediately raised her hackles—always had. "I would really prefer not to," she said as calmly as she could. "The owners are afraid of any negative publicity about the club. They have to be really careful and fly under the radar."

He nodded in understanding. "I can try to get ahold of my friend again to take a look, see if this is from the same IP as the other one. But, honestly, Paisley, if this is someone who knows what they're doing, they're not going to make it easy to find them. They haven't given you any explicit instructions yet, so maybe they're just trying to get a rise out of you?"

She had to fight to keep the tears at bay. She was not a crier and couldn't remember the last time she'd succumbed to her emotions. *After all I've been through, now this. Just when I thought I finally had everything under control.* She'd been on the verge of collapse so many times, but she'd never stacked her house of cards this high before. She had much further to fall, so much more at stake than she ever did in the past.

She swallowed hard and blinked away the wet, stinging sensation that threatened her eyes. "Can you just turn off the web form?" she asked. "I haven't gotten any other submissions besides those two. Most people either call or contact our Facebook page. So I don't think anyone will miss it."

"Of course, I am happy to do that." He reached toward her, touching the top of her hand with his smooth, long fingers. "Try not to worry too much, okay? At least until they make a more specific threat."

She nodded, grateful he wasn't overreacting. "I have to get to work," was all she could say, or else those tears she'd fought off would come back with a vengeance.

S he escaped into her work like it was her savior. Not having a family or even a best friend to lean on had never made her feel sorry for herself; it only reinvigorated her determination to succeed. She busied herself with survey results, trying to determine why people didn't renew their club memberships.

Casey had given her the task of calling former members of the club and offering them discounts to try it again. What she was learning over and over again was that most members who didn't renew were part of a couple who had broken up. It only solidified her long-held belief that relationships were doomed to fail.

No one could keep making sacrifices when their own needs were at stake. No one loved unconditionally. Eventually there came a time when a person had to choose herself first. Paisley knew this because she'd done it too. And that meant a broken promise.

She hung up the phone, ending yet another conversation about a severed marriage, only to hear a groan coming from the bathroom that shared a wall with her office space. She leaped up, concerned it was Leah, who was only two weeks from her due date.

She knocked on the door. "Leah? Everything okay?"

Her boss fumbled around inside the tiny staff bathroom, then finally unlocked the door to reveal her red, grimaced face. "I think I just had a contraction. Like a real one." She looked equal parts terrified and excited.

"Is Cap here?"

"No, he's on the boat. It's okay, let me just go sit in the

lounge for a minute." Leah bravely made her way out of the bathroom and headed down the hall into the large, open space of the lounge. She eased herself down onto one of the loveseats and let out a loud sigh.

"Should I call him? I don't know what the protocol is here." Paisley laughed. "Do you want a drink? A towel? Should I boil water?"

"I think you've watched too many movies." Leah giggled, then started to give Paisley instructions. Her face scrunched up, and she clutched her stomach as another wave passed over her. "I thought I had a couple more weeks," she said through her clenched teeth.

Paisley wished Cap or Casey were available. *How did I get chosen to deal with this?*

She watched the color return to Leah's face when the pain subsided. "Let me go get you some water." She headed over to the bar to grab a bottle from the refrigerator.

Leah gulped about half of the contents of the plastic bottle, still leaning forward with her elbows on her knees. Bent over like that, her perfectly round baby bump didn't look nearly so huge, much less like a balloon about to burst, like it did when she stood up. Tiny beads of sweat appeared on the edges of her hairline, and her hands and ankles looked swollen and uncomfortable.

"Are you going to call Cap?" Paisley asked again.

Another contraction began to crank up, gripping her tighter and tighter in its painful vise. Paisley watched her boss's face contort and wished there was something more she could do. She reached for her hand and let her squeeze it with nearly superhuman strength until the pain subsided.

A whooshing sound escaped Leah's mouth as all the air in her lungs rushed out. "Cap's out on the boat with a charter. I could try to call him, but chances are pretty good that it won't go through."

She stood up and began pacing around the lounge. "I think you're supposed to walk." Her hands clasped her lower back, her basketball-shaped stomach protruding. "The doctor said I should call when contractions are ten minutes apart. Do you know when that last one was?"

Paisley glanced up at the clock on the wall. This was such a surreal experience that the timeline seemed warped. It was 11:15 now. "I don't know, but I'll start timing with the next one."

Next she dialed Cap's number as she wasn't sure where Leah's phone was. It rang and rang, then went to voicemail. "Should I leave a message?"

When Leah nodded, Paisley spoke into her phone, "Hey, Cap, seems like it might be a great day to become a new dad! Leah's having contractions, and we just started timing them. Can you give us a call when you get to shore? Might want to call my phone. Thanks!"

Leah flashed her a thumbs-up sign as she suddenly stopped in her path and braced herself against the back of one of the chairs in the lounge. The pain was starting to cycle through her again. Paisley started the stopwatch on her phone. It was 11:22.

A minute later, Leah started another lap around the lounge and bar area. Watching a woman in labor pacing around a swinger club was a pretty hilarious sight. Paisley wanted to snap a picture, but she wasn't sure Leah would find it as amusing.

The phone rang in the office, so Paisley hopped up from her perch in the lounge to answer it. The caller had a long list of questions about membership, and midway through answering them, Paisley heard Leah calling her from the bar area, "Oh my gosh! Oh my gosh! Paisley!"

Paisley quickly excused herself from the phone call and rushed back to find Leah standing in a puddle of water.

"Oh, shit! I guess that was your water breaking!" Paisley exclaimed, glancing at her watch again. Leah was hunched over, breathing and groaning her way through another contraction. It was 11:31. "That's only nine minutes, Leah."

"Shit!" She exhaled and steadied herself against the bar as she pulled herself upright again. "Can you get my phone from my desk? I'm going to call the doctor."

Ten minutes later, Paisley was driving Leah in her Jeep to Atlantic General in Berlin. *I cannot believe I am the one doing this!* she thought as Leah directed her down the back roads of Berlin.

The panic and fear that had held her in their grips earlier in the morning had given way to panic and fear about getting this baby into the world safely, and getting the baby's father to the hospital before the baby came. She kept glancing down at her phone praying Cap would call and say he was on his way.

Leah was staying calm between contractions. She called Casey, who was showing a series of houses to a newlywed couple, but planned to head to the hospital as soon as she could.

She called her mother, who was trying to stay calm but was likely to hop the next plane to Maryland if the blaringly loud excitement coming from Leah's phone was any indication. Her mother stayed on the phone with her while she breathed her way through another contraction. They were holding steady at nine to ten minutes apart.

Paisley knew she should settle in for a long stay in the waiting room while they got Leah checked into her room, but she was so hyped up on adrenaline that she could barely sit. She found herself pacing the room much like Leah was doing in the lounge at the club only minutes earlier. At noon her phone finally lit up with Cap's number, and a wave of relief rushed over her.

"We're at the hospital!" she blurted out before he had the opportunity to say anything.

"I'm on my way," he answered just as fast. He was coming from the marina, and Paisley anticipated it would take him at least fifteen to twenty minutes to fight his way through traffic. *Shit, no, it's Friday on July Fourth weekend. It could take him thirty minutes.*

The nurse came out to retrieve Paisley and take her back to Leah's room. *It's weird to see my boss like this...so vulnerable. Our relationship doesn't seem at the right place for all this, but I guess it doesn't matter now. Here we are!*

She found Leah propped up on the bed with the IV running into a needle in her hand. The sheet was folded underneath her belly, which showed the outlines of the monitors and bands under her hospital gown recording her contractions and the baby's heartbeat.

"Your husband is on his way!" she said brightly. Leah already looked tired.

"As soon as they got me hooked up to all this stuff, my contractions stopped." The disappointment on her face was impossible to miss.

"But your water broke, right?"

"Yeah, if the contractions don't start getting regular again, they're going to start Pitocin. I'm only dilated to three, so it may be a long while yet."

"That's good though, right? Oh my gosh, you could have a July fourth baby!" Paisley gasped, thinking about the time-line. The holiday was now less than twelve hours away.

She watched a smile spread across her boss's face and a little color return to her cheeks. "I didn't even think about that. My Glory was born on July fourth. That's how she got her name, from Old Glory!"

"That's awesome!"

"Speaking of which.... We never got around to packing my bag or making arrangements for the dogs. You might need to run over to our house and feed them, take them out, and grab some things for me. Is that too much to ask?"

"I'd be happy to, of course. Let me stay here till Cap arrives, alright?" Paisley sat down on the edge of Leah's bed. It felt strange to be sitting so close to her in such an intimate setting.

Leah reached down and squeezed her hand. The two women smiled at each other silently as if they both knew a moment was happening between them. For the time being, the panicked visit to Calvin's office had totally slipped Paisley's mind.

"I really appreciate you staying with me," Leah finally broke the silence. "I hope the phones aren't ringing off the hook at the club though."

"Don't worry about it. That's what voicemail is for," Paisley reassured her. "Are you nervous?"

Leah's lips curled into a tentative smile. "A little, but billions of women have done this before, right?"

Paisley nodded. "That's one way to think of it."

They heard Cap's footsteps coming down the quiet hospital hall before they saw his silver-streaked beard and sparkling blue eyes. He was at Leah's side in a flash, and Paisley dutifully backed away toward the door.

He kissed his wife on the cheek. "How's it going, Sugar? Everything okay?"

"So far, so good," Leah answered. "Just waiting for my

contractions to get moving again. I think the doctor scared the baby back in!" They all laughed, and Cap affectionately patted her leg. "Paisley is going to run to our house to take care of the dogs and get a few things for me, okay? Can you give her your keys?"

"Oh, I'll have to drive your Jeep!" Paisley remembered, taking the keys from Cap.

"That's okay. We'll get everything straightened out later," she sighed, then her face began to twist again. She closed her eyes and tilted her head back against the pillow. The contractions were starting back up.

Cap was quiet as he held his wife's hand during the episode. Paisley slipped out of sight before Leah opened her eyes again.

TEN

Paisley heard the dogs barking as soon as she set foot onto the front porch. She was glad the Sheldons lived out in the country and not in the thick of the tourist season jungle that had taken over Ocean City. Her GPS had routed Leah's Jeep a back way from the hospital that avoided all the traffic of the major highways.

She felt awkward unlocking her bosses' front door and walking into their quiet, vacant house, wishing Casey would have been able to do it instead. After all, she made a living walking through people's vacant houses.

After taking care of the dogs, she filled up the small overnight bag with all the things on Leah's list. Then she heaped the dogs' bowls full of food and fresh water.

"Hopefully next time you see your daddy, he'll be telling you all about your new baby brother or sister!" Paisley stroked Keeper's back.

Glory was sniffing her shoes and acting like she'd rather go play than eat. "And I hear someone is a birthday girl tomorrow," Leah said, patting the beagle's head. "Wish I had a present for you, sweet girl, but I don't. Maybe I'll bring you a treat tomorrow."

She hated to leave the dogs when they were so thrilled to have company, but she knew she better get back to the hospital. She slung the overnight bag over her shoulder and began to head out to Leah's Jeep when her phone started buzzing in her pocket.

It was Calvin. "Hey, what's up?"

"Are you busy?"

"Yeah, kinda, my boss is in labor. I'm at her house grabbing stuff she needs at the hospital."

"Oh, wow, I guess this can wait, then."

"Well, what is it?" she asked, her curiosity now piqued.

"My buddy had a chance to look at the web form stuff," he explained, but his tone was so neutral she couldn't gauge whether he had good news or bad news.

"Well?" She didn't have time for suspense. "Just tell me what he said."

"Not good news, unfortunately. Whoever is behind the forms knows what they're doing. They're using a VPN and—"

"VPN? You can't do the geek lingo with me, okay?"

"Virtual Private Network, it basically routes everything through it so you can't see where it's really coming from," he explained.

"So, what, I'm screwed?"

"Look, there are hackers out there, professional ones who basically scam people out of money. It's possible these people don't even know you; they're just putting out feelers to see who they can get money from."

Paisley backed down the Sheldons' driveway and started to make the short journey back to the hospital.

"Look, they know my real name, Calvin. No one I've spoken to in the last eighteen years knows my real name."

He was quiet for a moment. "Just let me know if they send you anything else," he said. "They still haven't made any specific demands. Stay calm, okay?"

"It's kinda hard to stay calm when they know where I work, and my boss is in labor! This would be a really bad time for shit to go down," she yelled into the phone.

Her heart was pounding again, and now her temples were in on the act as well, forcing her to endure their dull throbbing. Any minute the force of blood flowing through her might find a weak point and come exploding out of her like a geyser.

"Go take care of your boss," was all Calvin said in reply.

Casey had arrived at the hospital by the time Paisley returned. It was two o'clock, and Leah had been given medication to make her contractions more regular. She was making progress, though, and was able to get an epidural.

Now, even though her contractions appeared like mountains on the monitor next to the bed, she was sitting serenely, laughing and joking with Cap and Casey while they tried to plan out The Factory's theme nights for the following year.

"Wow, you guys really plan ahead!" Paisley observed as she took notes on the same pad of paper that Leah had used to make the list for her earlier.

"There's nothing wrong with planning ahead," Leah defended herself. "Besides, it's a good distraction." She took another mouthful of ice chips and crunched them between her teeth. "I'm not in pain anymore, but I am hungry as heck. And I think I need to pee."

The nurse came in an hour later to check her dilation

and reported she was at six centimeters. "Four to go!" She smiled.

"It's so funny to be here with you two, Casey and Paisley. Neither one of you have squeezed a watermelon out of a hole the size of a lemon before, right? I thought experienced mothers were supposed to surround the laboring woman and impart wisdom and comforting words and all that crap."

"Maybe Paisley and I are even wiser. After all, we never put ourselves through the pain of pushing a watermelon through a lemon-sized hole!" Casey laughed and winked at Paisley.

"Yeah, hilarious, Casey, thanks!" Leah smirked.

Cap's daughters, Emma and Ashton, had just arrived, and the room was starting to become crowded. Casey turned to Paisley and asked, "You want to go grab some dinner with me? I think it's going to be a while yet."

Paisley nodded and left the growing family alone to await the arrival of its newest member.

The next several hours ticked by like they do just before Christmas or 5 PM on Friday. There were moments Paisley wanted to call it a night and retreat to her quiet apartment, but Casey seemed to be enjoying her company.

They were visiting with Leah in shifts as she prepared for delivery, but once it was time to push, they all got kicked out of the room except for Cap. Paisley, Casey, Emma and Ashton passed the time in the waiting room in the not-so-comfortable scratchy fabric chairs until their clocks all ticked well past midnight.

"Guess we're having a July fourth baby for sure!" Casey observed, looking at her phone.

"Oh, man, I'm jealous! My phone died a long time ago," Paisley complained.

After an hour passed... "How long does this pushing business last?!" Ashton whined.

"And now my phone is dead," Casey sighed. "Guess I won't be posting any photos of the baby on Facebook tonight!"

Just when the foursome was about to lose hope, a nurse in colorful scrubs appeared in the hall that led from the waiting room to the nurses' station. She was downright chipper with her bouncy black curls and shiny brown cheeks. "Hi, I'm Leah's nurse, Ebony! Would you like to see the baby?"

Emma gasped, "It's here?! Oh my god! Boy or girl?"

"Just follow me!" Nurse Ebony replied in her smooth, melodic voice.

She revealed a Norman Rockwell-esque scene when she opened the door to the new mother's room. Leah's wavy strawberry blonde hair was slightly damp and stuck to her forehead, and her face glistened from exertion, but the grin that stretched across her cheeks had the intensity of a thousand suns. She cradled a tiny bundle wrapped in a white blanket in her arms while Cap sat on the edge of the bed looking down adoringly at his wife and their newborn.

"Well, who do we have here?" Casey asked the obvious question. The four ladies encircled the bed, anxious for their introduction.

"Lincoln Thomas Sheldon," Leah said, the name rolling off her tongue with pride.

"That's a handsome name for a handsome boy!" Casey proclaimed, peeking down at the infant's tiny, pink scrunched-up face. "May I hold him?"

"Of course! Here's all eight pounds, eight ounces of him. Good thing I didn't go all the way to my due date." Leah watched her dear friend and long-time mentor rock her son gently back and forth while cooing softly in his face.

Paisley looked around the room, stunned that she was sharing such a precious, intimate moment with this family. She would expect Casey to be included; after all, she and Cap went way back. But she was a newcomer and still relatively unknown to the Sheldons.

She only walked into their lives three months ago, but here she was celebrating the birth of their son and being treated just like a family member. She'd never known such trusting people.

In that moment of sheer joy, she knew she must take care of whoever was threatening to expose her and The Factory. She couldn't let anything destroy the happy life the Sheldons had built.

ELEVEN

With Cap and Leah in their own little world, adjusting to life with a newborn, The Factory was busier than anyone had ever imagined. Paisley felt fortunate Casey was able to devote a half day to helping her manage club business, and she also was able to recruit some of the host staff to volunteer their time.

Complicating matters, Paisley's friend Allison insisted on coming down to spend a week at the beach. Despite it being the singularly worst week of the entire year for company, Paisley agreed, mostly out of boredom and need for distraction.

Allison took one look at Paisley's cramped apartment and staged an intervention. "You need to get a pet, and you need to get out more. And hang up some artwork or something, geez!"

"It's not any more dire of a situation than when I was on Long Island," Paisley insisted.

"You had *me* on Long Island!" Allison reminded her. "Who do you have here?"

Paisley didn't want to argue and swallowed back her

tendency to get defensive. She felt somewhat close to Leah, Cap, and Casey after all that had happened during the birth, but they were in different phases of their life. Casey was about to retire, and Leah and Cap had their hands full with a baby. She couldn't exactly show up with a bottle of wine and say, "Hey, let's hang out!"

She and Allison went out to the usual local hotspots, Seacrets, Fager's and Macky's, during the week to see if there were any interesting men afoot, but it was the same old twenty-something douchebags who lacked any real substance. In a fit of desperation, Paisley didn't mind shacking up with a muscle-bound six-pack ab-boasting jock who could barely form complete sentences, but she wasn't to that point yet. Neither was Allison.

Then there was also the conundrum of being "the fat friend" when Allison was around. Paisley didn't like the stares she sometimes got from shallow men who only wanted girls with fake boobs, fake tans, and hipbones that protruded from string bikinis. She also didn't care to be relegated to the wingman of whomever was itching to get in Allison's pants. That was why she preferred flying solo when it came to trolling for D.

But after Allison returned to New York, Paisley felt a sense of letdown. She still wanted to adopt a kitten, but she hadn't found the time to visit the animal shelter. She tried to pour herself into her work, but it was hard when every day was so draining, dealing with members and vendors and trying to make sure all the ducks were in a row for the next party, not to mention loose ends tied up from the last one.

It was a steamy mid-July day when she found herself nursing a throbbing headache after the phone rang repeatedly. Most of the callers asked routine things: "Can we register for Saturday night?" "Is the club having a beach-themed party again this summer?" "What's the nearest hotel to the club?"

But around 2 PM, she answered a call that left her heart pounding.

The voice was male, monotone and robotic, clearly masked with one of those voice-changing apps. "We are ready to collect our money from you. You may have turned off your contact form, but we still know how to find you. We know where you work. We know where you live. And we know what you did."

"Who is this?" she stammered, trying to harness some semblance of strength from the pit of her stomach instead of a spoonful of sour bile.

"Someone who knows who you really are. It's time to pay up. We're giving you two weeks to come up with the money. We'll make another call with instructions at the end of the month. If you fail to comply, we'll be calling your bosses as well as the local media and authorities."

Before she could say anything else, the line went dead. Her mind raced with thoughts of who could be behind the call. The male voice still pointed toward her high school boyfriend. She would need to find out if he had been released from prison.

But wait, those voice-changing apps can also change a female voice to a male voice, right?

Her stomach churned with the half-digested remnants of her lunch. She stood up from her desk and made her way to the bathroom, feeling as though she may pass out at any moment.

She locked the door and barely made it to the toilet before the contents of her stomach revolted, shooting up her throat with a sick, burning force. She coughed to get it all out, then flushed the toilet and shakily rose to standing.

I have to figure out who is doing this. I can't keep thinking this has blown over just to have it catch me in its web again. They're torturing me.

For the first time, she thought about the possibility of giving the blackmailer what he wanted, just paying the money. *But who's to say it would be enough, even if I was able to come up with 10K?*

A fleeting thought flickered to The Factory's bank account, and whether or not she could get access to it. Then she hated herself for even entertaining that disgusting thought.

Cap, Leah, and Casey have been nothing but wonderful to me. There's no way I could break their trust like that.

Desperation does funny things to people.

She knew that from experience. The only person she could think of asking for help was Calvin, but only because he knew about the situation already. But even that seemed like a reach because now that they weren't harassing her via the web form, it really didn't have anything to do with Calvin and the website he'd built.

If she couldn't tell her bosses, and she couldn't tell Allison, then who else did she have? *Exactly no one, that's who.*

She opened the door to the bathroom and practically ran into Casey, who appeared to be coming to check on her. "Everything okay?" she asked in her perky voice.

"I don't think my lunch agreed with me," Paisley stretched the truth. She had splashed cold water on her face and felt a chill when the breeze from the ceiling fans rushed against her skin.

"Why don't you knock off early today?" she offered. "I just got here and can handle the phones. There's no sense in having to talk to people when you're miserable."

Paisley nodded, grateful for her suggestion. A raw,

gnawing feeling was eating away at her stomach, plus she was desperate to brush her teeth. Home was definitely the best place for her. She just hoped the people terrorizing her were done for the day and wouldn't call back while Casey was there.

They said they know where I work and live. The website doesn't give an address for the club, and how could they know where I live?

Her head hurt from trying to untangle the mystery.

She drove straight home, paying careful attention to whether or not any cars were following her. She had a feeling their claims of knowing where she or the club was were bogus. Getting the club's phone number was easy – it was right there on the webpage.

Notice they called the club, but they didn't call my cell phone. They don't know as much as they want me to think they do.

"Maybe I should get a big guard dog instead of a cat?" she wondered out loud as she started to look up the address for the animal shelter again.

Before she could dial the shelter number, she got a text.

Calvin: We need to talk. Your stalker called me today.

Another shock of panic bolted through her like lightning.

Paisley: WTF?!

Calvin: Meet me tonight at Liquid Assets. 7 PM?

Thankfully, Liquid Assets, way up on 94th, was relatively dead for a summer evening. She found Calvin sitting alone in the open area between the bar and the wine racks on a bank of cushioned benches. He had already ordered a drink and was sipping it when Paisley approached.

"Sorry," he apologized, motioning to the chair next to him for her to sit down. "It's been one of those days."

"Tell me about it." She flagged the waitress down so she could order her own pain-soothing cocktail.

"I got a call around three o'clock, computerized voice. Basically said they knew I was the webmaster for The Factory's site, and that I better convince you to comply with their demands, or they'd come after me too."

The color drained from Paisley's face as she slumped down onto the chair next to Calvin and buried her face in her palms. Her long, dark curls gathered around her shoulders like a shawl. "I didn't mean for you to get involved in this mess."

"I know." He took another drink, then tapped her on the knee affectionately. "Paisley, it's okay, I'm not mad, alright?"

She looked up just in time for the waitress to deliver her cocktail. "Cheers?" she asked halfheartedly.

They clinked their glasses together, and she let the cold, fruity drink tingle her tongue, savoring it for a moment before the liquid slid down her throat. When she'd had a bad day at her old job in New York, she had a stable of men and couples she could call on to help her forget.

Paisley often repeated the mantra: *the best therapy is orgasms.*

She had been so happy at The Factory in the beginning, she'd not even bothered developing an outlet for dealing with work stress. Up until now, it'd been the good kind of stress, not the bad kind.

She was starting to reevaluate her need for a team of stress relief aides. Looking at Calvin's beautifully sculpted face, his features so perfectly aligned and symmetrical, she wished she could give him a spot on her team.

He leaned toward her, his head tilted and eyes wide. "I think you should go to the police," he said. "That's the only way we're going to get to the bottom of who's behind this."

There was a litany of reasons Paisley preferred to avoid the police. The obvious one, the one she felt she could share with Calvin, was that the club owners were very concerned about any public attention to their business. If they received any negative press, they were likely to get closed down. To borrow a euphemism Cap would appreciate: *she didn't want to rock the boat.*

But she also had a selfish reason for not wanting to go to the police. It was true, she had done things she was not proud of growing up in her hometown. She had gotten involved with people she shouldn't have given the time of day. She had done things that might have been illegal, but she was trying to protect herself.

Okay, yes, she broke the law. But she had a good reason. And then she left, changed her name, and started over so she never had to revisit her past. Why was someone forcing her to do it now?

"The owners just had a baby, okay? They're really preoccupied with that right now, and I'm running the show.

I don't want to give them anything to worry about, and if I did go to the police, I feel like I'd have to tell them."

"Okay." He leaned against the back of the upholstered bench, looking to his left, then to his right. "I think I know a way you can get the police's help without hurting the owners of your club."

"How's that?"

"My dad is a detective with the state police," he stated. "And they have ways of finding out online stuff, okay?"

She shook her head. "No, not okay. I don't want to get your dad messed up in this too!"

"If I get another call like the one I got today, I'm telling him about it, whether you're on board with it or not." His eyes narrowed, and his jaw tensed resolutely.

"I can't jeopardize my business either, you know. They could start trying to hack my clients' sites for all I know. They may already be trying to hack yours, and since you sell memberships on there, that means there's credit card info. Your members could be at risk too."

Paisley's skin prickled with anxiety. The cocktail was doing nothing to ease her nerves. "Well, that stuff is protected, right? With a firewall or whatever the hell you geeky people do?"

"It's a secure server," he answered, "but cyber criminals get more and more sophisticated all the time. And these people already used a VPN to contact the site and voice-altering software. They're not exactly scrubs."

She hailed the waitress for another drink. This was going to be a two-drink-minimum night; she could feel it. "If we went – together – to talk to your dad about what's going on, would he keep it quiet? Would he be all judgmental about the club's business?"

Calvin grinned. "My dad is cool. And he understands

what it feels like to be judged, trust me. He's a Black man who works in law enforcement, and he's married to a white woman. He's faced plenty of discrimination in his life, believe me."

She couldn't help but smile at the way his eyes lit up when he spoke of his father. "Okay, but he's not going to ask me a bunch of uncomfortable questions, right?"

He shook his head. "It'll be fine, I promise. We can go see him tomorrow if you'd like."

She was wary but starting to feel the effects of her second drink. "What is it about you that drives me to drink?" she teased him. "I hardly ever drink, and yet when I hang out with you—"

"Yeah, I know, I drive women to drink." He laughed along. "I guess I'm so ugly they need beer goggles to look at me."

"As if!" Paisley giggled. "You'd think a big girl like me could hold her liquor better. I'm going to have to wait a while before driving home. I've heard the OC cops are assholes."

He winked. "Yeah, but I usually just tell them I'm Detective Mitchell's son, and I'm off the hook."

"Lucky you!"

"And for the record, you're not a big girl," he said, the smile never leaving his face. "You're perfect."

His words rocked through her like an earthquake. She wasn't sure if it was just the alcohol talking, or if he was trying to elicit a particular reaction or...something else entirely. Her confusion over what he meant by it stole any words she might have managed to speak.

He promptly changed the subject. "Let's go walk on the beach. It'll help us sober up."

She nodded in agreement, and he signaled the waitress

for the check. She knew better than to argue with him when it came to paying the bill. There was no way he would relent anyway; his eyes told her as much. After they were settled up, she followed him out the door and across the busy Coastal Highway, the sunset behind them and the deep blue abyss of water and sky in their path.

The sand was cool and silver under the moonlight, which dappled on the waves at the horizon, making them sparkle like the stars overhead. She glanced back for a moment at the pairs of footprints they were leaving behind them. It made her think of a trail of evidence, and how hard it was to avoid leaving one. Hopefully the people responsible for blackmailing her had left enough evidence to be found.

"So, we're going to just waltz into your dad's office tomorrow and say, 'Hey, this is the deal'?" she asked.

"Just relax and don't worry about that right now. I can do the talking if you want. Things will be fine."

"I'm not a 'relax and don't worry' kinda person, though," she sighed.

He laughed and stopped abruptly, causing her to collide with him just as a wave rushed over their feet. She nearly lost her balance, but he caught her elbow and pulled her back to standing. Now they were facing each other, mere particles of air separating their bodies.

"It's not you, is it?" she asked suddenly, the idea popping into her mind like a kernel of popcorn erupting on a hot stove.

"What?" He laughed as if she'd just told a joke.

"You're not the one doing this so you can hang out with me, are you?"

It had not occurred to her before this very moment. After all, he was the one who had asked her about dating him during their original business dinner weeks ago. And he obviously had the technological capability to do it.

"Are you serious?" Even in the darkness, she was sure his smile vanished. "I hope you're just kidding around. I'd never be so unprofessional."

The longer the gravity of her accusation settled in, the angrier he became. He exhaled sharply and turned to head north on the beach, his footprints trailing away from her.

"Wait!" she called after him. She picked up her pace to catch up. *I'm a fat girl; don't make me run.* "Calvin, wait." She was slightly out of breath when she reached him.

He whipped around and raised his voice over the waves that were crashing on the moonlit surf. "I do want to spend time with you, that's the thing. But I would never stoop so low, and I can't believe you'd even suggest it."

She grabbed his arm, not firmly, just lightly to get his attention. "I thought you lost interest in me when you hired that new redhead receptionist."

"What?!" He searched her eyes for something that wasn't to be found. "Michaela is just an employee. She's a kid, for crying out loud. And not my type at all."

"She can't be much younger than you, and she's gorgeous! She's everybody's type!" Paisley argued.

"Well, not mine." He looked down at the scalloped waves as they soaked into the sand and then retreated back to sea.

"What *is* your type?" She was running a race, and the finish line was in view. She couldn't stop now. She had to see it through.

"Let's see..." He turned to face her, his eyes illuminated by the moonlight. "I like grown women. Confidence. Intelligence. No pretense. I like curves and smooth skin. I like long hair and round asses. I like a woman who isn't afraid to be herself."

Paisley was frozen by his words, except for the fact that she was sinking into the wet sand. She could do nothing but swing her high-heeled sandals back and forth in the grip of her left hand while searching the shadows on his face for a definitive clue. But when the moon passed behind some clouds, there wasn't enough light to see.

"Basically you," he said, when it was clear she needed confirmation.

A tiny incredulous laugh escaped her lips. No words would come, but her insides were screaming: *What? What does this mean?* It was right up there with "I feel drawn to you" in terms of being confusing.

"Don't be so shocked," Calvin said smoothly. "You're a catch, Paisley."

She shook her head. "You don't even know me." She laughed again, this time more of a reflection on the funny ignorance of his admission than the irony. *After all, he's ten years younger than me. What the hell does he know?*

He was resolute. "I'm a decisive person. And perceptive. Because I'm so perceptive, I can make decisions fast. I learned everything I need to know about you the first time we met."

"We are from totally different worlds. I have a... questionable past ...and I'm a swinger. You realize I don't just manage the club, right? I'm actively involved. I fuck people I meet in the lifestyle and have for years."

"Yes, that might very well be the deal breaker..." As the words fell out of his mouth, they were lost to the crashing waves. He drew closer, his eyes locked on her for a moment, closing as he reached her face. His hand gently trailed down her cheek as he brushed his lips against hers.

The spark raced through her body as if she'd shocked herself with static electricity. Goosebumps raised the hairs on her arms and neck as desire reverberated from head to toe. His lips felt impossibly full and soft against hers, unlike any pair of lips she'd ever kissed.

And I've kissed my fair share of people, both men and women.

He pulled her closer to him, smelling ever so slightly of vodka, cinnamon and musky aftershave. Something about the combination was more intoxicating than the cocktails she'd had at Liquid Assets. She was drunk all over again as his arms wrapped around her waist and his body pressed against hers.

Even so, a tiny portion of her sober brain was jumping up and down, waving her arms to get her attention: *Didn't he say something about a deal breaker?*

Her brain demanded that question be answered before she let him continue kissing her, yet she was paralyzed by his touch. She was consumed by him, every nerve in her body happy to give herself over to him, despite what her brain cells were urgently trying to communicate.

The tide, on its way in, suddenly sent a huge, cold wave to clobber the pair, drenching them both up to the waist and wrecking their tryst.

"Oh my god!" Paisley shrieked, her reflexes sending her bounding up the beach with the wet material of her skirt gathered in one hand, her heels in the other.

"Oh, man, you're supposed to be so into the kiss, you just let the waves crash over you." Calvin chuckled, joining her on higher ground. "Haven't you ever seen a cheesy romance movie?"

"I'm pretty sure the water would have to be a lot warmer for that to happen, no offense to your kissing skills," she advised. "And didn't you ever see the 'shrinkage' episode of *Seinfeld?*"

"The what?!"

"Oh, god. See, that's why this isn't going to work out. Among other reasons. You don't know *Seinfeld.* You're ten years younger than me! You were a baby when that show aired."

He grabbed her hand just as she was turning to walk up the shore toward the 93rd Street beach entrance. "Hey, my mom always tells me I'm an old soul. Don't make this an age thing."

"You're right. The other reasons I mentioned are much bigger barriers." It had turned cool, and the breeze blowing against her wet skirt made her shiver.

He wrapped his arms around her. "Let me keep you warm while I walk you back to your car," he offered.

She was getting tired from the long roller coaster of a day and didn't respond, just followed his footprints up the dune toward the wooden fence where the beach began.

His arm remained around her as they walked, holding her close to him. "I really like you, Paisley. I wish you'd give me a chance," he said into her ear while her long, dark curls blew into his face.

By the time they were under the glowing streetlamp, the swoon factor of their kiss had mostly disintegrated, evaporating into the night air like ice melting into a puddle. All she could think of was that the club was in jeopardy because someone from her past had decided to get revenge, and that this twenty-six-year-old man was kind enough to want to help her.

Giving him a chance meant one of them getting hurt. She couldn't do that to him.

"A chance to what?" she clarified but didn't wait for an

answer. "I'm not the girlfriend type, Calvin. I've tried it before, trust me, and it's just not for me. I'm good with fuck buddies, friends with benefits, booty calls, any of that. But please don't say the R word to me. It makes me break out in hives."

"I don't think I could do any of that," he confessed. "I'd be thinking of you with another man when all I want is to have you for myself." The way his body slumped, it looked as though reality had set in, and he was giving up his pursuit.

"Then I guess we've reached an impasse, right?"

He nodded reluctantly. "That kiss though..."

She mirrored him with her nodding head, feeling his disappointment wash over her. She hadn't felt a jolt of instant sexual chemistry like that with anyone for a long time. Maybe not ever, if she was honest.

"I'll text you in the morning to tell you where to meet my Dad and me. Not at his office. We'll figure something else out."

"Okay." There was a tiny part of her that wanted to wait to see if he would try to kiss her goodbye.

Even if she wasn't going to let him, she hoped he still wanted to.

TWELVE

Detective Mitchell agreed to meet them at an out-of-the-way coffee shop in West Ocean City. Paisley let Casey know she'd be a little late to work because she had an appointment. Casey didn't seem to mind, but she did sound tired. Paisley wondered how much longer the older woman could burn the candle at both ends.

Calvin and his father were already sipping coffee at a table in the most private corner of the shop. Paisley waved, and Calvin winked back. His father was a tall, imposing man with deep sepia skin, eyes to match, and some gray at his temples. He was dressed in a navy blue polo shirt paired with khaki pants, and she spotted a gun belt and holster around his hips.

She paid for her coffee and walked over to join them, feeling on display in her pinstriped navy blue suit. *I look like Casey dressed me today.* She glanced down at her shiny red pumps. She had wrangled her voluminous hair into a smooth, classy chignon at the nape of her neck.

Calvin gave her an approving glance as she held out her

hand to his father. "I'm Paisley Parker, Assistant Operations Manager at The Factory."

"I'm Detective Calvin Mitchell," he said evenly as he shook her hand. "This is all off the record here today, so please, don't be nervous, okay?" He had a warm smile that instantly put her at ease, for which she was grateful. "Now, my son tells me you've been the victim of extortion?"

Paisley nodded and told him all the relevant details: they knew her childhood name (she had legally changed her name when she was twenty-one); they had contacted The Factory through their webpage and also by phone; and they were demanding a sum of $10,000 or else they would expose Paisley's secrets in an effort to damage the club and cost her her job.

Detective Mitchell's eyes didn't leave Paisley's once. He hardly even blinked as he sat leaning forward with his hands folded together on top of the table. Paisley had to laugh, because she'd seen his son look at her with the same intense, engaged stare.

The apple doesn't fall far from the tree.

When she was finished and eagerly awaiting his response, he unfolded his hands and began to speak. He was a "talks with his hands" type of person, even more so than his son. "First thing, I want to ask you something, which I know you may not want to answer, but it's important for me to know how serious this is. Do these people really know anything that could incriminate you? Or, put another way: is there something incriminating to be known about you?"

"Uh...incriminating? You want to know if I'm a criminal?" Her eyes went wide, and a lump grew in her throat. Calvin placed his hand on her knee under the table, and instead of jolting away, she found it soothed her.

Detective Mitchell nodded. "Yeah, I just want to know what we're dealing with here."

She gulped in a mouthful of air. "Well, I guess so... Would it matter if I was a minor when it happened?"

"Did it happen in the state of Maryland?" he asked.

She shook her head. "No, no, back in my home state."

"Which is where?"

"Does it matter?"

Every time she spoke the name of her home state, she felt violently ill. She never wanted to go there again and didn't even want those three syllables to spring off her tongue. She was a New Yorker as far as anyone knew, including herself.

Can you disown a whole state? Well, if anyone can, it's me.

"As long as it's not Maryland, I suppose." He smirked. "Smart girl," he remarked to his son, who nodded and smiled in agreement. Then he looked back at Paisley, whose blue eyes reflected her relief.

"Alright, I have a bit of a secret weapon." The last two words and gestures were delivered as if he were the hero in a blockbuster summer action movie.

"And what's that?" Calvin asked. "You know, it's not just Paisley's club that's at risk here, but my business as well. They threatened me too, let's not forget."

"I know, and that's why I'm willing to pull out all the stops," Detective Mitchell said, grinning. It was obvious he relished the hero role. "I know someone – a hacker. He owes me a favor for not busting his ass when he tried to hack into the MVA servers. He ended up providing some information in a high profile case I investigated last year, but I think he'd agree with me that his debt is not fully paid. He has incentive to stay on the good side of MSP, that's for sure. I have no doubt he can get down to the bottom of who is behind the emails."

"Oh!" Paisley exclaimed, her eyes widening again.

"I wouldn't mind bugging your phone at work either," he offered. "In case they call again. It's pretty easy to trace phone calls."

She shook her head, "No, that can't happen. I don't want my bosses to know what's going on."

"It's not your fault that you're being targeted," he insisted with his arms waving in front of him. "It would be better if everyone was on the same page."

"I just started working there, and I'm still building trust. The owners just had a baby, and I'm supposed to be holding down the fort. I'm really uncomfortable with them being involved in any way. It's very important that the club not get any negative press because of this."

"Right," Calvin agreed. "Plus—"

His father cut him off, "So what's the deal with this 'club,' as you call it? What is it, exactly?"

Paisley and Calvin exchanged looks where it was obvious they were both trying to figure out the best way to word an answer. Paisley swallowed hard and went for it: "It's a lifestyle club," she simply explained, hoping to gloss over it as much as possible.

"What kind of lifestyle?"

Of course he'd ask that; he's a detective. "Um...does it matter?" She tried that trick again.

"Is it legal?"

Calvin laughed. "Of course, Dad, relax!"

Paisley's stomach was knotted so tightly that the acidic coffee she'd just drunk was gnawing away at her insides. *Why, oh why, did I get anyone else involved in this mess? It's so much easier when I just do everything myself.*

She tried smiling to cover up the discomfort of her stomach lining being eroded away. She could almost feel the ulcers forming. Detective Mitchell's brows were furrowed as if he was still trying to figure out what the club was all about.

Paisley seized the opportunity to wrap things up: "Is there anything else you need from me?"

He shook his head. "No, I think I can get the technical specifics from Calvin Jr. here. I'll definitely let him know if I find anything out. Fingers crossed." He smiled as if he'd accepted the fact that The Factory's M.O. was going to remain a mystery.

She focused on the armor she'd worn: shiny pumps, her crisp shirt, and her smooth chignon. The goal was to come across as polished and professional as possible. She shook his hand again with a firm, confident grip. "Thank you so much for making the time to meet with me, Detective. I can't tell you how much it means to me."

"It's my pleasure," he answered, his hand warming hers as he pumped it up and down a few more times for good measure.

Paisley smiled at Calvin and left the coffee shop. Despite being dressed in her Casey-approved outfit and having a secure smile plastered to her face, she felt more uneasy than when she first arrived.

Paisley considered Friday night's party at The Factory to be her escape from stress, which was saying a lot since managing the club mostly by herself on a busy night was anything but stress-free. She was being torn into two halves: half of her analyzing, worrying and generally freaking out about the threats she was receiving and generously peppered with inappropriate thoughts about corrupting Calvin; and the other half was dedicated to being the best assistant operations manager she could be.

Erik the Bartender winked at her from his perch as she made her rounds, stopping to ask members how they were enjoying their visit. She didn't mean to sashay quite so gratuitously, but the sparkly platform heels and the swingy red dress she wore made it quite challenging to avoid doing so.

"Looking good in red!" Erik called out, capturing the attention of a few ladies sipping their drinks from the wooden barstools.

"That dress is amazing!" exclaimed one of the women, a short-haired brunette with blonde highlights woven through her curls. "Where did you get it?"

"Torrid! Isn't it fabulous?" Paisley spun around so they could see how the circle skirt fluttered around her calves.

"I really admire your confidence. It's so inspiring!" one of the other ladies remarked. She was a heavier woman wearing a billowing peasant-style top and jeans. "I wish I could dress like that."

"I know, me too," their blonde companion agreed from the adjacent barstool. "How did you learn to be so sure of yourself?"

Paisley wanted to groan but maintained her professional smile. She hated having this conversation with women. "Your confidence is so inspiring," often seemed code for "Wow, I can't believe you have the nerve to wear that."

She was well aware that much of society thought plus-sized women were supposed to cover up their bodies and cower in shame. Every time people made referendums about what was okay for bigger women to wear and what wasn't, she wanted to weave a fine tapestry of expletive-ridden rebuttal, but she usually kept her mouth shut. The best way to fight fat-shaming, after all, was to wear whatever she wanted and to be more comfortable in her skin than women half her size.

"It's actually a choice," Paisley explained with the smile still plastered to her face. "You just decide you're worthy of self-love, then you stop giving a shit what anyone else thinks. Anyone can do that. It's up to you."

The three women looked as though they were in awe, as if she were a superhero. Paisley wished she could shake her fellow females by the shoulders, look into their eyes and make them see: "Just be yourself. Own it. Men will flock to you like flies." It undoubtedly worked for her.

After the night wound down, only Paisley, Casey, the two security guards and the bartender remained in the club. The hosts had gathered up all the dirty laundry, stuffed it into the two huge industrial-sized washers in the back, and left for a hotel room with another couple. Erik was wiping off the stainless steel counter when Paisley made her way through the lounge towing the yellow garbage bin behind her.

"Cleanup is always the worst part!" She smiled at him while studying the way his muscles flexed as he scrubbed a stubborn sticky spot.

"Hey, there you are." He smiled back, revealing his straight, white teeth. She would have bet money on him having had braces when he was growing up. "I wanted to say that I loved what you told those women when they complimented your dress."

"Oh yeah?" Her eyebrows shot up. Many a time she had

heard this sort of introductory statement and never knew if she was going to find herself humbly flattered or horribly enflamed. A man mentioning a woman's weight, even indirectly, was fraught with danger.

"Your confidence is not only inspiring, it's hella sexy," he offered, his green eyes meeting hers with a tiny flicker of desire.

She could sense flirtation like a shark smells blood from miles away. She never understood how other women could be so oblivious to it. *I mean, it's called women's intuition for a reason, right?*

"Well, thank you," she answered, trying to take his statement at face value, a compliment.

"This whole time you've been here, I've been watching you," he admitted, coming out from behind the bar. He was in full-on cowboy regalia again tonight with his belt buckle gleaming, Wranglers plastered to his thighs, and his boots clomping against the concrete. He wore a simple black t-shirt, no design, which was fitted enough to show the definition in his pecs, the armbands tight around his bulging biceps.

"That sounds a little creepy," Paisley giggled, stationing herself against the bar between two stools. Across the lounge, Jason was watching their interaction.

"I know. I can't believe I just told you that." His chiseled jawline was accentuated by his wide grin and stubble. She couldn't help but imagine what it would feel like scraping across her smooth, silky skin as he trailed his face down her stomach to its destination between her thighs.

"I'd be lying if I said I wasn't flattered." She smiled back, anxious to see what would come next.

She loved this dance, this negotiation. *How do people go*

from clothed to naked, from standing feet apart to bodies pressed against each other between the sheets?

She'd danced these steps a thousand times, but each time the sequence and lyrics were different. Every performance was a new version of an ancient ritual.

Jason ambled over to the bar where they were standing, trying to pull off a nonchalant attitude but clearly having an agenda. "I like your dress too," he stated, his eyes traveling up and down her body, hovering for the longest time on her ample cleavage. It wasn't hard to figure out what was going on here, and Paisley wasn't having it.

"Uh, thanks." She shot him a look that was meant to convey, *Get the fuck out of here. It's about to go down, and you're not invited.*

"Are you sticking around to play?" Jason asked, a hopeful twinkle in his eyes. Paisley wondered where his buddy Trent had gone off to. Maybe he would catch the clue Jason refused to comprehend.

"I think Erik and I are going to hang out back at my place." She shot Erik a beckoning glance. Still grinning with his perfect teeth, he nodded in agreement.

"Oh, I wanna come. I'd love to see the Paisley Parker lair," Jason remarked, growing animated. "I'm sure it's the stuff of legends."

He's really not getting it, is he? She wasn't sure how to make it any clearer.

"Oh, I think just Erik and me this time," she again clarified, trying to sound as pleasant as possible.

"Oh, I see how it is." He took another step toward her till they stood only inches apart.

Paisley wanted to back away, but she was pinned between the bar and the two barstools flanking her.

"Once you have a cock, you don't want it again, right?

Fucking slut." He mumbled the last two words under his breath as if he wasn't quite brave enough to say them at full volume.

"What did you call her?" Erik spat in Jason's face like a cobra spitting venom.

"It's okay, Erik, I can handle this," Paisley said calmly from her trapped position.

"Can you? You can handle both of us, if my memory serves," Jason continued, growing increasingly agitated. "You're just a fat fucking whore. Surprised you didn't ask Trent and me for money afterwards. Yeah, that's right." He turned to Erik. "Trent and I fucked this fat cunt right on the floor over there." He pointed to the spot in the lounge where their threesome had occurred.

Trent heard his name and appeared from the hallway leading to the offices and playrooms. "What's going on in here?" he shouted in a gruff tone, obviously still in security guard mode.

Paisley hoped Trent's presence might have the effect of resetting Jason's attitude, but it seemed to have the opposite effect as he now spewed into Paisley's face, "I bet you've fucked every man in this club, you fucking whore!"

Recognizing that his boss was trapped, Erik grabbed Jason by the arm and threw him down to the floor like he was a rag doll. Paisley's heart was pounding as the scene unfolded in front of her, and she experienced it in flashes: Jason's hand slowly gravitating to his skull, which had hit the corner of the bar and was now oozing blood; Trent's apparent conflict, torn between helping Jason up, punching Erik, or asking Paisley if she was alright; Erik's stunned expression that Jason had gotten hurt.

"I didn't mean for him to hit the bar." Erik sighed, backing away from the scene. "Fuck."

Paisley stepped over Jason's still writhing body to the other side where the three men stood in a triangle in front of her. "First of all," she said, looking down at Jason, "you're fired. Secondly, Trent, help him up and take him to the ER. He's going to need stitches. Thirdly, Erik and I are leaving. That's it. There'll be no further discussion."

The blood was starting to trickle down Jason's face, one drip caught in his bushy black eyebrows. His bald head didn't offer any resistance. Paisley spotted the small gash, and it wasn't that long or deep.

He'll be fine. She breathed a sigh of relief. *A few stitches and he'll be fine.*

"I cannot tolerate slut shaming of any kind," she said to the three men who stood with their jaws hinged open at her stoic demeanor.

"I'm sending the club my medical bills," Jason shouted over his shoulder as Trent escorted him out the door. Trent said nothing; Paisley assumed it was because he didn't want to lose his job too.

Once the two were alone, Erik shook his head as if he were trying to clear out cobwebs. "I cannot believe that just happened."

Paisley smirked. "I've seen worse."

"You have ice water running through your veins, woman! Fuck, that's really hot, you know that?"

"All in a day's work," she answered, slipping off her platform heels and returning to her normal 5'8" stature.

She was glad Casey had missed the show. Her mentor was in the office getting the deposit ready from the night's profits. Her hearing wasn't the best, so it was possible she didn't witness any of the altercation, especially since the giant fans in the main hallway of the club and over the lounge were so loud.

She came out of the office with her bag, ready to lock up for the night. "Well, if you don't look like two naughty kids with their hands caught in the cookie jar!" She grinned upon seeing Paisley and Erik.

Paisley laughed. "You missed all the excitement!" She hoped to get by with giving Casey only minimal details, but she knew she at least needed to explain why Jason was coming off the payroll. "I had to let Jason go."

Her perfectly groomed auburn eyebrows arched. "Oh? Why is that?"

"He said some pretty inappropriate things to me and was in my face screaming. I'm okay; don't worry. It was my first time firing someone, though."

"I trust your judgment." Casey smiled. "So I guess we'll need to find another security guard pronto, huh? It's our busiest month of the season."

"Yeah, I'll do some asking around and put an ad out if I need to." She noticed Erik's feet were firmly planted beside the bar. It appeared as though he was holding out for that tour of the Paisley Parker Lair.

"Can you guys lock up? I'm headed home," Casey called as she started for the door. She still looked fresh as a daisy in her spectator pumps and black and white print dress.

"Of course. See you tomorrow." Paisley turned to Erik. "Are you ready to go?"

His green eyes were shiny with expectation, confirming her earlier suspicions. *Might as well. It will be a good distraction, if nothing else.*

She did consider the ramifications of sleeping with another employee, but Erik seemed much more secure than Jason. She'd have a word with him about her expectations before anything happened. She should have done the same with Jason and Trent.

Erik followed her to the parking lot like a puppy dog. *Why do the strongest, most alpha guys suddenly become so demure and docile in my presence? It's so disappointing!*

She enjoyed more of a pursuit, a man who wanted her but didn't need her. If there was one thing she hated, it was any whiff of desperation. Erik didn't seem desperate, but he'd lost that cocky edge he had behind the bar.

Maybe he'll get it back once we get in bed. I need to be fucked hard, hard enough to feel it in the morning.

Paisley forgot to shut the blinds before bed and remembered in the most painful way possible: the light streaming through the slats blinded her upon opening her eyes.

Oh, so that's why they're called blinds, she thought, only semi-lucidly. The sun was at the perfect angle on its morning ascent to smack her in the face with its relentless brightness.

She felt around for her phone, and her hand landed on a limb, one that didn't belong to her. Then it all came rushing back to her, the tangle of sheets, the not-quite-as-big-as-she'd-hoped cock, the screaming "Fuck me harder!"

Her voice was a little hoarse, now that she thought about it. Somehow she had been convinced to let Erik spend the night, which was very much against her usual terms of play.

He stirred next to her, still looking rather delicious with his firm, round rump exposed to the sunlight and his messy hair matted to one side of his head. He rolled over to face her, and her eyes were immediately drawn to his morning wood, straining against his stomach muscles.

Without speaking, he pulled her on top of him, nuzzling her neck with his day-old stubble. He smelled faintly of the drinks they'd shared last night when they arrived at her apartment.

Inviting a bartender to your house means fancy cocktails. He used her as a guinea pig to try a few recipes he was considering for his second job at a bar in one of the hotels on the beach.

He reached into the glass bowl by her bed and retrieved a condom. "You want Round 2?" He waved the packet in her face.

She nodded. *I'm here, might as well.*

She took the condom from him, ripped it open and slid down his body so she could carefully unroll it down his rigid shaft. Then she climbed aboard like the seasoned cock jockey she was. She was surprisingly wet considering her level of dehydration, and his length slid into her smoothly, filling her up as her pelvis came to rest on his.

She pinned his arms over his head as she began to move her hips against him, lifting herself to slide up his cock to the very tip. Then she plunged back down till he was buried balls deep inside her again. Her pendulous breasts swung in his face until he captured a ripe, hard nipple with his teeth, causing her to wince at the initial shock. His scratchy stubble scraped against her breasts as she fucked him, still holding him down by his wrists.

She was riding his cock slowly, rhythmically, letting her orgasm build, but apparently slow wasn't what Erik wanted. "God, babe, you're killing me," he grunted as he struggled against her strong hands that bound him to the mattress.

"Patience is a virtue," she replied, her words smooth as silk as a smile crept across her face.

"Do I look like the virtuous type to you?" He used the fact that she was distracted by their conversation to his advantage. He broke loose of her grasp and flipped her over with one muscular arm, then pinned her to the bed. His erection pushed into the cleft between her full, round bottom as he pressed his weight against her back.

His hot breath blew into her ear along with the words, "Now we're going to do this at my speed." She shivered with desire as he pulled her to her knees and rammed his hard rod into her slit.

She braced herself against her wooden headboard as he continued to drive into her, faster and faster with his fingers dug into the soft flesh of her hips. "No better way to start the day!" he groaned, slowing just enough to punctuate each word with a deep thrust.

She barely heard him as her entire body was enraptured by her oncoming orgasm. It stole her breath, her vision, her hearing – all of her senses – as it sent her soaring through a purple sea of ecstasy. When it finally dissipated, she realized he had stopped, still buried to the hilt, to feel her pussy spasm around him.

"That's what I'm talking about," he growled as he began to thrust into her again.

"It's my turn now," he warned her as he started to pick up speed.

She envisioned what his muscular pelvis and ass looked like as they pummeled her forgiving flesh. His breaths were loud and raspy, and most of what came out of his mouth was either unintelligible or involved the F word, which was somehow clear as day. She felt him grow even harder as his release approached, then finally heard a gasp and a resounding moan as his cock jerked inside her.

As they lay together afterward, she rested her head on his arm. His eyes were closed; he had mentally left the bed for unknown lands, awash in bliss.

Despite their physical contact, she felt detached from him. She trailed her eyes up and down his body, admiring its masculine perfection, the peaks and valleys of his musculature. But he seemed like a different species from her, so hard and angular contrasted against her voluptuous softness.

As she studied their differences, she wondered if she could ever feel a sense of belonging with someone, if she could ever build a bond that bridged all chasms. *Love,* she realized. *I'm talking about love. I sometimes wonder if I'm not wired to feel it.*

On Sunday, Paisley had promised to meet Cap at the club to give a report about the weekend's activities. He also planned to pick up the deposit to take to the bank on Monday. She hadn't seen him since that night in the hospital when his son was born. The last time he'd come in to pick up the deposit, she hadn't been there, as it was when her friend Allison was visiting.

He looked even more tan and weathered than the last time she'd seen him, which made his blue eyes glow even brighter. He was wearing his trademark swim trunks, sandals and a t-shirt; he always looked like he belonged at the marina.

She still felt like he and Leah were a curious couple.

She seemed so prim and proper in comparison to him, not to mention a lot younger. Cap's daughters, Emma and Ashton, didn't look too much older than Leah, now that Paisley thought about it.

He gave her a warm hug, which was unexpected. He smelled exactly how she imagined he would, like sea salt and ocean breezes. He held her a little longer than she thought was appropriate, but then again, "appropriate" was a different animal in the lifestyle.

"How were things this weekend?" He finally broke away from their embrace.

"Good." She nodded with a smile. "Busy, of course. Had an issue with one of the security guards, so let me know if you have a lead on a new one. Casey took Friday night's deposit, but I have last night's ready for you."

She watched his face react as she spoke and noticed he seemed a bit sluggish. "How are things on your end?"

He sighed with that look of not wanting to complain but needing to. "Lincoln's not much of a sleeper yet, and Leah's been a wreck tryin' to keep 'im fed. That's all he wants to do...nurse, I mean. Though I can't say I blame 'im!"

Paisley laughed. Cap was the type to tell it like it is, which she very much appreciated, but he had a lighthearted way of doing it. He could find a smidge of humor in nearly everything, and it was all delivered with that twangy Eastern shore accent and dimples.

She suddenly wanted to tell him what was going on with the threats. She was slightly more hopeful now that Detective Mitchell was working to get to the bottom of it, but she figured Cap would be distressed by the fact that police were involved, even if it was off the record. She decided to keep it to herself, hoping it could be resolved without either the Sheldons or Casey finding out.

"Leah is hoping to come back to work the week after next," he stated, glancing around the club to ensure everything was in order. "She'll just bring the baby with her and go about her business."

"Oh! Well, she doesn't need to trouble herself with anything here just yet." Paisley had a momentary panic attack race through her when she thought about any phone calls coming through while Leah was here.

"I think she's going a bit stir crazy." Cap smiled. "It'll do her good to get out. Speaking of which, why don't you come over for dinner some night next week? She'd love to have some company now that the girls aren't coming around every day."

"Okay, I can do that," Paisley nodded. "Just let me know what night."

"I'll have her text you. You won't believe how big he's getting already." His blue eyes filled with pride. "He's going to be quite the ladies' man when he gets big; you can just tell!"

"How could he not with you as his dad?" She laughed.

"Good point." He winked as he gathered up the bag of receipts and cash. "Good point."

FOURTEEN

Though Cap had painted a picture of Leah as a frazzled, exhausted new mom, she seemed anything but that night at dinner. She seemed put together, already looking much slimmer in her smocked floral sundress. She wore her strawberry blonde hair twisted up and held by a tortoiseshell clip with a few loose tendrils gracing her neck.

The baby was snoozing peacefully in his sling, going with her wherever she went, to and from the kitchen. She looked like an earth goddess with no makeup and a natural peachy-pink glow emanating from her cheeks. Motherhood definitely suited her.

"My parents were here for two weeks," she sighed as she heaped another spoonful of potatoes on her plate. "Two weeks! I thought I might die!"

Paisley laughed. "Too long?"

"My parents are wonderful people, but they are very religious. I'd almost forgotten what it was like to be around them for an extended time. My brother and his wife are coming next week with their extremely rambunctious one-year-old. I wanted to get into the habit of coming back to work later this week so I have a place to escape if necessary."

"Gotcha. Well, things are business as usual at the club," Paisley assured her. "There's no hurry for you to come back."

"I know The Factory is in good hands, but I miss it so much!" She looked down at the golden-haired angel sleeping at her breast. "I thought about just coming in one night, maybe bringing the baby in his sling or leaving him with Cap for a few hours. Just to get out of the house. But he's nursing so often...I don't want to offend anyone."

"Do you really think anyone would be offended by seeing your boobs?" Cap chuckled. "On the contrary!"

"You'd be surprised. There are quite a few otherwise open-minded people who freak out as soon as they see a baby sucking on a nipple."

"Well, I wouldn't be offended at all. I think it's a beautiful thing." Paisley smiled.

It was as if Lincoln heard his cue and began to fuss, twisting his tiny body in the fabric of the sling. His cry was deep, lusty and sustained, most certainly hungry.

"Well, then, you won't mind me doing my thing, then." Leah pulled down the smocked top of her sundress, exposing her round, swollen breast. The baby's tiny head rooted for his mother's nipple, his cries extinguished as soon as he was attached.

"It's a shame, too," Leah continued, "because, although we're not quite ready yet, I think once I get the all-clear from my doctor for sex, I'm going to be ready to play."

"Thank god!" Cap cheered, raising his glass to toast the much anticipated occasion.

"Poor Cap, he's been so patient with me," Leah said,

glancing at her husband. "It's been three...four weeks since we've had sex, and I think he's crawling the walls."

"It's been five weeks and two days, but who's counting?" Cap's dimples popped out for emphasis.

"Oh, right, I forgot about the time before Lincoln was born when I was just too uncomfortable," Leah said. "Now we wait three more weeks for the doctor to say it's okay. We've fooled around a little, but no penetration."

Paisley admired the way they looked at each other, their eyes embracing. Most people would find it incredibly uncomfortable to listen to their bosses talk about their sex life, but that sort of openness was expected in the lifestyle.

That was one of the things Paisley loved most about it. Sex wasn't this secretive, tiptoed-around topic. It was a natural phenomenon and discussed openly with no shame and no pretense.

"So...now that we're talking about this," Leah began, looking directly at Paisley. "We wondered if maybe..."

Paisley's ears perked up when she noticed Leah shifting in her chair as her voice trailed off. She had a feeling she knew what was coming next, and it was adorable how much trouble her boss was having getting the words out. She had a feeling Cap would have blurted them out effortlessly by now.

"We wondered if perhaps you'd be willing to play with us," she asked, starting again after a deep breath helped her find her moxie. She looked at Cap again, and they both smiled and nodded as if presenting themselves as a package deal.

When Paisley interviewed for her job with the Sheldons and Casey Fontaine, they had asked her some unorthodox questions, attempting to discern whether or not she was actively involved in the lifestyle. They had prefaced the intrusion on her privacy with the promise that if at any time she felt uncomfortable answering, she could withdraw her application, no questions asked.

But Paisley was actually delighted that they were so committed to finding someone experienced with the life-style to fill a managerial role. They later told her that everyone they hired had some degree of involvement, obviously the hosts, but the bartender and security guards too. They wanted their employees to really understand lifestyle lingo, mores and etiquette.

"I would love to," Paisley answered without hesitation.

"Oh, good!" Leah sounded relieved. She switched the baby to her other breast, and Cap began to clear the dishes. "How's tonight?" she added sheepishly.

"Oh!" Paisley gasped, now finally understanding why she'd been invited. "I guess that's fine. I mean, I don't have any other plans." They all laughed.

Cap had a spring in his step as he completed his tasks. He didn't say anything, but Paisley heard him whistling as he carried the garbage out back. "I'm going to finish feeding Lincoln, and then get him bathed and settled in for the night," Leah said. "Why don't the two of you go enjoy the hot tub?"

Paisley shrugged. "Why not?"

Twilight was falling on Ayres Creek, turning the water a shade of indigo and the ripples into a mirror. Cap opened the French doors and ushered his guest out onto the deck, where the hot tub sat in the corner overlooking the dock. A small fishing vessel bobbed up and down on the silvery waves.

"I'll grab some towels and be right back," he promised.

She watched fireflies twinkling along the banks while she waited for him to return. It was finally beginning to cool after a viciously hot July day. Even though the sun was still sinking in the west, she spotted one or two early stars struggling to make themselves visible against the darkening skies.

She had tried not to think too much about the ongoing blackmail situation, although Calvin had texted her earlier in the day to say he had news. He suggested they meet in the morning. She figured she could drop by his office before heading into work. For some reason, she felt a little smug at the prospect of seeing his new receptionist Michaela again.

I'm more his type than she is, she reminded herself with a devious smile.

"You look lost in thought," Cap said, appearing at her side.

She nearly fell into the creek, he startled her so badly. "Sorry, I didn't even hear you come back out."

"Are you sure you're okay with this?" he asked. "We don't want you to feel uncomfortable."

He waited for her answer while he took the cover off the hot tub, as if he expected her to say yes and asking was just a formality. Still, she was glad he asked. It was always better to be straightforward about things, in her opinion.

The steam rose into the air as soon as the cover was taken away. He fired up the jets and turned on the lights, which shifted from purple to green to royal blue to turquoise to fuchsia and back again.

"Oohhh, pretty," she cooed as she dipped one toe into the swirling waters.

She saw the Sheldons' two dogs, Glory and Keeper, watching them from the glass doors. "You think they'll wonder what's going on if they see their daddy making out with another woman?"

Cap laughed. "Well, coming from two creatures who

constantly sniff each other's asses, I'm not too worried about offending them."

She giggled and let the steam fill her sinuses as she breathed in deeply. The jets were hitting her back muscles at the perfect angles. She sank down to bury her shoulders in the water, wishing she'd pinned her long hair up.

Oh, well, might as well go the full monty, and she slid completely underwater to get the entirety of her dark mane wet.

"Sorry if I look like a drowned rat," she apologized as she resurfaced.

"Quite the contrary. You don't look like a rodent at all," Cap assured her as he scooted so close, his thighs pressed against hers. "You're a remarkably beautiful woman, Paisley." He placed his hand on her thigh for emphasis.

She liked the weight of his arm on her. She had been curious about Cap for quite some time, and the prospect of finally having her curiosity satisfied was exciting. "Well, Leah is a beautiful woman as well. You clearly have good taste."

He didn't respond with words; instead, he used his still dry hand, rough from a lifetime of work on the water, to tilt her chin toward his face. His lips pressed against hers: hot, moist and hungry. As he began to kiss her more insistently, he threaded his hands through her wet hair, sending his tongue deeper into her throat.

She wasn't used to men being this aggressive with her. Because she tended to present a rather dominant persona, most of her lovers eased their way into sex with her, exploring their boundaries bit by bit. Either that, or they expected her to take control from the beginning. But not Cap. He was as bold as an astronaut on the moon, claiming his territory as his boots bounced off the rocky surface.

He pulled her on top of him so she straddled his legs, her knees resting on the fiberglass bench. They had climbed in nude, but he'd gone in facing the other way, so she hadn't gotten a peek at his manhood. But it was now wedged between her thighs, and she could feel it pressing into her lips, just shy of her clit. Without a doubt, Cap was well endowed, which did not surprise her in the least. She would have bet money on it, in fact.

He bent to bury his face between her breasts, biting and nipping her skin and sending her into a frenzy of desire. The steamy water bubbled up around them, heating up their respective bodies even more than the passion generated by their kissing. Paisley's entire pelvic region throbbed, and not just from the pressure of the jet spraying up between their legs.

She hadn't felt this much anticipation since... *Well, since Calvin, if I'm being honest. Though I really shouldn't think of him that way...*

But two minutes later she still was. Cap noticed she had slipped off into another world, so he stopped. He tilted her chin toward his face with one finger so their eyes could lock. "What's wrong, Sugar? Having second thoughts?"

"Not at all," Paisley moaned. "I just was thinking we should go inside before Leah thinks we've forgotten about her."

"Oh, very true, very true." He watched her dismount his lap and pull herself out of the water, where she wrapped herself in one of the fluffy beach towels he'd left on the patio chair. "Why don't you go on inside? I'll put the cover back on and join you in a few."

She nodded and used the towel to dry off before heading in the house. She found Leah in their master bedroom perched atop their king-sized mattress. She stretched her long, silky legs out against the comforter, wearing nothing but a black silk robe. She'd taken down her hair, which fell around her shoulders in copper waves. She had the slightest bit of roundness remaining from her pregnancy, but otherwise was sleek and fit. Except for her breasts, of course, which were lush and full from breast-feeding.

Though her breasts were still hidden in the robe, Leah's cleavage made Paisley thirst for more. She'd had a good glimpse at the dinner table, but now that they were alone, and the baby had taken his fill, Paisley wondered if she might have a turn to play with them.

Yet it was Leah's face, her high cheekbones, her glassy green eyes, the arch of her eyebrows, and her exquisitely curved lips that were even more alluring. She was a classic beauty, and Paisley never noticed more than she did in this moment.

"Hello, beautiful," she breathed, dropping her damp towel on the carpeted floor and stepping toward the bed.

Leah's eyes traced up and down her body, taking in her rounded white shoulders, her succulent breasts with their rose-colored areolae, and her ample, dimpled thighs. A woman of Paisley's stature might try to cover up, to minimize her curves and rolls, but Paisley stood with her arms open, her body in its full, natural glory.

Her wet hair was forming ringlets as it began to dry against her chest, but the wet strands clung to her as she crawled across the bed. She stroked a finger down Leah's cheek, watching her eyes flutter closed as her lips awaited meeting Paisley's. They were velvety soft as Paisley brushed against them. As she kissed her, her hand wandered down to Leah's black silk robe where she untied the belt and released her full, milky breasts.

Paisley heard Cap enter the room, but her attention never diverted from Leah. She slid the robe down Leah's shoulders and discarded it across the room. She planted tiny kisses along Leah's collarbone, and a smile spread her lips as Leah's back arched in response.

Then Paisley followed the trail she'd made with her mouth down to Leah's breasts. "Is it okay for me to touch them?"

"Yes," Leah moaned, "although I can't guarantee you won't get sprayed." She chuckled softly as Paisley ignored her warning and kissed each swollen nipple.

They instantly hardened under the pressure from her lips, and she couldn't help but wonder what would happen if she were to suck...only a little bit...gently, of course.

She spread her lips and took one into her mouth, just barely closing her jaws around it. Leah sighed, her head falling onto the pillow behind her. Paisley proceeded cautiously, her tongue darting over Leah's teats.

The bed shook as Cap took a seat on the bed to watch the show. "Go ahead, Sugar...it won't hurt you. She loves it."

Leah nodded her approval, and that was all the encouragement Paisley needed to suck the nipple deeply into her mouth. A few seconds later, her mouth filled with a warm, sweet liquid.

"Oh, my god, that's incredible!" She burst out laughing. It was like a science experiment that goes better than expected. "Oh, sorry, I don't mean to ruin the mood..."

Leah smiled. "It's fine. There's probably not too much since Lincoln just nursed."

"I have something you can suck!" Cap volunteered, rising to his knees.

"You always have the best segue ways!" His wife laughed. "Shall we, Paisley?"

Paisley was already licking her lips at the prospect of wrapping them around Cap's cock. He stationed himself in the middle of the mattress, thighs spread, his long, thick manhood already engorged with veins throbbing. He had a dense carpet of silvery hair on his tan chest and a look of lust filling his eyes.

The women flanked him, each running the tip of her tongue up his shaft until his eyes rolled back into his head with desire. "That's it, ladies, that's it." He sighed, his eyes fluttering open to witness the work they were doing on his organ with their mouths.

Once his tool glistened with saliva, Paisley made the attempt to swallow him whole. She had been known to easily take eight-inch cocks down her throat, but Cap was eight inches with nearly the same circumference.

"My god, Cap, my mouth doesn't even spread that wide! I'd need to unhinge my jaw like a snake to get that in!" Paisley laughed.

"That's why I need both of you!" he retorted, his dimples showing.

Paisley went to work on thoroughly sucking him while Leah rose to kiss him on the lips. Listening to the couple's muffled moans as their tongues entangled, she continued to suck and stroke him with her hands. Cap had managed to work his hand underneath his wife so he could play with her clit while they kissed.

Leah was panting as she rocked back and forth against his hand, her heavy breasts bouncing against her ribcage. Finally, she grabbed them with both hands, capturing her nipples between her thumb and forefingers and beginning to tease them, rolling them back and forth, expressing small quantities of milk that dripped down her stomach.

Then she stopped and got off the bed. Paisley's head

jerked up, letting Cap's stiff cock slip out of her mouth. "What's wrong?" She hoped she hadn't made a mistake.

"I'm going to grab my vibrator. I want to watch Cap fuck you while I get myself off."

"Are you sure? I could go down on you," Paisley suggested.

"Eh...probably not a good idea to do that yet, and besides, I want to watch you enjoy my husband. I don't want you to be too distracted. After all, he'll pretty much demand all your attention." She gave a quick flick of a devilish smile, then turned to open the bottom drawer of the nightstand. She pulled out a small egg-shaped vibe and arranged herself on the bed.

"Where do you want me to fuck this beautiful woman?" Cap asked, his fist encircling and intermittently stroking his cock, his need still evident.

"Right here beside me." She gestured to the space next to her. "I want to see both of your faces."

Paisley moved into position next to Leah while Cap grabbed a condom from the other nightstand. He climbed into place between Paisley's ample thighs and pressed his cock against her wet slit.

"Shouldn't I go down on her first?" he asked. "I feel like I'm missing out on tasting her."

"No, wait," Leah answered. "Let me." She got up on her knees and crawled between Paisley's thighs as soon as Cap gave up his place. "It's been a long time since I've gone down on a woman. Let's see if I still have some skills, shall we?"

Paisley was already shuddering just from the feel of Leah's hot breath against her clit. Cap stroked Paisley's still damp hair out of her face as his wife gently ran her tongue between Paisley's lips, letting the sweetness settle on her tongue.

"Damn, girl," she exhaled with more heat flaring against Paisley's nerves. "You taste delicious."

She licked all around her delicate folds and then teasingly placed the tip of her tongue directly on Paisley's clitoris, following it with more hot, steamy breaths. Paisley was gripping the sheets, her need growing with each passing moment. She placed a hand on Leah's head, urging her for more contact.

Deciding to make Paisley's wait even more agonizing, Leah ignored her unspoken demands and traveled away from her swollen pearl, her tongue blazing a trail down toward her ass.

Fucking tease! Paisley murmured only in the caverns of her mind, at once relieved she had managed to keep from saying it aloud.

She was nearly ready to throw Leah off and mount Cap's enormous cock when Leah finally took Paisley's throbbing rosebud into her mouth and began to suck it while also placing two fingers inside her, slowly but insistently rubbing her G-spot.

Paisley's hips nearly came off the bed, she was so overwhelmed by the sudden intensity of Leah's actions. Now both her hands tangled themselves in Leah's hair as she thrusted her pelvis up to meet her mouth.

"Oh, fuck," Paisley murmured again, this time out loud. "I'm gonna come..." No sooner had she spoken the words than she exploded in her boss's mouth, sending a gush of juices all over Leah's face. Leah, tenacious as she was, held on to the end, hanging on through the waves of pleasure rocking through Paisley's body until she finally sank into the sheets, totally spent.

Leah pulled away, sputtering as the air she breathed in hit the wetness all over her face. "I missed doing that." She smiled as she reached for a towel she'd left on the dresser.

"I would say your skills are as fresh as ever," Paisley commented, finally able to speak again. "Not that I was familiar with them before, but I don't see how they could be much improved."

"Now it's my turn," Cap said, licking his lips. He assumed the position his wife had just occupied. "I will clean you up before I get you all messy again." He buried his face between her thighs and began to lap up all the sweetness that hadn't ended up on Leah's face.

"Fucking gourmet," he announced, wiping his face as he emerged a few minutes later. "Do you want to come again before I fuck you?"

Paisley smiled as she watched Leah take her place beside her on the bed again, her vibe humming away against her clit. She looked so sexy with her arm crossed between her full breasts, slightly biting her bottom lip as the pleasure began to build between her thighs.

"No," Paisley decided. "I want your cock inside me."

"As you wish," Cap decreed and slid up her body, kissing her navel and breasts on his way. His cock was still rigid from before, and she felt the weight and thickness of it against her leg before he reached down to help guide himself into her warm wetness.

Paisley gasped as his thick eight inches began to slowly plunge to her depths till he was completely submerged. Her eyes flickered open just in time to see his close, a look of sheer bliss spread across his face.

"Feel good?" Her hands glided down his muscular back while Leah watched beside her.

"Oh, god, you have no idea." He sighed as he began to stroke slowly in and out of her pussy.

"Oh, but I think I do," she moaned as he struck a nerve deep within. "Holy shit, Leah, you are one lucky woman!"

"Tell me about it," she cooed from her perch. She had one leg bent at the knee, her foot flat against the sheets, and the other stretched out to the side, giving Paisley a nice view of how she was using the egg against her clit, rubbing it in tight circles. She used her other hand to twist her right nipple between her finger and thumb as she watched her husband and her employee fuck, her green eyes glistening with desire.

Cap not only had length and girth but stamina as well. He brought Paisley to orgasm three more times in the next several minutes, even after he warned her that he may not last long.

"I'm gonna have to flip you over though. I wanna look at that ass," he said, pulling out.

Paisley obliged by turning onto all fours, her ass on display. He playfully smacked it as he got in position again between her legs, and this time he shoved his cock in with no resistance, making her squeal from the sudden intrusion.

He smacked her again as he growled, "There you go; take it all, girl."

"That is so fucking hot. You have no idea," Leah gurgled beside them, her cheeks reddening, ravaged by her impending climax. "I'm trying to wait for you, honey, but I can't hold out much longer."

"I was trying to wait for you!" Cap answered, establishing a solid rhythm of deep thrusts that each elicited a low grunt from Paisley.

"Let's come together now," Leah suggested, rising to her

knees and inching her way toward him, the egg still pressed against her clit.

Cap's cock quivered as it hardened even more. Paisley could hear them kissing and moaning, even with her head submerged in the mattress absorbing Cap's relentless impaling. It turned her on so much to be the proxy through which Cap would find his release and to hear him and his wife perched on the verge of orgasming together. She too felt the pressure growing again in her body, despite her exhaustion.

"Oh god!" she screamed as he slammed into her, thankful the sound was muffled by the bed.

"Fuck, fuck, fuck," came the staccato beats off Leah's tongue as she buried her face in Cap's chest. He held her with one arm and used the other to steady himself as he pounded Paisley's pussy till his climax became imminent.

Moments later, the room was filled with the sounds of all three parties exploding in ecstasy, each trembling as their respective orgasms claimed their bodies and subsequently released them.

FIFTEEN

When Paisley drove home from the Sheldons' house that night, she was glowing. Her legs felt like jelly, and she had that delicious sore-ness between her legs that could only be caused by a large, aggressive cock.

It's always nice when your suspicions are confirmed, she thought as she tapped her fingers to the beat playing on the radio.

The drive back to Ocean City was dark. The straight two-lane highway was poorly lit and flanked by giant pine trees, which made her feel like she was driving blind through a tunnel. She opened her sunroof so she could catch little glimpses of the heavens conducting their starry symphony. It made her feel a little less claustrophobic.

For a moment, a tiny pain stabbed at her heart to know she'd go home to an empty apartment. She thought about Cap and Leah curling up together in that huge king-sized bed, their limbs entangling as they drifted off to slumber.

Until Lincoln wakes them up demanding to be fed. By

that time, I'll be snoozing away in my own bed of fluffy splendor.

Sometimes it was worthwhile to remind herself that the grass wasn't always greener. *Things are actually pretty good in my neck of the woods. I should be grateful for what I have.*

Her thoughts next drifted to Calvin Mitchell. She was due to meet with him in the morning to go over the information his father had collected. At the moment, all steeped in the afterglow of her intensely hot threesome, it wasn't anxiety that gripped her. Instead, it was an image of Calvin's piercing hazel eyes, his rich topaz skin, and his full, luscious lips.

I really have to get him over to the dark side. But how?

Her mind wandered to her staffing dilemma. She needed to hire a lifestyle-experienced security guard to take Jason's place. She had spent a few hours earlier that day scouring The Factory member database to see if any names jumped out at her.

She wished their member database included pictures, because truthfully, she didn't know everyone's names yet, only the regulars. Re-sorting the list by birthdate, she zeroed in on single men between the ages of twenty-four and thirty. Unfortunately, there were only a few names, and most of them were not local.

Maybe Calvin would know someone? Not someone in the lifestyle, probably, but perhaps he has an open-minded friend with security experience?

As she pulled into the parking lot next to her apartment building, she made a mental note to ask him in the morning. She started to turn off her engine but hesitated when she caught sight of a car screeching to a halt, then swinging into the lot. It parked a few spaces down from her, and the driver killed the engine. It didn't look like any of her neighbors' cars, and it didn't have a Maryland plate on the front. The back tag wasn't visible.

She glanced down at the clock in her car, which was still running. 12:05 AM, it read in neon green numbers.

Something told her to stay put with her engine on, waiting for the occupants of the strange car to emerge. She tried to gauge what was happening with her peripheral vision, but all she could tell was it was dark and shadowy in that corner of the lot.

Her heart began to pound against her ribcage, just as it had when she received the emails and phone call. It was nearing the August first deadline, and she had not been given any further instructions. She didn't have the money, anyway. She was hoping Calvin's dad would come through just in time to avoid a club scandal.

She heard the car door click open, surprised it was loud enough to be noticed over the sound of the blood rushing through her ears. Her engine continued to rumble as she readied her foot over the gas pedal just in case she needed to make a fast getaway.

She wanted to look over and see what the driver was doing – she only heard one door open and shut, the one nearer to her – but she didn't dare move her head. There was a streetlight not too far from her, on the other side of the strange vehicle, and it was casting an eerie orange glow into her Mazda.

Frozen with fear, her mind began running through different scenarios and escape plans. She had never thought about carrying any type of weapon, whether it be pepper spray or a gun, not even when she lived in New York for all those years. She was a woman of size, and people could generally tell she was not to be trifled with. But right now, in this moment, with her heart afire and tiny beads of sweat starting to glisten on her brow, she wished she had something, anything she could use if the person who got out of that car came at her.

At that precise moment, she heard a sharp rap on the passenger side window of her car. Her heart about to explode, she spun her head in that direction and saw a figure dressed in black with a hoodie pulled down over his face peering into her vehicle. She winced, eyes flashing to the door locks, *which, thank God, are locked,* she breathed.

"We're coming back for your money on August first," the hooded figure yelled. "If we don't get it, then your secret past is getting broadcast all over town. You don't want to know what we're capable of."

She had no problem hearing the voice because her sunroof was still open. A nanosecond passed as she tried to decide if she recognized it. After scanning her memory bank, she failed to find a match.

Then she did the next thing her reflexes told her: she hit the panic button on her key fob, which sent her horn and lights into a cacophonous symphony of obnoxious noise and flashes. The figure, still cloaked in shadows, calmly walked back to the vehicle and got inside.

She threw her gearshift into drive and peeled out of the parking space, her tires squealing as she floored the gas pedal after merging onto the main road.

I should have called the police. Her mind was stumbling and tripping over thoughts that were coming too fast, too sharp. *No, I couldn't call the police. That's what I've been trying to avoid this whole time!*

"Fuck!" she screamed aloud, slamming her fist down on her steering wheel. She tried to process each new idea as it wedged its way inside her gray matter. She didn't get the make and model of the car. *Strike 1.* She didn't see the tags.

Strike 2. She didn't even know for sure if the voice was male or female. *Strike 3.*

I am really fucking bad at this. And now I can't even go home to my amazing bed. Fuck.

Her head was pounding with regret that she had panicked so much, she failed to get information she could give to Detective Mitchell. But she had the more pressing issue of not having anywhere to go. Going back to Cap and Leah's wasn't an option, and she certainly couldn't go to Casey's.

I'm glad I never got a cat, she thought as her Mazda sailed down the highway. *At least that much I can be sure of.*

Paisley pulled into the apartment complex off Bayshore Drive where Calvin lived. It was almost 12:30 AM, but she texted him anyway. *It's either this or check into a hotel, and there probably aren't too many vacancies since it's the height of summer and all.*

> Paisley: Hey, can we move our meeting up a little?

She sat in the dark car, hyper-aware of her surroundings and consumed with paranoia, her breaths shaky and uneven. She was fairly certain no one had followed her this time. The person who approached her in her own apartment parking lot appeared to have been following her.

Did they tail me all the way from Cap and Leah's house? Oh, god. Her heart seized again with fear. *They better not try to hurt the Sheldons. Come on, answer, Calvin!*

As if on cue, her phone buzzed.

She let him know she was in the parking lot, and he came down wearing only a pair of basketball shorts. She tried to keep her eyes from bugging out at the sight of his finely chiseled torso, managing to accomplish that feat by throwing her arms around his neck and squeezing him tight against her body in relief that he answered her text.

"What's going on?" He stepped back from her, bewildered at seeing her so late at night and in such disarray.

"He followed me," she stammered, finding it difficult to keep her lungs inflated with air. "I got home late, and this car followed me into the lot. He approached me."

"Come inside," he offered, staying calm and taking her hand into his.

He got her settled on his sofa with a bottle of water and asked her to start from the beginning. "Take a drink first, though. God, Paisley, you're shaking all over."

She looked down at her hands and could see they were visibly trembling. "You know, I don't think I really took this whole thing that seriously until tonight. I mean, yeah, I was upset and anxious, but it didn't feel so real until that creep was leaning against my car."

"So he followed you into the parking lot, and then what happened?"

"I immediately suspected something was up, so I kept my car running in case I needed to make a quick escape. The car pulled into a space about three down from me and killed its engine. I was waiting for whoever it was to leave before I went inside, then I planned to get out after he was gone. I was trying not to look over there, but then I heard him pounding on my window on the passenger side."

"Did you get a look at him?"

"No." She shook her head. "It was dark and he was wearing a big hoodie. It was just sort of an amorphous figure, and to be honest, I'm not one hundred percent sure it was a man. It sounded like it was either a guy with a high-pitched voice or a woman with a low one. Does that make sense?" She buried her face in her palms. "I can't believe how stupid I was not to get a better look at him or the car and tags."

He put his arm around her like a hook, pulling her toward him. She came to rest with her cheek pressed against his bare shoulder. "You've been shaken up. It's okay; you did the best you could do under the circumstances."

"After he yelled that they were coming back for the money on August first, I hit the panic button on my key fob, and he just sauntered back to his car like it was no big deal. Then I fucking peeled out. I wasn't thinking straight..."

He squeezed her tight to his body and held her for a long minute, only the sound of their breaths and faint music from the television in his bedroom filling the air. Then he sat up straight, and she pulled away to hear what he had to say. "My dad got back to me yesterday with the information he found."

"Okay?"

"He looked into that blocked number that called me. Unfortunately, it's one of those pay-as-you-go cell phones, and we don't know who it's registered to....at least not yet. We did find out that the caller was somewhere near the state line in North Ocean City, though."

"Great, someone local then," she surmised, looking down at her hand, which was resting on Calvin's thigh. She couldn't remember putting it there. It just sort of gravitated in that direction.

"Well, maybe," he answered. "But the more interesting finding is that the emails came from an IP address in Kentucky of all places."

Her heart felt like it might explode at the mention of the State Which Shall Not Be Named. She had spent many years cringing whenever she heard it casually mentioned in conversation or on the news. Listening to Calvin say it rendered her tongue useless.

"Uh, Paisley, you just turned as white as a ghost." His hand gently brushed across her cheek with concern. "What is it?"

She felt the lump in her throat give way just as she managed to confess, "It's where I'm from."

"I thought you said you were from New York?"

She shook her head, the tears starting to burn against her eyelids. She hated every single one of them. She promised years ago she would never cry again over what happened to her in that godforsaken place. She hated breaking promises, most of all to herself.

"So are you going to tell me what the hell you did and why this person is blackmailing you or what?"

He probably sounds more exasperated than he means to. But she was still trying to figure out what to say, how to react. It was nearly 1 AM, and they were both tired. She didn't know if she had the energy to start back at the beginning.

And where was the beginning, anyway? Was it the year a baby girl was born to a low-life drug user in the backwoods of Kentucky? Was the year that baby girl was abandoned at her grandparents' house never to see her mother again? Or was it when that teenage girl met a man who promised her the moon if only she'd give herself to him?

Calvin sighed and pulled her close to his body, absorbing her shakes. She was trembling to keep the tears from falling. She had to be stronger than her emotions. *That is the only way I've survived this long,* she kept telling herself.

"Why don't we get some sleep, okay?" he suggested. "You can tell me the story in the morning, then we're going to go talk to my dad again."

She nodded, her bottom lip just barely quivering from the force she had to exert to keep herself from crying. She was filled with gratitude for his kindness in not pushing her any further, and that made her want to cry all the more.

SIXTEEN

She didn't remember consciously having a discussion with Calvin about sleeping arrangements. All she knew was that every time she woke up, she was in his arms. She kept pulling herself out of his embrace, trying to wall herself in with the sheets and comforter, only to find herself reeled back in the next time her eyes fluttered open. It went on like that all night.

By the time dawn broke and meandered its way in through his sheer curtains, he was spooning her, his chest pressed against her back and arm draped over her waist. When she was finally lucid enough to realize what was going on, she also noticed he was still wearing the basketball shorts. But only the basketball shorts. They weren't thick enough to disguise the fact that his rather stiff morning wood was knocking on her back door.

She was still wearing the summery dress she'd worn to Cap and Leah's the night before, complete with bra and panties underneath. She experienced a momentary flash of disappointment that he hadn't attempted to take advantage of her, but then again, she was certain that was not Calvin

Mitchell's style. She knew him well enough to know that. She turned to face him, accidentally yanking the sheets off his body.

He jolted awake and snatched the sheets back, then his eyes sprang open. "What the hell?!"

"Sorry," she mumbled sleepily.

"What time is it?"

She scrambled for her phone and squinted as she read the numbers. "Almost eight. Shit. We're supposed to be meeting in five minutes."

"Never had an official meeting in my bed before." Calvin smirked.

"Come to the dark side." Paisley winked, surprising herself at how relaxed she felt lying next to him considering their relationship. But as the memories from the night before rushed back to her with growing intensity, the smile faded from her face.

Calvin lay stretched out on the bed, chin propped up on the palm of his hand. "So, first you promised to tell me this crazy secret you've been keeping from me."

She sat up and arranged herself crossed-legged facing him, buying herself some time as she weighed her options about what she should reveal. There was something about Calvin that made her trust him, maybe because he hadn't judged her when she'd walked in off the street, handed him a business card for a swinger club, and asked him to build her a website.

He just said, "Sure, no problem," and made it happen. Not only that, but had she ever woken up next to a man who hadn't expected to have sex with her? No, never.

On the other hand, she couldn't help but wonder if she was being naïve. Maybe trusting someone had gotten her into her current predicament. She knew all the pieces to the puzzle of her life, and she still didn't know who could be harassing her. Telling Calvin her secrets could further compromise her safety.

If there was one thing she had learned from both Casey and Leah, it was how to be truthful and direct without showing her entire hand. She could explain some of the situation to Calvin, leaving out a few of the more troublesome details, and it would satisfy his curiosity. Perhaps he'd have some insight into unlocking the mystery of who was blackmailing her.

So she took a deep breath and began: "I grew up in a small town in rural Kentucky. I was raised by my grandparents, and my grandmother was an elementary school teacher, so she was pretty particular about my schoolwork. I was bright and skipped a grade, so I would have graduated when I was only seventeen."

He was watching her mouth move, her nostrils flare, and her pupils expand as if she was the most fascinating show in the universe. He rested one hand on her knee as she wove her tale. "Why were you raised by your grandparents?"

This was one detail she didn't want to share. "My mother got pregnant with me when she was seventeen, and she was all messed up with the wrong crowd, doing drugs and stuff. You know, back in the '70s."

Her eyes rolled, and then she caught herself remembering that Calvin wasn't around in the '70s, and not really long enough in the '80s to have a clue about that decade either.

"My grandparents tried to get her straightened out when she was pregnant, but when I was a baby, she went back to her old ways. When I was almost one, she left me on their doorstep, rang the doorbell, and disappeared by the time they got to the door. They always told me that her leaving was the best thing to ever happen to me."

His eyes, normally calm and measured, were wide with shock. "That sounds like something straight out of a movie!"

"I know." She nodded. "So, anyway, when I was a teenager, my grandparents got super strict with me, probably because they didn't want me to turn out like my mom. They gave me this crazy unreasonable curfew and forced me to go to church camp, and all kinds of other measures designed to keep me in line."

"Yeah, that usually goes over well." He stroked his hand up and down her leg, still completely absorbed by her story.

"Right. Well, naturally, when I was about sixteen, I met a guy a few years older than me. I'm sure you saw that coming."

He nodded. "Of course, beautiful girl like you... That was bound to happen."

She had come to the part of the story she preferred to gloss over. "Bottom line is the guy was bad news. I ended up dropping out of school. We got messed up in some shit, and right before my eighteenth birthday, I took every cent I could scrape together and bought a bus ticket to New York. I changed my name and never looked back."

He stopped nodding and kept his eyes locked onto hers. "What kind of shit?"

The discomfort was setting in. Calvin wasn't about to let her off the hook that easily, and she wasn't the least bit surprised. *This is why I kept my mouth shut for so long.* She searched his face for a clue to how she could get through this roadblock.

"Paisley, my dad will need to know what we're dealing with here if he's going to help you, okay?"

"I still don't want any official reports filed," she breathed in a voice just above a whisper.

He took her hand into his. "Whoever is doing this is here in Ocean City. They know where you live. If he's going to help you, he needs to know everything you can tell him. And they're going to have to make some shit official, okay?"

Her lip was trembling again. "I don't know why this is so hard for me. I mean, it's not like I killed anyone!" She laughed nervously. "At least I don't think I did…"

"What?!" He leaned toward her, staring at her even more intensely than before, looking for some evidence she was teasing him.

"I'm kidding, I'm kidding, relax!"

"So is it the ex-boyfriend who is blackmailing you?" he asked.

"I considered that, but last I heard, he was in prison, and I didn't think he was getting out for a long time." She had compared her blurry image of the hooded monster from the night before to every archived memory she had of her ex-boyfriend, but it didn't seem to be a match. He was taller and lankier than the person who had knocked on her car window. *He could have filled out, but I doubt he shrank.*

"Ten thousand isn't a lot of money, either. I mean, compared to how much they could ask for," Calvin observed, finally looking away as if he was trying to work something out in his mind. "Why terrorize someone over ten grand?"

"I come from a really poor town, Calvin. Ten thousand dollars is a lot of money for people back home. Trust me on this. And it's also an amount that I could reasonably come up with." She had spent a lot of time analyzing the figure, and she had come to the conclusion there was a specific meaning behind it. She just didn't want to tell him exactly what it was.

"So could it be one of his buddies going after you? Someone who knew what you guys were up to?"

She shrugged. "How much of this am I going to have to tell your dad?"

"More than what you told me. Let me go call him so he knows to expect us. Do you want to take a shower or what?"

"Okay, okay. But I don't have anything else to wear..." Her voice trailed off as she tried to mentally review the catalog of items she kept in her car at all times. "I may have something in the car, but can't promise it's meeting-with-your-dad appropriate."

"Just do the best you can," he advised.

"I always do," she replied.

Detective Mitchell agreed to meet his son and Paisley at the same coffee shop as before. Paisley remembered the uneasy feeling she'd had when she left the shop the first time—it returned threefold upon entering its doors. She tugged at the tight skirt of the dress she'd found in her car.

It's not what Casey would have chosen, that's for sure. She'd tried to subdue her look by wearing minimal makeup, but as her grandmother would have said, "You still look like a hoochie-mama!"

Detective Mitchell didn't seem to notice her attire, though; he just had the same kind, patient look in his deep brown eyes as he greeted her. "So tell me what happened last night," he said as soon as she and Calvin were seated.

Paisley relayed the story, along with her regret that she hadn't gotten more information. She felt Calvin's hand on her thigh under the table, like he had done before. He was an anchor, helping her find her foothold in a sea of uncertainty. She felt his eyes on her, full of concern.

She wasn't used to men being so kind to her, not ones who didn't have expectations. Yes, Erik the Bartender had stood up for her the other night at the club, but A) she could have held her own against Jason, even if he was a security guard and B) Erik had expectations that were revealed as soon as they were alone.

"Did he have a weapon?" Detective Mitchell asked.

"It was so dark, I really couldn't see any details at all," she answered apologetically. "I feel like such a failure!"

Calvin patted her on the back. "Quit saying that. You did the best you could!"

"So he said that they'd be back on August first for the money, right?"

Paisley nodded.

"Well, then we'll just be there too," Detective Mitchell smiled. "Will you be able to go to your apartment today?"

She shrugged. "I just feel...watched. I don't know. I haven't ever felt this powerless before. I'm a big girl, and I'm used to taking care of myself, and maybe that's why this has caught me so off-guard."

"Calvin, why don't you go with her to her apartment tonight and help her get some things? She stayed with you last night, right? She could just stay with you till this blows over, couldn't she?"

Paisley was astounded Detective Mitchell would volunteer his son's apartment like that. But Calvin nodded, a determined expression on his face. "Whatever it takes to keep you safe," he answered, looking at Paisley.

"Do you know anyone in Kentucky?" Detective Mitchell asked just as Paisley began to feel some relief.

She glanced at Calvin and then back to his father. "I'm from Kentucky. I grew up there."

"Oh, I thought Calvin said you were from New York?"

She shook her head. "Sorry, I just had a very...uh...difficult childhood, and I don't like to talk about it."

"Is there someone in Kentucky who could be responsible for this? You said whoever it is knows your real name, and that would mean someone from your past, right?"

She nodded. "I have an ex-boyfriend, but as far as I know he's in prison."

"Maybe I should contact the local authorities there. We could do some digging around."

"No, I—" This was what she was afraid of. This was why she had stayed away from the police. "I don't really think that's necessary. Can't we just get them on the first when they come for the money?" She grabbed Calvin's hand underneath the table as a way of asking for backup.

"The more information we know going in, the better. I haven't filed any paperwork on this yet, but if we're going to do a stakeout on the first, I'm going to have to get the ball in motion," he explained.

"I'm really worried about my workplace," she blurted out, hoping to take the conversation in a different direction from Kentucky. The Factory was certainly on the opposite side of the map. "My bosses are really good people, and I don't want to jeopardize their livelihood over this whole thing."

"Are you worried about being followed to work?"

"Yes, of course I am! My bosses don't know what's going on, and I would really like to resolve this matter without them knowing. I'm already down a security guard there and—"

"Are you going to be able to hire another guard soon?" Detective Mitchell asked.

"It's a long process. I just did get the job posted yesterday after failing to find a suitable candidate from among our membership. We have a thorough screening process and have to vet all employees, of course. There's no way we'll have one in place before tomorrow night's party. It could be a few weeks."

"Do they just work on weekend nights?" Calvin asked.

She nodded. "It's only a part-time job, fifteen hours a week max. The other guards we've had have been former military or cops, for the most part."

"I was a bouncer at Seacrets in the summers when I was in college," Calvin answered. "Maybe I could do it?"

Paisley whipped her head in his direction. "What?!" She couldn't help but laugh, which, if nothing else, lightened the mood a tiny bit.

"Yeah, how hard could it be? I'm guessing your club isn't as rowdy as Seacrets on a busy Saturday night at the height of tourist season!"

Paisley was reeling. First, there was the suggestion she stay with Calvin for a week; Next, he was asking for the job at her club. She'd tried so hard keep her walls firmly in place where he was concerned, and now he was tearing them down left and right.

His idea isn't a bad one either. It would solve a lot of problems and would help me avoid having to tell Leah, Cap, and Casey what's really going on.

And that is why she reluctantly said, "Alright. You're hired, but you're going to have to come to the club today to fill out the paperwork and go through some training."

He shot her a smug smile. "Eh, it would have been a slow day at the office anyway."

I can't believe this is happening. What tangled webs we weave...

She thanked Detective Mitchell for his help, and on their way out the door, she thought, *If only I could be the spider and the not the fly about to be dinner. I'd much rather be the spider.*

SEVENTEEN

Every time Paisley caught sight of Calvin in the hallway, she did a double-take. Then a cyclone of emotions would start churning toward her, only to suck her into its funnel cloud and spit her back out on the other side, dazed and disoriented. She couldn't remember the last time someone made her feel so conflicted.

After they'd met with his father a few days prior, Calvin had followed her to The Factory. He stepped out of his car, took one look at the building, and shook his head. "So, this is a swing club?!"

Paisley had smirked at him, remembering how unimpressed she was by the outside of the building the first time she saw it too. "Reserve judgment till you've seen the inside, okay?" She took his hand and pulled him in the direction of the glass doors. Opening the one on the right, she waited for him to step inside and fully absorb his surroundings.

He pivoted in a complete circle, taking in the sight of the glowing interconnected gears sign; the impressive mixed metal chandelier; the sleek, stylish furniture; and the large monitors broadcasting a club infomercial.

"This is incredible! I guess I'd seen the photos for your website, but they did not do it justice. I can also see why you didn't want any photos of the outside of the building on the site."

After a brief tour, she'd taken him to her office space, where she had him fill out an employment application. She was glad neither Casey nor the Sheldons were in yet because she needed to ask him to do something for her.

Leaning toward him, she whispered, the utmost seriousness on her face, "I need you to act like you have some lifestyle experience."

"Uh, what?" He squinted as if that might help him understand. Her words didn't seem to register with him.

She cleared her throat and said in a normal volume: "If anyone asks, you just need to say that you're lifestyle. You can say you've been to a few house parties or something."

He had laughed at her. "Why is it I feel like you're speaking a different language?"

"We only hire people who are familiar with the lifestyle, so you're going to have to fake it till you make it to work here. So to speak. And no, I'm not talking about orgasms." She stifled a giggle.

"Okay, so by lifestyle you mean swinging; I got that much. What, I need to get my swagger on, or what exactly are we talking about here?"

"Just don't act like a newb, that's all," Paisley had advised, her former seriousness returning. "You've probably fooled around with a couple of girls at once, right? I'm sure you had a few wild nights in college. That's close enough. Draw on that."

His face surpassed hers in seriousness until it looked like a dark cloud had just consumed him. "No, Paisley, I have never fooled around with more than one girl at a time."

He seemed offended that she would even make such a suggestion.

And that was why a few days later when it was time for their first Friday party with him at his post, she had considerable reservations about him being able to pull it off. She'd tried not to worry herself to distraction, but Cap and Casey insisted on coming in to meet the new security guard toward the end of the evening. There was a tiny part of her panicking that they would ask him a series of uncomfortable questions, and he'd stand there looking like a kindergartener in a class full of PhD students: cute but clueless.

For the end of July, the club wasn't as crowded as it could have been, which was an unexpected blessing. Someone told Paisley that one of the members was hosting a party at her house on the bay that boasted a beautiful outdoor pool overlooking the water.

"Oh, I certainly didn't get an invitation!" Paisley complained to the source of the gossip.

"You're not the only one," the informant commiserated. "Guess we're not popular enough." Then she winked. "I'd rather be here, though. You guys throw one hell of a party! A pool would be a nice addition, come to think of it..."

She had already suggested to Cap and Casey that building a pool on premises should be a priority. Casey spent a great deal of time shaking her head about the liability and the insurance. Cap added it to Paisley's ever-growing list of must-haves. "Bring me a hundred more members – not seasonal ones. Year-round ones. Then we'll talk about pools."

Calvin seemed to be adjusting to his new station, and Trent was showing him the ropes without complaint. Every time she circled past him, she winked and mouthed the words, "You okay?" He always nodded affirmatively.

On one rotation, Erik the Bartender pulled Paisley aside to inquire, "So, you knockin' the boots with the new guy?"

"What kind of question is that?" Paisley had no intention of answering.

Erik shrugged. "Just curious. I'd love to come see you again sometime." He leaned back against the counter with his arms crossed over his chest, a flirtatious smirk curling one corner of his mouth.

Paisley smiled politely, but in her mind she retorted, *Sorry, my curiosity was completely satisfied last time.* She managed to keep from blurting out her internal monologue and continued with her rounds to make sure everything was running smoothly.

At the end of the night, Cap, Leah and Casey all showed up at closing time. Paisley hadn't seen Leah since the night she'd been invited for dinner and playtime. She wore Lincoln in his sling, and he appeared to be sound asleep.

"Little booger was awake when Cap left, so I decided to come too. Sure enough, now the baby's asleep, and I'm wide awake!" she lamented.

Casey was decked out in a long, flowing floral print maxi skirt and an apple green camisole with delicate pin-tucks and matching sandals. *Is there no end to this woman's wardrobe?* Paisley wondered.

"This is Calvin Mitchell," Paisley interrupted. "Calvin, this is Chris 'Cap' Sheldon, his wife Leah, and their partner Casey Fontaine, who is a local real estate agent."

"Oh, my gosh, it's THE Calvin Mitchell!" Casey shrieked, nearly loud enough to disturb Baby Lincoln. Leah shot her that maternal death glare all mothers give when their child is prematurely awakened.

"Usually people consider my father to be THE Calvin

Mitchell but, thank you, I'm flattered," Calvin replied with a charming grin as he extended his hand to shake Casey's, then Leah's and Cap's.

"You don't remember me, do you?" Casey laughed. "When you first set up shop, I came around as part of the Chamber of Commerce Ambassadors to welcome you to town. You about had me convinced I needed a new website, if my memory serves."

Paisley couldn't believe that they knew each other, but then again, Ocean City was a small town. And Casey Fontaine was a social butterfly with lots of connections. She hoped this didn't mean Calvin's cover was blown. The last thing she needed to do was raise her bosses' suspicions.

"Oh, yes, I do remember now that you mention it. I'm so sorry, Ms. Fontaine. I hope you'll forgive me." He flashed her his perfect smile with a twinkle in his gorgeous hazel eyes, and it was immediately apparent his apology was accepted. "Oh, and for the record, you *do* need a new website. Lucky for you, I know a guy!" He playfully winked at her.

"Quite the catch, this one is," Casey continued, still gushing over Calvin. "Word on the street is you're one of the most eligible bachelors in Ocean City. Now I know why you stay single. Looking for the perfect lifestyle unicorn, aren't you?!"

Paisley's heart began to thump inside her chest as she held her breath awaiting Calvin's response. He chuckled lightly. "Something like that," he answered and winked at her again.

His coolness factor was X to the thousandth power, yet it came with understated charm and an elegance few men his age could achieve. Paisley couldn't believe what a natural he was schmoozing with Casey; she was clearly smitten with him.

Leah began to quiz Calvin on his background, and he passed her inquisition with flying colors. Yes, he had done security before. Yes, he had been in the lifestyle for a few years now. Yes, he knew Paisley through designing The Factory's website. He would have won her over based on that fact alone.

Leah is a big fan of the website, Paisley remembered. *I don't know why I was so worried!*

Paisley breathed a sigh of relief as Cap ushered his two co-owners out the doors of the club. He turned back to Paisley with a dimpled smile and simply said, "Nice work, Sugar."

"The owners are cool as fuck," Calvin offered as soon as they were out of the building. "No wonder you want to protect them."

"Yeah, I know a good thing when I see it," she answered.

He looked right at her with his eyes glowing. "Is that so?"

It wasn't until later that night when she had climbed onto the futon in his guest room that she realized what he had meant.

EIGHTEEN

Saturday night's party started off busier than Friday, but by midnight, it began to fizzle out. Having gotten a hall pass from his wife, Cap came to play, though he frequently checked in with Paisley to make sure everything was running smoothly.

"We're still waiting for her doctor's visit," he reminded her. "I couldn't help but light up when she told me to go out and play tonight. I'm like a kid in a candy store!" He grinned, rubbing his hands together with excitement.

"Did you scare off all the members or what?" Paisley laughed. "Where did everybody go? I just checked all the playrooms, and they're mostly empty. What gives?"

"It's like fishing. You can know all the currents and seasonal patterns and think you understand where the fish'll be biting and when, but sometimes those boogers just surprise you and do something entirely different. The club is the same way." He shrugged.

"So you're saying our members are like fish. Got it." She laughed. One thing she liked about Cap was that he almost always seemed to be in a jovial mood. "So did you have some fun tonight, then?"

He nodded with enthusiastic dimples popping, and she couldn't help but wonder if there was a chance she would get a turn with him after the party ended. Her experience with Cap was definitely one she'd like to repeat. And she couldn't help but feel some degree of sexual frustration at having had to watch Calvin walk around half-naked the past four days.

Speaking of the devil, Calvin came around the corner in his security uniform. The guards wore fitted gray polo shirts with The Factory logo stitched just over the right breast. She liked the way the arm bands clung to his biceps and the way his ass filled out his black dress pants.

She also appreciated the way he seemed to be establishing a nice rapport with the members. She had observed several ladies ogling him when he passed by. He had been told it was fine to flirt with the female members since he was supposed to be like-minded, but that playing with them during club hours was off-limits.

He'd smirked and replied, "No worries there."

Doesn't this man ever get horny? Paisley wondered as he peeked into the Jungle Room. There were two couples on the round bed, their naked bodies twisting in passion as both of the men were going to town on their respective partners' pussies.

"Let's watch," she suggested to him, giving him a little push inside the room.

He looked uncomfortable, a perplexed look contorting his face. His pupils were so dilated from the dim light, his eyes nearly looked black rather than their usual light golden hazel. "Is that allowed?"

"Of course." She smiled, the words oozing past her lips as if they were dripping with honey.

He gave a little shrug and stepped farther inside, making room for Paisley to join him. She couldn't help but train her eyes on the crotch of his pants, wondering if his observations would get the blood pumping to his manhood. Unfortunately, between the low lighting in the room and the dark color of the fabric, she couldn't tell. She inched closer to him, hoping she could somehow bump into him with her wide hips, creating a diversion that allowed her to cop a feel.

Calvin mouthed the word "Damn," as the bodies on the circular bed rearranged themselves.

The curvy brunette, with her burnished tresses brushing the top of her full, shapely ass, climbed on top of the statuesque blonde with thick thighs and burgeoning breasts. The pale ivory skin of the brunette melded with the golden tan of the blonde as they began to taste each other, their tongues delving into each other's pink-lipped treasure boxes as their mates watched with approval.

The men stood on either end of the 69, both stripping down and revealing their engorged cocks. One was tall with rich mahogany skin and a deep, booming voice. She had the impression he was with the blonde, while the shorter man with reddish-brown hair and a matching beard belonged to the brunette. The taller man reached out one long, muscular arm and delivered a firm slap to the brunette's buttocks, causing her to squeal with delight.

"Oh, she loves to have her ass smacked." Her partner nodded, eyebrows wagging. He reached down and took his short, fat cock into his palm, wrapping his fingers around it slowly. His eyes never left the two women as he began to stroke it.

The room was filled with their sounds of pleasure, high-pitched gasps and lower-register moans. The Black man, whom Paisley thought was named Devon, slid a condom onto his long, velvety shaft and worked his tool into the brunette. He buried his hands in the flesh of her hips as he began to pump in and out, his tongue just barely visible in the corner of his mouth and his eyes half-closed with lust.

Paisley shuddered with desire. She loved the way it felt to have a tongue on her clit and a cock inside her at the same time. It was so overwhelmingly stimulating, especially when the cock was buried nice and deep.

She shifted her eyes over to Calvin, who was enthralled as the scene played out before them. The white man, who was apparently named Adam, emulated his friend and edged himself closer to the bed so he could slide his cock into the blonde. It took a bit more maneuvering for him to get into position, but after he planted his knees on the mattress, the foursome was off and running, each taking their pleasure from another's body.

"What do you think?" Paisley leaned in closer to whisper in Calvin's ear, "See anything you like?"

"I'm not gonna lie; that's pretty fucking hot," he whispered back. Paisley was fairly certain Devon had heard him and could have sworn he winked.

They both stood there, wordless, watching the foursome as the women's voices rose and fell with each orgasm that rocked through their bodies. Again and again they cycled through the stages, starting softly at first, then ushering in a crescendo of ecstasy that rose toward the ceiling and reverberated through the room.

"Wonder if the guys get a turn?" Paisley whispered. She tried to get another look at Calvin's pants to see if a bulge had appeared, but she still wasn't able to tell. She wanted so badly to reach out and put her hand there, to feel if he was hard and throbbing. It took every ounce of restraint she had to keep her hands to herself.

Later, after everyone had left, Calvin and Paisley found themselves alone in the club finishing up the nightly clean-up effort. "So was that your first time watching people have sex?"

He scratched his head as if he had to think about it, but he was only playing around. "Uh, yeah, especially four people."

"Did it turn you on?" She'd never been able to tell for sure, so she decided to stop beating around the bush and just ask.

He shrugged as a little smirk appeared on his lips. "It was erotic, but... I wouldn't say it turned me on."

"No? It was like live porn!" Her eyes trailed down his body, eliciting a smile at the way he was standing: propping himself up on a broom and looking at her with sparkles in his eyes.

"It was, but I'm not a porn guy." He shrugged and finished sweeping a pile into the dustpan and emptying it into the big yellow bin.

"Don't you ever get really horny? Horny enough you just want a nice wet hole to fuck?"

He dropped the broom and dustpan and locked eyes with her, his jaw slightly open with surprise at her audacity.

"Come on," she urged him. "Just tell me the truth. There's no shame in needing to fuck."

"You really like saying that word, don't you?" Calvin asked her, grinning. He seemed to be proud of his ability to dodge her question. "It just floats off your tongue and then pops with that nice, hard K sound on the backside." He shook his head and picked up the broom again, this time carrying both implements to the supply closet.

"Well, maybe I do," she reasoned. "And there's no shame in that either. And as for the swinging thing – don't knock it till you've tried it!"

He closed the closet door and made his way down the hallway toward her as if what he wanted to say next demanded proximity. "I prefer making love," he claimed, standing close enough to her that she could smell his cologne, which had faded away to where only the bottom notes remained.

"Fucking is okay, but it's not my style. I prefer something with substance." She watched his eyes gleaming as he continued to speak, passion dripping from his tongue, "I don't just bring my cock to bed. I bring my mind, heart, and soul too. It's a whole other animal than just plain fucking."

She stood staring at him, stunned by his words. For once, she was speechless.

Allison: So let me get this straight. You're staying with a guy? Hold on, I'm calling you.

That's what Allison said when Paisley failed to adequately elaborate on her current situation. Her phone immediately buzzed with her friend's duck-lipped selfie all lit up.

Paisley considered not answering her call, but if she failed to answer, there was the very real threat of Allison getting in her car and driving down to see what was going on. She was impulsive like that, whereas Paisley was only impulsive when it came to sex.

"Hello, darling," Allison cooed into the phone. "Now, I thought we'd talked about you getting a pet, not shacking up with your web dude!"

"I know, but I just couldn't settle on a kitty cat," Paisley joked.

"So what's really going on?"

There was no way she was going to tell Allison what was *really* going on; she needed to improvise. "Nothing. They're fumigating my apartment because my neighbor had fleas, and they had started to invade my place." *Where do I come up with this shit?* she asked herself, duly impressed with her improv skills.

"It's funny, 'cause I meant to call you anyway. I heard something weird through the grapevine at work I wanted to tell you about."

"Oh, yeah? What's that?"

"I don't know how long ago it was, but a while back apparently, someone was in here asking about you."

"What?!" The hairs on the back of Paisley's neck instantly stood on end.

"Yeah, it was some woman who said she was an old friend. Boss-man just told her you'd taken a job down in Ocean City, Maryland, and that was the end of that."

It was everything Paisley could do to keep the gasp trying to break free securely locked inside her mouth. "Oh, that's weird," she managed, nearly choking on the words.

"Yeah, I thought so too. Anyway, what's the deal with this guy? Is he hot?"

Paisley tried to shrug off the creepy feeling infiltrating every nerve in her body from Allison's news. As if he knew he was being talked about, Calvin plopped himself down on the couch right next to her, wearing only basketball shorts. That was his usual attire at home, she had quickly learned.

"Well?" Allison demanded.

"Yeah, but he's a security guard at the club, so I can look but not touch."

"That didn't stop you before!" her friend insisted.

"Why do you think I had to hire a new guard?" Paisley retorted.

"Oh, she wants to know why we're not fucking?" Calvin asked, gesturing for the phone to indicate he wanted to have a turn at speaking with Allison.

Paisley vehemently shook her head no and clung tight to her phone. When he persisted, she yelled, "No, no! No, you're not talking to her!" *God knows what kind of trouble that would cause.*

"Oh, he wants to talk to me?" Allison's high-pitched voice squealed.

"Hey, Paisley's friend!" he bellowed into the phone from inches away. Then he succeeded in prying the device out of Paisley's hand.

She sat with her arms crossed tightly over her chest, scowling. *No good can come from this.* She felt like a kid who had been left out of a schoolyard game.

"I'm Calvin; what's your name?" he schmoozed into the phone in his sexy voice.

Is there no limit to this man's charm?

"Well, hello, Allison! No, Paisley hasn't said anything about you, but I plan to get the full scoop as soon as we get off the phone." He paused while she spoke. "Oh, okay." He pulled the phone away from his face to look at the screen. Glancing down, Paisley saw her friend had texted a photo of herself practically topless.

"For fuck's sake," she demanded, "give me back my phone!"

"Oh, yes, you're definitely a hottie," Calvin said. "Thanks for sharing. Okay, Paisley wants her phone back." He held it outstretched to her like it was a peace offering.

She rolled her eyes at him, then focused her efforts on getting Allison off the phone. The absolute last thing she wanted was for Allison to think she needed to rush down to Ocean City to bed her new security guard. Well, it was *almost* the absolute last thing she wanted.

"Sorry," Calvin apologized as he sat back down next to Paisley on the sofa, so close their thighs were touching.

"She's my only real female friend, and she's a royal pain in the butt. But she'd do you in a heartbeat," Paisley said. "I could have her down here in a flash. You only have to say the word."

"How many times do I have to tell you?" He took her hand into his, his eyes zeroing in on hers. "Meaningless hookups are not my thing."

"Define meaningless," Paisley retorted, then saw Calvin wasn't joking.

"Let me ask you a question, okay? And please don't get mad."

"Why would I get mad? I'm an open book!" Paisley scoffed.

He shook his head while still grinning. "Maybe you need to check your definition of 'open book,' 'cause that's not you. You won't even tell me what happened to cause this whole blackmail thing. I feel like I don't know anything about you at all, only the tiny bit you've let me see, which is that you're a very competent boss and manager. Oh, and I know you used to be a burlesque dancer. And I guess I know you're in the lifestyle, and you don't use the word 'swinger.' And you grew up in Kentucky."

"Well, sounds like you know quite a bit then, Mr. Mitchell. About as much as I know about you." She crossed her arms over her chest again like she had when he was on the phone with Allison.

He leaned toward her, stroking his fingers down her cheek affectionately. "Why won't you let me get close to you, Paisley? What are you afraid of?"

"Is that the question you wanted to ask me originally?" Her bright blue eyes were dancing with mischief, reveling in the game of chase they were playing.

"I want to ask you a *million* questions," he answered, his voice just above a whisper.

She sighed. He was drawing her in like a magnet, having expertly identified her weaknesses. It was rare that a man stood in awe of her independence and confidence instead of being intimidated by it.

Every time she had been close to letting her guard down in the past ten years or so, that had been the magical combination she'd responded to. And here he was making matters so much worse with his *gorgeousness. Is that a word?* She decided that it was indeed a word, and Calvin was its very definition.

She stared at him, trying to figure out why and how he could push her buttons in just the right way. *And now his sexy eyes are all aglow.* She could feel the warmth he projected. And a sense of *groundedness. Not sure that's a word either, but what the hell—it fits.*

"You always give me this look like you're about to give in to me," Calvin observed. "I always think we are *this* close to something happening." He made a gesture with his finger and thumb to indicate a very small amount.

She couldn't help but laugh at him; his persistence was flattering. And he was right, but she didn't know if she wanted to admit it and further stroke his ego. "It's not like I'm not tempted..." she offered as consolation.

"Just tell me what man made you swear off relationships," he said, "so I know who to blame."

"It wasn't just one man," she sighed. "That's the problem. It was a half dozen men, starting with my high school boyfriend, then my first manager when I was dancing, and then – "

She stopped and peered at him. He was taking notes inside his head, his wheels always turning, always adding information to the file he maintained on her. He reminded her so much of his dad in that moment, it was almost frightening.

"The specifics aren't important. Just too many men who took advantage of me being naïve and weak. So I decided to be aware and strong, that's all."

"You know, being in a relationship and being strong aren't mutually exclusive," he pointed out.

She let a tiny smile curl her lips. "What about you? I don't see you as Mr. Relationship either."

"I was almost engaged when I finished college...but we decided we wanted different things. She wanted to go to grad school on the west coast, and I didn't want to leave my family. So we parted ways amicably. And I had a pretty serious high school girlfriend too."

"So that's it? Two girlfriends?" She couldn't believe it. *Surely he'd had his share of flings?*

"Well, you know, a couple others here and there, but nothing long-term. But if you add those two together, it's like six years of relationship experience. Not too shabby for someone my age, right?"

She smirked. "It's more than I have. But wait, you haven't seriously dated anyone since college? Didn't you graduate like four years ago?"

He nodded. "We already discussed the dating situation here on the Eastern Shore."

"Yes, yes, we did. See anyone at the club who caught your eye?" She was teasing him but wanted to see how he would react.

"Just a certain beautiful brunette manager..." He grinned so wide, his teeth were gleaming between his full, dark lips.

"You're incorrigible, you know that?"

"Oh, I love those big words. So damn sexy!" After he said that, his smile faded, and a serious look took its place. "You know, Paisley, you have a lot to offer. I hope you won't keep yourself closed off forever. Even if you don't want to try a relationship with me... I bet you'd be happier than you think with a man in your life. And, no, I'm not saying you *need* a man, just that you might be surprised how—"

"You don't think I'm happy now?" she cut him off, feeling a little annoyed that he would suggest otherwise. "Well, I am," she added sheepishly, "aside from the whole blackmail thing."

He put his hand over hers. "Being in a loving, healthy relationship is the most joy I've ever known. It may not be right for you, but... well, didn't you say something about 'don't knock it till you try it'?"

"Touché." She pulled her hand away.

The conversation had taken an unexpected turn, one that made her uncomfortable. She went to the kitchen to make herself a drink, but her hand still felt warm where his skin had pressed against hers.

NINETEEN

"I just got the weirdest phone call," Leah said as she stepped out of her office. Lincoln was curled against her body, sound asleep in his sling, as usual. Most of the time, it didn't seem much different from when Leah was pregnant. Just that she now carried Lincoln on the outside of her body, rather than the inside.

"What was it?" Paisley looked up from her expenses spreadsheet. She was shopping for vendors to see if they could cut their budget on paper goods, not exactly the most titillating activity she could imagine doing on a hot late July afternoon.

"It was this weird computerized voice, and it told me the 'contact us' form was down on our website. Then it said I should ask you why."

Paisley's body stiffened. "That *is* weird. I don't know why they'd say that." She tried to keep her voice smooth and even. "I guess I'll call Calvin and have him look at it."

"They said you'd pretend like you don't know about it," she said, her voice shaking a bit.

She sighed. "That's really strange. They mentioned me by name?" She knew if the caller had mentioned her real name that she was done for.

"Yeah, they said to ask Paisley."

"Well, unfortunately, I'm still not sure what they're talking about, but I will check with Calvin to see if he knows anything a—" Her cell phone rang on her desk before she could get the whole sentence out. "Oh, it's Calvin, what do you know?" She laughed, hoping Leah would walk back to her office so she had some privacy.

"Hey, what's up?" she spoke into her phone, still eyeing Leah to see if she would return to her office.

"I think they just hacked into The Factory's website," Calvin said.

"What?!" She was on the verge of panic, but Leah was still standing there staring at her. *Oh my god, why can't the baby start crying or something?*

Paisley's mind suddenly resembled scrambled eggs. She tried to nonchalantly click the home button on her browser to pull up the website. Sure enough, the home page now featured her high school yearbook photo with big, black, bold letters underneath that read "Paisley Parker (a.k.a. Rebecca Bridges) is a murderer, thief, and whore!"

It took every ounce of strength Paisley had not to let on that her insides were about to implode. "Calvin, any idea why our web form might be down? Someone just called here to let us know."

On the other end, his voice became scratchy with panic. "What do you want me to do? Fuck, Paisley, I'm so sorry. I thought everything was secure."

"Oh, so you have to take the whole website down to figure out what's wrong?" Paisley asked, tapping her pen against her desk to expend some of the excess energy coming from the adrenaline flooding her veins.

"I guess I can do that. When can we meet? Will I see you before we get back to my place?"

Paisley ignored him, instead putting the phone down so she could address Leah, who was looking at her with bugged-out eyes. "Yeah, I'm going to just stop over at his shop when I run out for lunch. There are some programming bugs, I guess. He says it will be a fairly simple fix, something about updates to the database, but the whole site might be down for a few hours."

"Okay," Leah answered, looking partially relieved. The other half of her looked like she was still trying to work out some part of a puzzle as she walked back into her desk.

"I'll be there as soon as I can," Paisley said, pressing the phone to her ear. As soon as she did, the landline phone on her desk rang from the main club number. "Shit, hold on, Calvin."

"The Factory, this is Paisley Parker," she answered, trying to sound as bright and pleasant as she could.

"Good afternoon, Ms. Bridges," the computerized voice said. "Did you get a chance to see the brand new homepage we made for you? I hope you haven't forgotten our agreement. In two days, we'll be meeting you at your apartment. We know you're shacking up with that web guy, but you will be at your apartment alone in two days for us to collect the money. If you are not alone and unarmed, and if any cops or any other people are there, then we will immediately go to the police and media with the secrets from your past."

When she didn't answer, the voice demanded, "You need to confirm that you understand."

"I understand," her voice trembled. And then the line went dead.

Paisley hadn't been to Calvin's shop since she'd started staying with him over a week ago. Michaela, the receptionist, was painting her nails, and the entire room was filled with the strong scent of polish when Paisley stepped inside. The pert redhead just barely lifted her chin when she saw a customer had arrived.

"I'm here," Paisley shouted past her, hoping Calvin would hear her.

Her whole body vibrated with a volatile mix of chemicals surging through her bloodstream. It was a toxic mixture of adrenaline, cortisol and who knows what else, and it made her feel like she'd just downed a gallon of coffee.

"What the fuck happened?" she demanded as soon as he appeared from his office wearing a navy and white checked dress shirt and a brightly striped tie. *No one else could get away with that combination*, she thought, giving him a once-over.

"Come on back," he said stoically, raising his eyebrows as he nodded toward the receptionist, whose back was toward him. She just barely looked awake and certainly didn't seem to be paying attention to their conversation. That was when Paisley noticed she had earbuds firmly implanted on either side of her head.

Calvin ushered her into the conference room where he threw his weight into the gray leather chair with an air of defeat. "I'm not sure how this could have happened." He closed his eyes and rubbed his palms against his temples. She'd never seen him look so upset before. He was as distraught as she was. Maybe more so.

"It's not your fault, Calvin. Just chill out," she said softly, reaching out to lightly touch his arm.

"It's my responsibility to keep my clients' web pages secure, and I let you down in a big way." He looked up long enough for her to see that his eyes were misty with emotion, like he was straddling the fence between tearing up and choking them back.

"Did you tell your dad?"

He nodded and then took a deep breath, trying to clear away all the negativity. "I took the page down, like you requested. Did anyone at the club notice it?"

"Leah got a weird phone call from the computerized voice saying our contact form was down and she should ask me why. She had just come over to tell me about that when you called."

"We have to figure out what we're going to do on Saturday when they come. Do we know what time they're planning for?" he asked.

"They said they're coming to my apartment – though they didn't say what time – and that I must be alone. If anyone is with me, they're immediately contacting the cops and media with my secrets." She put the last word in air quotes.

"Yeah, about that. Look, Paisley, you have to tell me. My dad is all over me, wanting to know, especially with the accusations on that homepage they put up. I screenshot it for him before I took it down. He really needs a new lead, okay? We need more information from you, or we can't help."

She shook her head. "Calvin, I told you, I—"

"He wants to call you in for questioning, okay? I told him you'd rather tell me and not have to come in... since you're so worried about compromising the security of the club. So far he's been treating this as an extortion case against you, not The Factory. I know that's the way you prefer it, but he has to have more info, otherwise he's not going to be able to protect you or figure out who the hell is doing this to you."

"Fuck." It was the only word that seemed suitable under the circumstances.

"Please," he pleaded with her. "Do you remember what I told you that very first night you came over to my apartment? The time we watched the sunset together?"

The very fact that the sunset they shared was the landmark by which he remembered that night softened her. That moment made an impact on her; it was one of dozens of images that flashed in her mind when she thought of Calvin.

There was the "business" dinner where they'd picked crabs, the moonlit night on the beach when he'd kissed her, the first morning she'd woken up in his bed after being stalked by the scary hooded figure. How was it she'd only known him for a matter of weeks and her mind was so full of him already? No matter how hard she'd tried to pull away, he came back to her more intensely.

His question was still ringing in her ears when she finally uttered, "What?"

"I told you I'd never judge you," he reminded her. "Whatever you did when you were seventeen, no matter how bad it was, it doesn't change who you are now. And who you are now is a strong, independent woman whom I've grown to admire and respect a great deal."

Paisley's cheeks flushed from his words, and she never, ever blushed. How could she strip in front of hundreds of people and never feel the slightest embarrassment, but his words pushed the blood from her veins to the very edges of her skin?

"Okay," she finally relented. "But not here. We have to go somewhere quiet."

"No problem. Come on." He grabbed her hand and led her down the hallway. "Just close up at five," he told Michaela, whose eyebrows were extra-arched as she wondered where her boss and the older, overweight lady were going. Or at least that was what Paisley imagined was running through her mind as they sailed through the lobby and out to Calvin's car. He revved up the engine and whipped the vehicle onto Route 50, heading away from town and toward Berlin.

He took a sharp right onto a desolate road that wound its way into the country. After several twists and turns, he pulled into a long driveway that snaked back through a grove of pine trees until it landed in a clearing. There was a two-story white farm house with navy blue shutters and a small red barn behind it.

The driveway was empty, and the house stood quietly on its lot, flanked by cornfields. A blue porch swing just barely moving in the late July breeze invited company. As soon as she spotted it, she realized that was where they were headed.

"What is this place?" She felt like she'd stepped onto the set of *The Waltons* or some other fictional rural family.

"It's my parents' house," he explained. "They're not home yet. They had some charity function tonight after work. I figured it would be a quiet place to talk."

She nodded. *No wonder Calvin is kind of a throwback*

to a more traditional time, she thought, studying every detail from the flower pots suspended from hooks between each of the columns supporting the porch, to the perfectly trimmed hedges lining the front of the house. On the far end underneath a bay window, a huge hydrangea bush drooped with heavy blue and purple blooms.

He apparently grew up in Mayberry.

The swing creaked back and forth as Paisley settled herself in. She glanced up at the chains it hung by and prayed they'd hold all their weight.

"I'm just trying to decide where to start," she explained.

"Take your time." He breathed in deeply. "Mmmm... this country air. It's good for your soul, isn't it? I grew up in Baltimore in a dirty, crowded neighborhood. When we moved out here, I remember being completely fascinated with all the agricultural elements. Combines on the road, cows dotting the landscape. All the damn chicken trucks around here. It's totally different than what I was used to."

Her eyes followed the curving rows of corn stretching to the horizon. "This place actually reminds me a lot of my grandparents' farm. It's a little eerie, in fact. Their house wasn't as big or nice as this one, though. They didn't have a lot of money, and they certainly weren't expecting to raise another kid after my mom and my aunts and uncles flew the coop. There were five of them in all, and my mom was the youngest. I know I already told you about her, and I told you about my high school boyfriend, Jimmy."

She couldn't believe how easily his name slipped off her tongue after all these years. Even though she'd been thinking about him a great deal since the blackmailing began, she hadn't dared utter those dreaded five letters that she equated with pure evil. She gauged Calvin's reaction so far and saw nothing but interest as he leaned toward her, one hand resting on top of the swing and the other on her thigh.

"I told you Jimmy was bad news, your garden variety thug. He did drugs, sold them, was a petty thief—you know, your typical career criminal, even though he was only twenty-three."

"How did you meet him if you were so much younger?" Calvin asked.

"When I was sixteen and got my license, I started hanging out with the druggie crowd at school. They were stoners and punks and goths, I don't know what the right label is, but they were basically the kids who didn't fit into the jock or prep molds that were deemed acceptable in our little town. I was chubby, you know? I was bullied about my weight by the jocks and the preps, and these other kids, well, they accepted me. And that was that. It wasn't a hard sell.

"My whole life I felt like I was a burden. My mom abandoned me, and my grandparents didn't really want me. They were good people, but they didn't have the energy to put up with my strong-willed self."

"You? Strong-willed? Get outta here!" Calvin joked as he squeezed her thigh affectionately.

"Yeah, I know, hard to imagine, right?" She smiled at him even though her eyes were burning with tears that she forced back down like she always did. When she swallowed, she felt them slide down her throat, all raw and slimy.

"Let me back up a bit for some context. When I was twelve and started developing, my grandparents tried immersing me in the church - literally. They baptized the shit out of me. I think they thought they could wash away any of the wild tendencies I'd inherited from my mother, but I'm pretty sure their efforts backfired." She gestured at her body and rolled her eyes.

"Anyway, Jimmy was the older brother of someone in the group I hung out with, and I met him at some party I snuck out of the house for. It was just so cool to have this older guy infatuated with me. He said I was beautiful. And no one had ever said that to me before."

Calvin nodded as if he knew where the story would go next. A crop-dusting plane zoomed overhead, and for a moment they paused and waited for the loud sound to disappear into the clouds.

Then Paisley continued, "So, naturally, I slept with him. And I got high. I did a lot of things when I was high that I probably shouldn't have done."

"Like what?"

She groaned, knowing how bad it was going to sound when she put it into the words she had to use. But she was this far in already, and she had committed to telling him the story. "He made me let all his friends fuck me too."

"What do you mean by 'made you'?"

"He was pretty rough with me. When he was angry, he'd slap me around. I always had bruises and marks on me, and honestly when he told me to do stuff, I didn't think I had a choice. Though he never threatened me with it, he had a gun. And I just—"

He placed his hand on her shoulder. "Jesus, Paisley... okay, okay." He shook his head as if the motion could make the anger welling up inside of him go away. His whole body stiffened with it, as if her pain was coursing through him, setting all his nerves on fire.

She took a deep breath and exhaled till her lungs were empty, then filled them again. It was exactly the way she'd gotten through that period of her life: *one breath in, one breath out. Repeat.*

"So in the spring semester of my senior year, I finally just dropped out of school. I was stoned or high most of the time, so I couldn't see the point in going. I was living with Jimmy since my grandparents had kicked me out. They washed their hands of me, and who could blame them? They didn't know what to do with me, even though I was a minor, and they were still responsible for me. They were just hoping I could make it to my eighteenth birthday without anything happening that would get them into trouble with the authorities. But then shit went really south."

"How so?"

"Jimmy pissed off the wrong person. I don't know if it was a gang; honestly, I don't even know what happened. Like I said, I was fucked up most of the time back then. Anyway, he needed some cash or else they were going to kill him. At least that is what he told me, and I didn't feel like I had any choice but to follow his instructions. He wanted me to steal ten thousand dollars from my grandparents."

His eyes bugged out. "But that's the same amount—"

She nodded. "I know."

"Paisley, you should have told me all of this before. We could have caught him."

"He's still in jail, Calvin. I checked. He's serving two lifetime sentences. He's not getting out anytime soon."

"But still—"

She ignored his interruption and continued her story. "So, my grandparents did have a stash of cash. They didn't keep it in the bank. My grandfather was weird like that, distrustful of banks and all that. It was their life savings, just a measly ten grand, and I knew where it was hidden. So I took it because I didn't know what Jimmy would do to me if I didn't. Not only that, but I was afraid the men after him would come after me too."

"So then what happened?"

She stared off in the direction of the cornfield, her eyes glazed over as if the memories were playing out in front of them. She saw herself in her rusty blue Honda hatchback driving away from her grandparents' house. She'd broken in on a Sunday morning when they were both at church so she could take every last penny they had.

Her stomach twisted into a million knots as she drove down the country road, up and down the hills that rolled with corn and soybeans, one field after another. She rounded the curve by her neighbors' hog farm, and the pungent fumes filled her car, then she sailed through a wooded valley where the leafy boughs hung over the roadway like sentinels.

She remembered the very second it all crystallized. Her life went from fuzzy and out-of-focus to clear and sharp in an instant.

She only needed two words to explain the course of history: "I escaped."

"You drove to New York?"

"I knew they'd come looking for me, and having my car, which was registered to my grandfather, made me an easy target. So I ditched the car at the bus station in Louisville, paid cash for a ticket to New York, and I didn't look back."

"Fuck, Paisley, that is the bravest thing I've ever heard anyone do."

"But, Calvin, I stole my grandparents' money. I—"

And then there came the point that she could no longer hold the invading army back. A single tear slid down her cheek, but it was the General, and all its troops followed.

"That's not all that happened," she sobbed. He pulled her into his arms and rocked her back and forth, her tears soaking his dress shirt.

After several minutes of her shuddering against him, letting out the pain that had built up like layer after layer of sediment eventually becomes hills, then mountains, she pulled back. "That isn't where my story ends, unfortunately."

Her eyes were puffy, and her cheeks were red, but she straightened up on the wooden swing so she could finish telling him the long-buried truth – her truth that she tried to forget every single day of her life but that would always haunt her no matter what she did or who she became.

"Go on," he instructed, moving his hands back to their original positions on the back of the swing and her thigh.

"Jimmy was livid when I didn't show up, as you can imagine. The next day, after failing to find me in town, he drove over to my grandparents' house. With his gun."

"Oh, fuck..."

"My grandfather had a gun too, a shot gun."

"If you were gone, how did you find out about what happened?"

"Because it made the news, Calvin. It made the news," she repeated, her eyes closed as the vivid memory of what she heard and read in the media came back like a graveyard full of ghosts. "He shot them, Calvin. He shot my grandparents when they couldn't tell him where I was or where the money was." She was shaking with a whole new batch of tears as she spoke the words; they exploded out of her mouth like a spray of bullets from a machine gun.

"Dear God," was all he said, pulling her into his strong embrace again.

When she recovered for the second time, she continued,

"My grandfather got one shot off, which hit Jimmy in the leg. My neighbors called 9-1-1 after hearing all the gunfire. From what I understand, the police showed up to arrest him at the same time as the ambulance to take him to the hospital. But my grandparents were dead by the time they arrived. And it's all my fault. I killed my grandparents."

"You didn't kill them, Paisley. You were seventeen, and you were trying to save your own life. There's no way you could have known what would happen."

She finished the story as it came to her in flashes: "My picture was all over the news. Fortunately, they didn't have a very current one of me – remember, this was before the days of cell phones and selfies. When I got to New York, I cut my hair off and dyed it blonde. Remember, I had the money I stole. If I hadn't, there's no way I would have been able to get an apartment and get my life back on track. The police never found me..."

She opened her eyes and locked them with his. "Now you understand why I didn't want to tell your dad..."

He nodded. "Yes, but now we have to tell him. Whoever is behind this knows what happened back then. I know you said Jimmy is in jail, but could it be someone you guys hung out with, or maybe a relative? Didn't you say you had aunts and uncles?"

"Yes, but—" She had never been able to wrap her head around how she'd been tracked down. She had changed her name and started her life over from scratch. How would someone from her past find her?

"But what?"

"I can't figure out how they found me, that's all. There was a period of three years that I still used my birth name in New York, before I had it legally changed. So my first couple of jobs and my first few leases were the only places who had it. I didn't even get a New York driver's license until I changed my name because once I moved to New York, I didn't drive anymore. That was so long ago, I have no idea how to get in contact with my landlords or former bosses to see if any of them gave me up. That was over fifteen years ago, Calvin."

She watched a cloud of dust billow up from the driveway from two cars making their way toward the house. "Your parents?"

He nodded. "Yes, and after dinner, you're going to tell my dad everything you told me."

"Calvin, I can't—"

He took her face in between his palms and looked into her red-streaked eyes. "You're the strongest person I know, Paisley. If anyone can do this, it's you."

Mrs. Mitchell was a short redhead with an ample bosom and matching backside. She had a smile so bright, she lit up the room when she introduced herself to Paisley, and the younger woman was pulled into the older woman's embrace before the words "Call me Patty" left her mouth. Patty's nose was smattered with freckles as were her shoulders, Paisley noticed when she took off her white linen jacket to reveal a light pink tank top.

Calvin clearly got his looks from his dad, she thought to herself with amusement.

Patty bustled over to the large, old-fashioned farmhouse kitchen where pots and pans began to clatter and clang. Paisley followed her. "Didn't you and Detective Mitchell already eat at your charity function?" she asked. "Please don't go out of your way to—"

"This is the first time Calvin has brought home a girl since college!" Patty exclaimed. "I'm making you dinner!"

Paisley couldn't help but chuckle at her enthusiasm. Calvin appeared by her side and leaned over to give his mother a peck on the cheek. "Whatcha making, Mama?" he asked with an adorable grin spread across his face.

"Pork chops, baby. How long have you two been dating?" Patty questioned as she breaded the meat and slid it into a frying pan. She already had potatoes boiling on the stove alongside six ears of sweet corn in a tall stock pot. Fresh green beans from the garden were in a bowl nearby, ready to be steamed.

"We're just friends." Paisley laughed. "I think your mom wants to see you married off!" She smiled, turning to Calvin to gauge his reaction.

"One of his younger brothers is married, and the other one is engaged. This one, though. I'm not sure what to do with this one!" She pinched his cheek, then whirled back to the stove to flip the sizzling pork chops over. A savory aroma began to fill the kitchen, and despite her stomach being uneasy, Paisley's mouth started to water.

After dinner, the four sat around the hefty oak table in the adjoining dining room. "I can't believe you made me eat two dinners!" Detective Mitchell sighed as he patted his stomach.

"Oh, yeah, really put a gun to your head," scoffed his wife, which was followed by laughter all around the table.

"We all know those catered charity event dinners pale in comparison to your cooking, love," he gushed, looking at her with pride.

Paisley couldn't get over how normal Calvin's family

was. Family dinners when she was growing up were hastily slopped together, then during the meal she had to listen to her grandfather spouting off his conspiracy theories, which ranged from how the government used jets to fill the sky with chem-trails to poison and control the citizenry, to what *really* happened to JFK (*he insisted it involved the CIA, FBI and LBJ.*)

She hadn't allowed herself to think about her grandparents for years, but now she was inundated. The memories she'd shared with Calvin piled up around her like the rubble leftover from a tornado that destroyed everything in its path. Some of the memories made her smile, and others sliced into her like she'd punched her fist through glass. Her mind echoed with the ghosts of her childhood.

When Patty began to clear the dishes from the table, Calvin alerted his father that Paisley had a lot more information to provide for her case. She prickled at the sound of the words and the way Detective Mitchell's deep brown eyes pierced hers with expectations. She breathed deeply, and Calvin's hand found hers under the table as he squeezed, urging her to share her story.

She was somehow able to find the words to tell it succinctly and without all the emotion that had bubbled up when she'd told Calvin earlier. *I think I spent all my tears on the porch swing,* she thought as she wove each piece of her history, binding the words up tight with as many relevant details as she could muster, which Detective Mitchell jotted down in a small notebook.

Afterward, he simply leaned back in his sturdy oak chair and nodded, as if her story wasn't too far off from what his imagination had already concocted.

"I've been in contact with a detective from the Kentucky State Police," he finally said, "as well as some buddies of mine up in New York. I'm going to relay all this tomorrow and see what we can dig up. In the meantime, we have to figure out what to do on Saturday. That's the first, right?"

Paisley nodded, feeling her dark curls bounce around her shoulders. She entertained a momentary compulsion to cut her hair, dye it, and flee across the country just like she had so long before. She could go out west, change her name again, and leave Paisley Parker buried in the dust just like she had Rebecca Bridges all those years ago.

"I have to work Saturday night," she said, "and I'm afraid they're going to come to the club, which I want to avoid if at all possible."

"They said they were coming to your apartment though, right?" he clarified.

"Yes, but they also know I have to work that night, and I have a feeling I've been followed to the club. I can't let them come there. I can't let the Sheldons and Casey find out what's going on."

"I'm hoping with the information you just gave me that we can figure out who is behind this and get to them before they get to you. But time is running out. In the meantime, I want Calvin with you at all times, okay?"

She nodded, biting her lip to keep the tears at bay. Somehow she had managed to refill the reservoirs between finishing her story for the second time and the onslaught of Detective Mitchell's questions.

She didn't know what made her want to cry more: the fact that this was happening, that she was being stalked, targeted, and blackmailed; or the kindness of the Mitchells, who were all so devoted to helping her. Detective Mitchell didn't seem the least bit judgmental about Paisley's past. He hardly said a word about it, and his wife also remained silent on the subject. Paisley wondered if she knew anything about her situation. If she did, she didn't let on.

That night as they left to return to Calvin's apartment, he placed his hand on her thigh as they drove. Her eyes were glued to the cornfields that flashed by her side of the car, and her ears were listening to voices inside her head telling her it was time to run again.

As if he could hear them, Calvin turned to her. "It's going to be okay," he said. "Trust me, okay?"

TWENTY

When they arrived back at Calvin's apartment, the sun was gearing up for its nightly swan dive into the bay in a blaze of glory. Paisley was emotionally drained from her afternoon, starting with the creepy phone calls at work, to the teary confession she'd made to Calvin and spending the evening with his delightful parents. Her reserve of energy and words, not to mention tears, had been depleted.

Now she just wanted to drift off to dreamland for a respite from the emotional roller coaster she'd been riding. Only one problem prevented her from collapsing on the futon in Calvin's guest room in utter exhaustion. Okay, two problems. One: the futon had left her with a sore and aching back and two: she hadn't had an orgasm in several days. She felt like her whole body was made of granite, she was so tense.

Calvin pulled her out onto the patio to watch the sun sliding down to the horizon, plying her with a glass of wine. "You deserve it after the day you've had." He swirled the pale beverage in the glass before he handed it to her.

"You can say that again," she sighed.

Puffy cloud formations had filled the skies all afternoon, so it promised to be a spectacular show. Broad brushstrokes of mauve and rose were painted across the sky already, setting the stage for the grand finale. She took a sip of the wine and savored its sweetness as it eased down her throat.

"Thank you for everything, Calvin. I know this isn't over quite yet, but I just want you to know, no matter what happens, I will never forget your kindness." There, she had reached deep inside her word bank and managed to pull out a few choice ones of appreciation for the man who had turned out to be so much more than she had fathomed.

He smiled humbly and clinked his wine glass against hers. "It's been my pleasure." He gulped down the contents of his glass in one swallow, then set the empty goblet down on the patio table.

He stared across the bay at a few geese who had swooped down onto the water. They were both silent as Mother Nature wrapped up her overture, and the main event began, saturating the skies with its glorious show. Paisley wondered what could be going through his mind; he was unusually silent. She assumed he'd depleted his reservoirs of words and energy as well.

Twenty minutes later, the skies over the bay had turned a dusky purple streaked with thin bands of magenta. Frogs were churning up their chorus of solicitation, and fireflies were beginning to sparkle in the reeds. Nighttime was blanketing the Eastern Shore, making way for the moon to rise and the stars to pierce the heavens with their tiny lights.

One more day to get through, and then it's showtime for me. Now if the director would just give me my copy of the script...

"Are you going to bed?" Calvin asked as Paisley headed toward the guest room to change into her pajamas.

She'd tried to be respectful of him by wearing long t-shirts with shorts underneath to bed as opposed to something skimpier. She didn't want to tease him after all the kindness he'd shown her. He'd made it abundantly clear that nothing was going to happen between them as long as she was a swinger and refused to date him in the traditional sense.

"I'm not sure. My back is a little sore from sleeping on the futon. Maybe I'll finish my wine and have some ibuprofen before I try to fall asleep. It's only nine o'clock, after all."

"Why don't you come join me in the living room? I'll rub your back," he offered along with a sincere smile.

"Oh, that's very sweet of you." She returned from the guest room wearing a sleeveless nightgown that billowed loosely around her curves as she'd run out of clean shorts and t-shirts. She thought about passing on his offer, but the idea of having a bit of her tension relieved, even if it was only a drop in the bucket compared to what she really needed, was a compelling notion.

She plopped down on the floor between his legs, noticing that when she crossed hers, her nightgown rode up on her thighs, exposing quite a bit of skin. She hoped she wasn't crossing any lines, but he didn't seem to complain. He turned on the series they'd been watching on Netflix together and began to knead her shoulder muscles with this strong hands.

His fingers digging into her tender flesh felt incredible, breaking down all the knots that had formed during the day. She was beginning to think, despite how gifted he was at web design, that he may have missed his calling. The tension in her body was melting away like butter in a hot frying pan.

Speaking of which.... "Your mother's pork chops were amazing, by the way" she sighed, remembering them fondly as he continued to rub her upper back.

"She's an incredible cook, lucky for me. My parents really like you, by the way," he shared as he concentrated on a problem area around her right shoulder blade. "Relax!" He tapped on the spot with his fingertips for emphasis.

"They told you that?"

"Mmmhmmm," he murmured, still pressing into her muscles with the pads of his fingers, trying to release the tension.

"It's been a long time since I've met anyone's parents." She laughed. "Damn, that feels so fucking good." She moaned as he moved from one side of her back to the other, devoting attention to a different trouble spot.

"Why was it so hard for you to tell me about your past?"

Her body stiffened as soon as he revisited their conversation on the porch swing. "God, Calvin, what kind of question is that?" She immediately knew where his mind had been during the quiet time on the patio. He was still trying to piece together the story she'd shared. He stopped rubbing as he waited for an answer.

"Because it haunts me, that's why. That whole period of my life, those two years or so I spent with Jimmy—" She struggled to find the right words without the emotions bubbling up again. "Honestly, I just don't like thinking about the person I was before I was Paisley."

"What happened when you got to New York?" he pressed as he resumed digging his fingers and thumbs therapeutically into her flesh.

She sighed. *Why does he keep forcing me to dredge up*

the past? This is killing me. The questions were undoing all the work he'd done to relax her back muscles.

"It sucked, okay? I spent half of the money I stole on drugs, and I was taken advantage of by my landlord and my first boss. It's a wonder I made it through that first year, to tell you the truth. It's all kind of a blur."

"Is that why you don't think you can date me? Because you think I'm too naïve and straitlaced? You don't think I can deal with your past?"

His hands suddenly felt as hot as branding irons. A searing shock of anger bolted through her as she scrambled rather ungracefully to her feet. "Why are you so fucking relentless?"

He rose from the couch to face her. She felt naked in her thin cotton nightgown with no bra or panties underneath. It may have hidden her curves, but it wasn't doing a good job of concealing her hard nipples. Even though she had once stripped for a living, she couldn't remember the last time she felt as exposed as she did right there standing in Calvin Mitchell's living room while he pierced her eyes with his own, searching for answers.

"I don't see you as some bad girl with a troubled past. I don't see you as tainted." Taking one of her hands into both of his, he bore into her eyes so intensely, she couldn't bear to meet his gaze.

"Well, that's what I am," she insisted, inching away from him. Her eyes darted to the floor where she noticed the polish on her big toe was chipped. "I'm sure, even if your parents do like me, they'd be less than thrilled to have me as a daughter-in-law. I'm positive they'd rather have someone clean-cut and...oh, I don't know, fucking normal marry their son."

Still holding her hand, he pulled her back to her

previous position. "Why do you act like that? You have so much confidence in your body and in your work, but for some reason you have absolutely zero in your character. I just don't get you, Paisley."

Breaking eye contact for a moment, he shook his head while he glanced down at their bare feet, which met each other toe to toe. The contrast was striking: her creamy white skin with delicate toes and chipped crimson nail polish next to his size-thirteen dark-skinned feet with long toes.

Seconds later, his eyes zipped back up her body and burned into hers again. "I want to, though. I want to under-stand you. I wish you'd let me in."

She'd never had someone dissect her like this, trying to separate the different facets of who she was. Nobody in her adult life had known enough about her past to be able to do it. But now Calvin held the keys and had unlocked all the doors. He'd stripped her down bare, and she couldn't hide who she really was underneath her strong exterior from him. Inside she was still that baby abandoned by her mother on her grandparents' doorstep, who grew into a little girl who just wanted to be understood and loved, but had only been used and abused instead.

"Don't you understand?" she whimpered, feeling that carefully constructed exterior begin to crumble around her. "My mother didn't want me, my grandparents threw me out, and Jimmy fucked me over. The only person I've ever been able to count on is myself."

"So you can't trust anyone. You don't think you're worthy of love?" he asked, his voice soft and trembling with compassion.

She collapsed. The structure she'd built so high and strong, girded with resolve and sheer stubbornness, imploded as she fell into his arms weeping. If the tears she'd shed earlier in the day had been a mighty river, then this was the ocean, with waves thundering onto the shore.

He held her as she shattered, their bodies pressed together for what felt like an eternity, until finally a small but earnest voice emerged from her mouth, one that may have not been heard in her lifetime. "I think you know me better than I know myself."

His eyes begin lit up with understanding, as if he'd finally cracked the mystery. "You are, you know," he said. "Worthy of love, I mean. And I know because..." He tilted her chin up so their eyes aligned again. "I haven't been able to stop myself from falling in love with you."

She wanted to back away from him; she wanted to run. He'd said words she previously refused to hear, but something had changed. Her ears had suffered a tiny crack, letting a whole new world of ideas fill her head.

Instead of escaping, she allowed Calvin to sweep her into his arms and press his lips against hers as if they were made to kiss her. She felt herself opening to him, though the tears were still streaming down her face.

It was one of those course-altering moments, like the instant she knew she must escape her life in Kentucky, her life as Rebecca Bridges. Only in this moment, she knew it was her heart that had escaped. It had escaped its prison cell, where she'd been punishing it for her entire adult life.

"I feel it too," she murmured against his lips. It was only a whisper, but still a tiny first step.

She buried her face in his chest as he squeezed her tight to his body, caressing her curves with his fingertips. She couldn't mistake his arousal as it pressed into her, separated by only two thin layers of fabric. The exhaustion she felt earlier faded as a new energy ignited within her, a hunger the likes of which she had never experienced. She wanted him so badly, she was trembling with her need.

"Calvin, will you make love to me?" she asked, desire seeping out in her voice.

He pulled away just enough to look her in the eyes, searching the contents of her heart. "Only if you're absolutely ready...and absolutely sure you can give yourself to me, Paisley. I don't just want your body; I want your heart, mind, and soul too."

The emotion pooled in her throat as she stood on this rocky ledge looking down at a city of golden splendor below. He was asking her to take the leap, to commit to him, and she had to decide whether or not to jump. She saw the hope and expectation etched on his face, the love and desire emanating from his eyes, and she felt a sense of peace as she sailed over the edge into the wide expanse of sky.

"I'm ready," she whispered.

He took her hand and led her to his bedroom, where he pulled the thin cotton nightgown off her body like it were made of air. He slid his shorts down his body and stepped out of them, leaving them both nude and exposed to each other for the first time.

She marveled at the way his body was crafted: tight mounds of muscles perfectly sculpted and proportioned from his head to his toes. In the dim light, shadows lingered in the valleys of his rippling musculature, and his magnificent cock strained toward his stomach with need.

A soft moan of approval escaped his lips at the sight of her, his eyes caressing her body as if she were a treasure, a rare masterpiece of art. He started by lightly grazing his fingertips across her cheek, then pulled her into his arms where his lips found hers again.

"I've wanted to do this for so long," he whispered into

her ear as he nuzzled her neck, breathing deeply the scent of her long, dark curls.

She couldn't believe how sensual his hands felt as they explored her body. His lips made a path of kisses from under her ear, down to her collarbone, between her full breasts and down the center of her torso as he fell to his knees to worship every inch of her. His steamy, hot breath fell on the smooth triangle crowning her thighs, and her pussy began to swell in response. She could only imagine how wet he was making her with his careful attention to detail.

He gently pushed her toward the bed until she collapsed onto the mattress. Spreading her legs, ravenous to taste her, he filled his lungs with her body's natural perfume, inhaling as though the molecules he breathed in were necessary to sustain his life.

As he explored her body, he spoke to her in a soft voice, praising every discovery he made along the way. "Your thighs are so soft, baby; I want to spend as much time as possible between them."

He covered the tender flesh with kisses as his hands wandered up to her breasts, leaving a firestorm of electricity in his wake. "Your nipples are exquisite. I can't wait to see how they feel in my mouth."

Every word he spoke sent shivers down her spine. She couldn't believe this was happening, that it was so real and so much more in every sense than anything she had ever experienced before. How could someone ten years her junior, who had only been with a handful of women in his entire sexual career, elicit such strong, electric responses from her body?

Calvin slid down the length of Paisley's figure until his face came to rest between her thighs again. "I can't wait any longer to lick and suck your pussy," he claimed, running the tip of his tongue up her wet folds, which were saturated with desire.

As he began to taste her, he adjusted his pressure and rhythm to the signals her body gave him, reading her like a bestselling novel. He was completely absorbed in the task of bringing her to climax, patiently, without rushing. He seemed to understand how to gently guide her down the path until her body involuntarily exploded.

His hands buried underneath her hips, he held her firmly while she bucked and quaked against his face. Even when she thought she was done, he continued to apply just the right amount of stimulation to prolong her ecstasy until she thought she might go mad.

After her quivering finally dissipated, he returned to her face, where his lips found hers again. Tasting herself on his mouth made her desire for him swell again, a hunger only he could satiate.

"I want to return the favor," she gasped, finally regaining her breath and ability to speak. He held her tightly to him so she could feel his need throbbing against her. "Please."

"God, Paisley, I just want to bury myself in you right now. I have waited so long; I'm not sure I can wait a minute longer."

Though she wanted to take his cock into her mouth and gift him the same intense pleasure he'd just given to her, she could hardly argue with him wanting to be inside her. "Okay," she relented, ready to surrender herself to his passion.

"But I won't be fucking you," he reminded her as he climbed between her thighs again, this time aligning his pelvis with hers. "I'll be making love to you. And I need to make sure you're okay with that."

"Yes," she whispered into his ear as his weight sank into her. "I am."

What transpired as he worked himself between her lips and began to penetrate her core was virtually indescribable. It was a sensation that, despite her vast catalog of sexual experiences, she had never felt before. There was a rightness, a perfection to the way he fit inside her that she didn't even know was possible.

He stayed still for a moment as they both adjusted to the feeling, precariously balancing on a fine line between urgency and restraint. And when he finally began to move within her, it was all she could do to keep from crying out, not only from the sensations radiating throughout her core, but those bursting in her heart.

Her hands stroked down the deep, muscular indentations of his back, across his bulky shoulders, and down his strong arms as he found his home within her. Her hips rose to meet his as they came together fully, then tilted back to give him the space he needed to plunge into her soft, warm depths again and again.

The music they generated together rivaled the greatest symphonic masterpieces; neither Mozart or Beethoven – nor any composer living or perished – had anything on the melodies and harmonies their bodies created.

He held her flush against his body, his fingers laced in her long, curly locks as he thrust into her, occupying a space inside her that had somehow never been discovered. Her entire body clung to him as if her climax was utterly dependent on his, as if the two were inextricably linked together. There was a symbiosis between their individual bodies, two parts of one machine bringing their awe-inspiring duet to an inevitable and exquisite finale. After a few more minutes passed, that finale was so sure, so imminent, that no earthly or heavenly power could have prevented it.

And then, it happened. The passion swirled around them both so fiercely that it swallowed them up together in a spiraling whirlwind of ecstasy. Their bodies soared to unfathomable heights, riding parallel waves of pleasure as they slowly floated back down to earth, still wrapped in each other's arms.

The experience was so consuming, so physically and emotionally draining, they remained intertwined for several minutes before any words could be exchanged. And when their hearts and lungs finally returned to normal functioning, they found there was no need for words after all.

TWENTY-ONE

Paisley awoke the same way she had fallen asleep: her limbs entangled with Calvin's and her head on his arm. At first she felt a bit disoriented, as though trying to wake up from a dream that was actually reality. But after she got her bearings, it felt more natural, like something she could quickly become accustomed to. It was quite a metamorphosis from her previous self who hated having fuck buddies stay the night.

Calvin is not a fuck buddy though. This is a legit relationship.

She felt a bit swoony invoking the formerly dreaded "R word." She'd tried to avoid it for so long, it still seemed like a foreign concept.

Despite being emotionally drained from yesterday's events, she had a busy day of trying to figure out how to dodge her blackmailers to look forward to. Oh, and she needed Calvin to restore The Factory's website. She was afraid once it was back up, she'd check it a hundred times to make sure they hadn't usurped control of it again. And she needed to get ready for the Friday night party at the club while also reconciling the July books.

By afternoon, Calvin and Paisley had heard from his father that they were close to making a breakthrough in her case. They were interviewing a few people, tracking down some additional leads generated from Paisley's information, and were hoping to make an arrest by nightfall. They believed the suspect was in Ocean City, and it was only a matter of time before he was found.

"Who is it?" Paisley asked, her heart pounding with the possibilities.

"We can't say at this time," Detective Mitchell replied. "But we do have an out-of-state license plate we're looking for. That's all I can tell you."

Kentucky or New York, she guessed. She would have been put money on it. She wondered if the gang that was after Jimmy all those years ago was now after her. She wished she could remember more details about that period of her life so she could let Calvin's father know, but it was fuzzy for a reason. She had done her best to bury those memories so deep they'd never be accessible again.

She looked at her phone approximately four million times throughout the course of the day as she tried to prepare for that night's party at the club and run the end-of-month reports. Fortunately, Casey was in the office helping with the preparations, and Cap was planning to be at the club that evening. They were expecting a huge crowd and had already run out of space in their reservation system for everyone but single females.

Calvin arrived at The Factory at five, earlier than expected, already wearing his security uniform. Casey spotted him giving Paisley a peck on her forehead after he whispered in her ear that he got The Factory's website back up and running.

"Well, what do we have here?!" Casey gushed. "What's going on with Mr. Mitchell and Ms. Parker? Is there something I should know?" The twinkle in her eyes revealed she had witnessed their moment of affection.

Paisley's first impulse was to brush it off, but Calvin spoke up first. "Only the hottest item at The Factory." He shot her a wink.

As soon as Casey passed them to head into her office, Paisley grabbed Calvin's hand and asked if he had any new information from his father. He shook his head. "No arrests yet, but he did ask me if the name Jones means anything to you?"

Her eyes widened. "That's Jimmy's last name. But he's still in prison, so—"

"Well, it is a pretty common last name. Maybe just a coincidence?"

Her mind was flooded with images of people she knew from her hometown: people she'd gone to school with, people affiliated with the crowd she hung out with. No one other than Jimmy had that last name that she could recall.

"One way or the other, they're getting close. Hopefully by the end of the night."

"What are we going to do if they don't track down the suspect before tomorrow?" Her voice trembled with worry.

"They will, relax," Calvin assured her, drawing her into his arms again. She wanted to trust things would be okay, but in her past, when people promised things would be okay, they were decidedly *not* okay.

If things did end up being okay, it's because I took matters into my own hands. It was because I took care of myself.

She was thankful for the busy night at The Factory to distract her from the worry settling in like a long spate of rainy days. If she thought she was anxious before, it was nothing compared to the impending sense of doom permeating every thought. She found herself staring every club patron in the eye, wondering if her tormenter could possibly be among them.

She had thought about telling the hosts to watch for anyone trying to buy a membership with a Kentucky or New York driver's license, but she didn't want to raise any suspicions. So far she had managed to keep this entire operation a secret from her bosses, and all she needed was for an arrest to be made before anyone beyond the tight circle of her, Calvin and the Maryland State Police could find out.

"Do you think they followed us here tonight?" she asked Calvin when she managed to pull him aside three hours into the party.

"I don't think so. We drove my car, not yours."

"But they know I'm staying with you. They probably know your car too."

He sighed. "Paisley, please. Just trust me that this is going to be okay. I'm not going to let anything happen to you."

She was reminded of those first few years she spent in New York before she officially changed her name. She was constantly looking over her shoulder. The paranoia became so normal that after she did finally change her name and got a new job and apartment in a different part of the city, she didn't even realize how paranoid she'd been until she experienced the relief of being able to let her guard down. She was so sure at some point that either the police or Jimmy's enemies were going to come after her. Now she supposed she was finally getting her comeuppance from the latter.

Maybe they're using Jimmy's name or his car?

That night when they'd crawled into Calvin's bed, she once again brought up her trepidation. "Your dad didn't get in touch."

"He texted me at midnight and said they were close and not to worry."

"That's what he said at noon," she sighed.

Every muscle in her body was clenched so tight, she felt as though she were made of stretched-to-their-limits rubber bands that might snap at any given moment. Calvin sensed her tension and began to work the knots out of her shoulders with his strong hands, just as he had the night before when they ended up making love for the first time.

"I wish I could be as sure about it as you are."

"I know a good way to distract you," he murmured in her ear, pressing himself against her. The feel of his rigid cock on her thigh gave away any secret about what kind of distraction he had in mind.

She groaned, but not out of desire. She could only think of a handful of times she had ever passed up sex with someone she liked, but her stomach was twisted in pain. She felt anything but turned on.

"Calvin, I...I'm sorry..." She pulled back from him until they were no longer touching.

The times she hadn't felt like having sex when she was younger, whether it was with Jimmy or any of the asshole guys she'd dated before declaring lifestyle unicorn status, she'd ended up giving in. Men had a way of making women think their dicks might fall off if they didn't get relief from their sexual aches. She used to fall for it when she was younger and inexperienced, and part of her expected Calvin to plead his case, to coerce her into taking care of his needs.

Instead, he wrapped his arms around her. "Cuddling is good too. Whatever you want, baby."

Fuck, did he just call me baby?

Part of her was as nervous about their developing relationship as she was about her blackmailer coming to collect his money. *Which I don't have*, she reminded herself, the panic surging through her again.

"What's going to happen tomorrow?" Her voice came out like a timid squeak into the silence of his dark bedroom. She swallowed down her nerves and added, "We keep talking about how there's going to be an arrest. What if there's not?"

"Then I'm going with you to your apartment, and we'll wait for him together."

"But I don't have the money."

"I know. You're not paying that lowlife pond scum. Get real!"

"What if he has a gun?"

"I have a gun too," he retorted.

"What?!" she shrieked.

"I'm not going to let anything happen to you," he reaffirmed. "It's almost three in the morning, babe. We have to get some sleep now, okay?"

She didn't say another word; her mind just kept reviewing every life choice she made that brought her to this pivotal point. She left Kentucky two months before she turned eighteen; she beat addiction; she learned to support herself through dancing. It was a battle waged through a series of stumbles and small advances.

She remembered meeting a girl on the subway who was a dancer shortly after arriving in the city: Nicole. *Whatever happened to Nicole?* She had gotten Paisley her first dancing gig at some disgusting bar in the Bronx with its handsy manager, Kurt.

That was not burlesque dancing. It was just plain stripping. Not to mention going home with drunk clients who slipped her extra money. *It's a wonder I didn't end up dead in a dumpster at any point during those two years.*

Then she met Samantha. Samantha worked at a classier joint that happened to be hiring, and she let Paisley move in with her. That was when Paisley decided to legally change her name to the one she'd been using since she started her dancing career. Samantha's boyfriend was a real piece of work and...

Paisley slammed the door to that memory shut as soon as she started to open it. There was no reason to dredge up that particular nightmare. Suffice it to say, she ended up leaving Samantha's because she was afraid her roommate's boyfriend was going to assault her. Then she'd have to call the police and risk having her past discovered.

Fortunately, she found an amazing opportunity at a different club and moved into another place on a whim with a man she barely knew. *Big mistake, as rash decisions typically are.*

When she ran down the catalog of all the mistakes she had made in the past eighteen years, it was really quite a miracle that she'd gotten as far as she had. Somehow, just the right people came into her life to either help her get ahead or teach her a lesson she needed to learn.

She would never forget the friend who first suggested she go back to school. Lyndsay was a dancer who used the stage name "Luscious Lulu." She was remarkably curvy and knew how to dress her body to accentuate her best features; Paisley learned a lot from her in that regard.

Lyndsay was taking classes at the local community

college with the hopes of transferring to a four-year school. She wanted to be a veterinarian, which Paisley recalled thinking might have been a bit beyond her reach but... *I wonder if she ever did it?*

Yes, Lyndsay was one of the first to convince her she needed to plan for her future. "You can't dance forever," she had warned. "No guy gets off on wrinkles and saggy tits!"

Paisley suddenly regretted not keeping in touch with all the friends she'd made during her first decade in New York, the people she met in clubs or in college. The only person she'd really kept in touch with since she moved was Allison, and Allison was someone she met long after her dancing days, when she began working for the event management company. Allison gave their circle of friends updates about her from time to time. But the cast of other characters from her years in New York was virtually lost to time and eroding memories.

Oh, the can of worms Calvin has opened, she thought to herself as she felt his body jerk and surrender to sleep. It was only their second night of sleeping together as a couple, and she was still getting used to feeling him in the bed beside her. He had idiosyncrasies, same as anyone else, endearing little twitches and ticks. She lay beside him, listening to his breathing become deep and regular, wondering what he was dreaming about, if it was her.

She saw his phone flash on the nightstand with an incoming call from a blocked number. Her heart began to pound as she impulsively snatched it up to answer it. "Hello?" she whispered.

"We know you've contacted the police, which you were told not to do. We know your boyfriend is the son of a cop. We will be contacting the management of The Factory first thing in the morning unless you show up at your apartment alone by 5 AM with ten thousand dollars in cash. And do NOT tell anyone where you are going."

She winced as the robotic voice ended the call, then a flood of adrenaline surged into her bloodstream. She wanted to scream as loud as she could, to let her frustrations pierce the silence of the room and give the anger bubbling up within her someplace to go. Before, she had felt fear, a gripping, paralyzing fear. But now that fear had been replaced with pure, unadulterated rage.

It seemed so unfair that Calvin had gotten dragged into this. He was hell-bent on protecting her, but she suddenly felt protective of him. The blackmailers had his cell phone number because it was on his website; they did not have hers. They could only reach her via The Factory's number. And obviously they were following him, too, and knew of his connection to the state police. The hole she'd dug herself into just kept getting bigger and bigger, dragging more and more people into the abyss.

Cap and Leah were next.

Well, that hole is as big as it's going to get.

She swung her legs off the bed as gently as she could so as not to disturb Calvin. She grabbed her purse and keys from the bar in the kitchen and slipped on the clothes she had worn the night before. She contemplated taking Calvin's gun with her but thought better of it. She had already caused enough problems in her life by taking something that didn't belong to her.

And not only did she want to avoid getting Calvin in trouble, she also felt his safety was more important than her own. She wanted him to have the gun in case he needed it.

I guess I do love him.

She stepped into the dark bedroom to take one last look at him. He was stretched out on his stomach with one leg bare on the sheets. The comforter was spread across his lower back and thighs, covering his perfectly muscular ass.

I am going to miss fucking him. I only got to do it once.

Okay, fine, I'm going to miss all of him, not just the fucking.

Before she could change her mind, she slipped out of the room and out the door, being extra careful not to make any noise as she shut it. She glanced down the stairwell outside his door to see if she saw any shadows lurking in the bright orange light coming from the front of the building.

Her car was parked several rows away because there hadn't been a close visitor spot when they'd returned from his parents' house. She planned to get down to her car like ripping off a Band-Aid: with lightning speed and without thinking too much.

It was 3:30 in the morning. She had to get to her apartment, then she'd decide what to do about the most recent call. *Stay or go?*

She didn't know. The two options crisscrossed in her mind until they were tangled together like Christmas lights after sitting in the basement all year. Pointing her key fob toward her car, she clicked to unlock it. The horn beeped, and the lights flashed on, giving her a target in the crowded parking lot to aim for.

She began jogging toward her car, and suddenly headlights flashed from the opposite direction. There was a screech of tires, a deep, rumbling rev of an engine and then those blazing lights came barreling across the lot in her direction. As her heart began to pound and panic froze her limbs with fear, a dark-colored car whizzed past her, nearly knocking her into a large black SUV.

She could barely catch her breath as she sprinted the last fifty feet to her own vehicle, jumped inside, and fired up the engine. After backing out carefully, her tires squealed as she gunned the gas pedal. Her Mazda took off like a lightning bolt, and she barely had a chance to whip it around a curve before she slammed into the sidewalk.

Looking behind her, she was fairly certain the other car was racing around the next row of vehicles so it could pursue her out of the parking lot.

"Fuck!" she screamed out loud and tried to formulate a plan as she floored her gas pedal and shot toward Bayshore Drive like a bullet.

Ocean City was a long, narrow strip of land with one side facing the bay and one side facing the ocean. Resorts, restaurants and shops lined both sides of Coastal Highway, the main street running north and south. The cross streets were short, often ending in the water after only one or two blocks. She didn't have much hope of being able to lose her pursuer without a great deal of luck as there simply weren't many places to hide, nor very much traffic to get lost in.

Her heart threatened to burst out of her ribcage and her lungs to explode as she flew through the stoplight on yellow and peeled out onto the highway heading north, hoping she'd lose them when the light turned red.

Where am I going? Maybe I can lure them up to New York, away from Ocean City where they could hurt Calvin or The Factory.

Shit, I have to go to my apartment first.

She hadn't been back to her apartment since the day after she was confronted by the hooded figure late at night in the parking lot. She and Calvin had returned to grab a suitcase full of clothes, which she'd left at his place. Now she desperately needed to grab her mail and get another load of clothes if she wanted to skip town. She was fully aware that they'd be following her, hoping to collect the cash before she could get away.

From what she could tell, there were two figures in the car that nearly rammed into her. One looked to be a female. She only knew because she saw the outline of long hair illuminated by her headlights when the car zoomed past. She assumed that meant she'd face two people at her apartment if they managed to get there before she could leave.

Her mind raced with different scenarios: *What if they get physical with me? What if they have a weapon? Is there really anything I can do to protect myself or the club anymore... or is this all over?*

She flew down the highway at nearly eighty miles per hour. *Where are the over-eager OC cops when you need them?* If she got pulled over, the bad guys would have to stop following her. She couldn't believe after running from cops for her whole adult life, she now felt like they were the only ones who could help her.

Maybe this is good. Her mind spun with a million thoughts per second. *If they're in the car the police are looking for, drawing them out into the open on the main highway is a good thing. Maybe they'll get pulled over, and I won't?*

She continued to pray for red and blue flashing lights and the shrill, piercing sound of a siren until the moment she pulled into the parking lot of her apartment complex. But there was only darkness and silence greeting her when she arrived.

"Fuck." Her heart sank deep into her gut. She looked down at her phone at a text as it came in:

Calvin: Where did you go?

"Fuck this." She pulled the key out of her ignition. *If they want their money, they can't kill me. The only way they can keep threatening me is if they keep me alive. Plus, maybe I can finally find out who is behind this bullshit.*

She wasn't sure where her sudden bravery was coming from, but she conjectured it had something to do with her anger over all the upheaval this had caused in what was supposed to be her brand-new start in life.

She had convinced herself the third time was the charm. *I failed in Kentucky, and I ended up stagnating in New York. Moving here was my first chance to really make something of myself, and I'm not going to let these assholes take it away from me. What's the worst they can do?*

Calvin's dad knew her secrets, and he didn't whip out the handcuffs. Cap, Leah, and Casey were at greater risk than she was. They could hurt her bosses more than they could hurt her. If she headed back to New York, they would probably follow her up there. Otherwise, she would have to trust MSP to come through with an arrest before they could do too much damage.

She opened her car door, a sudden bolt of courage surging through her. She glanced around the parking lot but didn't spot any other newly arrived cars. The night sky was still dark with a half moon slung beneath some scattered clouds. The stars were all too shy to appear, either that or the lights on the outskirts of the parking lot had hidden them.

Using her peripheral vision to keep an eye on her surroundings, she hurried to the doorway that led to her apartment. She had her key ready to go and her first stop at the mailboxes just inside the door planned out. After quickly grabbing her mail, she'd hustle down the hall to her place at the end of the building.

As soon as her key turned in the lock of the mailbox, she heard the footsteps behind her. She bit her lip to keep from gasping and slowly whirled around as if in slow motion. Relief spread through her nerve endings as she recognized her crazy neighbor with an obvious drinking problem. He was apparently just getting home after a night out.

"What's up?" he slurred, nodding at her. He reeked of alcohol and looked a mess, but she felt a little better just having another human standing near her.

She mumbled hello to him as she collected an armful of mail from her box, then she practically ran down the hall to her apartment. She jabbed the key into the lock, threw open the door and rushed inside, deadlocking it behind her.

Her entire lung capacity of air rushed past her lips as she collapsed against the countertop that separated the kitchen from the dining area.

Okay, I don't have much time before five o'clock. Get in and get out before they get here.

Her apartment was frozen in time, documenting exactly what was going on in her life a week prior. Unwashed dishes sat in the sink; an empty coffee mug lingered on a small table in her living room. She rummaged through the hallway closet until she found a duffel bag, into which she stuffed clothes from a basket of freshly laundered items she'd never gotten around to folding.

Then she headed into the bathroom, which she'd never gotten around to cleaning, and dumped a handful of toiletries into the side pocket of the bag. She quickly thumbed through the mail she'd left on her counter, then took a deep breath. Now she just needed to make it back to her car.

In the lobby near the mailboxes, she saw her drunk neighbor had vomited all over the carpet, then proceeded to pass out near the stairs. *That's attractive.* She stepped over him, trying to avoid breathing in the foul stench of puke. Her eyes darted to every corner of the hall and down the path toward her car, searching for lurking shadows.

Across the parking lot, there was just enough illumination from the tall light posts to make out the front doors of a midsize burgundy sedan opening. She hadn't gotten a good look at the car that nearly plowed into her because its headlights were blinding her at the time, but she suspected it was the same one.

She kept walking to her Mazda, her head down but casting furtive glances in the direction of the burgundy car. Two figures stepped out and began walking toward her.

"Fuck."

She reached her car and slid inside, but fumbled with the keys as her hands shook with nervous energy. Her body was so hyped up on adrenaline and endorphins, she could barely control her limbs.

The fumble gave the approaching figures time to get within view. One was a tall man with shaggy, mousy brown hair. He had a wiry build and wore a charcoal gray t-shirt with baggy, ripped-up carpenter jeans. The other figure appeared to be a middle-aged woman with dark, shoulder-length hair suffering from a grown-out perm. She wore a ribbed camouflage-print tank top showing two lumpy rolls around her midsection and ill-fitting cut-off denim shorts that exposed thick, pale white calves. They weren't close enough to make out their facial features.

Paisley turned the key in the ignition and started up the engine as they continued to approach. As they got closer and closer, the finer details of their faces came into focus, which triggered synapses deep in Paisley's brain that she didn't have time to decode. Their figures were brightly illuminated as they approached the nearest light post, and the male reached into the large pocket on his thigh to pull out a small handgun.

When the fact that he now held a gun registered in her head, the anger and rage she felt when she left Calvin's apartment was replaced again with a gripping, pulsating fear. The blood drained from her face, and her nerves turned into a million sharp spikes piercing her flesh as her phone began to ring in the seat next to her. With one glance, she determined it was Calvin calling.

With trembling hands, she threw her gearshift into drive and began to pull out of her parking space just as the man raised his gun into the air, pointing it toward her. Everything felt like it was happening in slow motion, like an action scene from a summer blockbuster.

Seeing that her companion had raised his gun, the woman screamed so loudly that Paisley could make out the words even with her windows rolled up: "What the fuck are you doing? Put the fucking gun down, Billy!"

Paisley had two choices: pull out and drive away in the opposite direction, where she risked getting shot from behind – or pull out and head right toward them, giving her the option to mow them down like they'd tried to do to her back in Calvin's parking lot.

She always chose having more control over having less, so she jerked the car backwards, slamming on her brakes just before plowing into the car behind her. Then she cranked her steering wheel to turn and began to fly toward her stalkers, who were still making their way toward her with the gun drawn.

Just as she swerved to miss them, the woman slapped the gun out of the man's hand. Paisley was positive she heard her scream, "Don't fucking shoot my daughter!"

TWENTY-TWO

Paisley's phone was still ringing as she sped north up Coastal Highway. She glanced in the back seat to make sure she'd managed to get her duffel bag in the car and, much to her relief, there it sat. She was having trouble remembering what happened between the time she left her apartment building and when she began driving like a maniac toward the two people pursuing her.

The only thing blaring through her mind was what the woman screamed: "Don't fucking shoot my daughter!"

I think that lady is my mom.

It was an idea so foreign, it was like waking up aboard a spaceship to a band of aliens hell-bent on probing all her orifices. And not in a fun way.

Evelyn Bridges was more of a myth in Paisley's mind than an actual human – *at least she was until a few minutes ago.* She never thought she'd come face to face with this mythical maternal creature, and especially not in the circumstances that just transpired.

After dropping her infant daughter off on the front porch of her parents' house, Evelyn had vanished. But living in a tiny, rural town, Paisley's family would occasion-ally hear reports of Evelyn sightings. She'd pop into town for a week or two after excursions to exotic locales such as Texas, Louisiana, or Las Vegas. A few times she made a sheepish return after serving time at the Kentucky Correctional Institute for Women. But she never came around to see her daughter or parents. Not ever.

Paisley knew the whole town pitied her for being Evelyn's abandoned daughter. She could tell by the way they looked at her with sad, disapproving eyes that seemed to say, "Oh, there's that Bridges girl. Poor thing." But it was widely accepted that Evelyn Bridges' daughter had a much better chance of making something of herself in the care of her grandparents, and so, for that fact, sometimes people would say she was actually lucky.

Just as she had been abandoned by her mother, so too Paisley's grandparents had abandoned hope of their daughter returning. Evelyn's photographs and personal items were hidden away, and neither her parents nor any of her siblings dared speak of her.

When she was thirteen or fourteen, Paisley embarked upon the typical adolescent quest to explore her roots and find her true identity, during which, an interest in learning about her mother was sparked. But there wasn't much of a story to uncover.

Evelyn Bridges had fallen in with the wrong crowd when she was a teenager. She'd gotten pregnant, and then she chose a life of crime and drugs over her daughter. It was a cautionary tale that, in retrospect, Paisley wished she had better heeded.

At least I finally woke up and saved myself.

But not before I got my grandparents killed.

She had no idea how her mother had tracked her down,

but she could only guess that the woman who gave her life blamed her for the death of her parents. Who knew what nasty rumors still circulated about her in that godforsaken town she'd called home for the first seventeen years of her life? Who knew what lies Paisley's own aunts, uncles, and cousins had spread about her?

She passed the state line into Delaware before she asked herself exactly where she was going. The Indian River bridge with its two triangular masts rose into the early morning sky, all lit up in a mesmerizing blue glow that would soon be swallowed by the dawn. Once her car hit the bridge, she accepted the choice her subconscious mind had made when she'd been paralyzed by fear: she was leaving Maryland and heading to the only place that had ever seemed like a refuge: New York City.

She stopped just north of Dover to get gas and stretch her legs. There was something strangely comforting about being in a different state, as though she were safe. She knew it was a fallacy; if they'd tracked her down in Ocean City, they could track her down anywhere. And they would likely follow her; she was prepared for that.

But who knew what they might do to Calvin or the club beforehand? Taking a deep breath, she decided to check her messages. There were three texts and a voicemail from Calvin, the latter warning if she didn't check in soon, he would assume her blackmailers had kidnapped or otherwise incapacitated her. If that were the case, not to worry, MSP would find her.

A sick feeling gnawed away at her stomach as she considered the trail of damage she had now left in Ocean City.

No one is dead, but there's going to be a lot of anger, resentment, confusion and god knows what else because of me. I can't believe how good I am at truly fucking people over. It's really quite a skill.

She decided to send two texts before getting back in her car. One was to Allison:

> Hey, chica, I'm heading up to hang out. Need to get away and clear my head. Hoping I can crash with you? Let me know.

Then one to Calvin:

> I'm so sorry I had to go. I'm not the woman you need me to be. I wish I could be, but I'm just not.

After she settled herself on the leather seat and fastened her seatbelt, she sent one more, a group text to all of her bosses:

> I'm very sorry for causing you any trouble. I never meant to hurt anyone.

And with that, she turned off her phone and proceeded to drive north.

The drive to New York wouldn't be nearly so terrible if not for the abomination known as the New Jersey Turnpike. Paisley cranked up her radio, letting the sounds of classic rock drown out the voices in her head while she continued to weave her way in and out of traffic, always searching for the fastest lane.

She tried to concentrate on what she was going to tell Allison – she had already convinced herself there was no way in hell she could tell her the truth – but the mental image she'd snapped of her blackmailers kept popping back into her head no matter how fervently she resisted.

There was no denying that she looked like her mother. The mythical Evelyn Bridges turned out to be an older, rougher version of Paisley.

The man with her mother reminded her of Jimmy. *God, Jimmy has to be in his forties by now.* The mystery man had the same build as him and the same thick, muddy brown-colored hair. *His son, maybe?*

But Jimmy had been in prison since she had last seen him, and he'd never had any children. As a matter of fact, he'd always told her he couldn't have children, which was his way of assuring her she would never get pregnant when they had sex. Since she never had, she believed him.

She wanted to take all of the memories, the fears, and the guilt that were twisting her stomach and brain into knots and dump them in some random cesspool in New Jersey so she could never dwell on them again.

She'd have to start her life over yet again. *Finding a job without a good reference from the Sheldons or Casey Fontaine is going to be rough. But I'll just have to be patient.*

By the time she crossed the bridge to New York, she was already feeling better about her prospects. She'd made the right choice removing herself from a situation where she might ruin her bosses' lives and break Calvin's heart.

Soon she'd be at Allison's, and she could put all the crazy mess of the last few months behind her. The consummate party girl, Allison would be the best person to help her forget.

Maybe she'd even change her name again, just for good measure.

N ot surprisingly, Allison was still in bed when Paisley arrived at her apartment. She had a male roommate, Ian, who was fastidious and quiet, never ruffling any feathers. He answered the door when Paisley knocked.

"Hey, Paisley," he greeted her in his flat, monotone voice.

"I guess Allison didn't get my text. Paisley mustered up a warm smile for Ian. "I tried to warn her I was coming."

"She got home late last night and crashed. You know how she is. The sky could be falling, and she'd sleep right through."

Paisley nodded, knowing exactly what Ian meant. She was sure the roommates only got along because Ian was such a marshmallow that Allison always got her way. She found her friend asleep, naked and tangled in the sheets, one arm under her pillow and the other wrapped around a man.

Ah, I should have known.

At this point, she was exhausted from her drive, not to mention the emotionally draining circumstances that made her flee Maryland. All she wanted to do was to curl up in the bed and sleep off the trauma she'd just survived. She nudged the unknown male's foot with her own foot until he opened his bleary eyes into narrow slits.

"Hey, you have to go," she told him authoritatively. She recognized the tone as the one she used the night she had to fire Jason. It had also served her well whenever a member got out of hand at The Factory.

"Why?" he groaned. Allison didn't so much as twitch a

muscle when the naked man began to sleepily pull himself up from the mattress.

"I'm Allison's girlfriend," Paisley stated, "and you're in my spot. Get the fuck out!"

His eyes widened, and he bolted to his feet. "I didn't know; I'm so sorry. Fuck, that's hot though!"

She couldn't help but notice his cock was stiff and jutting up against his stomach. He apologized again as she watched him leave, her hands on her hips with exasperation.

After he was gone, she slid into the warm spot he'd left and wrapped her arm around Allison. Mere seconds later, she was asleep too.

It was noon when Paisley felt Allison stirring next to her. She wearily flipped her body toward her friend's as her eyes fluttered open. "What? Where'd Nick go?"

"I sent him home," Paisley mumbled groggily.

"What the fuck are you doing here?"

"Some hospitality." Paisley wearily pulled herself into a cross-legged position while her friend pulled the sheets around her naked body and sat up to join her.

"It's a guy, isn't it?" She seemed rather confident in her guess.

She chose to nod and stare out the window dramatically, as if she needed to be prodded to talk about it. It bought her some time to come up with a half-truth explanation that left out anything so crazy as being stalked and blackmailed by her mother, whom she hadn't seen since she was a baby.

"That guy you were staying with?" Allison questioned. "Calvin, right?"

She's making this too easy. She nodded again. "Yeah, I knew sleeping with him was a bad idea."

Allison patted her hand. Paisley forgot how nurturing she could be when she wasn't entirely self-absorbed. "It'll be okay," she reassured her friend. "You know what? Let's get the gang together tonight. We'll make sure you forget all about what's his name! How does that sound?"

Paisley squeezed her friend's thigh and smiled. "Yes, that'll be perfect!"

She felt nostalgic getting ready for a night out in the city. It had been several months since she'd spent a weekend night anywhere but The Factory. Speaking of which, when she turned on her phone, she had missed calls from both Leah and Casey. Their voices were filled with concern on the messages they left. They didn't understand what her text was about, but they hoped she was okay and that she'd check in soon.

The voicemails had been left in the morning, so the blackmailers hadn't contacted the club owners...yet. Perhaps they were still holding out for the money and had followed her to New York.

There had been no further communication from Calvin, so Paisley assumed he decided to let her go gracefully. After all, they had barely gotten their relationship off the ground.

Leaving was the right decision, she told herself as she pulled the mascara wand through her lashes, making them thicker and longer with every stroke. *It's better for everyone if I'm gone.*

Allison chose to wear the tightest, reddest dress in the universe. Paisley couldn't help but sigh when she came out of the bedroom with the fabric clinging to her curves for dear life.

"Can you walk in that thing?" Paisley asked.

"Don't be a hater!" Allison snarled as she slid her feet into four-inch platform heels that were as red as the dress. "If I can walk in these, the dress should be no problem whatsoever!"

"So what we're saying is that I'll be carrying you home." Paisley laughed.

Next to Allison, she felt almost frumpy and demure in the black dress she'd chosen for their night out. It had spaghetti straps and a sweetheart neckline, which showed off ample cleavage with her breasts smooshed together in a lacy black push-up bra. The bodice and skirt were made up of layers of chiffon that fell in ruffles skimming her waist then floating out to her knees.

She wore sparkly rhinestone sandals, trusting she'd be able to dance in them all night. And dancing all night sounded more appealing than anything else. She wanted to lose herself in the beat of the music, let it soak into her soul and move her limbs as if she were merely a marionette under the command of an invisible master.

"You look gorgeous, by the way," Allison assured Paisley, smoothing her long ringlet curls over her shoulders.

Paisley almost slipped back to Allison's room to retrieve her phone from the nightstand, but at the last minute decided against it. *If I truly want to lose myself tonight, I sure as hell can't take my fucking phone with me.*

A short subway ride later, they were standing in line to

be admitted to a club that was literally throbbing with a heavy bass beat even from the sidewalk. There was an energy circulating through the crowd, the energy of the city that Paisley had sorely missed, though she'd appreciated the slow, laidback pace of the Eastern Shore for other reasons. No matter how crowded The Factory was on a Saturday night, it didn't hold a candle to the urban electricity being generated up and down the block where they were standing.

Once inside with their small posse of friends, Paisley and Allison headed directly to the bar to start their evening with a shot. Then Paisley settled herself on a barstool to enjoy her martini while she waited for the alcohol to permeate her cells. Allison was soon riding high in her element, flickering like a firefly flashing its call for a mate. It wasn't long until men responded, and the entire group was pulled onto the dance floor.

Allison shimmied her body up and down Paisley's wicked curves as a ring of hungry men formed around them. Ordinarily Paisley wouldn't like being used as a prop in Allison's sexual exploits, but the liquor was kicking in, and she was beginning to feel the rhythm of the music pump through her like a heartbeat.

Even though Allison had a tight little body, she didn't know how to move it like Paisley moved hers. No one taught Paisley how to dance; her moves were instinctual, primal. Her hips began to undulate to the beat, her body writhing and twisting until she was but a whirlwind of motion, captured in flashes by the pulsating lights.

Foreign fingers rippled down her curves, sweat beading along her hairline and the back of her neck, and her muscles burning from the energy surging through her. She closed her eyes, giving herself over to the power of the bass thumping so loudly, it shook the floors beneath her feet.

She wasn't sure how many songs had elapsed, maybe two or three, then one of the men dancing alongside her bought a tube of effervescent pink liquid from a vendor circulating around the floor. She poured it down her throat, feeling it burn all the way down to her stomach. And then she was handed another tube, which suffered the same fate.

It didn't take long for Paisley to become completely disoriented, the songs bleeding into each other, the faces of the men dancing with her a blur. Though the other women they'd arrived with had disappeared, Allison was still there, and she became Paisley's beacon. From what she could tell, she was Allison's only focal point too. They were two lighthouses beaming signals at each other in a choppy sea of testosterone and spectacle.

Finally, Paisley noticed Allison had been swallowed up by two men so that only flashes of her red dress appeared between beats of the music. Paisley was too inebriated to panic, or have much of a reaction whatsoever, other than a fleeting thought of the last time she had been sandwiched between two men.

Suddenly, she felt someone grab her by the wrist, and her nerves spiked with paranoia. A surge of sobriety rushed through her, only to be extinguished when she discovered it was Allison taking her by the hand to lead her out of the club.

They got into a cab, squished between the two men who had enveloped Allison on the dance floor. They were tall and broad with foreign accents. Or they may have been speaking a different language entirely; Paisley was having too much trouble processing anyone's words to know for sure. A thrill coursed through her, displacing any fear she'd had when Allison grabbed her.

I'm going on an adventure! It's been a while since I've had a good adventure.

The cab stopped outside a hotel in Midtown, and one of the men grabbed her hand to help extract her from the seat where she'd been wedged between him and Allison. Her legs didn't quite want to cooperate with her, so the man put his arm around her, coaxing her up the steps to the lobby of the hotel, which was lit up with a glowing brass chandelier hanging with drops of crystal.

A spark of memory flickered, filling her mind with the image of the chandelier in The Factory's lobby, but she dismissed it as quickly as it appeared, refusing to let her intoxicated mind travel back to Maryland.

She experienced everything that followed in flashes: shiny marble floors, cool air blowing from a row of ceiling fans high overhead, the ding of the elevator when the doors slid open. There was a hand on her back as she stared into the mirrors that surrounded the elevator car. It looked as though the elevator was full even though there were only four people aboard.

Is it possible I'm getting more drunk? Is it possible there was something besides alcohol in those shots?

The flashes continued as they made their way down the hall: her jeweled sandals sinking into the mesmerizing geometric pattern of plush carpeting, pearlescent sconces illuminating the bland striped wallpaper, and door after door after door. The taller of the two men inserted a card, and the handle flashed green, granting them access. She was prodded inside the dark room, which was cool and smelled of cleaning products. As a dim light came on in the bathroom, she caught sight of two fluffy white beds and imagined what it would feel like to cascade into the softness, letting sleep consume her like a decadently rich dessert.

She watched Allison's skin-tight dress being pulled over her head, her platform shoes discarded by the side of the bed. Deep moans slipped past her friend's lips as two strong hands trailed down her supple skin. The man twirled her to face the bed, then pressed her down until her hands reached the mattress.

He caressed her hips and ass as they jutted out on display in front of him. "So beautiful," he murmured, the first words Paisley had been able to comprehend since they'd left the club. Then he said something to his companion that sounded like Spanish.

Paisley's brain slowly began to unclog until she finally felt capable of scrutinizing the two men who accompanied them to the hotel. Both dark-skinned with angular features and thick, slicked-back hair, they appeared to be Latino. One was quite tall, perhaps 6'4" or 6'5", while the other was closer to the 6-foot mark. They were well-dressed with finely woven button-down dress shirts, crisp black trousers and shiny black shoes. She wondered if they were brothers as much as they looked alike. The shorter of the two had unfastened his black leather belt and was making his way across the room toward her.

She was sober enough to recognize her body responding to his looks and the hunger in his eyes. His full, slightly parted lips sent the message that he wanted to devour her; his dark eyes smoldered, brimming with lust. Her breath hitched as he took her into his arms, his fingers weaving through her long tresses and guiding her lips toward his. Upon impact, a spark raced up her spine as he coaxed her mouth open with his tongue.

But before she could get carried away, the remaining cells in her brain still under the influence seemed to drain themselves of their fuzzy, liquefied stupor. And in the place of that drunken daze, a crystal clear image of Calvin rose to a place of prominence that could not be ignored.

She saw Calvin's piercing hazel eyes bore into her, his strong hands claim her flesh, and his full lips press themselves against hers. It was a strikingly vivid flashback to the night she'd bared her soul, and he'd promised her she was worthy of love, of his love. She felt his earnest longing for her thunder through her body so powerfully, it nearly took her breath away.

Stumbling back from the gorgeous man, she watched his expression change from one of desire to one of confusion, his eyes narrowing and eyebrows furrowing. He turned to say something to his companion in Spanish.

"I'm so sorry," Paisley gasped, as surprised at her reaction as he was. Allison barely turned her head to acknowledge what was going on.

"I'm sorry, I can't," she attempted to explain. "Please, enjoy my friend." She gestured toward Allison with a reassuring smile on her face.

She wasn't sure if Allison had ever indulged in a threesome with two men, but Paisley couldn't imagine a more golden opportunity than the one laid before her like a red carpet leading to the Oscars. Allison appeared on board as the shorter man sandwiched her between his body and his brother's. Paisley thought she'd heard the taller of the two called Juan, and the shorter, Marco. Even if that wasn't quite what she heard, she decided those would be the names she called them in her head, and she began to think of them as a pair out on the town in Manhattan, hoping to come away with tales of wild and salacious adventures they could boast about when they were old men.

Marco practically ripped Allison's lacy red bra from her body with one hand as Juan pulled her matching thong panties down her slim thighs. Once she stepped out of them, she was completely nude and wedged between the two men. Marco pressed his pelvis into her ass, still wearing his well-fitting black pants, while Juan grasped her face in his palms as his tongue explored every nook and cranny of her mouth.

Allison seemed overwhelmed by the attention, her moans rising to the ceiling with such volume, Paisley wondered if they'd get a knock on the door from hotel management asking them to tone it down. *That never happens at The Factory,* she mused as if it were a source of pride, then quickly swatted the thought away like a rogue fly in the kitchen.

She reclined on the bed for a better vantage, watching as Juan slowly pushed Allison down onto the bed until Paisley caught her head in her lap. She cradled her friend, stroking her fingertips down her collarbone and arms, whispering in a soft, soothing voice, "You're about to be taken by two men. You up for that?" She wanted to make sure Allison was still capable of giving consent; otherwise she was shutting the entire show down.

"Yes, ma'am," came her garbled, but still perfectly coherent reply. "Yes, I am, and it feels incredible."

She arched her back as Juan spread her legs with his palms. He planted a series of kisses on her inner thigh while Marco finished removing his pants, laying them over the wingback chair that sat at an angle next to the bed. When he was completely nude, he made his way onto the bed, his erection and tight, round balls slightly bobbing with his movements. He edged himself toward Allison's mouth, then tilted her head toward him to feed her his engorged cock.

She moaned as Juan's mouth made contact with her clit, which gave Marco just the opening he needed to slide his length deep down her throat. She sputtered and choked as it hit her tonsils, the saliva she'd generated glistening on her lips and chin. Paisley stroked her hair as she recovered.

"Please, baby, suck it some more?" he groaned in his thick accent. She grunted and tried again to swallow his thickness, meeting with the same result as before.

Damn, Paisley thought, *I could have swallowed that thing whole by now*. She laughed to herself thinking about how vanilla Allison was. She expected her friend to be a more accomplished cocksucker with as much experience as she had.

Juan was licking Allison's pussy with the primary goal of getting her wet enough to fuck. He climbed onto the bed, positioning himself on his knees with several inches of his stiff cock jutting out the top of his hand. It was obvious he had but one intention, and that was to slide his manhood into Allison's now dripping cunt.

"Uh, you need to put a condom on," Paisley scolded him with her eyebrow arched to show she meant business.

"Oh, of course!" he apologized. He went to find one in his pants pocket and returned victorious with a gold packet. She looked on approvingly as he unrolled it down his shaft.

"You like to watch me fuck your friend?" Juan asked as he guided his cock into Allison's waiting hole. She groaned with the intrusion, but Marco quieted her by stuffing his thick tool farther down her throat.

Paisley nodded. She hadn't spent much time as a

voyeur, but right now watching these two gorgeous men have their way with her friend did offer a certain degree of titillation. She couldn't believe she wasn't compelled to join in, but every time she considered it, she thought of Calvin again.

I just need a little time to get over him. I'll be back in the saddle in a week or two.

Allison clearly wasn't thinking about anything other than the two men taking pleasure from her body. She reached one arm up to wrap it around Paisley's neck, which meant she felt each forceful thrust of Juan's cock as it moved Allison's lithe body up the bed. The energy soaked into her as if she were a shock absorber.

Watching the expressions on the men's faces as Allison serviced their cocks was so hot, it made Paisley want to touch herself. She managed to get one hand underneath Allison and attempted to weave her way up the layers of her skirt and between her crossed legs. Finally, she was able to slide one finger under her panties and swipe it down her moistened slit. Not surprisingly, she was soaked with desire.

"Let's switch," Marco suggested. He seemed somewhat frustrated by the fact that Allison couldn't maintain a solid rhythm deep-throating his dick.

"I've got a better idea." Juan had a gleam in his eye. "You ever do DP, mami?" he asked Allison, who definitely appeared more sober than she had when this delightful ménage à trois first began.

"No?" She shook her head, looking a bit nervous. "I've done anal plenty of times, though."

"You wanna try?" Marco's words were laced with hope.

Allison turned to Paisley. "Why aren't you fucking?"

"I...I just don't feel like it tonight. I thought it would be more fun to watch you enjoy yourself with two men. It's your first threesome, right?"

She nodded, suddenly thrilled with the idea of having everyone's attention devoted to her. She loved being the star of the show. "So, yes to DP?" She looked to Paisley again for confirmation.

"Well, I certainly enjoy it, but don't do anything you're not comfortable with." Paisley said it with the perfect tone to make it seem like a dare. She licked her lips in anticipation of watching something she'd never seen done live in person before, at least not from the vantage of observer.

"Anyone got lube?" Marco asked as he unwrapped a condom and rolled it down his cock. Though he was the taller of the two, his cock was slightly less girthy, which would hopefully make the anal part of the experience more comfortable for her friend.

"Oh, I have lube!" Paisley chimed in, nearly forgetting that she never left the house without a travel-size vial of it along with a few condoms. She was a veritable Sex Girl Scout.

She retrieved the lube from her pocketbook and handed it to Marco, who gave it a generous squeeze, dripping it onto his cock and Allison's ass once she turned onto her hands and knees and presented it.

"What do I do?" she asked, rocking back slightly and looking toward Paisley for guidance.

"Let him penetrate your ass first. It's going to take him a little time." She shot him a warning look before saying, "Go slow."

"Sí, sí, of course." He spread her cheeks and pressed the tip of his cock against her puckered hole.

Allison gasped as she felt the pressure against her anus.

"Ahhhhhh, not so fast," she winced as she squeezed her eyes shut.

Paisley lay down on the bed facing her friend. "Relax," she advised. She reached down and began to fondle Allison's clit with her index finger. Her friend's thighs began to tremble from the competing sensations of pain and pleasure. "Relax," Paisley said again. "When he's in all the way, it will start to feel good, I promise."

She moaned as Marco made a little more headway, his hands grasping her hips to hold him steady. His face was contorted in a grimace, the veins visibly throbbing on his shaft even through the thin layer of latex. She glanced at Juan, who was stroking his cock patiently while he watched the show.

Allison screamed as Marco broke through. Once the head of his cock passed the tight ring of muscles, the rest of him slid in easily. Suddenly he was balls deep inside her ass with an unmistakable look of ecstasy painted on his face. He waited for her to adjust to his size, making the slightest moves back and forth as Paisley continued to rub her clit. Once she began to buck against his cock, he knew it was safe for him to start thrusting into her.

Juan also knew it was his signal. Paisley moved out of the way so Juan could very carefully slide beneath them. Marco helped by pulling Allison up against his chest, his cock still buried to the hilt inside her ass. She slowly eased herself back down, and Juan helped her guide his cock between her lips until she was sitting on top of it. For a moment, she was suspended between the two, impaled by cocks on both sides and breathless with pleasure.

When her tongue finally worked again, she could only manage to say, "Holy fuck," as the two men began to move inside her.

Paisley perched at the head of the bed, propped up on some pillows, her legs spread so she could reach her clit. She couldn't get over how sexy her friend looked in the throes of passion with two enormous cocks pumping in and out of her from both sides. Finally, she was able to forget about Calvin as she concentrated on how amazing it must feel to have both of those sexy men buried deep inside.

Allison was carried away by orgasm after orgasm as the men struggled to keep from blowing their loads. The looks of concentration on their faces, the way their brows knitted with determination as sweat beaded at their temples was so erotic, not to mention the chorus of animalistic moans and grunts that filled the room. Paisley loved being a fly on the wall, the quiet observer of this gratuitous display of raw sexual energy, beautiful bodies working in sync to create a glorious, thundering vortex of orgasmic delight.

She held back, waiting to explode at the precise moment the two men did. Allison had already come a half dozen times by Paisley's count, and she was thoroughly impressed by the restraint the men showed. Finally, Marcos shouted that he was about to explode. He pulled out of Allison's ass and flipped her over with one hand while the other ripped off the condom.

As choreographed as Juan's reaction was as he gracefully glided to his knees, Paisley would have bet money the friends had performed this scene before. Sure enough, both leaned over her stomach, cocks in hand as they sent streams of thick, white semen flying across her body, landing in pearly stripes on her abdomen.

Their cocks continued to jerk in their hands as they coaxed out every last drop, which was hot, but not as hot as the looks of satisfaction on their faces. That sent Paisley over the edge, and she groaned when the waves crashed through her, her body convulsing with each intensely plea-surable spasm. While she was still recovering, Marco eased himself off the bed to retrieve a stack of towels so everyone could clean themselves up.

"Well?" Paisley managed to articulate as soon as air could fill her lungs again.

"No regrets." Allison smiled, still splayed out on the bed. "No regrets at all."

TWENTY-THREE

On the subway ride back to Allison's apartment Paisley's numbness shattered like glass. Once the shock wore off – she hadn't even realized she was numb – the tears attacked.

She thought she was just being the badass adult she knew herself to be, pushing aside all the confusion, hurt and guilt over what had happened in Ocean City to make way for a fresh start. But when she completely sobered, her cells depleted of that soothing tonic, she recognized the emptiness left behind. Which is why, when Allison glanced her way, she found her friend sobbing discreetly into her palms.

"Oh, my god, what's wrong?" She sounded so bewildered because she had never once seen her friend cry.

Paisley tried to do her usual blowing-it-off thing. Shaking her head and forcing a smile, she answered, "Nothing."

"Tell me what happened with Calvin," Allison asked, remembering his name.

"I'm sad because I'm not good enough for him," Paisley admitted. Even though she'd thought up those words a dozen or more times, there was something seriously liber-ating about speaking them aloud, something that gave them more credence.

Allison seemed surprised. "How can you say that?"

Paisley took her friend's hand in hers, which was a little cold from pressing against the metal bar on top of the subway bench. She didn't expect Allison to understand since she was virtually clueless when it came to Paisley's past.

"Let me tell you about Calvin Mitchell," she offered. "First of all, he comes from an absolutely adorable family, where he's the oldest of three sons. His parents are still married; his dad's a detective with the state police, and his mother is a nurse. Secondly, he's a self-made businessman who is quite successful, especially considering he's only twenty-six years old. Thirdly, he is in no way, shape, or form a swinger, and even though he's worked at the club for a couple weeks now, he has no desire to try it himself. He's a one-woman man."

"I'm failing to see any negatives," Allison answered. "So what is the problem?"

"The problem is that I come from a nut-case family. I'm ten years older than him, and I like to get it on with a multi-tude of men. See the problem now?"

"Only with the last excuse." Allison tilted her head thoughtfully. "But you just gave up a chance at two hot guys. I knew something had to be wrong with you!" She smiled with sudden understanding.

"I feel guilty for fucking him over." She let another tear slip down her cheek.

And it wasn't just Calvin she'd let down. What about her bosses? Who knew what kind of havoc her blackmailers had wreaked since she skipped town? Part of her didn't even want to know.

"How have you fucked him over exactly?"

Paisley sighed. She couldn't explain the entire story to Allison, so she didn't even know why she was bothering. She tried to wipe away her tears with the back of her hand.

She felt something rush through her just then, and it wasn't the subway car grinding to another obnoxious, jerking halt. It was a spike of panic rippling through her nerves that made her think something bad – something outside of her control – had just happened. She couldn't put her finger on what it might be, but she felt certain she was about to get some bad news.

A few minutes later when they arrived at their stop, she crawled into Allison's apartment feeling on the verge of collapse. Cursing herself for the tight dress and high heels, Allison wasn't much better off.

Stripping off the now infamous red dress, Allison disappeared into the bathroom to shower, while Paisley fell like a zombie into her friend's bed, forgetting to check her phone. She'd survived the drive and night out on only a few hours of sleep, not to mention the weeks-long emotional roller coaster she'd been riding. She'd get back to trying to sort things out in the morning.

"What did you do?!" Paisley's voice thundered down the dark hallway at the ungodly hour of 4 AM. "What the fuck did you do?"

Grabbing her phone on the way, Paisley had stumbled into the kitchen for a drink after waking up with an incredibly dry mouth. She finally felt brave enough to look at the messages she'd missed during their night out on the town. She wasn't surprised to have missed a call from Leah, one from Casey, and one from Cap, as though they placed some sort of bet on whose call she would answer.

But what she *was* surprised to find was a text sent to Calvin at 1:45 AM, which would have been around the time they'd arrived home and Paisley had crashed.

Only one person could be behind this travesty, and that was, of course, Allison. She'd said:

> Paisley misses you so much, but she doesn't think she's good enough for you. She probably won't answer your calls, but if you want to come up here yourself, the address is ...

She'd proceeded to give him the address of her apartment.

As her feet crossed the bedroom's threshold, she hissed again, "What the fuck did you do?!"

Allison was just barely stirring beneath the tangle of sheets.

"Why are you screaming at me?" Allison barely lifted her blonde head off the pillow so she could get the words out without being muffled.

"Why did you text Calvin?" Paisley plopped down on the bed, her weight shifting Allison's entire body on the mattress.

"Hey, watch where you're parking that big ass of yours," Allison groaned. Then she got defensive: "Look, it's pretty obvious you're in love with him. And how the hell are you ever going to be happy if you don't swallow your pride and go after somebody who's probably perfect for you?"

"It's too late now," Paisley insisted. "I don't want him coming up here."

"Well, maybe you won't have a choice." With that, she harrumphed and threw her body over to face the opposite way.

Paisley wished her head would stop throbbing. She noticed Calvin had not texted back, and he should have gotten the message around the same time the club closed up for the night. Now it was four in the morning, and he should be asleep.

If he'd wanted to respond, he'd had ample opportunity, but Paisley was certain he figured it out for himself.

After all, he's a bright kid.

Sunday slipped into Monday, the former made notable by intense thunderstorms that rocked the city throughout the course of the evening. Paisley ignored two phone calls, one from Casey and one from Leah. They didn't leave voicemails. She assumed her bosses were so angry that they wanted to deliver the full brunt of their fury in person.

Little did they know, she wasn't coming back to work and would, in fact, only be returning to Maryland to clean out her apartment and tie up loose ends. She planned to draft a resignation letter at some point during the day and send it out the next morning, but she was having a hard time getting started.

She was having a hard time doing anything, if she was honest with herself. Allison and Ian had gone back to work and left Paisley alone in the apartment to brood. The thunderstorms had left lingering clouds that obscured her ability to think clearly. After all the chaos of the last few days, it was strange to sit in utter silence.

Allison had promised to ask their boss if there were any positions open for Paisley. She sighed with frustration at the thought of having to return to the event management company where she met Allison and worked for two years before she took the job at The Factory. She wasn't happy there, which is why she'd taken a chance on something totally different in a whole new location.

But returning to her old position would be easy, and at least she would know what to expect. Plus, any threats to expose her past would likely be met with apathy as it was a huge company, and no one cared what she did unless she wasn't doing her job.

Maybe just being another faceless number at a big company is the right place for someone like me, a place where I can blend in.

If The Factory ended up closing down over all this, she would never forgive herself.

Despite how hard she tried not to think of him, she was disappointed she never heard back from Calvin. It was one thing for him to ignore her on a romantic level, but he'd been the conduit between herself and his father.

After binging on a silly, mindless, but nevertheless entertaining series on Netflix, Paisley decided to log into Allison's laptop to draft her resignation letter and update her resume. She was struggling to decide how to handle her most recent stint of employment. She decided it might be better if she left it off.

Her train of thought was derailed by her phone ringing. "I thought I turned that damn thing off," she snarled to the empty room.

Considering it might be Allison, or even her old boss, she decided to take a peek. It was Casey again. *Damn it.* With trembling fingers, she grabbed the phone off the counter in the kitchen and managed a nervous hello.

"Oh, thank god you answered. Paisley, I'm standing downstairs in the lobby, but I guess you have to buzz me up?"

Paisley's stomach flip-flopped. "You're where?"

"I'm downstairs. I need to talk to you."

"You drove all the way up here?" she asked, incredulous. It was at least a four-hour drive. She wasn't used to anyone going out of their way or making any extra effort for her.

As the reality sank in, her heart started to pound. *If Casey came all the way up here to talk to me, it can only mean something very bad has happened.*

Her mind flashed with images of the man with the gun and the older woman who may or may not have been Evelyn Bridges knocking it out of his hands. She sucked in a breath as she pushed the button near the door to let Casey in.

"Thanks," was all Casey said, and then Paisley had no choice but to station herself at the door and wait for her to arrive.

By the time Casey knocked, Paisley's heart was beating as wildly as it had during the encounters with her black-mailers. Instead of the impeccably dressed, perfectly coiffed and glammed-up, award-winning realtor and manager she fondly remembered, she found a frazzled, disheveled shell of the woman known as Casey Fontaine.

"Oh my god, what's going on?" Paisley ushered the older woman inside the small apartment. Casey followed her to the living room where she collapsed on the loveseat as if she'd just run a marathon. Paisley remembered her manners and offered her guest a drink.

"Something cold – just water – would be divine," Casey answered with gratitude. She wiped the sweat from her forehead. Paisley was shocked her mentor perspired. Even in the blistering heat they'd had at the beach that summer, she'd never seen any evidence Ms. Fontaine even had sweat glands.

Paisley came back from the kitchen with a glass of ice water and handed it to her boss. "I still can't believe you're here, that you drove all the way up here."

"You wouldn't answer our calls, and this conversation would be better in person," she answered, then took a long sip of the water.

Every nerve in Paisley's body was on fire as she awaited the words about to form on Casey's lips.

"Well, I'm all ears now, so please fill me in."

"When we first got your text Saturday morning, we were pretty baffled. Then you didn't show up for work, and neither did Calvin. We were really afraid that something terrible had happened to you both. Cap even called his buddy who's an OC cop to see if he could go check on you.

"That's when we found out you were gone. No one could get ahold of Calvin either. Of course, all that was going on while we were trying to run the Saturday night party without you and with only one security guard. Even Leah and the baby came in to help clean up because it was a busy night, and we were short-staffed."

Her heart sank as guilt filled every cell in her body. "I'm so sorry to leave you guys in such a bad position—"

With a dismissive wave of her hand, Casey plodded on with her story. "Calvin came in around midnight, and he was acting so weird, like he wanted to tell us what was going on, but he couldn't. I asked him if he'd heard from you, and he just shook his head. I was planning to confront him again when we were closing up, and there weren't so many people around, but I didn't get a chance to."

At that, Paisley's heart nearly burst from her chest. "What happened?"

"We had the club cleared and were starting the clean-up. I was in the office getting the deposit ready when I heard a scream coming from the front of the building. I rushed into the lobby and didn't see anything, so I stepped out into the parking lot. Leah was standing there with Lincoln in his sling, and there were three people, couldn't really see their faces, all in a line confronting her. They were making some demands and yelling."

"Oh, god," Paisley gasped. She thought it would have been two people, the man and woman from the parking lot at her apartment. *Who the fuck was this third person?*

"They told me to get up against the wall next to Leah, and I swear to god, Paisley, I thought I might soil myself! I kept wondering where Cap was, or even Calvin or Trent. I asked them what they wanted and tried to reason with them, you know.

"The one man, he was young, I could hear it in his voice. He had a gun – otherwise I would have told Leah to make a run for the car. Thank god the baby was asleep! Oh god, Paisley, I have never been so scared in my entire life."

Paisley noticed she was trembling, her pale, veiny hands literally vibrating with fear as they lay in her lap. The further along Casey got in her story, the more physically ill Paisley became. The amount of guilt she felt for getting Casey and the Sheldons involved in such a horrible situation was like the weight of the world resting on her shoulders.

"I'm so sorry, Casey," was all she could murmur.

"So he told me they wanted all the cash we had on premises. Then he said that you were a criminal, and they had plans to expose you and the club to the media if we didn't cooperate. He said you had stolen money and had been an accessory to the murder of your grandparents."

She shook her head as her eyes began to fill with tears. The secret past she had tried so hard to keep hidden had been unleashed, and in the worst way possible.

"I didn't kill my grandparents," was all she could say. She looked into Casey's eyes, trying to see if there was any empathy or understanding there, but all she saw was a frightened woman who needed to spill her guts.

"Then I realized that one of the three people was Jason, the security guard you fired. He stepped forward out of the shadows, and I recognized him. He said he was going inside to get the money while we stayed there at gunpoint."

"What?!" She could scarcely believe her ears. Somehow they'd gotten connected with Jason, and he'd given up the club location? It was all too much to take in. She felt so nauseated, at any moment she might need to jump up and run to the bathroom to relinquish the contents of her stomach.

"Oh, Paisley, it was so damn scary. So, Jason went through the front doors, and the two other people just started yelling...the younger man and a middle-aged woman. They were yelling about all the horrible things you'd done, how you'd been on drugs and stolen your grandparents' life savings, and how you deserved everything you had coming. They said you ran away to New York and changed your name so you could dodge the police, and that you've been running your whole life.

"I didn't know what to believe, Paisley. I didn't think

you were that type of person, but I was just standing there against the wall listening and hoping to god they didn't shoot me, or god forbid Leah or the baby – and then it started to rain. Lincoln woke up crying, and it was just a huge mess.

"When I heard a gunshot go off inside the club, I thought I'd die right then and there. Leah was so brave, though, she held Lincoln and tried to get him to be quiet, and she asked if they would mind if she nursed him."

"Who got shot?!" Paisley interrupted.

"Then we heard a huge commotion and yelling coming from the side of the building. As soon as the two holding us were distracted by the noise, Leah threw open the door to the club and bolted inside. I have never seen anyone move so fast in my entire life, and, of course, she had the baby with her.

"I was petrified, still glued to the wall. I heard footsteps and voices coming around the building, and then the man took the gun off me and fired a shot in that direction. It was so dark; you know there's not good lighting on the sides of the club. I couldn't see a damn thing!"

Paisley could have fallen off the couch, she was so caught up in Casey's story. "Where was Calvin?"

She suddenly realized he was probably still there during all of this. But Casey's eyes were glazed over, and she didn't even seem to hear Paisley's question. The poor, traumatized woman was reliving the scene in fine detail, myriad emotions tearing through her body all over again.

"A shot came from the side of the building, from the shadows, and the man who was pointing his gun at me went down right in front of me." Casey's lips trembled as tears welled in her eyes.

"Then there was screaming. I will never forget the loud, ear-piercing wailing. The woman was yelling, 'You shot my son! You fucking shot my son!' and there was other screaming too – coming from the side of the building where the shot was fired, but I couldn't figure out who it was. And all I could think of was that Cap might have been shot."

"Oh, god!" Paisley couldn't choke out any other words. "Was it Cap? Was it Calvin?" She was on the verge of leaping off the sofa and grabbing Casey by the shoulders if she didn't hurry up and relieve her worry.

A searing pain bolted through her as if lightning had struck her heart. If something had happened to either one of them, she didn't know how she could go on. *If Calvin got shot* – she couldn't even complete her thought.

In that moment, her feelings for him became completely undeniable. She cared for him in a way she had never cared for another human being. And it was much deeper and more complex than friendship; it was a feeling she had never truly experienced. One she had always been afraid to hold to the light and accept as truth. She'd never trusted her heart with it before.

"They came out from the shadows dragging Jason with them, and he was kicking and screaming. He'd been shot, and the other man was lying in a pool of blood while the woman collapsed on top of him. That's when I finally pulled out my phone and called 9-1-1." Casey shuddered as the tears spilled down her cheeks.

She sighed and tried to clear her throat while wringing her hands together in her lap. "I honestly don't know if I will ever recover from this nightmare."

Paisley could think of nothing but Calvin. She hated elevating him over her bosses, but the thought of losing him was more than she could bear. "Calvin didn't get shot, though? He's okay?" she finally asked in a weak voice, unable to handle the question marks churning like blades, ripping up her insides.

Casey nodded, sniffling with the onslaught of mucus that accompanied her tears. Paisley handed her a box of tissues from the other side of the couch. "Everyone was okay, except Jason and –" The older woman's face grew as dark as a graveyard on a moonless night. "Paisley, do you realize who was blackmailing you?"

Paisley nodded, her face equally grim. "It was my mother."

"Yes," Casey answered. "But the man who died, his name was William Jones, and he was your mother's son, so –"

She hadn't put two and two together when Casey was relaying the events of that wretched night. But if what she said was true, then the other blackmailer had been her brother.

TWENTY-FOUR

The rhythm of the wheels spinning against the pavement was beginning to numb her mind. She'd thought so long and hard about what Casey said that she wasn't sure she ever wanted to think so deeply again. After filling Paisley in on everything that had happened since she'd left Maryland, Casey was disappointed when Paisley announced she'd be tendering her resignation effective immediately.

Her boss's eyes clouded over like a hurricane threatening to make landfall. Casey was not a person you wanted to let down, and Paisley hated seeing the disappointment on her face. She expected her to try to talk her out of resigning, but not in the way she did. Casey really knew how to appeal, not to the mind, but to the heart.

It was late afternoon, and the sun streaming through the windows silhouetted the older woman, giving her an ethereal glow. Without her thick layers of makeup and her perfectly set hair, she looked her age. She was a woman turning sixty who had spent a lifetime exceeding expectations and breaking down barriers, not to mention forging relationships. Paisley respected her opinion perhaps more than anyone else's, which was why she was patiently waiting for her to speak her piece in response to Paisley's resignation.

"So that's it. You're just quitting," she finally broke her silence. "What they said about you is true?"

"What?! No!" Paisley resisted. "Not all of it." She exhaled with a heavy sigh as she realized she needed have this conversation for the second time in the last week after avoiding it at all costs for years.

Wow, when your past comes back to haunt you, it's a persistent motherfucker, isn't it?

"So what is it? What are you hiding? What are you running from?"

"That woman – my 'mother,' if you can call her that – left me on my grandparents' porch when I was a baby. They raised me and tried really hard to keep me from becoming what my mother was, which was basically a loser. But I guess those genes run pretty deep because I got involved with a horrible guy when I was sixteen. He forced me to rob my grandparents' life savings so he could pay off some gang members who were threatening to kill him.

"But once I had the money in hand, I decided to escape Kentucky and my shitty life. When Jimmy found out, he went over to my grandparents' house to try to get the money himself. When they refused to give him anything, and they didn't know where I'd gone, he was irate. My grandfather had a gun, and anyway, Jimmy ended up shooting both of them dead, but not before my grandfather shot him. I was already in New York by the time it happened."

"Oh, Paisley," Casey whispered, her eyes glassy with

tears, "that must have been traumatic. I don't even know what to say."

"I started my new life with their money. It had their blood on it," Paisley explained, a lump firmly embedded in her throat.

"Have you ever considered talking to someone, you know, like a therapist, about this stuff? It sounds like you're harboring a lot of guilt."

Paisley smirked. "Uh, no. I don't think therapists are my style." She smiled graciously at Casey even though her suggestion left a bad taste in her mouth. "I'm sure therapists are great for other people; don't get me wrong. I just don't think it would help me."

"I see." Casey straightened her spine. "I think I'm going to need to see mine after the events of the weekend, that's for damn sure!"

"You have a therapist?" Paisley wasn't able to hide her shock. She couldn't imagine anyone who had their life more together than Casey Fontaine did. If *she* needed a therapist, there was definitely no hope for a mere mortal like herself.

"Most successful women I know do," she said with a laugh that sounded like a wind chime. "Seriously, Paisley, there's no shame in therapy. I have dealt with my share of issues too..."

She didn't want to pry into Casey's personal business, but she was pretty sure her face conveyed her burning curiosity about what those issues could be. It was hard to fathom what Casey may have overcome to transform into the woman she was. But her knowledge of Casey's background was limited. All she knew was she was single and didn't have any kids. She remembered her saying that when Leah was in labor with Lincoln.

Casey took a deep breath, and in a flash there was something about her that looked almost delicate, fragile. "My ex-husband was an alcoholic," she explained, "and he abused me, physically and emotionally. I actually fled New York to get away from him. That's when I ended up in Ocean City, where my parents had moved back in the 80s. So I know all about escape, my dear. I ran away from my problems too."

Paisley could scarcely believe her ears. Casey was such a strong, imposing woman – much like herself – it was difficult to picture her as a victim.

"I'm so sorry," was all she could think of to say, but it felt woefully inadequate.

"There are some situations where it's best to run," Casey continued. "That's what my therapist told me. When your adversaries are dangerous and irrational, when no amount of sitting down to talk through things would change the situation, then the best thing you can do is leave. You're not going to win a battle against an irrational person."

"That makes sense."

"But," she continued, her eyes gleaming, "when the people you're facing are reasonable and rational, that's when running away is weak. You owe it to them and yourself to be equally reasonable and rational, to throw your whole self into working things out. Especially if you were the one at fault."

"So you're saying I shouldn't be running away from Ocean City."

"Running away from your blackmailers makes perfect sense," she clarified. "It was a terrible situation that wasn't going to have a good resolution for you. Now your mother is in custody, and your brother is dead. You have to deal with that, and I know it's not going to be easy. But there are other people in Ocean City who care about you and who did nothing wrong. Leaving them high and dry is not fair."

"I see." Her whole body stiffened as she considered what going back to face Cap, Leah and Calvin would be like. "But I'm sure everyone is angry with me. I don't know if I deserve their forgiveness."

"I can't tell you what to do," Casey answered. "But I know you are a strong woman who is perfectly capable of facing her problems head-on. I have every confidence you'll make the right choice."

And that conversation was why Paisley was speeding down to Ocean City, her tires rumbling on the endless black pavement. Casey had decided to stay a few days in Manhattan to visit some old friends, so Paisley was returning by herself to a great unknown. She hadn't been in contact with anyone, and she had no idea what to expect when she got there.

I hate not knowing what to expect. But she pressed on anyway.

Monday was a good day to return to Ocean City. The weekend tourist traffic had cleared out, leaving only the regular weekday visitors to clog the streets and the boardwalk. Paisley dropped her stuff off at her apartment, which she'd abandoned with the air conditioner switched off and all the food rotting in the refrigerator. She opened the windows, emptied the refrigerator, and headed down to the beach.

The sun was still blazing high in the sky, but there was a nice breeze coming off the ocean. As the surf rushed across her toes, she noticed the water was warmer than the last time she'd been down to the shore. It was hard to believe summer was already on its downswing toward fall. Soon the tourists would be packing up their stuff, and another season would be over and done with. She struggled to remember how dead things were when she had first arrived at the end of April, but she knew it was an entirely different world than tourist season.

There is something cleansing about the ocean.

Her eyes took in the vast blue that stretched to infinity. Maybe she associated it with healing because her grandmother always extolled the virtues of salt water for fixing everything from a cut to a sore throat. Maybe it was because being washed in the waves was a baptism of sorts. Either way, as the surging tide rushed over her, licking her wounds, it destroyed that tiny voice she'd allowed to become too loud in the past month. It was the voice that said she wasn't good enough.

She was surprised she hadn't heard a peep out of Calvin or the Sheldons since the weekend. Casey said she'd tell Cap and Leah that she was headed back down to Maryland to sort things out.

I guess they're waiting for me to come to them.

So, as she sat on the beach, the sun beating down on her and the water cleansing her soul, she pulled out her phone and sent both Calvin and Leah the same text. It simply asked, *Can we talk?*

Leah was the first to respond. She suggested Paisley come over to their house that evening, as the police still had the club closed down while they processed the crime scene. Paisley didn't know who she was more nervous to face: Cap or Leah. Taking them on at the same time was going to require every ounce of strength she could muster, but she felt her time spent at the beach earlier that afternoon had rejuvenated and prepared her for the challenge.

Very little traffic impeded her progress out to Berlin, where Cap and Leah lived on the shores of Ayres Creek. Their stately house looked exactly as it did the other times she had visited: grand but welcoming as it waded into the reedy waters of the creek.

The door swung open, revealing Cap in an old t-shirt and fraying olive-colored shorts. He held his son in one arm like a football. The baby had filled out since birth and now had the slightest chubbiness around his thighs. His bald head was perfectly round and smooth, and his creamy white skin contrasted against Cap's tan.

"Hey, Cap, thanks for having me over. Can I come in?" Paisley asked meekly.

"Of course." Cap had a weariness about him. There was no smirk or dimples on his face, and that worried her.

"Where's Leah?"

"She's in the shower. She just got in from a run."

"Oh." *I wish things didn't feel so awkward.*

Cap walked into the living room, where he sat down on the beige loveseat and shifted the baby so his little chin rested on his dad's hulking shoulder. He gestured for Paisley to sit down, but she remained standing to admire the cherubic infant tucked into his father's arms. He was sleeping so peacefully, his little round cheeks bunched up and his lips slightly moving as if he were suckling at his mother's breast.

"He dreams about boobs, just like his dad," Cap joked. She appreciated his attempt to lighten the mood.

Leah rushed into the room from the hallway that led to

their master bedroom with a towel wrapped around her head and moisture clinging to her shoulders. She wore a plain navy tank top and plaid shorts that showed off her shapely thighs.

"Sorry, I was trying to hurry. Thanks for waiting." She placed herself next to her husband on the loveseat, and Paisley took that as a signal to choose a seat across from them in the armchair.

"I don't know where to start," Paisley began, trying to smile and set a light tone, though she wasn't sure there was really a way to do that under the circumstances.

She expected Cap to do the talking, but it was Leah who opened her mouth first. Then Paisley remembered Leah had managed a large staff at The Pearl, an upscale hotel on the north end of town. She likely had more experience supervising staff than her husband did at his little fishing shop just blocks off the boardwalk.

"We kind of feel the same way. You put our club – and really, our lives – in a lot of danger, Paisley."

She wasn't surprised that Leah was cutting to the chase. "I know, and I am so sorry for the way things turned out. I was trying to circumvent anything – "

"We know about Calvin and his father, Detective Mitchell," Leah shared. "I know you were trying to handle everything and to protect us from finding out, but we're disappointed you didn't come to us in the very beginning to let us know what was going on, especially since our business and our reputations were in jeopardy. And not just Cap and myself. Casey too. You know her father is a retired congressman, right? She has worked really hard to keep her two lives separate."

Paisley's bottom lip began to tremble. Most of the time, she tried to act selflessly. That was one of the reasons she excelled at her job in event management and also in her position at The Factory, at least up until she was attacked. But when she objectively examined her motives for not telling her bosses about being blackmailed, she knew she'd been scared of having to tell them about her past. She wanted to protect the club too, of course, but not telling them what was going on had more to do with protecting her own reputation than theirs.

She took a deep breath and prepared to defend herself without coming across defensive. "I regret how I handled it," she admitted. "I acted selfishly because I didn't want you to know where I came from and what I'd been through. But now I realize all that stuff made me who I am today, and it was overcoming the demons of my past that made me the manager you were looking for. Now that I've gotten to know you, Cap, and Casey better, I realize I should have trusted you not to judge me for things that happened when I was just a teenager."

"Calvin told us," Leah said, her voice still a bit thin, as if she were trying to emotionally disconnect herself from Paisley and the situation at hand. Paisley recognized it as the cool, businesslike tone she'd heard Leah employ from time to time when dealing with club members, vendors, or other staff.

"Speaking of which, hiring Calvin under false pretenses – he's not in the lifestyle – wasn't an example of exercising good judgment either."

Paisley let out a heavy sigh as she studied her bosses' faces. She could see in Cap's clear blue eyes that this was as hard for him as it was for her. Leah was more difficult to read. She could put on an incredibly cryptic poker face when she wanted to.

"I was told repeatedly that they would be making an

arrest before the August first deadline I'd been given. I truly believed the suspects would be in custody before they were able to hurt me, and certainly before being able to damage the club. I really didn't think they knew where it was, and I have no idea how they hooked up with Jason."

"Well," Leah continued, "one thing that's coming out of the investigation, from what Calvin has told me, is that your mother and her relatives have been tracking you for quite some time. She'd been to New York and spoken with some of your associates there. She was in Ocean City figuring out your connections for a few weeks, and while it's not clear how she first contacted Jason, we've now learned that he is not the only person affiliated with the club that she spoke with."

"Wow, really?" Her eyes widened, wondering who at The Factory had thrown her under the bus – and if they'd done it knowingly. It sounded as though Cap and Leah had been in close contact with Calvin.

She had tried to suppress her worry that Calvin wouldn't speak to her, but it was flaring up with a vengeance. "How is Calvin? He didn't return my text earlier."

Cap cleared his throat and spoke up, "He's having a hard time with all this, Paisley. He's a real good guy; we all like him quite a bit. But he is the one who fired the shot that killed William Jones, and that's going to weigh on him for a long time."

"Oh no!" she gasped. For some reason, she had assumed it was Cap who fired the shot. But then again, she knew Calvin had a gun. Casey hadn't told her that part of the story, and she hadn't asked.

"He's having trouble reconciling everything, so I'm not surprised you haven't heard from him," Leah offered. Paisley noted an undercurrent of protectiveness in her voice. "From what I understand, you had developed a close relationship with him."

Her heart rate quickened at the thought of Calvin, and despite trying to breathe in deeply, she wasn't able to control it. A slight blush crept across her cheeks, and it wasn't from the sun she'd soaked up on the beach. She didn't give Leah and Cap a real answer, but the flush on her face served as one.

"I know he's quite a bit younger than you, and he's not lifestyle," Leah continued. "I'm just concerned, that's all."

"You're saying you don't approve?"

"It's not my place to comment on your personal relationships," she answered, "but I don't want either of you to get hurt. Though it seems it may be too late..."

"That's why I resisted him for so long," Paisley sighed. "But I guess it doesn't matter now. He probably doesn't want anything to do with me."

"Just be patient with him," Cap piped up. "He may not be lifestyle material, and you don't want to push him."

"I wasn't planning on it," Paisley retorted. Talking about Calvin was not adding to her comfort with the conversation. "So what about The Factory?" She was anxious to change the subject.

Leah shifted on the loveseat pulling one leg up onto the cushion and wrapping her fingers around her shin, hugging her knee to her body. She glanced at her husband, then back at Paisley. "We don't know yet. The story is still unfolding in the media. We've received a few personal calls from hosts who had our cell numbers and did as much damage control as possible.

"I'm guessing the club's phone is ringing off the hook, but the building hasn't been released yet, so we haven't been able to monitor how members are reacting. We sent them all an email; Casey wrote a rather judicious explanation before she left for New York. We tried to calm them without providing too many details. And we turned off commenting on the Facebook group so things don't get out of hand there. So we don't really know how it went over – yet."

Paisley was impressed that they seemed to have their bases covered, at least what they could control. "What are they saying in the media?"

"So far just that a man was shot at a private club in Berlin," Cap answered. "Detective Mitchell has really been our savior as far as releasing limited information to the media is concerned. He told them the investigation is ongoing, and the man's identity will be released pending notification of his next of kin. It's not even been forty-eight hours yet, after all. We're hoping since he's not a local, people won't dig too deep."

Paisley shook her head, trying to stabilize the whirlwind spinning inside it. She stared past the loveseat where her bosses sat to the little wooden fishing boat docked on Ayres Creek. As she watched it bob up and down on the rippling tide, an enormous puffy cloud all but obscured the majesty of the early evening sun. She wondered if another storm was coming in.

A long, breathy sigh escaped her mouth. "I should have just taken the bullet myself in the parking lot..."

"What?! Why would you say that?" Leah snapped.

"They confronted me in the parking lot at Calvin's apartment the night before they came to the club, then followed me to my apartment. They nearly hit me with their car, then the man pulled his gun on me when I was trying to make my escape."

"Oh, god, Paisley. Why didn't you come here instead of going to New York? We would have helped in any way we could."

"I didn't want them to follow me here," she answered. "I feel positively horrible that this is happening. I know I don't deserve your forgiveness – not to mention my job – but I will do anything I can to help you save the club."

"I don't know what can be done," Leah said, her face forlorn. "I'm not sure we can do anything but wait it out and see. I just wish this had happened in the dead of winter instead of at the height of our busiest season. If we're not open by the weekend, we're going to lose a lot of money. But who knows if we'll ever open the doors again at this point?"

Cap put his arm around his wife and pulled her close to his body as the baby sleeping on his shoulder began to stir. Lincoln reached his tiny arms with perfect fingers curled into fists toward his head and stretched, arching his back and yawning with his miniature mouth opened in a perfect O.

Here's this beautiful little family, and I have ruined their lives. Just fucking blew it. The guilt and insecurity she thought she'd washed off in the surf had come back full force.

"We've all been through a lot in the past few days. It's going to take some time for the smoke to clear. I'll tell you, yesterday, I was about ready to pack up the whole family and just start over someplace new," Cap chuckled. "But I've got the shop here and the charter business, and we'd be okay without the club. It's just that we invested a lot of money in it. Casey and I would be out a lot if it failed. And I don't want to see that happen, especially to her when she's so close to retirement."

"What do you want me to do?" Paisley wished they had a simple answer for her, but she knew they wouldn't.

"First thing's first. You need to go talk to Calvin," Leah said. "He needs you right now, even if he's too stubborn to admit it."

"What if he won't talk to me?"

"You have to try. You owe him that much."

TWENTY-FIVE

Twilight was falling like a lavender blanket over Delmarva by the time Paisley got into her car. She shuddered when she remembered the last time she'd left Cap and Leah's house at night, her body surging with endorphins from their wild romp that started in the hot tub and ended in their bed. And then she arrived at her apartment only to be stalked in the parking lot.

That night changed everything. That was when she drove to Calvin's house, and he took her in. Now she knew she needed to return to his place, again unannounced, but she wasn't sure if she'd receive as warm a reception.

I should go home and get my apartment back in order. But everything is so fucking up in the air right now, and there's nothing I can do to control what happens to the club, so I guess I should at least try to tie up a few loose ends.

Those words, "loose ends," tolled like a bell in her mind as she drove down the tree-lined highway back toward Ocean City. She hated to think of Calvin that way, as if he was so trivial. Of all the people she'd met since she moved to Ocean City, he was the one she'd spent the most time with.

And despite her original resistance to feeling anything for him, she had finally accepted that it was futile. She already felt more for him than she ever thought she'd allow herself – than she ever thought herself capable of feeling.

And this is why I kept telling him – not to mention myself – that we couldn't get involved. I knew one of us would get hurt. Now it seems like we both have. I hate it when I am so right.

Once she hit West Ocean City and headed toward the Inlet, she wondered if she might be better served by hitting Seacrets or one of the other clubs. She nearly let the siren lure of Pain in de Asses and Orange Crushes capture her Mazda in their tractor beam of fruity goodness before her good sense forced a turn onto Bayshore Drive toward Calvin's apartment.

She sat in the parking lot for a few minutes in awe of the audacity her classic rock station had to play "There's Gonna Be a Heartache Tonight."

You've gotta be fucking kidding me, she mumbled to herself. It wasn't the first time The Eagles had been a soundtrack for her life. *"Desperado" much?*

When she'd last sat in that parking lot, early on Saturday morning, she thought she was doing the right thing. She'd hoped she could get her things and skip town, maybe incite her blackmailers into following her north, distracting them from Calvin and the club. It just didn't go down how she imagined it would. She thought they might call Calvin or The Factory again, but she didn't expect them to show up there on a night they were open for business and demand all the money in their coffers.

She glanced at her phone to make sure he hadn't responded to her earlier text, but her message to him still floated on the screen with no answer underneath. She considered sending him another to alert him that she was there, but decided she'd rather take her chances just knocking on his door. His car was in the lot, parked only a few spaces from hers.

There's no time like the present.

With a deep breath, she climbed out of the car and pressed the key fob to lock the doors. If nothing else, she had to get in touch with him because she'd left a ton of her things in his apartment. If nothing else, she needed to get them back.

She echoed that phrase in her mind on repeat – *if nothing else* – and she could think of at least a half dozen endings to that sentiment. *If nothing else, I can get some closure and tell him goodbye…*

The walk up to his door was excruciating. Her heart was pounding almost as wildly as it did when she was being confronted by her blackmailers. *My mom and brother,* she corrected herself as she knocked on his door. *My fucking family. What the fuck kind of person has a mother and brother who would pull a gun on her and demand money? Me, that's who.*

She was still deeply entrenched in her pitiful soliloquy when the doorknob turned.

He was wearing his ubiquitous basketball shorts, but with a t-shirt this time, no bare chest in sight. *That's for the best, otherwise I'd want to do naughty things to him instead of figure out where we stand.*

His face was drawn, his jaw tight with tension. She had hoped to see a warm smile spread across his face upon seeing her, but there was nothing there. His lips were straight and frozen in place. She knew that first glimpse at him would give her a lot of answers, and there were so many in his expression, she wondered if she should even bother with the questions she had for him.

"I'm sorry for just showing up," she apologized. "But you didn't answer my text, and I wasn't sure you would even speak to me. If nothing else, I need to get the things I left when I was staying here." Her heart fluttered at hearing the words *if nothing else* come off her lips.

"I've been at my parents' house all day and just got home a few minutes ago," he explained with a stiffness in his tone. If he did have emotion pent up inside, his words were not yielding to it.

"I see." She glanced around his apartment and found it to be messy, which wasn't like him. In the week or so she'd stayed with him, she found him to be a very tidy individual. He'd playfully snapped at her for leaving a wet towel lying around or forgetting a glass in the living room. But it seemed he had abandoned his own fastidious rules since she left.

"Do you want me to go?" she asked. "I can come get my stuff another time if now isn't good."

"You're here now," he answered. "So you might as well do it now."

His coldness gave her a chill from the inside out. She sucked in a sharp breath and breezed by him, trying to convey that she was unaffected by his frosty demeanor, even though inside her heart was breaking. Then she whipped around after the thoughts circulated in her mind: *what if this is my last opportunity to talk to him? What if I never see him again?*

"Are you okay?" Her eyes trailed up his lean but muscular body to meet his. She didn't find his usual bright, sparkling gaze. Instead, his eyes were muddy pools, clouded with the emotions he was struggling to keep inside.

"Yeah, I'm fine."

It was obvious he was not fine. She was overcome with desire to make things right, to restore the sparkle in his eyes. After so many years of taking care of herself, it was a strange sensation to want to take care of someone else, but here it was. She stepped toward him, her feet pressing deliberately into the hallway carpet as she made her way, his face broadcasting a confusing array of emotions as she approached.

"You're not fine."

She was close enough to touch him but refrained. She could feel his body heat rising from the surface of his skin, and she wanted so badly to take his hand into hers and promise things would be okay. But she knew she had no right to make such a promise, and no way of keeping it.

He let a shaky sigh escape his lips as his eyes flashed to the floor. When he lifted them to her again, they were full of tears resting in his lower eyelids, but refusing to fall. She was amazed at how he could balance them there, to have his eyes filled to the brim but still manage to keep the tears back.

"I may not be now, but I will be," was all he said.

She pulled him by the hand to the sofa where they'd been sitting the night she spilled her guts to him about her past. This time the shoe was on the other foot. "Please?" she pleaded with him when there was some resistance. "Please talk to me."

He grunted in acquiescence as he firmly planted himself on the cushion farthest from her. "Why did you leave me?" His voice nearly cracked on the word "leave."

She hadn't expected him to start with her leaving him, but she saw the pain in his eyes still trembling, threatening to spill down his cheeks. She wanted her answer to do those tears justice.

"Oh, god, Calvin, I—" Her voice broke when her own eyes filled with warm, salty liquid.

Just tell him what happened. Tell him why you had to run.

"They called your phone early Saturday morning, and I intercepted it. They were demanding the money by 5 AM. I decided to get my things and head to New York. I was hoping they'd follow me and leave you and the club alone. When I got there—"

"Why didn't you wake me up? I would have come with you."

"I just didn't think—"

"When I woke up to find you missing, I was so scared they'd gotten you. I wasn't supposed to let you out of my sight. I thought I'd failed."

"You didn't fail, Calvin. I'm a grown woman!" She nearly laughed. "I'm not used to being taken care of. I've always done everything on my own. And besides – I felt the same way when Casey was telling me what happened at the club that night. I was afraid I'd lost *you.*"

He ignored that revelation. "Why didn't you answer me when I tried to get in touch with you on Saturday morning?"

"Look, I was wrong to push you away, but please try to understand..." she said, not able to disguise her exasperation. "When I left and went down to my car, they were in the lot waiting for me. They almost hit me with their car, then they followed me to my apartment, where they pulled a gun on me. The guy would have shot me too if the woman hadn't knocked the gun out of his hands."

"You mean your mother?"

She took his statement and ran with it, the emotion rising within her like magma pushing its way up the center of a volcano. "Here I was, fleeing my *mother* and apparently my *brother,* who were threatening and blackmailing me. What kind of person has a family so fucking messed up?"

She didn't give him a chance to answer her rhetorical question. "Me, Calvin. I do. Who comes from a family where her boyfriend murders her grandparents? I do, Calvin. I'm a fucking mess."

Her entire body trembled with a volatile combination of rage and regret: rage from being imprisoned by such horrible circumstances and regret because there was not a damn thing she could do about it.

"I know it's fucked up," he said, his voice finally sounding rich and soothing again, the coldness having melted away. "But it's not your fault, Paisley."

"But it *is* my fault. If I didn't have such a fucked-up past, this wouldn't have happened. I never wanted to get you, or Casey, or the Sheldons involved in any of this. It's amazing that none of you got hurt. I don't know how I would have lived with myself if something had happened to any of you."

"I know how you feel…but I *did* take a life." His voice grew quiet again, and his eyes shifted back to his feet.

"I just found that out. When Casey first told me, for some reason, Cap took the shot."

He shook his head, and finally, a single tear made a gallant escape down his cheek. "I took my gun to work that night. I just had a feeling I might need it since I hadn't heard from you, and I knew from my dad they were having a hard time finding the suspects.

"All night during the party I was on edge, especially since I was the only one who knew that something might go down. I got that club cleared in record time. I didn't want anything to happen while members were there. Trent kept asking me what was wrong, and I wouldn't tell him. Probably a mistake now, as he was pretty blindsided."

She detected a need for him to talk about it. "So what happened?"

"I didn't know anything was going on until this man busted through the side door and started shouting at Trent. It was apparent Trent knew him, and from what I could tell, they were yelling about whether or not Trent was going to help him get the cash from the office. He kept promising Trent would get a cut, but Trent was having none of it. So I approached them and asked what was going on, and that's when I found out the dude had a gun."

Paisley's eyes were just as wide as when Casey shared her side of the story. She leaned toward him, hanging on every word that flew out of his mouth. Casey hadn't disclosed that Jason had a gun too. Maybe she hadn't known.

"Then Cap came from behind him and just took him down – bam – literally knocked the fucking wind out of him. He dropped the gun, but not before it went off once—fortunately, it didn't hit anyone. Cap kicked it away from the guy, then Trent picked it up. Trent said he was going to the office to secure it, and that's when Cap pulled Jason to his feet and shoved him out the side door. Cap is a total badass, by the way. Wow, I was impressed at how strong he is for an old dude."

"He's not *that* old." Paisley laughed, then let him continue with his riveting account.

"Well, he's got almost twenty years on me." Calvin smirked, and Paisley began to see some of the life come back to his eyes. "So when we got outside, we heard the baby start to cry, and it sounded like it was coming from the front.

I thought Cap was going to go ballistic. He was shouting at Jason, demanding he tell us who else was with him.

"As they were yelling at each other, we heard a gun fire two shots from the front of the building, and a bullet struck Jason in the lower leg. About that time, I felt all of my senses get shoved into fucking overdrive. I don't know what came over me, but I ran toward the front of the building, still under the cover of darkness, thank god.

"I saw the two guys – or I thought they were two guys at first. The one was pointing his gun right at me. I heard Leah and the baby screaming, and, fuck, Paisley, I was so scared something was going to happen to them, I pulled the trigger. I probably should have aimed lower, but I was afraid he'd get off another shot and hit us—or Leah—and I just couldn't risk that. I think I ended up hitting him in the chest."

"I am so sorry you had to do that, but thank god you were there. Who knows what would have happened if you hadn't been?"

"I don't know because Cap didn't have a gun, although by the time I got around to the front of the building, Trent had come out the front doors, and he had the other dude's weapon."

"So then what happened?" This was the part Casey glossed over, leaving Paisley with a lot of gaps in her understanding.

"Casey called the cops. I called my dad, who was at home. He beat MSP there and immediately took charge. The ambulance showed up, the coroner; it was pretty fucking chaotic there for a while. They took your mom into custody right away, and then I didn't see her again."

Paisley grew quiet. She was playing the scene out in her head, watching it like a film reel. "I still can't believe it. It sounds like an action movie, not something that happens in real life."

"Art imitates life," Calvin observed. "I'm so sorry about your brother and your mom."

She shrugged. "Well, I never really knew either one of them, so, whatever..."

"I still don't understand why you left." He turned toward her and locked his eyes onto hers. "I thought we were in this together."

"Maybe I don't know how to do 'together,'" she whispered, another tear rolling down her cheek. "I've been left; I've done the leaving. That's why I tried to tell you not to get involved with me."

"I know, you warned me," he agreed, stroking a finger down her cheek. "You'll have to stick around OC for a while, you know. My dad wants to talk to you. You're probably going to have to testify."

Shit. She hadn't even thought about that. Evelyn Bridges was going to stand trial, and god knows what all charges she had racked up.

"Is my mom in jail?"

"Yeah, she couldn't make bail. Flight risk," Calvin explained. "Are you going to talk to her?"

"What?!" Paisley's eyebrows shot up. "Why would I do that?"

"Don't you want to know why she did it? What she has to say for herself?"

She shook her head. "Fuck, no. That bitch is crazy. I don't want any more of the crazy to rub off on me than already has."

"You don't think you'll regret that someday? She's still your mother. She gave birth to you."

"So what?" Paisley was appalled he would even make

the suggestion that she see her mother. "Look, not everyone has a happy, cute little family like you do. Some of us have fucked-up families that are better off forgotten."

"I just thought maybe you'd like an opportunity to hear her side of the story. Now that you've heard mine and Casey's. And, I don't know, maybe you'd like to know more about your brother."

"He was obviously as big a piece of shit as she is," Paisley spewed. Just talking about them left a bitter taste in her mouth and made her head feel like it would explode.

He shrugged. "I just don't want you to regret it, that's all. When she's sentenced, she's probably getting sent over to Jessup. That's across the bay, at least a two-hour drive."

Paisley's face twisted at the thought of confronting her mother. When she was little, she used to dream of what she would say to the woman if she were to return. She had this wild fantasy of her mother showing up in a fur coat and dripping with diamonds, then she would take Paisley by the hand and tell her that she'd had to leave so she could go and make all this money. She would explain how she had returned to her precious daughter and would be taking her to live happily ever after in her mansion in New York City.

Maybe that's where I got the idea to go to New York. I always thought that's where you went to make something of yourself.

She couldn't help but laugh at the strange notions about the world that little kids concoct. *But it turned out my mom spent more time in jail than anywhere else. And look where she is now!*

What makes some people choose to be fuck-ups?

It wasn't like her mother hadn't had a stable childhood with two parents who loved her. No, there was never enough money, but there was no reason she couldn't have put herself through school and gone on to a modest but happy adulthood. As far as Paisley knew, her aunts and uncles hadn't turned out to be worthless thugs.

"Paisley?" Calvin asked, breaking her trance.

Her blue eyes met his hazel ones, and she gathered up a fistful of her dark curls, arranging them over one shoulder. She was beginning to realize how sunburned she was from her time on the beach. It just took a long time for the color to fully appear.

"So you don't want to talk to your mom," he said. "What *are* you going to do?"

She shook her head and shrugged. "I don't know how secure my job is these days. I thought about just going back to New York permanently and trying to get my old job back."

"My dad thinks the club will be fine. They'll finish up their investigation tomorrow."

"What about the media? Cap and Leah are pretty afraid of the backlash. They've been in touch with members and asked them to be as low key as possible about it, but they're afraid of it blowing up once the papers and TV stations get some more information."

"On Sunday, there was a little blurb on WBOC, but there was minimal information. The same day there was a shark sighting in North OC, and some drunk teenagers all got arrested down near the inlet for starting a huge brawl. Those two things were all over the news. You know how easily distracted people are."

She brightened a little. "Honestly, Calvin, I want to stay here. I like it here. I love my job. I love Cap, Leah and Casey, and I –" She caught herself before she said the L word in conjunction with his name. "I don't know if everyone will welcome me back, though. I caused a lot of trouble." She wasn't sure if he would pick up on the fact that he was included in "everyone."

"Good, well, I hope you *do* stay here." He squeezed her hand. "I'd miss you if you left."

She wanted to feel relief, that maybe he had forgiven her, but something in his voice was closed off. His body language reflected the same sentiment. He was sitting a few feet away from her, his shoulders against the cushion, his elbow resting on the arm of the sofa. He used to sit with a hand on her thigh. Now this squeeze to her hand was his only touch, and it felt warm but platonic.

"So..." She hated to address the elephant in the room. "What does all this mean for us?"

She watched the expression on his face change, every muscle contracting and rearranging to get to a state that was equal parts disappointment, frustration, and resolution. His full lips parted to let carefully chosen words spill out before he could replace them with others he hadn't rehearsed.

"To be honest, I think you were right about us."

She felt the color drain from her face, even the parts that were red from the sun. He was still squeezing her hand, as if trying to soften the blow.

"I'm sorry I left the other day." She let the words hang light as feathers in between them, wishing they could change his mind. She didn't want to argue with him. She was certainly not going to beg. But sitting there, she realized that every fiber of her being was clinging to the hope he would take her back.

"I know," he answered, the stiffness in his voice from earlier returning. "I thought a lot about you when you were gone, Paisley, and..." He sighed as if he had to force the words out. "I just need someone I can count on."

Calvin's words stabbed through her heart like a sword.

She had never thought of herself as unreliable—quite the opposite, in fact. She understood why he would think that, but he had the wrong picture of her. She *was* loyal. After all, she was here right now, wasn't she? She had come back to face Leah and Cap, and now Calvin.

"I see," she choked out, unable to find any other words.

"I want us to be friends, though, if you're down with that." The corners of his mouth turned up into an optimistic smile, a peace offering.

"Okay," she relented.

She wished she could plead her case for giving her another shot at being his girlfriend. If someone would have told her a few months ago she would *want* to be someone's girlfriend, she would have dismissed it as the funniest joke she'd ever heard. But here she was.

She had already convinced herself she wasn't good enough for him many times over, so why was she so upset that he had finally convinced himself?

TWENTY-SIX

Paisley stared at the woman across from her. To say she was skeptical would be an understatement, but she had it on good authority Dr. Dawn Townsend was the best therapist on the shore, that good authority being Casey Fontaine. She was small and wiry with graying hair at her temples and the rest a mousy brown that she wrapped into a knot and clipped at the back of her head.

She wore tiny, frameless glasses that made her gray-green eyes look smaller than they actually were. Her mouth naturally turned down at the corners, making her seem critical, as if everything she heard was a disappointment. Except when she smiled, then her whole face lit up with triumph. This was the first time Paisley had seen the smile, and its appearance was as much a victory for her as it was for Dr. Townsend.

It came on the heels of Paisley's observation: "So, you think the reason I joined the lifestyle and am 'so obsessed with sex,' as you put it, is because that way I can get my physical needs met and never have to risk being hurt in a relationship."

"Bingo." Dr. Townsend grinned as if she'd just cured cancer.

"Couldn't it just be because I enjoy sex?" Paisley's nose wrinkled up in frustration.

"Of course that's part of it, and that's fine. It's perfectly acceptable to enjoy your sexuality. I never said it wasn't. It's just that with everything you told me about your mother, your grandparents, and your past romantic relationships, it's obvious you have a huge fear of abandonment."

"Uh, yeah, well, that's not rocket science," Paisley scoffed.

"No, I suppose not," she answered, undaunted by Paisley's less-than-impressed attitude. "The first step is identifying the problem; the next is accepting that it's a problem you want to fix; and then, finally, working to fix it. So we have one down and two to go. The last one is a real doozy though."

Paisley had been talking for almost an hour straight. It took that long for her to tell Dr. Townsend her story from its humble beginnings, to the royal mess it exploded into circa present day. She had just gotten to the part about the stalking, blackmail, and her brief but influential relationship with Calvin. After all, that was why she was here.

After talking at length with Casey and Leah, she had grown to realize that if she ever wanted to have a successful relationship – and she knew now that she did, so that was progress – then she needed to get herself straightened out.

"And, I suppose you've realized your fear of abandonment is why you like to break things off first, why you find yourself running away when feelings might be too deep."

Paisley nodded. It wasn't that she didn't know the problem down deep in her heart of hearts. But knowing what the problem was and doing something about it were two entirely different ventures.

"Our time is almost up for today, but I want to ask you two more things."

"Okay?" Paisley's brows rose in suspense. She expected Dr. Townsend to ask her to keep a journal, or read a book, or some other standard therapist operating procedure. Not that she'd ever seen a therapist, but she'd watched enough television shows and movies.

"First, I want to know if you really want to change – if you want to confront your past and learn from it. Then, will you be able to use that knowledge to get closure and move forward to the point of letting others get close to you – even though you might get hurt?"

Paisley nodded. "That's exactly why I'm here."

"Okay, good. Then the other thing I have for you is your first assignment."

"And that would be?"

"I want you to go see your mother."

Paisley's face fell at the mere mention of Evelyn Bridges.

Dr. Townsend proceeded with her instructions despite the look of dismay on Paisley's face. "Go in without any expectations; I just want you to listen to what she has to say. You don't have to forgive her. I only want you to see that she is a human being, and maybe walk away with a little insight into who she is.

"Right now she's a huge source of resentment and anger, something of a monster. I want you to see she's just another human, and that who *she* is has no bearing on who *you* are. It's all part of that getting closure thing we just talked about."

It made sense. And it hearkened back to what Calvin

suggested when she last saw him. She still didn't think it was a good idea, but the whole idea of therapy didn't seem particularly palatable either, and yet here she was. Casey had told her to expect to stretch herself.

"Oh, one more thing I want you to do," Dr. Townsend said, snapping Paisley out of her mind-clogging thoughts. "Actually, seeing your mother is something I want you to *do*. But there's something else I want you to *avoid* doing."

"What's that?"

"I don't want you to have sex this week. Or actually, for a while, till we've gotten a few more sessions under our belts."

"What?!" Paisley's eyebrows shot up to the sky. "You've got to be kidding me!" She'd already put off getting back in the saddle after her break-up with Calvin for three weeks and was ready, more than ready, to sink her teeth into someone new.

"I don't want you to have sex with anyone unless it's part of a deliberate, conscientious desire to be intimate with someone and therefore emotionally vulnerable," Dr. Townsend explained firmly, "which you're not ready for yet."

She blew out a long, exasperated breath. "I don't understand. I thought we agreed I wouldn't be slut-shamed." There was nothing more infuriating to Paisley than being slut-shamed, except perhaps for being fat-shamed, and Dr. Townsend had agreed not to do that either.

"I want you to relearn your sexual motivations and response," she explained with a tiny little grin on her face that Paisley found slightly sadistic. "I don't think swinging is wrong – not at all – but if you are going to learn how to connect sex with intimacy, then you need to retrain yourself from square one. Do you think you can do that?"

She shrugged. "I don't know. I like sex quite a bit. And I've never forced myself to abstain."

"Do you want to heal? Do you want to be in a healthy relationship?" She peered at Paisley over the top of her glasses, making her eyes look bigger and more demanding.

Paisley bit her lip and nodded, sighing and rolling her eyes for good measure. "I'll try," she promised. That was the best she could do.

❦ ❦ ❦

There was no denying that the detention center where her mother was being held reeked. It smelled like cheap cleaning products attempting to mask an assaulting combination of mildew and B.O.

The guard doesn't exactly smell like roses either, she noticed as he led her down a hallway to the visitation room. She had already gone through the metal detector and been stripped of her cell phone and dignity. She was pretty sure the guard had purposely grabbed her ass when he frisked her, and though she was desperately missing cock in her life, she wasn't that desperate.

She was escorted to a small plastic table with two plastic chairs. One of them was occupied by none other than Evelyn Bridges, this time wearing a loose-fitting orange top and matching pants that resembled shapeless scrubs. Her lackluster brown hair was pulled back with a faded black scrunchie, and her face was etched with tiny lines around her eyes and mouth.

This is what a lifetime of drug use will do to you, boys and girls.

She glanced down at a tattoo across the woman's wrist.

She couldn't read it because of the way her hands were folded together on the table. All she could see was the letters "be."

"Rebecca," Evelyn said as Paisley took a seat.

"Please don't call me that. My name is Paisley now. You gave up your rights to my name when you gave up your rights to me." She didn't mean to start off on such a sour note, but it was hard to keep a lifetime of resentment buried inside.

"You're right; Paisley it is." Evelyn smiled, revealing nicer teeth than Paisley expected to see. "I can't believe you're sitting here across from me."

Paisley could spot the tears in the woman's eyes, but they didn't alleviate any of her suspicions that the therapist's assignment was a mistake. "I'm not really sure why I'm here, to be honest," she confessed.

"I'm just glad you came so I c'n apologize before the trial. Might be my only chance to see ya," she said in a thick, backwoods Kentucky accent. She moved her hand just enough so the tattoo on her other wrist became visible. It said *William* in a curly script.

"Well, I'm here. Apologize away," Paisley answered with a sharp tongue. She wasn't feeling particularly generous, and she wasn't about to make this easy for Evelyn.

"When I found out Mom and Dad was dead all them years ago – and how they died – I was in shock." Her eyes glazed over with tears. "Not sure if you realize it but...yer brother was Jimmy's son."

Paisley was glad she hadn't eaten that morning. Her stomach was so twisted that if she'd had the slightest amount of food in it, there would have been a revolt. As it was, enough bile was creeping up her throat to steal her words.

After the nausea, came the anger, followed by her mind trying to work out the particulars of the situation.

Jones. That was why Detective Mitchell asked me if I knew anyone by the name of Jones.

She'd heard them say *William Jones* a dozen times, but never once put it together. Jones was a common name, and the thought of her mother sleeping with her ex-boyfriend was far too disgusting to fathom.

"I know it's weird, but I met 'im several years before you did. He didn't know I'd had his kid 'cause I got locked up shortly after gettin' knocked up. Billy was in the system while I got myself straightened out. Jimmy didn't know till Billy was four or five, but he was never part of his life till after you."

"You forgave him for shooting your parents?" Paisley asked, disbelief painted thickly across her face. Her knee began to shake under the table, and it took every ounce of strength she had not to overturn it and storm out of the building.

"He always told me it was all yer fault." She crossed her arms over her chest and waited for Paisley's response.

"What?! I wasn't even there!" She knew she sounded defensive, and it surprised her considering she had spent a lot of time blaming herself for her grandparents' death. But to hear it coming from him, the asshole who had created the entire situation, made her burn with rage.

"He said you run off with the money and disappeared. He gone over there to find out what happened to you, and Dad up and shot 'im. He's always said he shot back in self-defense, that if you'd just given 'im the money like ya was supposed to, he wouldn't even went over there in the first place."

"If it was self-defense, why did he shoot Grandma? She didn't have a gun. That's bullshit."

Evelyn shrugged. "I gone to see him a few months ago for the first time. Billy used to go up there once a month'n kept telling me Jimmy wanna see me. So I finally go see 'im, and he's all like 'you need to get that money back.' And Billy said he already started lookin' for ya. He was a computer genius. Fuck, he could do anything with technology. I kept hopin' he'd put them skills to good use and get a real job, but he actually been hired to hack into a bunch of different banks and other business computers. He'd made a shit ton of money that way."

That explained how he was able to hide his identity when fucking over The Factory's page. "I still don't understand how he found me."

"We knew you gone to New York after you left Kentucky," Evelyn explained.

Paisley cringed at her mother's blaring redneck accent. "How in the world did you know that?"

"My brother, you know, your Uncle Phil, seen you when he used to go up there for work. He kept track of ya for years, knew ya was dancing, knew ya changed yer name and all that. He blamed you for killin' Mom and Dad too."

"What the fuck?!" *No wonder I always felt like I was being watched. I was! And he saw me dancing?* She shivered with disgust.

"He kept track of yer roommates and yer jobs. And then when we needed to track ya down, we had connections, knew who to talk to. It was some woman named Tonya you'd gotten fired who told us ya gone to Ocean City to manage some swinger club."

"But how did she know that?" Paisley wasn't sure this exercise was having the effect Dr. Townsend anticipated.

"People talk, babe. That friend a'yers – Allison, is it? Yeah, she got a big mouth. We didn't talk to her, but we talked to people she talked to."

Great. Just fucking great. See? I can't fucking trust anyone.

"We gone to Seacrets and some of the other hot spots, struck up convos with club members. We met Jason that way too. He was all too eager to help us out."

"But why? Just for the money? And if so, why did you guys need a gun?"

"That was Billy and Jimmy's idea, and I had no part of it. He said he was just gonna use it to scare ya..."

"That gun got him killed. Calvin wouldn't have fired at him if he hadn't shot first." Paisley shook her head, thinking about what a waste the whole thing had been. "I wasn't going to give you guys any money – gun or no gun. I don't have that kind of cash laying around. And now you're in jail, and your son is dead."

And I lost my boyfriend and nearly lost my job, she silently added.

Evelyn nodded, a tear sliding down her cheek. It was the first one she'd given up, though her eyes had been wet the whole time they'd been speaking. "I told 'em he was gonna get himself shot up. Fuckin' mother's intuition," she lamented. "On the other hand, I wouldn't wanna see him rot in jail like his dad. But I'm glad Jimmy's not gettin' out 'cause I'm afraid he'd come after ya."

"Even though he knows I'm your daughter? What a fucking scumbag." Her skin felt like it was crawling when she thought about how Jimmy Jones had ruined her entire life, taking over from where Evelyn Bridges had put a pretty big dent in it.

"I think we can both agree gettin' messed up with 'im

was the worst decision we ever made," Evelyn said, the whites of her eyes crisscrossed with red streaks.

"Yeah, I guess," Paisley sighed. "Just tell me one thing: he didn't know I was your daughter when he first got involved with me, did he?"

Her sad, bloodshot blue eyes met her daughter's younger, brighter ones and locked onto them, searching for a clue as to whether or not she should tell the truth. Then she let the words slip out nonchalantly, like skipping a flat stone across a lake: "He got off on it."

Paisley grimaced, her whole face twisting with disgust. She hated to admit it, but she realized Jimmy had controlled Evelyn the same way he controlled her. And it sounded like the apple didn't fall far from the tree where Billy was concerned.

Evelyn rubbed her temples as if soothing away an oncoming headache. "Wish I had a better reason fer doing what we done, but it mainly come down to greed'n revenge. And I admit I got caught up in it too. I'm jealous you made somethin' of yourself, and I can't take no credit fer it. You turned out so successful an' so goddamn beautiful. Okay, I guess I c'n take a little credit fer the beautiful part, but the rest was all you." She gave a half smile as though her daughter might find her compliment endearing.

Paisley shook her head. She had never heard anything so ridiculous in her life than this grown woman sitting across from her admitting she was jealous.

"You know, you could have made something of yourself too. It's a choice. I made the choice to do something with my life, to go to school and get an education, to try to be a goddamn professional. It was a fucking choice." She couldn't help but seethe the last few words, spewing them out from a clenched jaw.

Evelyn trembled as the tears quaked through her body. She had obviously been struggling to keep them at bay. She turned her hands palms-up and reached toward her daughter as if she wanted to grab her hands.

Looking down, Paisley saw that while her left wrist spelled out *William,* the other said *Rebecca.* Even though this woman had no part in raising her, she still considered herself a mother, one worthy of tattooing her child's name on her wrist.

That was the final straw. Paisley stood up, her legs shaking as noticeably as Evelyn's entire body was. "I think I've heard all I can for today," she said. "Good luck, Evelyn." With that, she nodded to the guard and headed for the exit without looking back to see the woman breaking apart in the plastic chair.

"How did your appointment with Dr. Townsend go this week?" Casey wore an expectant look as Paisley headed into the club for the Friday night party.

"I think I have my work cut out for me," Paisley sighed, poking her head into the office to wave at Leah.

It had been three weeks since the shooting at the club, and things were finally settling back to normal. Fortunately, the club never missed a weekend being open, and the media soon forgot about the whole debacle, having been supremely distracted by a shark sighting, a teenage brawl on the boardwalk, a political scandal, and a sinkhole on Route 90 all in the same week. For once, Paisley was glad for the short attention span of social media users.

"I'm just glad I could pull a few strings and get you in.

Dr. Townsend's normal wait time for a new patient is three months. But I send her a lot of business, so she always tries to accommodate my referrals. She knows her stuff, and I hope you'll listen to her."

"Of course." Paisley smiled. She was grateful Casey had helped her get back on her feet after the blackmailing incident. Leah and Cap had also been very supportive and, of course, were also relieved the club didn't suffer any damage.

"So did she impose a moratorium on sex?" Casey's eyebrows arched with curiosity.

Paisley couldn't help but giggle. "How did you know?"

"I had a hunch. She asked me to do the same thing when I first started seeing her. I'd been involved in the lifestyle for a few years, and she wanted to make sure I wasn't using sex as a crutch to distract me from the healing process of recovering from the abuse. I abstained for about six months, and it really helped me get my head on straight."

"Six months without sex?!" Paisley gasped, trying to fathom a worse fate.

"Six months without sex?" Leah repeated as she slid out of the office. Lincoln was in his normal spot in his sling draped across her chest. "And I thought six weeks was bad! We survived, though...with a little help from our friends." She winked at Paisley, who winked back.

"Dr. Townsend knows what she's doing; trust me on that," Casey reiterated. "You can do it." She gave Paisley an encouraging pat on the back. "And who knows? After some time has passed, maybe you and Calvin will find your way back to each other?"

"Ohhh..." Paisley couldn't prevent her face from falling at Casey's well-meaning suggestion. "I am pretty sure that ship has sailed."

"That's too bad," Leah remarked. "We sure miss him around here. Was he freaked out by the lifestyle stuff?"

"No, he liked it here too. It's just, under the circumstances, he didn't feel it was right to stay. Our new security guard has the personality of a wet mop," Casey complained, referring to Kyle, the new guard Leah hired. There weren't a lot of choices among the applicants, and Kyle was the most qualified, plus he and his wife were both members at the club.

"Whereas Calvin is quite the catch!" Leah laughed. "I checked in on him a few days ago, actually. He says he is doing well. His father has been nothing short of a miracle worker in helping us keep the club out of the press."

"That's good to hear," Paisley replied, but she couldn't help but feel a few pangs of regret rock through her. It had only been a few weeks since she'd visited his apartment and gotten his take on the incident at the club, when he'd told her he just wanted to be friends. Since then, neither had reached out to say hello or perform any of the other functions typically associated with friendship. The Factory's website was up and running smoothly, so there was no using that as an excuse to contact him, either.

Since being welcomed back to the club with open arms, Paisley had tried to concern herself with her job and the upcoming trial where she would testify against her mother and Jason. She wasn't sure she'd come away with closure from her visit with Evelyn in jail like Dr. Townsend had hoped, but she had developed a sense of contemptuous pity, if that was such a thing.

Evelyn Bridges had not turned out to be a sympathetic character. She was just a selfish, lazy woman who never had the discipline to make something of herself. In some ways, talking to her in person had solidified Paisley's belief that she was nothing like her. And in that one, simple way, perhaps there was a bit of closure after all.

That night while traveling her normal route through the club, she looked from Erik the Bartender; to Trent and Kyle, the security guards; to Cap, Leah and Casey; plus the hundred and fifty members in attendance, and realized that she, for the first time in her life, belonged to an extended family who accepted her for who she was. No, they were not blood relatives, but they loved her just the same.

She couldn't go more than a few feet during her rounds through the club without someone stopping to ask her how she was doing. Most did not know the details surrounding the shooting. They had played it off as a failed robbery attempt. No, these were just people with whom Paisley had developed friendships, who cared she was there and that she was happy. And that meant more to her than she could have ever expressed in words.

I t was hard to believe summer was winding down. *Where the hell did August go?*

Paisley had finally gotten her apartment the way she wanted: new curtains, rugs, artwork, bookcases and shelves, plus the last few miscellaneous boxes unpacked. To reward herself for accomplishing that feat, she fulfilled her early summer dream of adopting a kitten.

The day she picked the furry creature up from the humane society, she was filled with a sense of joy she hadn't felt for as long as she could remember. The tiny little furball was tiger-striped with the roundest, brightest green eyes she'd ever seen, magnificently outlined in a thick ring of white.

When she brought the kitten back to her apartment, the first thing she did was run to hide under Paisley's bed. After lots of coaxing, she was finally able to convince the shy, tentative creature to come out and sit on her lap. The next thing she knew, she was purring, then dozing next to her on the sofa while she answered work emails.

A text from Allison popped up on her phone:

> Did you pick a name yet? Where are my pics?

Allison loved animals, but her roommate Ian was practically allergic to life in general, so she hadn't been able to get her own pet. She had warned Paisley that she planned to live vicariously through her feline ownership.

It was obvious the little one was going to have no problems wrapping her owner around her tiny little striped paws. She took a photo of the curled-up ball of feline fluffiness and sent it to her friend. Then she very nearly popped the photo into a text to Calvin as a way to start a conversation with him. Despite the weeks that had gone by without any communication, she still thought of him every day.

After she'd left Calvin's apartment that night, she'd not seen or heard from him, but she did meet with his father a few days later to go over some lingering questions he had about her case. He was warm but professional and didn't ask her anything about her relationship with his son.

"I guess we'll see you at the trial, if not before," he'd said to close out their conversation. She couldn't help but wonder what he meant by that.

If not before? Like he knew something she didn't.

Allison texted back immediately with emojis for cats, hearts and smiley faces:

Allison: So cute!

Paisley: What should I name her?

She had never thanked her friend for texting Calvin her address that night after their excursion into Manhattan. She was angry at first, not only about that, but also about how Allison had blabbed information that helped her mother and brother track her down in Ocean City. But then she realized, in both cases, Allison was only trying to help. She wanted Calvin to be able to connect with Paisley, although he ended up passing along the address to her bosses instead, which was how Casey had known where to find her.

And as far as sharing Paisley's whereabouts with her old coworkers was concerned, Paisley underestimated how attached they had gotten to her. They'd pumped Allison for information about how Paisley was doing, and Allison obliged. But that information had fallen into Tonya's hands, and that was where things went south. It wasn't Allison's fault.

Allison: How about something beachy?
Shelly? Sandy? Shrimp? She looks tiny!

Paisley contemplated her friend's suggestions as she stroked her fingers down the kitten's soft fur. "What's your name, little girl?" she asked, but the kitten continued to doze away, her fuzzy belly moving up and down with each breath she took.

A few hours later, she found herself browsing pet name websites, then baby name websites for ideas.

Let's just see how I do with a cat before I get all carried away wanting a baby.

She laughed to herself as she scanned down the list of names. One caught her eye that she had never heard of before: "Cordelia."

She read that it had two origins: Latin and Celtic. The former origin was from the Latin word for "heart," whereas the Celtic meaning was "daughter of the sea." She wasn't sure that the tiny fluff ball could carry the mantle of such an impressive name, but the meanings seemed absolutely perfect.

"I hereby dub you 'Cordelia,'" Paisley announced in her most royal voice, touching her fingertips to each fuzzy ear. The kitten's eyes slowly opened as if she was accepting her christening, then they drifted closed again.

TWENTY-SEVEN

Two weeks into her therapist-imposed abstinence, Paisley felt like she might climb the walls with sexual frustration. She wasn't sure Dr. Townsend could adequately appreciate how hard it was to resist indulging herself in carnal delights when she worked in a building expressly designed for those pursuits – not to mention the veritable parade of man candy she saw traipse through the club on any given weekend night. She warned Leah to keep a tight rein on Cap so she didn't attack him when they were working late.

Leah had laughed. "No need to resist Cap's charms on my account."

"No! Resist you must!" Casey had insisted. "There's a method to Dr. Townsend's madness, my dears. Let's trust her wisdom."

"Dr. Townsend never had to work in a swing club!" Paisley protested with a smirk.

She did understand the point of the exercise, and yes, perhaps it had cleared her head and allowed for a degree of introspection she hadn't felt comfortable attempting in a long while, if not ever. *But damn I'm horny!*

The upside of all that self-reflection meant answering Dr. Townsend's relentless questions had become infinitely easier. "Where do you see yourself in five years? If you had to change one thing about your personality, what would it be? What do you think are the most important qualities in a mate?"

"You sound like a dating app questionnaire," Paisley joked with her at their third session.

"Does that mean you've tried online dating?" she fired back.

Paisley shook her head. "Oh, hell no. I have heard horror stories about those sites. Never gonna go down that path."

"Where do you expect you'll meet your next partner?" the doctor quizzed, a curious look on her face.

"Probably at the club once I'm allowed to get busy again," Paisley answered truthfully. Throughout her celibacy, she had been fully anticipating a glorious return to the lifestyle.

"So your heart is set on finding someone to share the lifestyle with, then?"

It wasn't as though Paisley hadn't thought about leaving the lifestyle before starting therapy. That would have been a deal breaker had she continued her relationship with Calvin. *But in an ideal world, I would have my cake and eat it too.*

She gave Dr. Townsend a thoughtful, measured answer: "I guess I'm open to someone who isn't lifestyle, if they're not judgmental about my past and truly open-minded about trying it together in the future."

"Fair enough," the therapist replied. "I want you to be

able to identify what it is you get out of the lifestyle and whether those are needs that could be met within the context of a committed relationship. And, Paisley, for the record, I'm not knocking it, okay? Our goal here is a healthy relationship, and your sea is going to have a lot more fish in it if you consider the - what do you call them - vanilla? guys as well."

"I understand, though I've never been accused of being closed-minded." She laughed. "The lifestyle is my family; that's the simplest explanation. I haven't ever had a real family before now. To be honest, Casey is sorta like the mom I never had, and Cap and Leah have become like a big brother and little sister to me. The club members themselves are like cousins, in a way. It's the first time I've ever felt a sense of belonging and connection."

"I certainly can't argue with that," she said, smiling. "One more thing before we wrap up today's session..."

"Okay?"

"What did you do to take care of yourself this week?" Dr. Townsend asked, sounding like the quintessential therapist.

"Well," Paisley's face brightened as though a fire was lit within her, "I adopted a kitten. It's my first pet since I was a little girl. And the first time I've ever been solely responsible for another living thing."

"That's great, Paisley! What's his name?"

"It's a girl, and her name is Cordelia," Paisley shared.

"Oh! Like from *Anne of Green Gables*?"

"From what?"

"*Anne of Green Gables*, the classic literary series by Canadian author L.M. Montgomery," Dr. Townsend shared, hoping to spark her patient's memory. Her face scrunched up in disbelief at Paisley's lack of recognition. "It was my favorite book series growing up; it's about a spunky redheaded orphan named Anne – who always wished she could be called Cordelia, by the way—"

"Ah, okay. I found it on a baby naming website," Paisley admitted sheepishly.

"You know, you're not too different from Anne yourself, being a spunky orphan from a small, rural town. Only you actually *did* change your name. If only you had red hair!"

"Thank you...I think?"

"It's a compliment, trust me," Dr. Townsend assured her. "Now we just need to find your Gilbert Blythe!" She winked.

"I have no idea what you're talking about, but if it means I'll get laid again, I'm all for it!"

Paisley stepped out of Dr. Townsend's office surfing a wave of contentment. Everything seemed to be settling down to a normal routine, and she was surprised by how much she was getting out of therapy, even if it did mean cobwebs had grown in her girly bits. She came around the corner from the hallway and stopped dead in her tracks as her eyes fell on rich, topaz skin and long, muscular limbs sprawled out in the waiting room.

He lifted his glittering hazel eyes to hers just about the time she found herself frozen in place, then she watched his lips spread into a huge grin.

"Paisley!" He put his phone down on the little table next to his chair and leaped up to greet her with a hug.

Feeling his arms wrap around her sent a wild thrill

reverberating through her body. It all at once felt familiar and exhilarating. She pulled back from him slowly, hoping to read the thoughts on his face when she noticed Dr. Townsend was standing in the entrance to the hallway observing them. She wore a warm smile and not an ounce of surprise.

That was when it hit Paisley that Casey had orchestrated this reunion.

"Are you...going in?" Paisley gestured toward the hallway when she finally regained the use of her voice.

He nodded. "So you got a referral from Casey too, huh?"

She laughed. "Yep. Kinda feels like a set-up, doesn't it?"

"I would never want to disappoint Casey Fontaine." Calvin grinned. "Maybe we can catch up over dinner after my session? I'll be done in an hour."

"I'd like that. I have to run back to work, actually...got a late start today." Her heart fluttered within her ribcage, but she managed to get the words out smoothly, much to her surprise.

"Why don't we meet at that crab house where we had our first business dinner?" he suggested, his eyes sparkling like gemstones. "Say six o'clock? Does that give you enough time?"

The hole-in-the-wall restaurant where they'd met to go over his initial designs for The Factory's website was just around the corner from the club. "Sure, that's great. See you soon!"

She pushed her way into the parking lot and didn't look back, choosing to let him watch her backside disappear out the door, just as she had the first day they met. So much had happened since that early summer day back in June that she could scarcely believe only a few months had passed.

Struggling to keep her heart rate in check knowing they

were to spend the evening together, she drove back to The Factory to finish up the reports she had started to run prior to her therapy appointment.

Casey was still at her desk wrapping up a phone call with a new vendor who wanted to do some onsite sales of lingerie and sex toys. It wasn't every day one could observe a woman of Casey Fontaine's stature throwing around the words "dildos," "butt plugs" and "lube" as nonchalantly as she might toss out real estate terms during her day job.

Paisley camped out at her desk until the conversation was complete, as much for the entertainment factor as actually having something to say.

"Yes?" Casey asked, her face lit up with a grin. She knew Paisley had come from therapy, and her sly smile indicated she knew what the younger woman was about to say as well.

"I can't believe you!" Paisley laughed. "You knew exactly what you were doing."

"Yes, ma'am, and considering that you both need Dr. Townsend's services as much as you need mine, I believe it's killing two birds with one stone," she sang with her melodic arpeggio of a laugh.

"I'm going out to dinner with him tonight."

Casey executed a spry little fist-pumping gesture that made Paisley laugh. "Don't worry, I'm still sticking to my sex hiatus," she assured her boss.

"I am pretty sure Dr. Townsend wanted you to avoid emotionless hook-ups. I really doubt that would be the case with Calvin..."

"Are you encouraging me to have sex?" Paisley gasped. Then she sighed. "I doubt anything like that will happen, anyway. He told me a few weeks ago that he just wanted to be friends."

"I wouldn't rule anything out." Casey winked at her.

The restaurant was just as quiet as the first time they'd met, that first time feeling like it happened in some parallel universe where Calvin and Paisley were slightly different versions of themselves. So much had happened since that night Calvin showed off his web designs, and Paisley shot down his romantic advances.

In some ways, she would have loved to travel back in time to that night so they could start over from there. In other ways, she felt as though the trauma they'd survived that summer was necessary to shape them into the people they were at that very moment, sitting across each other and staring into each other's eyes.

"So what made you decide to try therapy?" he asked after the waitress delivered their heaping tray of Old Bay-coated crabs.

"I figured it was time, you know. Someone as messed up as me is a therapist's dream." She laughed at herself, which was something she was learning how to do. Therapy was teaching her not to take herself so seriously. "Honestly, I just want to put my past behind me once and for all, and to move forward with my life, believing I'm worthy of being happy and being loved."

"I think that's an admirable goal," he answered with a smile and raised his drink in a toast to her journey.

She clinked her glass against his and took a long sip of the fruity concoction. Dr. Townsend had also been working with her to stay in the moment, so she wasn't constantly rewinding or fast-forwarding. "You're not a VCR tape," she'd admonished her.

And she was so right. I had a bad habit of being in another space and another time.

"Was that your first session with Dr. Townsend?" she asked him as he cracked open one of the crab claws.

He nodded. "Yeah, it was interesting. I definitely never thought I'd need to go to therapy. But I also never thought I'd – "

He can't say the words.

A sharp, spiky guilt dug its claws into her as she grappled with the fact he'd have to shoulder this burden every day for the rest of his life, and that it was basically all her fault.

"There are no words that can express how sorry I am, Calvin." She lowered her eyes to her folded hands, hoping to keep them from filling with tears. She had cried more in the past two months than ever before in her entire life.

What the hell has happened to me? I used to be tough.

But she and Dr. Townsend had been talking a lot about how it was okay for her to express what she was feeling. She was definitely getting the hang of it, even if she hadn't mastered control of it yet.

"Please," he asked softly, luring her eyes up to meet his again with his smooth voice. His glowing hazel irises were intense balls of emotions, a mixture of feelings she couldn't begin to unravel, but she thought she saw a flicker of hope. "It's not your fault your family is crazy...not any more than it's my fault I'm still crazy about you."

Her heart nearly burst through her ribs at his statement. Speaking of video tape, she wanted to rewind to make sure she'd heard correctly as she watched the tension that had been in his eyes moments before dissolve. It seemed as though the chains holding him back had just broken.

"What are you saying?" she asked, tiny words dotting the space between them, each one capped off with a question mark.

He cleared his throat and laid his crab mallet back on the table, then he covered her trembling hand with his own. "I've tried to move on and stop thinking about you and that one amazing night you spent in my bed, but I can't, Paisley. It was by far the most intense lovemaking I've ever experienced."

She watched his expression change as if he were peeling off layers of himself, undressing his soul before her eyes.

"I kept thinking that night was tainted because you obviously didn't feel the same things I felt. But I've slowly realized that, whether you felt them or not – "

"But I did, Calvin. I did feel them. That was what I was trying to tell you when I returned from New York. I just didn't know how to say it."

After dinner, the pair ended up on Assateague Island, which was only a few miles down the road from the crab house. There wasn't a lot of thought or discussion behind it; Calvin just said, "Let's drive down to the beach," and then it happened.

By the time they parked, the skies over the ocean were a canvas swooning with rose, lavender and heather. A fiery sunset over the bay was exploding on the other side of the island, but there was something so tranquil about what was unfolding right there over the rippling waters of the

Atlantic. And in the east, fledgling stars were beginning to emerge in the deepening twilight.

The sand had begun to cool and felt soothing between Paisley's toes as she slid her sandals off. Calvin intertwined his fingers with hers as they pressed their bare feet into the wet sand near the shoreline. For a while, they just walked, leaving tandem impressions as they made their way down the beach.

And for a while, there was silence between them, an unspoken script about second chances that they didn't feel the need to act out just yet. They were both operating under the assumption that the past was the past, while the future stretched before them like the endless miles of ocean that extended far past the horizon.

Until Paisley abruptly stopped, a niggling voice inside her head telling her she needed to make sure they were squared away. It may have been Dr. Townsend's voice tickling her ears, reminding her how crucial communication was in relationships. In any case, she felt inclined to ask Calvin a series of questions that she prefaced with, "I want to make sure we're on the same page."

He straightened his back, looking strong and tall as his figure was silhouetted against the remnants of the dying sun. He grasped both of her hands in his and faced her, his eyes entranced by hers. "Of course, good idea."

"Does this mean we're...dating? Boyfriend and girl-friend? All that good stuff?" she asked, her voice coming out a bit smaller than she anticipated, as though she hadn't been able to extinguish all the glowing coals of fear inside her.

His lips curled up into a smile, and his eyes glittered with hope. "Well, that was kind of my intent all along – but only if you're ready."

It had taken losing him to realize the heart that beat

wildly in her chest didn't fully belong to her anymore. He had claimed so much of it, snatching up tiny little pieces here and there. She couldn't quite put a finger on the exact moment his ownership reached critical mass, but what she did know was that she fully trusted him to cherish it. And that was something she feared she'd never be capable of.

"It doesn't matter to you that I have a fucked-up past?"

He shook his head.

"Or that I've been a swinger?"

"Nope."

"It doesn't bother you that I'm so much older than you?"

"Not at all."

"How about that I'm a fat girl?" She ran her hands down her ample curves.

"I think you're absolutely beautiful."

"And you don't care that I work at a swing club?"

He shook his head. "You're brilliant at your job; this much I know."

"Then I'm yours. Unless there's some other catch I'm not aware of?" Her eyebrows arched as her heart thundered in anticipation of his response.

"My turn," he said. "Can you deal with the fact that I'm a perfectionist and a bit of a workaholic?"

She laughed. "I have to or I'd be a total hypocrite."

"My race isn't a problem for you?"

"Seriously? That's never been a consideration whatsoever!"

"Just checking." He smiled. "What about the fact my family is so incredibly important to me?"

"I'm good with that. I love your family! So far, anyway." She winked.

"Are you open to starting a family of our own... I mean, someday, if we get married and all that?"

She hesitated just slightly, thinking of the tiny kitten she'd adopted and how much she already cared for that precious little creature. "I think so. We'd have some pretty fucking gorgeous kids, that's for damn sure."

He grinned as they both conjured up a mental image of what a Calvin/Paisley spawn might look like. Then his smile faded, and his expression grew serious.

"What about only being with me…only making love to me…" He peered into her eyes, searching for the answer on her heart before one emerged from her lips. "At least for now?" he added.

"I wondered for a while if I would be able to promise that," Paisley admitted, returning his intense gaze. "But I haven't been with anyone else since the night we were together. And it's mostly because I knew any other experience would pale in comparison to what I shared with you."

There was no further need for words. He wrapped his arms around her, pulling her tightly against his body as she lifted her chin to seal their agreement with a kiss. His lips felt like magic against hers, igniting every nerve in her body and sending waves of desire cascading through her as he threaded his fingers through her long, dark curls. Their breaths synchronized, their bodies melded together in such perfect unity that neither of them even remotely flinched when a cool, starlit wave crashed over them.

An hour later, they found themselves intertwining their limbs beneath the sheets of Paisley's bed. "I've been waiting to do this again ever since the last time," Calvin whispered as he nibbled at her earlobe.

She could barely respond, the shivers down her spine were so powerful. She felt his cock throbbing against her thigh and knew he was moving into position to slide it into her.

"Wait, there's something I want to do first," she managed, though he'd stolen her breath with his kisses.

"Ah, the word 'wait' is not the one I wanted to hear, babe." He smirked as she struggled to extract herself from underneath him. "What's wrong?" His eyes searched the length of her body, gliding over her luscious curves, his hunger for her growing more and more urgent.

"I want to suck your cock," she whispered, sliding down his torso until her face was in line with his rock-hard manhood. Licking her lips, wondered if she would even be able to fit the entirety of his impressively thick head in her mouth.

She ran her tongue around the crown and relished the groan that resonated from deep in his throat. "Damn, Calvin, I didn't get a close enough look at you last time."

"Uh...is there something wrong with it?" He was barely able to squeak out the words as her lips were poised over him.

She licked him again, eliciting another tremor. "No, no, quite the contrary. It's quite the masterpiece."

"I'm so glad you approve." He laced his fingers through her hair, guiding her mouth down on his shaft. "Now if you could just – ah, there we go," he moaned as she engulfed the first few inches, stretching as wide as her lips would spread. "That's more like it."

She worked her mouth up and down the top third of his cock that she could manage to swallow and used her hand to stroke up and down the rest of his length. She used her other hand to explore his body, gently fondling his balls. Then she trailed her fingertips down his legs and finally up toward his muscular chest. She could feel his thighs tensing and his balls tightening as she picked up speed.

"If you don't stop, I'm going to come," he warned her.

"You say that as if it's a bad thing." She laughed, the words garbled due to her mouth being intermittently full of cock.

"Oh, fuck, Paisley," he murmured as he lifted his hips toward her while simultaneously pushing her head farther down on his shaft. She held her breath as he began to fuck her mouth, deeper than she thought she was capable of. Finally, he groaned and erupted down her throat, his seed filling her mouth until she was forced to swallow.

"That was delicious," she sighed, licking her lips to collect the last drops that had oozed out around her mouth.

"Really?"

"Really."

"I bet you taste even better." He smiled, his breath still ragged as he worked his way back to homeostasis. "Come here," he urged, pulling her up on top of him. She pressed her mouth to his knowing full well he could taste himself on her. He kissed her, then brushed his lips against her ear. "Sit on my face."

"What?! No." Because of her size, the one and only sexual thing that made her feel uncomfortable was being on top. She would occasionally ride a cock, but she never, ever sat on a man's face. She hadn't done that since she was in her twenties and much lighter.

"What do you mean, 'no'?" He sounded shocked that she would refuse his request.

"I don't want to suffocate you, silly," she answered, half-joking but mostly serious.

"You won't; come on. It'll turn me on, I promise. I'll be hard again in no time."

She sighed. She hated to deny him when they were finally embarking upon the relationship she desperately wanted, one for which she had been willing to see a therapist to help her get her shit sorted out.

"Okay," she answered as she tentatively climbed aboard, aligning her pelvis with his face, her thick thighs resting on either side of his head.

"Mmmm," he moaned as he planted a hand on each side of her, lifting her so her balance was thrown off, and she had no choice but to press her weight against him. He used his tongue to spread her already drenched lips, then delved inside to lap up the honey that had collected there while she was sucking his cock.

"I was right," he said, moving his head back into the pillow. "You taste amazing. Will you be able to come this way?"

"I don't know," she answered, but her voice was mostly stolen by the intense pleasure bolting through her when his tongue penetrated her folds again. She gently rocked her hips back and forth against his mouth, her hands instinctively gravitating to the headboard for better stability and leverage.

"That's it, baby," he encouraged her as her ass got in on the action too, her muscles working together to grind her pussy against his face. His muffled moans signaled he was clearly enjoying his work, which compelled her to fuck his face even more aggressively.

Still using one hand to grip the headboard, she twisted back with the other hand to feel his cock, which had begun to swell again against her soft, fleshy ass cheeks. Knowing she was turning him on so much heightened her own arousal as well.

"I want you to come on my face," he directed her as she continued to writhe on top of him.

She couldn't speak; her climax was gradually beginning

to take shape. It had humble beginnings deep in her core as a tingle that soon became a burning. Then, at long last, when his mouth was sucking her clit in the most agonizingly perfect rhythm, every nerve surged within her until mountainous waves of ecstasy broke, drenching him in her juices. She remained suspended, straddling his face as the pleasure so very slowly subsided, his tongue still buried deep inside her well.

She pulled away as gracefully as she was capable of moving with her thighs still trembling from the sheer intensity of the orgasm he'd delivered. She slid her body down his, still surprised she was able to relax enough to get to that state.

He was speechless, his face covered in the product of her climax, and his cock proudly waving like a flag. She didn't wait for him to direct her again; she just moved down far enough to slip his length into her core until she was perched on him like a queen on a throne. He gasped at the sensation of her walls closing in around him as his hands buried into her fleshy hips again.

"Make love to me," he uttered, his voice just a few decibels louder than a whisper.

Her lips found his as she began to move against his tight, muscular body with tiny motions, just enough to get their pelvises used to grinding against each other. He was so deep inside her, it took her breath away.

She remembered a time someone told her that her body had been designed for sex. She had begun to believe it. After all, when she was with a partner, her instincts took over, the same as they did on the dance floor. Her body intuitively knew how to move to whatever rhythm was thrown at her.

But that night, looking down into Calvin's eyes and

finding his admiration, respect, and tender care for her reflected in them, she realized he had rendered her body capable of something beyond sex, something much more beautiful and pure. They were making love. And what was more, it was a love that was strong and true, one that would never abandon her.

Theirs was a love with no boundaries, a love that would endure.

EPILOGUE

ONE YEAR LATER...

She stood in front of the mirror to catch the first glimpse of herself. Her dark hair fell in ringlets all around her shoulders, and her face was exquisitely made-up, cheeks blushing the perfect shade of rose and eyes as blue as the deepest ocean waters. Her creamy skin was only slightly darker than the ivory lace that framed her bosom, sparkling with pearls, sequins and beads that spilled down the bodice of her gown. The silk fabric with a delicate lace overlay gently smoothed over the generous curves of her hips, landing in a waterfall that barely grazed the floor.

Leah leaned in behind her and whispered, "Are you ready for your veil, beautiful?"

Paisley nodded, trying to hold back the tears that glittered in the corner of her eyes; she didn't want to mess up her makeup. Leah placed the pearl and rhinestone tiara on top of Paisley's head, adjusting the sheer tulle layers until they cascaded over her shoulders and down her back, gently obscuring the view of the tight V of laces that closed the bodice of her gown.

When Paisley turned to face her boss, friend and

matron of honor, she saw her eyes were just as damp. "You're simply breathtaking," Leah gasped. She looked over her shoulder at Casey and Allison, the other two bridesmaids, and the women made a circle around the bride, all showering her with compliments.

Moments later, Cap appeared at the door. "Is the bride all ready?" he questioned, dimples flashing in his cheeks.

He stepped into the room to join the ladies, a little strawberry blond-haired boy clinging to his legs. Leah scooped up the child and balanced him on her hip. "Doesn't Miss Paisley look gorgeous?" she asked him. He nodded, his blue eyes sparkling just like his dad's.

"I can't believe this is actually happening!" Paisley gulped, looking into the faces of all her favorite people. All her favorites except one: the handsome groom who was sure to be waiting for her at the end of the aisle.

"Oh, it's happening," Cap assured her. "The men are getting into place. You're sure about this, right?"

"Absolutely!"

"Good, that's what he said too." Cap grinned.

They followed the procession, led by Casey, out of the room. Leah handed Lincoln off to his aunt Emma, who ushered the little boy outside and onto the sand.

Paisley was stunned by the sight as soon as her eyes fell on the huge bay window of the oceanfront condo they'd rented for the weekend. The sky looked just as it had the first night she and Calvin had walked on the beach at Assateague together. In a swirl of rose, mauve and periwinkle, the clouds rose like spires into the heavens, and the first hint of stars appeared in the east along with the ghost of what would become a full moon.

The foam-crested waves reflected the pink skies as they crashed along the beach. A few yards from the scalloped shoreline were a smattering of flickering lanterns dotting the beach with their dancing flames. A hundred white chairs in two perfectly mirrored formations filled in the space between the lanterns, the aisle between them marked with more lanterns hanging from tall metal hooks bedecked with flowers.

As a bride, she'd tried many times to envision this moment when time and her planning converged, the moment when she would pledge her eternal love to her betrothed. No matter how vivid or wild her imagination was, it paled in comparison to the reality stretched out before her. The beauty of the skies and beach were unparalleled, something out of a fairy tale.

She watched Casey make her way onto the sand, her gauzy coral dress catching the breeze and floating around her. Then Allison followed, clutching her bouquet of roses, lilies, shells and starfish. Finally, Leah moved into place to make her trek down the aisle. She turned back to look at Paisley, her green eyes glowing with a combination of joy and pride.

"See you on the other side," she whispered, "when you're Mrs. Calvin Mitchell."

Paisley sniffled, wishing she'd grabbed a tissue. "Don't make me cry!" she ordered, then laughed. "Alright, alright. I've got this. Gonna suck it up now and get it done! You ready, Cap?"

Cap looked down at her, a smile spreading his lips. Holding out his elbow to her, she threaded her arm through his and squeezed him affectionately with her other hand. "Thank you for giving me away."

"I'm not giving you away, Sugar. I'm keepin' ya. That's part of the deal, ya know."

"I know, I know." She giggled. "I'll be back to work in a week."

"Damn straight you will!" He leaned down to plant a kiss on her cheek. "I think it's time."

She nodded, and they began to move, her lacy train swishing behind her. As she proceeded forward, she saw her jewel-strewn feet peek out from underneath her gown as they sank into the soft, cool sand. The strains of the guitar playing her processional filled her ears as she put one foot in front of the other to propel herself down the aisle. Though on Cap's strong arm, she felt more like she was floating.

Her eyes fell on the crowd perched in anticipation on their white chairs and picked out familiar faces: club members, a few friends from New York, Cap's daughters and son, Calvin's family. She had a fleeting thought of her mother, who had been convicted of extortion and other crimes and sat in a cell serving a ten-year sentence across the bay in Jessup.

No, no, I'm not going to think of her, Paisley decided, sucking in a deep, cleansing breath like Dr. Townsend taught her to do. *I'm not going to think of Kentucky at all, except for the fact that I survived and wouldn't be the person I am today if not for that entire mess.*

She had often tried to imagine what her life would be like had she grown up in a normal family with normal parents and had led a normal existence. But no matter what, she kept coming back to the realization that she wouldn't be able to fully grasp what a treasure she had in Calvin and her family at The Factory if not for having done without for so many years.

As they moved closer to the seashell, starfish and rose-studded arch that opened up to the sea, her groom came into focus. He stood tall with broad, capable shoulders, his suit accentuating the masculine cut of his figure. But the best part was the beaming smile stretched so wide across his face, it looked as though he might crack.

She'd never seen him look so excited, so proud. His eyes locked onto hers as she and Cap took each step closer, and if she wasn't mistaken, when she finally reached him, she thought she saw tears sparkling in them as well.

The minister, Mary, who happened to be a member of The Factory, began by sharing a story about the first time she met Paisley. "She was fierce," she recollected, her eyes full of the memory. "I remember thinking, 'There's a lady who knows how to get things done.'" The crowd laughed. "But I also remember there being a bit of hardness to her, like she had walls up and would kick anyone's ass who tried to scale them."

Paisley glanced over at Calvin's elderly grandmother and thought she might pass out from hearing the minister's salty language, but instead, she was smiling and nodding. Calvin's mother had tears in her eyes. And looking next to Calvin at his father, who was serving as his Best Man, she found his eyes matched his wife's.

Who would have thought Detective Mitchell would cry when his oldest son tied the knot?

"Then Calvin came along," the minister continued. "He must be one hell of a climber, because he not only scaled those walls, he climbed right into her heart. And what a difference! That hardness has gone away, and I've noticed a light inside her that wasn't there before. It's a light we all have inside of us, my friends, one that just needs to be lit so it can shine across the universe as a beacon of love and joy."

Calvin squeezed her hand as they stood before the minister. Mary's story ended, and she moved on to the next part of the ceremony, the vows. With trembling words and hearts, Calvin and Paisley pledged to love each other until death parted them. And in a flash, Mary was pronouncing them husband and wife to the elated cheers of their guests.

Calvin pulled Paisley into his arms, and she wrapped hers around his waist so their bodies pressed together as one. With the waves crashing just yards away, a seagull crying overhead, and hearts melting all over the beach, they sealed their union with a kiss. Before pulling away so the happy newlyweds could be presented, she whispered in his ear, "I can't believe I'm finally your wife."

"Believe it," he whispered back.

Her face lit up with joy as a single happy tear slid down her cheek. Squeezing his hand as they turned toward the crowd, she shouted to her husband over the applause, "Let's go show them what happily ever after looks like!"

THE END

Read Siren Call, Book 3 of the Eastern Shore Swingers Series
You can also follow Calvin & Paisley's next adventure in Loyalty & Lies (crossover in my Spicetopia series)
Join my newsletter for updates!

AUTHOR'S NOTE

Another book is in the books, so to speak. I am overwhelmed by all the support I've received for this story. It all began when I was texting with my amazing book lover friend after she read *Fisher of Men*. I don't remember the particulars of the conversation, except she said she really wanted to see what happened with Cap and Leah, and I'm pretty sure she mentioned Leah needed to get pregnant!

I didn't feel like I had a whole sequel in me, but I had been toying with the idea of a feisty plus-size swinger heroine ever since I finished *The Playground*. It seemed absolutely perfect to combine the ideas into a spin-off. I had originally conceived Calvin as more of a nerdy white kid computer geek, but for some reason I kept picturing him as this hunky bi-racial guy, and once that image crystallized along with his name, the rest was history. I had no idea that the suspense part of the book would become all it did, so tangled and tied to Paisley's past, but once it started to reveal itself to me, I went for it. This was my first attempt at romantic suspense!

I couldn't have written this book—or any of my books—

without the love and support of my husband, who has been my biggest motivator from the get-go. He is the one who inspired me to write *The Mountains Trilogy*, and many of you know that the first two installments of that series are what brought us together. I really don't know if he and I would be married now without those two books. Talk about writing your own happy ending!

I also want to take a moment to thank my loyal, dedicated, and relentlessly positive Personal Assistant, Jared Gallant. He and my street team, Phoebe's Angels, make my job as a writer so much easier and more rewarding by helping me spread the word about my books to readers. I couldn't do what I do without them.

I also need to give some love to others who help make my dreams become reality: my proofreader and friend, Tina Kissinger, and those who have helped me with promotion: Kelli Smith of Totally Talented Promotions, Jessica Baldwin of Beach Bum Book Promotions, Veronica Williams of Heavenly Sent Promotions, and Colleen Noyes of Itsy Bitsy Book Blog.

Being an indie author may seem like an isolating proposition, but it's really not. Or, I should say, it doesn't have to be. I have found the most amazing group of fellow writers with whom I can share my joys, victories, frustrations and challenges. I started Indie Author Support on Facebook at the beginning of the year, and it has been an endless source of beautiful connections with kindred spirits. We've grown from a handful of members to nearly 500, and I hope I can give back to them as much as they have lavished upon me.

What's next for me? You may or may not know that I write women's fiction/clean romance under the name K.L. Montgomery. My next book will be under that moniker, due out next spring. I really hope you will follow me on my author social media platforms so you can keep up with all my latest news:

Phoebe Alexander

- Newsletter: https://bit.ly/PhoebeAlexanderNews
- Readers Group: www.facebook.com/groups/PhoebesAngels
- Facebook: www.facebook.com/phoebealexanderauthor
- Instagram: authorphoebealexander
- Bookbub: www.bookbub.com/authors/phoebe-alexander

Thank you again for reading the story of Paisley and Calvin, and I hope you enjoyed it as much as I enjoyed writing it. All my love to you, dear readers; you're why I keep dreaming and writing!

Xoxo,
    Phoebe

ABOUT THE AUTHOR

USA Today Bestselling Author Phoebe Alexander writes romance about characters like her: with extra curves and life experience. Her stories often include themes of ethical nomonogamy, such as polyamory. She believes love is love, and everyone deserves a happily ever after, no matter your size, shape, age, or color.

Phoebe lives near the beach on the East Coast with her husband and multiple fur babies. When she's not writing, she works as an editor and consultant for indie authors. She also volunteers to run a 6000-member indie author support group.

Phoebe enjoys hanging out with her three adult sons, as well as travel, Broadway musicals, dark chocolate, swimming, hiking, college basketball, and making Seinfeld references whenever possible, especially in her books. Her single greatest fantasy is just having some free time. Join her newsletter for bodypositive memes and plenty of dog pics!

facebook.com/phoebealexanderauthor

instagram.com/authorphoebealexander

bookbub.com/authors/k-l-montgomery

amazon.com/stores/author/B00ANN43WK

threads.net/authorphoebealexander

tiktok.com/@authorphoebealexander

Mountains Series

Mountains Wanted

Mountains Climbed

Mountains Loved

Christmas in the Mountains

The Navigator

The Explorer

The Adventurer

Mountains Transcended

Eastern Shore Swingers Series

Fisher of Men

The Catch

Siren Call

Sailors Knot

Turning the Tide

Alpha Bet Guys Series

A Hole

The Big O

Need the D

Hard F

Ride the C

9 781949 394795